"It's possible your life is in danger." Paul took one of her hands in both of his.

She didn't believe it, but the intensity in his eyes told her that he was dead serious. Madison liked to think she could take care of herself, and she could, but something cracked inside her. Knowing Paul cared appealed to her softer feminine side—the side she liked to. deny having.

His expression darkened with an unreadable emotion. "So much is going on, a perfect storm of events, and you're at the center. I don't want anything to happen to you."

His look was so galvanizing it sent a tremor through her. The concern reflected in his eyes became smoldering desire. She was gathered against a warm, rock-solid body and he covered her mouth with his. He kissed her urgently, hungrily, as if he couldn't get enough of her. She eased her arms around his shoulders and returned the kiss.

In a heartbeat her blood thickened to warm honey. Kissing him was even better than she'd imagined....

MERYL SAWYER

DEATH'S DOOR

HQN™

Recycling programs
for this product may
not exist in your area.

ISBN-13: 978-0-373-77374-9
ISBN-10:   0-373-77374-9

DEATH'S DOOR

www.HQNBooks.com

Printed in U.S.A.

This book is dedicated to Dave Wells
and to my close friends, Pamela and Ricki.
Where would I be without your friendship?
A special thank-you also
to the real Keith Brooks Smith
for his humor and his inspiration.

The best way to love anything
is as if it might be lost.
— G. K. Chesterton

PROLOGUE

"THERE'LL NEVER BE another you."

The killer's words were spoken softly, almost lost in the darkness. The dead were lucky. Death stopped time and their mistakes were ended. They were forever young and unchanged in the minds of those left behind. They were immortalized. Especially beauties like the woman slumped across the floor nearby.

What might she have become?

That unfulfilled promise would be seared into the memories of her loved ones. So young. So sad. So tragic.

So necessary.

Death meant life everlasting. Didn't it?

"Don't look at her body. Don't allow this to become personal," whispered the killer.

Death divides time like nothing else. Closing doors irreversibly. Before and after. No doubt her family, friends, a lover—if she had one—would always say her name accompanied by those words. Never, ever would "before" return.

Silent as a shadow, the killer moved toward the door, unable to resist a quick look back. Inhaling deeply, the killer absorbed the sweet perfume of death.

Take it in. Make it last until the next time.

This murder had been much harder and messier than the others, but in a way the difficulty of the task—the challenge—made the kill more satisfying. Life did not go smoothly. Why should death?

Had the dead woman seen this coming? the killer wondered. People believed terrible things happened to others—not them. Still, humans did retain remnants of their ancestors' primitive instincts. Fear—first among those vestiges of survival. She must have sensed…something.

THIRTY-SEVEN MINUTES earlier, at almost three in the morning, the victim had driven up the short, narrow driveway. Her front porch light must have burned out. She had turned it on before leaving, hadn't she?

It was difficult to remember just what she'd done when she'd raced out of the house to meet the others. She'd been too keyed up to pay much attention to anything but what she had been instructed to wear. A black stocking cap to go with her black pants and T-shirt and black soft-soled shoes. They promised to provide the night-vision goggles and latex gloves.

She idled in the driveway, gazing at the burned-out light, and almost put the car in Park before remembering she'd had the garage door opener replaced last week. Thank heavens. She didn't know if she had the strength left to hoist the heavy old door. The job tonight had been much more physical than anything they'd attempted in the past. Her body was in great shape, but working so strenuously against the clock consumed more energy than she'd imagined.

She pressed the remote control and the garage door creaked upward. "We're home, big guy," she told the dog on the seat beside her.

The retriever cocked his head slightly as if he understood every word. She gave him a quick pat as the Toyota rolled into the garage. His golden fur was matted and he smelled as if he needed a bath. Not your show-quality golden retriever, but he was precious just the same.

"Home sweet home," she said to the dog when she stepped out of the small car and held her door open for him. The retriever hesitated, again tilting his head toward her as if expecting another command. "Here, boy. Come on."

The dog lumbered across the driver's seat, sniffed the humid air, then cautiously lowered himself to the garage floor. The single-car garage dated back to the twenties and had a dank, musty smell. The heat of the day was still trapped inside, making it like breathing through wet wool.

She turned and punched the button beside the door leading into the house. Behind her, the garage door groaned shut as she stepped into the laundry room and hurried through the small space into the kitchen. The dog hesitantly followed, sniffing at her heels.

"Thirsty?" She put the manila envelope she was carrying on the counter before filling a cereal bowl with water. She set it on the floor, but the dog didn't move toward it. "You feeling okay?"

The golden retriever hitched one ear. He couldn't have to go to the bathroom, she decided. She'd stopped at a park on the way home. He'd relieved himself while she'd pitched the outer layer of her clothes and gloves into a nearby trash can before using the pay phone. She'd been warned numerous times to never—under any circumstances—use her home phone or cell to make a call that could be traced back to the others.

"You stay right here," she instructed as she walked out of the kitchen and closed the door behind her.

The rest of the small house was dark, the air only slightly cooler than it was outside thanks to the window air conditioner. She flicked the switch that lit the tiny lamp across the room. Suddenly the hair on her arms prickled. Something didn't seem...right. She refused to allow the tidal pull of memories to interfere with rational thought. Her unease was just the residual effect of the past few hours, she decided. She was safe now. No one could link her to the job. But if she'd been caught in the act—

"Don't go there," she whispered to herself. The reward was worth the risk.

Feeling silly for being so jumpy, she walked into her bedroom. And stood still. Something slightly ominous seemed to hover in the air like an unseen ghost. She looked around at the drifts of clothes tossed over a chair and underwear slung onto the bed. She had the housekeeping habits of a frat boy. She really ought to make an effort to be neater, she thought, still battling her nerves.

What was giving her the willies?

It was ridiculous for a grown woman to be afraid, but she tiptoed over to the closet and put her hand on the knob. For a moment she merely stared at the door. *Stop being an idiot,* she told herself, and jerked open the closet.

Nothing. Just clothes haphazardly shoved into the small space. On the floor was a jumble of shoes and a few purses too large for the overhead rack. No one was hiding in here.

In the small bathroom off her bedroom, she ran a bath and filled the tub with magnolia-scented bubble bath, then lit lavender-infused candles, known for their calming fragrance. Even though she'd showered before she'd left, the adrenaline rush had left her sheathed in sweat that had since dried and made her skin itch. She peeled off the short shorts, tank top and underwear she'd worn beneath her dark clothes, then swung her leg over the side of the tub.

She had the unsettling sensation that someone was watching her. Of course, that was impossible. It was merely her mind playing tricks. She'd purchased new locks and dead bolts when she'd had the garage door opener replaced. This was a safe neighborhood, considering it was Miami. Still, you couldn't be too careful. The others in the group believed they were under surveillance. It came with the territory. If the authorities were spying on her, they were outside the house, monitoring her comings and goings to build a court case. They were *not* hiding in the house.

The bathroom door was open. She pushed it and the door would have shut, except the tangled cord from her blow-dryer on the counter got in the way. Hadn't she returned it to the drawer? Obviously, she'd been in such a rush to meet the others that she'd forgotten.

She eased into the tub and turned off the taps. Leaning back, she closed her eyes and let the warm water and fragrant air soothe her taut nerves. This was it, she told herself. The last job. From now on, she would lead a normal life. It might even be time to settle down, she silently admitted. That meant a steady, down-to-earth guy, not one of the club rats she usually met in South Beach.

A faint, muffled noise outside the bathroom made her eyes fly open. Her pinched throat kept air from entering her lungs and she trembled. Then she remembered the dog. Aspen. A great name for a honey-colored golden retriever. She'd given it to the dog even before she'd seen him. She had it put on the collar she'd bought. She'd chosen "Aspen" because when the leaves on Aspen trees changed color each fall, they were the same golden shades she associated with golden retrievers. Aspen wasn't trying to get out of the kitchen, was he?

She kept listening, straining to hear another noise, but the only sound was the muted whir of the air conditioner in the living room. What was throwing her world out of whack? She'd never been this disturbed before, and the group had engaged in missions that had been just as dangerous as the one tonight.

Closing her eyes again, she settled back, allowing the warm water and the fragrant candles to do their magic. She was bone weary and soon almost nodded off. She forced her eyes open so she wouldn't fall asleep in the tub.

Hadn't the bathroom door been almost closed a few moments ago? She stared hard at its reflection in the mirror partially fogged by steam, then looked over her shoulder directly at the door. Her red robe hung from a hook on the back. Maybe the door wasn't quite balanced and the weight of her robe had caused it to open several inches. What was going on? She was more jittery than she ought to be.

She settled back, closed her eyes once more and inhaled deeply to take the calming scent of the candles into her lungs. Her tense muscles relaxed and her mind almost purged itself of the sight of all those forlorn, pleading eyes riveted on her.

Almost.

Don't drift off, she warned herself. She needed to scrub away the sweat, crawl into bed and set the alarm for seven-thirty. She struggled not to close her eyes, but gave in for just a moment.

A mechanical whir jerked her upright, the sound reverberating against the ceramic tile. Her eyes flashed across the short distance to the counter. Her blow-dryer was on. How had that happened? She grabbed the towel bar and heaved herself upright in one quick jerk. Instinct told her to get out of the tub NOW!

"Wh-what?" The serrated blade of fear shredded each syllable. The vapor from the candles scorched her throat as if she'd been suddenly transported to the desert. She attempted to make sense of what her eyes told her, but the dark glaze of panic blacked out the edges of her vision. Hot, white noise rumbled through her head, awakening a terror unlike anything she'd ever experienced.

A gloved hand appeared from behind the door and grabbed the blow-dryer off the counter. The next instant the dryer was hurtling through the air at her. It splashed into the bubble-filled water at her knees with a serpent's lethal hiss and an eruption of sparks. Instantly, little popping sounds battered her skull like fireworks exploding in her brain.

CHAPTER ONE

Before becoming a world-famous photographer, what did Ansel Adams aspire to be?

MADISON CONNELLY STARED out the window from the largest enclosure in the cube farm at the shimmering waters of Biscayne Bay visible over the rooftops of nearby buildings. As copresident of TotalTrivia, she was entitled to a large private office, but she and Aiden had agreed long ago that doors encouraged isolation. Togetherness inspired innovation—the healthy exchange of ideas that led to creativity.

Maybe, she thought, but right now she wished she could slam her office door shut and make the world go away. She was burned out by what her father would have called "premature success." Her company was barely three years old and it was already being touted as a triumph. If only her personal life was as glorious.

Get a grip, Madison told herself. *There's no reason to feel sorry for yourself. Concentrate on what you're doing and forget past mistakes.*

Madison forced herself to stare at her computer screen as she waited for inspiration. The software program she'd invented culled obscure facts from numerous sources for their online game, but every so often she liked to throw in a zinger. Her favorite was "what if." What if Ansel Adams had his wish? He would have become a concert pianist. Lucky for the world, he hadn't.

If she'd had her wish, she would have pursued a doctorate and—

"Madison, there's a man here to see you. How cool is that?"

She swiveled around in her chair to face Jade, TotalTrivia's receptionist. Short blue-black hair gelled up like a rooster's comb and deep red lipstick combined with Cleopatra eyes gave the girl an unfashionable Goth look that was rarely seen in South Beach these days. Jade could easily have told Madison she had a visitor with the interoffice telephone, but the girl never lost an opportunity to sashay by the cluster of cubicles the programmers used, just as she never failed to add how "cool" something was, even when delivering bad news.

"Who is it? I'm not expecting anyone."

Jade consulted a business card she held between bloodred nails that could have doubled as letter openers. "Paul Tanner. He's with Tanner Security Solutions, Inc."

Another geek trying to sell them software that was supposed to prevent other online trivia sites from hacking into their database. Online protection. What a joke.

"Tell him we take care of our own security." She was about to give Jade another lecture on how to screen people, but she spotted Aiden Larsen coming toward her office.

"Hey, Madison," her ex-husband called in his usual upbeat voice. "Got a minute?"

"Not really," she fibbed as Jade ducked out of the cube and began to saunter down the aisle toward the reception area.

Aiden ignored Madison's response and parked himself in the chair opposite her desk. She tried not to notice how handsome he looked. Chloe really knew how to make him dress in a way that emphasized his best features, his height and surfer blond hair.

The irony of the situation irritated her. Aiden would do anything for Chloe, but he'd stubbornly refused to make the smallest change for Madison. Instead, he'd insisted she be the one to alter her looks and life for him. He'd wanted her hair long and ruler-straight, even though it was naturally curly and at the mercy of Miami's humidity. He'd wanted to go out to SoBe's clubs almost every night. It was a scene she hated. Madison had resisted, of course, but it didn't seem to matter now. Aiden was on a new path in life—Chloe's course.

"Where've you been? I tried to get you all weekend."

"Busy." She didn't want to tell Aiden she'd wasted another weekend searching for a place to lease. She couldn't decide on anything, because each property she was shown made her think of the fabulous house in Coral Gables that she'd permitted Aiden to keep in the divorce. Retaining half the business they'd started together had been more important.

"You didn't answer your cell."

"I left it at Erin's on Friday."

The mention of her best friend's name caused one blond eyebrow to quirk. Aiden's brows were less scraggly than they had been on Friday, she noted. Over the weekend, Chloe must have convinced him to go to one of SoBe's stylish spas for a professional wax.

Madison could see Aiden was biting back another negative comment about Erin. For an instant, Madison's brain replayed something she'd heard on the morning news as she'd been getting ready for work. It made her think about Erin and wonder if her friend could have been involved in the incident.

"Why were you looking for me?" She knew it had to be important. Since their divorce they spoke only when necessary. So much for the "togetherness" they'd envisioned when starting the company. She struggled to keep her tone civil. Their last conversation had ended with Aiden accusing Madison of using her tongue like a whip.

"I had such a great idea that I wanted to run it by you immediately. That's why I kept calling. TotalTrivia needs a shot in the arm, right?"

"I guess," she reluctantly conceded, although she knew he was correct. Advertising banner sales were level but she perceived a lack of momentum. On a per-week basis they weren't drawing new gamers the way they once had. They were still raking in a bundle, but similar Web sites were invading the territory they'd once dominated.

"How's this for an idea?" He rocked back in the chair opposite her desk and put his feet up on the rim, the way he used to when they'd been developing ideas for TotalTrivia. "Add betting to our site."

"We've been down this road before." How could he waste her time with this? They'd known when they created TotalTrivia that Internet gambling and auctions made boodles of money. They'd defied the odds by making money with a game that didn't feature gambling.

He chuckled nonchalantly, but she knew better. Aiden handled the business end of their site. He could smell money the way a bloodhound picked up a fresh scent. "True. We have avoided gambling, but now Trivia Mania has added it to their site."

"Interesting," Madison hedged. Trivia Mania had been their chief rival *before* their competitor added gambling. She had no doubt gamers on TotalTrivia would flock to a site where they could place bets. "Who's handling their finances?"

"They've contracted with Allied Miami Bank."

"Why am I not surprised?" Madison knew the bank was owned by a group of YUCAs—Young Urban Cuban Americans—with a reputation for financing shady gambling operations. Not all young and ambitious Cubans skirted the law, of course, but some did. It was a temptation unique to Miami, where many immigrants had settled and were making new lives.

"We're thinking that adding betting to TotalTrivia is the way to go. We know Allied Miami has the most experience."

Madison didn't have to ask who "we" was. This must be Chloe's idea. Well, she could say many things about Chloe, but not being one of God's brightest creatures wasn't one of them. Madison had personally hired Chloe, but she hadn't counted on Chloe stealing her husband.

"We're making money. Why risk associating with questionable characters?"

"What if I tell you—"

Bzzt-bzzt. Jade was buzzing her from the receptionist's desk. Madison picked up the phone, relieved at the interruption. "Yes, Jade?"

"Mr. Tanner is still waiting to see you. He says it's not about business. This is a personal matter."

"Yeah, right. That's what they all say." She never failed to be amazed at how many creeps crawled out of the woodwork once they sensed a computer game had hit the big time. She must get ten of these guys a week.

"I think he means it." Jade was whispering now.

"Tell him to call me. We'll discuss it on the phone." Madison hung up and turned back to Aiden.

He was watching her intently, and she wondered if she was wearing an outfit she'd had on last week. She tended to wear half a dozen outfits that she liked over and over and over. No wonder she'd never been able to turn geek Aiden into *GQ* Aiden the way Chloe had. Twice a year Erin forced Madison to donate her old clothes, then took her shopping.

Don't let him make you feel inferior, she told herself. Both Madison's mother and Erin always described her as pretty. Not that they fooled her, but natural blond hair and wide blue eyes did manage to turn a few guys' heads. Unlike Chloe, Madison didn't have much to brag about in the chest department. Chloe was pinup material. Madison didn't care; her brains set her apart. She had no intention of competing in the body department.

"Well, what do you think?" Aiden asked, and though his tone was still casual, she knew his manner meant he was ready to move on this immediately.

She stood up. "Let's do a bit more research. I'm still not in favor of gambling or Allied Miami, but maybe—"

"Why? Allied Miami handles all sorts of betting operations. They even have a division set up to process, then pay every bet."

"Wait!" She threw up one hand to stop him. "We don't want to hand over a chunk of our business without thoroughly investigating the situation. It's an invitation to steal from us or ruin our reputation. This isn't something to leap into without careful thought." She picked up her purse. "I've got an appointment."

"Wait. I—"

"Later. I'm in a hurry."

She rushed out of her corner cube and took a left. She headed for the back door to avoid the software salesman. She needed time to think about Aiden's proposal. She might as well swing by Erin's and pick up her cell phone.

Madison climbed into her BMW and lowered the windows to air out the car. Even though it was barely ten o'clock, the Miami sun was scorching a path across the blue April sky. She allowed her mind to drift for a moment. She'd wasted yet another weekend. She was never going to be able to replace the home she'd shared with Aiden.

Why was she trying?

She should lease the condo that she'd reluctantly allowed the Realtor to show her, Madison told herself. She didn't need a yard. This way she could come and go easily. She punched the AC button and reached for her cell phone with her other hand to call the Realtor. Then she remembered she was on her way to pick up her cell.

"I'm losing it," she said out loud. She backed out of her parking space and drove away.

TotalTrivia was located several blocks off trendy Ocean

Boulevard in South Beach's low-rent district—if such a thing existed. They'd leased the office space nearly ten years ago, before she had married Aiden, when TotalTrivia had been just another blip on the information superhighway. Aiden had insisted locating in SoBe would lure programmers they could hire for less.

Her ex had been right. Talented programmers often made sacrifices, living in studio apartments or sharing run-down flats just to be in the area. As Erin always said, SoBe was "hip to the max." It was amazing what people would give up to live here.

Maybe Aiden was right about adding gambling to Total-Trivia, but she didn't think so. Letting an offshore bank collect the money was evading the law. Wasn't that the same as breaking the law? Sooner or later the government would catch on and come after them.

South Beach traffic was light—no doubt a fair number of residents were inside nursing hangovers—which meant Madison had to wait a mere two cycles to drive through most traffic lights. By evening, when the club set went on the prowl, it would take at least six cycles to move through a light.

From ten until dawn, the clubs would be full of tanned guys and women wearing next to nothing, slurping mojitos and chocolate martinis. Sexual energy would pulse through the air like a drumbeat in the tropics.

Madison didn't like the club scene, but last Friday, Erin had wanted to check out two new clubs and she'd gone along. Her best friend since they'd been in diapers, Erin Wycoff had always been something of an enigma. Like a butterfly, Erin was beautiful but difficult to pin down. As close as they were, Madison often didn't know what Erin was thinking. Even when they were young, Erin had kept her thoughts to herself, unlike most teenage girls, who told their best friends all their secrets. But since Madison's split with Aiden, Erin had been the only one who could lift her spirits.

Erin had insisted on going to Sweet Cheeks and another club whose name Madison couldn't recall, but as soon as they were there, drinks in hand, Erin had wanted to leave. Too hot. Too crowded. Too many airhead guys.

Well, that was the club scene for you. A club wasn't "in" unless it was crowded with hunky guys and scantily clad babes. And jam-packed places were hot. That was a given.

They'd gone back to the little cottage Erin had rented and ordered pizza from an all-night pizzeria. They'd sat chatting about the move Madison couldn't seem to make, but Erin had seemed distracted, on edge.

Still, Erin had scored a major point when she'd claimed Madison was in denial. By searching for a large home to replace the one she'd shared with her ex-husband, Madison was attempting to hang on to the past. The last time Madison's mother had telephoned from some remote island in the South Pacific, she'd told Madison the same thing—in different words. "Oh, baby doll. Try something new. Get on with your life."

Madison had admitted Erin was probably right and had left after finishing a slice of cardboard-tasting pizza. She'd only realized the next day that she'd forgotten her cell phone. She'd tried to catch Erin on Saturday and again on Sunday but hadn't been able to connect. Maybe she hadn't even wanted to reach Erin, hadn't wanted to explain why she was still asking the Realtor to show her large homes.

A bit of trivia popped into her head, which often happened when she was thinking of something distressing. How much wine does one grapevine make? The average vine yielded twenty-four pounds of grapes. That was enough to make ten bottles of wine. She hadn't used this fact on TotalTrivia because inexact measurements like "average" caused arguments and players would claim their answer was correct.

She told herself to forget about trivia and concentrate on

finding a place to live. The owners of the house where she was staying would return soon. Gambling and trivia could both wait until she'd settled her life.

At this hour of the morning, Erin was probably out making sales calls for the sunglass company she represented. It didn't matter if Erin wasn't home. Madison had a key to her friend's place. She could pick up her cell then call the Realtor. Signing the lease on the condo and making arrangements would take the better part of the day, but Madison didn't care. She didn't want to return to TotalTrivia until she'd had a chance to consider Aiden's proposal.

It was quieter in the middle-class neighborhood in South Miami where Erin lived. People were at work, children in school. She turned into the narrow driveway and shut off the engine. The white cottage with an attached single-car garage was a legacy of the early twentieth century, when snowbirds from the North built small, inexpensive bungalows where they could wait out the winter in Miami's warm sun. Snowbirds now clustered like bees in the hives of condos that riddled the state. This neighborhood had morphed into a working-class section of the city.

She slung her purse over her shoulder and got out of the car. On her way up the walk to the front door, she selected the key Erin had given her from the seldom-used ring of keys at the bottom of her purse. She rang the bell and heard its chime echo through the small house. As she expected, Erin wasn't home. She attempted to put the key into the lock. It didn't fit.

Suddenly, Madison remembered her friend mentioning getting a new garage door opener and new locks. Erin had forgotten to give Madison a new key.

"Great, just great," she muttered under her breath. Standing on the small porch, Madison noticed a silver Porsche had pulled to the curb across the street. It seemed out of place in this neighborhood. A tall, dark-haired man stepped out. He glanced in her direction, then locked the car.

Madison wondered if Erin had hidden a spare key in the small yard behind the cottage. She went around back, but didn't bother to check under the flowerpots. Erin wouldn't hide a key in such an obvious place. She looked around, thinking, then spotted a dog turd over by a bush. Erin was an animal lover and always had been, but she didn't have a dog. The landlord wouldn't allow any pets. Erin got her pet fix by volunteering at an animal rescue facility.

She toed the dried pile and it rolled over. Just as she suspected, there was a latch on the bottom. These rock-hard devices had become popular with pet owners. A close look revealed they were molded pottery of some kind, but to the untrained eye, they looked like a deposit a dog would make. She picked up the fake turd and opened it. A shiny new key was inside. Leave it to Erin to hide a key in plain sight—in a fake dog turd that looked disturbingly real. So real, you could almost smell it.

She rushed up to the back door. For a moment she paused and gazed up at the flawless blue sky, feeling inexplicably troubled. The key fit in the lock and the door creaked open inch by inch. She brushed her odd reaction aside and stepped into a small service area with a washer and dryer.

A noxious odor she couldn't identify hung in the close, humid air and made her stomach roil. Obviously, Erin had burned a funky candle. She opened the door leading into the kitchen and was greeted by a golden retriever with runny eyes. A small pile of dog poop accounted for the odor. Why hadn't Erin let this dog out?

"Hi, there. What's your name?" When had Erin gotten a dog? She hadn't mentioned a word about it when they'd gone out on Friday. She'd probably found the retriever at the rescue center and couldn't resist even though her lease specified no pets. With Erin, you never knew what was going on.

"Erin, it's me," she called out, in case her friend was still home but hadn't heard the bell. No response.

The dog kept scratching at the door. She opened it and he charged through the service area and out to the small backyard. He immediately lifted a leg on a low-hanging bush.

"You're a boy," she muttered, more to herself than the dog. He trotted back to her and she bent down to check his collar. It looked brand-new. "So, your name is Aspen."

The dog cocked his head and looked up at her. His eyes were tearing the way some poodles' did, leaving brown stains on their fur. She wondered if something was wrong with the retriever. Maybe that's why Erin had brought him home.

She led Aspen back inside. The odor she'd smelled earlier was worse now. She covered her nose with her hand. On the counter was a fly-covered pizza box clearly left over from Friday night. Typical Erin. She wasn't much for housekeeping.

Next to the box was a manila envelope marked "Aspen." Coiled beside it was a nylon leash. She held her breath while she opened the unsealed envelope and found a bill of sale inside for a male golden retriever, age three years and seven months.

Erin had purchased the dog for twenty-five dollars. Interesting. It wasn't much for a purebred, but maybe something was wrong with it, like an eye problem. And it wasn't Erin's style to buy a dog. She didn't believe in buying from breeders when there were so many homeless animals, many of whom had to be put down when homes weren't found for them. Yet she had purchased this dog. Very odd.

Madison returned the paper to the envelope and closed it. On the back flap, Erin had written something so quickly that it was difficult to read. "Rob—Monday noon. Don't be late."

Interesting, she thought. Very interesting. Madison had always believed Erin and Robert Matthews were meant to be together, but they'd broken up. Erin hadn't mentioned the veterinarian in months.

Madison decided to leave the dog in the kitchen. Obviously, Erin had her reasons for keeping Aspen there. She opened the door to the small space that served as a living room with a dining area off to one side. With all the blinds drawn, it was hot, dark and uninviting.

She let the kitchen door close behind her. A denser cloud of the horrible, cloying smell saturated the air. The stench sent her stomach into a backflip. A fly zoomed by her nose, closely followed by a second one. The odor of urine was also present. That must be why Erin had left the dog in the kitchen. He wasn't properly trained.

Despite the room's darkness, she managed to spot her silver cell phone gleaming on the coffee table where she'd left it. She charged forward to pick it up and nearly tripped over something protruding from the shadows between the sofa and coffee table.

A bare foot.

The thought scarcely registered when she saw something on the floor. A naked body? She squinted, her eyes adjusting to what light had stolen into the room. The form was sprawled across the carpet, dark brown hair streaming like a banner. Her limbs were splayed, one arm bent beneath her and the other flung outward, palm up. The open hand seemed to capture a shaft of light that was seeping in from between the blinds. Around the neck was a red scarf pulled so tight the head torqued to one side.

All Madison could make out in the semidarkness was the side of the woman's face. Erin! No. It couldn't be.

She sucked in a terrified breath as goose bumps pebbled her skin. For a heartbeat she couldn't move. A burning, wrenching sensation gripped her stomach and a wave of throbbing dizziness hit her. Madison heard a jagged, high-pitched shard of sound rip through the air, but it was a second before she realized she'd screamed.

A thousand thoughts pinwheeled through her brain. Erin. How could she be dead? Her friend had always been there—a constant presence in her life—even more reliable than her own mother.

She forced herself to edge closer just to be sure. A few strands of hair covered the naked woman's face, its skin like white candle wax. Erin. No question about it.

Why? Why? Why?

She stood near her friend, her mind barely taking in what she saw. Details registered like freeze-frame images. A wet stain pooled around Erin's thighs. A drop of dried blood lingered at the corner of her mouth. One knee was swollen, the purplish skin so tight that it seemed ready to burst. A bulging blue eye stared sightlessly at the beige carpet beneath her. The white part of her eye was bloodred.

Madison's vision had grown accustomed to the dark. Now, she noticed evidence of a frantic struggle. Furniture was knocked out of place. Pictures on tables had fallen and plants were overturned. By some quirk of fate, the coffee table where her cell phone had been was still upright.

Suddenly, a hand clamped across her lips. Pulse misfiring, her mind attempted to grapple with the situation, but panic shredded her brain like shrapnel.

A single thought registered: the killer!

All her instincts told her that she was a heartbeat from death. The will to survive kicked her body into gear. She flailed, biting the huge hand over her mouth and jabbing her elbows in a futile attempt to free herself. Powerful arms locked around her and brought her against the solid wall of a big chest.

"Be still," a deep, masculine voice ordered. "I'm not going to hurt you."

She wasn't buying that bridge—not with her murdered friend less than a foot away. She kicked backward and landed a blow with the heel of her shoe.

"Stop it!" He had a death grip on her now, squeezing her so tight the air in her lungs turned to cement. "I'm trying to help you."

"L-lemme go." She worked hard to keep hysteria out of her voice, but detected its shaky undertone in every word.

"Screaming isn't going to bring her back."

Suddenly, it dawned on Madison that she hadn't stopped screaming from the moment she'd spotted her friend's body.

CHAPTER TWO

How far away can a fly smell a dead body?

MADISON TEETERED, feeling light-headed, grabbed the back of the sofa for support and closed her eyes for a second, her fragile barrier of control slipping. Get a grip, she told herself. The air was so tight in her lungs that she could hardly breathe. But the thump-thump of her heart filled her skull and made it difficult to think. Even with her eyes closed, she kept seeing Erin's lifeless body. She opened them and found the dark-haired man from the street gazing down at her.

He handed her a cell phone and calmly said, "Call 911. I'm going to check the rest of the house just in case."

The man's calm, cool attitude told Madison that she'd been mistaken. He really was trying to help her, as he'd said. He wasn't the killer. That man was long gone but his evilness remained, hanging over the small house like a noxious cloud.

Madison's eyes dropped to the body prone on the carpet. "Don't leave me."

The man touched her arm and prodded her in the direction of the kitchen. "Go out back. You'll be safe."

Madison stumbled toward the kitchen, managed to open the door and lurched to an upright position on the other side. She gulped hard and air rasped down her throat, then thundered into her lungs. She swayed for a moment, the numbers on the keypad of the small cell phone swimming in front of her. Something brushed against her leg and she gasped out loud but managed not to scream when she realized it was just the dog, standing beside her, tail swishing.

She gazed down into his soulful eyes and something unexpected tugged at her heart. Erin must have cared deeply about the dog to bring him home even though she knew a pet could mean eviction from a bungalow she'd described as "perfect." Had this poor animal seen the killer, heard the desperate struggle in the other room?

The screech of tires on the street outside jolted her. *Call the police!* She punched the numbers and hit Send.

"Nine-one-one. Please hold."

Hold? Erin was dead. Getting an ambulance here fast wasn't important, but what if someone—

"What is the nature of your emergency?"

"M-my f-friend's been killed." Madison choked on the words. It was almost as if saying them made it true. If she didn't utter them, Erin would still be alive.

"Does your friend have a pulse? Have you cleared the air passages?"

Madison mumbled her replies, trying to make the overly calm, patient woman understand. Erin had been murdered. As she talked, she spotted the envelope and leash on the counter and made a split-second decision she hoped she wouldn't regret. She shoved the envelope into her purse, which by some miracle was still slung over her shoulder. She snapped the leash onto Aspen's collar.

"What is your address?" the emergency operator asked.

Madison went blank. She could find her way to her best friend's house easily but didn't recall the number on Sawgrass Terrace. "I'm on a cell. I'll go outside and check the number." She plowed through the small kitchen and service area, Aspen in tow. Outside, the sun was blistering a path across the sky. In shimmering waves, moist heat rose from the grass in back of the house.

Madison squinted. How could it be so bright and sunny when Erin was dead?

"You're at fourteen eleven Sawgrass Terrace. Correct?"

From back here, Madison couldn't see the house number but knew it was correct when she heard it. The man's cell phone must have a GPS chip in it. Most cell phones couldn't transmit the location so quickly. "Yes."

The operator told her help was on the way and to stay on the line. She snapped the phone shut. Why remain on the line? Nothing the operator could say would help Erin now.

The door behind Madison slammed and she spun around. The man who'd heard her frantic screams walked toward her. She'd been so upset that she'd only had the vague impression of a tall, powerfully built man with dark hair and eyes. His hair was indeed dark brown, almost black, but his eyes were a deep blue that had only appeared brown in the gloomy house.

She told herself again there was no reason to be afraid. The man merely looked intense, the way anyone would at a murder scene. Yes, his size implied strength and threatened her even though she wasn't the type to be intimidated. But she could see he was trying to help. And finding a dead body had to be as shocking for him as it was for her.

The hollow *thunk-thunk* of blood in her temples made it difficult to think as quickly as she usually did. Somewhere in the back of her mind, a thought managed to register. Most women would say this guy was hot. Not that she cared. Being with Aiden had taught her that a handsome man couldn't resist the temptation thrown into his path.

"Whoever killed your friend is long gone," the stranger told her in a concerned voice, but she felt trapped by his unwavering stare. "Did you call—"

"They're on the way." She returned his cell phone.

"We'd better go around front where the police can see us."

Madison started to move but couldn't. He stared at her for

a moment and Madison wondered if he expected her to again cut loose with a shriek loud enough to be heard in New York. She forced herself to put one foot in front of the other and headed toward the street, bringing the dog with her.

"If only I'd gotten here sooner," she muttered more to herself than to him. As sharp as a blade, a lone siren cut through the still air, coming closer and closer.

"It wouldn't have mattered. She hasn't been alive for some time."

Madison stopped and Aspen plowed into the back of her legs. "How can you tell?"

"I'm Paul Tanner with Miami PD."

"Oh," she said simply, remembering the flies hovering around Erin's body. A pinprick of a thought flashed through her brain the way obscure facts often intruded. A fly could smell a dead body a mile away. They'd been buzzing around Erin's lifeless body for hours.

A police car followed by an ambulance, lights flashing, screeched to a stop at the curb. Two uniformed policemen emerged from the squad car just as a gray sedan drove up. They waited until two men in suits got out of the second car.

"Yo, Tanner," called one of the men in suits to Paul Tanner.

The man was who he claimed he was, she thought. How could she have mistaken him for a killer?

"Her friend's been strangled." Paul lightly touched Madison's arm. "The back door's open. She came over to—"

Madison realized everyone was staring at her, expecting an answer. "I came over to get my cell phone."

One detective remained with her while Paul led the other detective and the uniformed officers to the back of the house.

"I went in and found Erin on the floor in the living room. Sh-she had this cord or sash around her neck."

"So she was dead when you arrived?"

"Yes. It looked like she'd been strangled."

The detective jotted a few notes in the small notebook he held in his hand. His face registered no emotion. Obviously, dead bodies came as no surprise to him.

"What is the victim's full name?"

"Erin Allison Wycoff."

"How'd you get in?"

Madison ran through the story of the newly changed locks and how she'd found the hidden key. She was coming to her senses a little bit, her mind grasping the gruesome reality of the situation.

The two policemen came out of the front door, followed by the other detective and the Tanner guy. From their impassive, almost frozen expressions, no one could guess the grisly scene they'd discovered in the house.

"Medical examiner's on the way. The tech van will be here to process the scene," announced one of the men in uniform.

The men gathered a few feet from Madison. She took a step back and bumped into Aspen. She leaned down and stroked his head. The men conferred for a moment, speaking so softly Madison couldn't make out what they were saying.

The detective with the notebook continued asking questions as the men moved closer. "When was the last time you saw the victim?"

"Erin. Her name was Erin."

The men looked at one another. *Hysterical female,* they silently telegraphed.

Madison took a deep breath, then told them, "I was with her on Friday night. That's when I left my cell phone. I called her Saturday and Sunday, but I didn't get her. I also tried to reach Erin on her cell. It kicked into voice mail."

"Did you find that unusual?" asked the detective.

"No, not really. Erin often turns off her phone. She isn't—wasn't—the kind to talk on it all the time." Madison couldn't help blaming herself. She should have driven over yesterday instead of house-hunting for a home she could never replace. If she had, Erin might still be alive. Surely the killer wouldn't have tried to murder two women. She could have saved her friend if she hadn't been obsessed with replacing a home—and a life—that was gone forever.

"When I couldn't make contact this morning, I drove over here," Madison told them.

"Do you have any idea where she's been or who she was with?"

Madison shook her head.

"Boyfriend? Parents?"

Before she could respond, Tanner asked, "Do you know anyone who would want to kill your friend?"

"No, no. Of course not." She heard her voice crack and with it came the threat of tears.

The men were silent for a moment, waiting for her to compose herself. A Miami PD van marked Crime Scene Investigation pulled to the curb. The uniformed officers went over to meet it, and Madison was left with the detectives. It seemed to be straight out of a *CSI: Miami* episode—only this was horribly real.

"Erin doesn't have a boyfriend. Both parents are dead. I'm all she has."

None of the three reacted—exactly—but they silently regarded her with keener interest.

She suddenly realized how it sounded. "I—I mean, Erin has had boyfriends in the past, and she would like—would have liked—to find a guy. That's why we went out clubbing on Friday night. But as far as family, I'm it. We grew up together." She looked at Paul Tanner, feeling more of a connection with him than the other two men. His expression said he was measuring every word. "Our mothers met when they were pregnant with us. I've known Erin my whole life."

Two men and a woman in navy jumpsuits with Crime Scene

Investigator stenciled on the back had emerged from the van with a video camera and bags of gear. The crime scene techs headed toward the open front door. While she'd been talking, someone had strung yellow crime scene tape across the porch.

"We're close," Madison continued, "just like sisters."

The detective taking notes arched one thick eyebrow. "Where were you last night?"

It didn't take a rocket scientist to see where they were heading with this. "Wait a minute. You don't think I—"

"They're just doing their job," Paul interjected. "This is a question they'll ask everyone associated with your friend."

"I spent the night alone. I'm house-sitting for a friend. That's where I was."

The detective taking notes asked, "Make any phone calls?"

Madison knew that could establish her whereabouts. "No. But I wouldn't have any reason to kill Erin. She doesn't have any money or anything of value to inherit."

She could have added that the dog on the leash was her friend's only valuable possession, but she didn't want to draw attention to Aspen. Erin had gone out of her way—and violated her lease—to rescue this dog. Madison couldn't bring herself to give up the retriever. She knew he'd be sent to some pound and kept there for who knew how long. Erin wouldn't have wanted the dog to be distressed. The animal was all she had of her friend; she had to protect him from more abuse.

"We're going to need a set of your fingerprints," the detective said.

"Eliminating your prints and your friend's may leave them with the perp's," Paul added.

"All right," she said, but something in their attitude told her that she was a suspect. "A man had to have killed Erin, right? She was strangled."

Silence greeted her statement. Then the detective taking notes said, "We'll take you down to the station for the prints."

"I'll come in this afternoon," she told them in her firmest tone. "Aspen has to go to the vet's." She tugged on the leash, making this up as she went. She had to get away from here. "He has an eye infection."

"It'll have to wait," the detective said.

Maybe it was just her imagination—misplaced anxiety over her best friend's death—but Madison needed to get away. Perhaps she should consult a lawyer. Why, she couldn't imagine, but something was going on here that she didn't understand.

"I said I would come into the station. Unless the department wants to be slapped with a lawsuit for causing blindness in a champion show dog, I insist on taking Aspen to the vet."

The word *lawsuit* detonated on impact. The men exchanged indecipherable looks. "We'll need those prints by four o'clock."

It took all Madison's willpower to lead Aspen to her Beamer without running. Who'd killed Erin? How could she possibly be a suspect? It didn't make sense.

Something else had been niggling at the back of her brain. She was behind the wheel, driving away from the cluster of police vehicles when it hit her. Paul Tanner. He wasn't some former cop who just "happened" to live in the neighborhood. He claimed to be a policeman. This morning Jade had said a Paul Tanner wanted to see her about selling her security software or something. He'd driven up in a Porsche. He'd followed her here. Why?

CHAPTER THREE

"THERE'S NO SUCH THING as a perfect crime. Little things—the unexpected—stand in the way of a flawless murder." The killer spoke the words in an undertone, although there was no one around to hear.

Erin Wycoff's murder had made headlines. People feasted on the brutality of the crime and lapped up every gory fact. It was to be expected. Death was fascinating, especially if it wasn't yours. The details had captured the city's imagination. Many identified with the victim and felt lucky to have escaped her fate.

"The devil is in the details. Always has been, always will be."

Not many people realized blow-dryers were no longer instruments of death. He certainly hadn't. He'd been too consumed by his life's work to read the papers or watch mindless television that might have given him the information he needed.

An enterprising manufacturer would advertise the fact. But the truth was most people didn't recognize their potential—big corporations included. Never mind. The blow-dryer didn't electrocute Erin, but the mission had been accomplished in spite of the unexpected development.

The killer stared out at the series of waves tumbling one after another onto the white sand, remembering and reliving the instant the blow-dryer hit the water and hissed like a cat with its tail on fire. The killer had anticipated a guttural scream, then a body collapsing into the water. Dead.

The earsplitting cry had erupted from Erin's throat as expected. But instead of dying, she'd vaulted from the tub and streaked out of the bathroom with wild, unfocused eyes, reminding him of a rabid dog. She had to be stopped, had to be shut up before she awakened the neighbors.

Luck was always with those who planned and noticed details. The red sash for her robe had been right there on the bathroom door. She'd fought like a hellcat, but she was a small woman. Her struggle had been exhilarating but brief.

A strange twist of fate. Death was always exciting but not this thrilling—so stimulating that nothing could match the experience. It was the struggle that was so captivating. The others had died well-planned deaths—they hadn't even been listed as murders. This time there was no mistake.

When you didn't anticipate having to physically attack, the chance of leaving incriminating evidence grew exponentially. Still, the killer had considered the situation many times and decided there was no way the police could solve this crime. Certainly, there was no chance they could link it to the previous murders. They wouldn't figure out the common denominator between the victims.

PAUL TANNER WAITED in the Porsche as Madison pulled into the driveway of the Fisher Island home where she was house-sitting. She still had the golden retriever with her. He shut off the air-conditioning and got out of the car. His leg hadn't quite healed and it was stiff from being in the small enclosure for so long. Madison's head swung in his direction, a puzzled expression on her pretty face.

Paul had known she would be surprised to see him. No doubt she was wondering why he was here and how he'd gotten into an enclave famous for its exclusivity. The small island was linked to the mainland only by ferry service. He'd driven off the boat with a gaggle of Rollses and Bentleys. Parking valets washed the salt spray off the overpriced cars while uniformed guards checked visitors' credentials. He'd flashed his badge and implied this was official business even though his mission didn't have a damn thing to do with the murder.

Madison opened her car door and tugged on Aspen's leash. It took the dog a minute to gauge the distance from the driver's seat to the ground. His eye problem must really be bothering him.

"How's his eye infection?" Paul asked as he walked up to them.

"The vet gave him drops." It was evident the used-car-salesman's smile Paul was practicing on her wasn't working. She beelined to the front door. "What are you doing here?"

"I need to talk to you."

"What about?" She rammed her key into the lock of the Mediterranean-style villa. "I've already given the police a statement. Now I have to plan a funeral. Erin doesn't have anyone else to do it."

"If you'll give me a minute—"

She spun around to face him with a look that could have frozen lava. She was exhausted, grief stricken, and probably wanted to curl up somewhere to cry. Her shoulders unexpectedly sagged and he could almost feel the fight go out of her. His entire body tensed with the urge to reach out and put his arm around her, but he resisted.

He didn't know what he'd expected when he'd followed her to Erin Wycoff's home and heard Madison's five-alarm scream followed by anguished, keening cries like those of an animal caught in a trap. He'd seen several pictures of her in the file his father had given him. Nothing had prepared him for the woman he'd found when he'd rushed through the back door. She'd been on the verge of debilitating hysteria—who could blame her?—but she'd fought him with more courage than most guys he'd taken down.

He hadn't gotten a good look at her until they were outside.
Then a mind-numbing attack of...of what? Aw, hell. He might
as well be honest with himself. A jolt of sexual awareness had
shot through him, despite the inappropriate time and place.
There was something undeniably appealing about that storm of
blond hair and those baby blues. He'd instantly wanted to help
her. This from a man who was about as sentimental as Attila
the Hun. Okay, so a lot more than help had crossed his mind.
But he'd tamped those thoughts down and reminded himself
that this was business.

He had no illusions about his profession. Homicide—his
usual line of work when he wasn't temporarily sidelined and
helping out his father—occurred at all hours, night and day. A
detective couldn't hope for much in terms of a private life—a
lesson he'd already learned. You took women where you found
them and walked away. Romancing a woman like Madison
Connelly wasn't in the cards.

"Sorry," she said now in a tight, pinched voice. "You were
great this morning. I wasn't thinking clearly enough to thank
you. I appreciate the way you helped me."

He nodded, noticing she hadn't yet asked him why he'd
followed her to Erin Wycoff's home. Undoubtedly she was too
shaken by finding her friend dead to make the connection.
"Glad I was there. No wonder you weren't thinking clearly. You
had a great shock." He reached around her and shoved the door
open. "Let's go inside and talk for a minute."

The air conditioner was on and ceiling fans with paddles
shaped like palm fronds circulated the cool air in the semicir-
cular living room with walls entirely of glass. The house faced
the ocean and the faint tang of salt air drifted through the room
even though he didn't spot any open doors or windows. The
area he could see was bigger than his entire apartment.

She bent over and unhooked Aspen's leash. "What do you
want to talk to me about?"

He hesitated, reluctant to hit her with this immediately and trying to decide the best way to break the news. Hell, he'd had plenty of time to think while he'd been waiting for Madison. He'd prepared enough bullshit to bury Fisher Island, but being face-to-face with her was different.

Something cold gripped his gut. *Why me?* he asked himself. He should have convinced his father to send someone else. He would have if he'd known he was going to find himself at the scene of a brutal murder beside a knockout blonde who didn't deserve to be clobbered with another problem right now.

"The police think I have something to do with Erin's murder, don't they?"

"Why do you say that?" His was voice guarded now, her question surprising him.

"They took my fingerprints, then kept grilling me, asking the same questions over and over and over."

"Was there something you didn't tell them? Something they were fishing for?"

"No," she replied just a little too quickly.

What wasn't she revealing? he wondered. Paul had taken a careful look at the scene and he'd been at Madison's side within seconds after she discovered the body. He knew she hadn't killed her best friend.

"Do you have any idea what happened? They won't tell me anything." She sank down onto the sofa, the retriever at her feet.

"It's not my case," he replied, set to sidestep her questions, but her pleading eyes got to him. Then he decided gaining Madison's trust might help him when he delivered his news. "This is off-the-record, okay? You didn't hear it from me."

She measured him with those melt-your-heart baby blues. "All right. Tell me."

"From the looks of the crime scene, the killer caught the vic—your friend—taking a bath. He threw the blow-dryer into the tub."

"Oh Lord, no!" She slapped her hand over her mouth, then sucked in a stabilizing breath. "It's a wonder she wasn't electrocuted." Her eyes went empty for a moment, then she asked, "Aren't blow-dryers fitted with a gizmo that makes them shut off if they're in water? Seems to me that I read something about it."

"She received a shock before the dryer quit. That's why her knee was so swollen, but she managed to get out of the tub."

"Oh my God. Poor Erin." Madison gasped and he could see her struggle anew to comprehend the violent and brutal death. She didn't know the half of it; she hadn't seen the bathroom. "Do you have any idea…how long she fought?"

"Several minutes at least. Long enough for blood to keep pumping and the knee to swell."

"Once the heart stops beating the body shuts down, right?" she asked, and he nodded. It took her a minute to add, "Erin must have been terrified."

Paul couldn't disagree. "Throwing a blow-dryer is the kind of thing a woman would do."

"Why? Couldn't a man have done it?"

"Absolutely, but a killer's method can often tell us about his or her identity. For example, women use guns at times, but if someone is killed with a less direct method like poisoning or lethal drug doses, the responsible party is usually a woman."

"But Erin was strangled. That hardly counts as less than direct. The police should be looking for a man. Ninety-three percent of all murders are committed by men."

That stopped him cold. She was correct. He knew she and her ex had developed a wildly successful online trivia game. Obviously, Madison was a trivia buff herself to know the statistics so well.

"Odds are a man killed your friend," he conceded. "But most people don't know blow-dryers have shock interceptors in them and have had since 1991. The perp tried to electrocute her. Strangulation was a last resort."

Paul studied her closely for a moment. He could almost see Madison's brain working, imagining her friend running, desperately fighting for her life. Her tormented expression hit him like a sucker punch to the gut when it shouldn't have. He'd seen more than his share of devastated family and friends. Madison Connelly should be just another woman. Except she wasn't. He'd read her file and knew the woman better than she knew herself. What he couldn't predict was how she would react to his news.

"The killer strangled Erin with the sash from her robe that was hanging on the back of the bathroom door." He kept his voice pitched low in an effort not to upset her more than necessary. "Your friend was a very small woman. A bigger woman could have overpowered her."

Madison frowned at him for a moment, then asked in a voice so thick with emotion that it was difficult to understand her, "Not bringing a weapon to the crime scene—doesn't that mean the killing wasn't premeditated?"

Madison didn't miss a damn thing. He'd been prepared for a smart woman. One look at the file his father had on this woman made that clear. But she was a lot sharper than he'd expected. A hell of a lot.

"Often lack of a weapon suggests a crime of passion or a crime of opportunity. But this case is unusual. You wouldn't bring a blow-dryer to the scene if you knew one was already there. It still could have been premeditated."

"The killer was hiding, lying in wait, watching." A frown crinkled her smooth forehead. "But how did he know she would take a bath?"

"Good question. He could have spied—"

"Erin loved a long bath. She was a big believer in the relaxing powers of various sea salts and herbs. She would light candles with special fragrances and soak in the tub. But her fondness for aromatherapy wasn't common knowledge."

"Her boyfriends must have known, and other close friends like you."

Madison released a long, frustrated sigh. "I gave the police the names of every guy I knew about. Erin didn't have any close female friends except me."

"Why not?"

Madison shrugged. "I don't know. It was just her personality."

Paul had the feeling there was more to it, but he didn't press. He settled himself at her side on the plush white sofa, facing the panoramic view of Biscayne Bay and the sea burnished to a honey color by the setting sun. Neither of them said anything. The retriever reached up and licked Madison's hand.

"I found Erin's body. How could I be a suspect? One look and you knew she'd been dead for hours. The others must have realized this. Why would they suspect me?"

"Sometimes killers 'discover' the victim to throw off detectives and provide a reason for their prints and other trace evidence to be at the scene." He watched her slowly nod. A heavy beat of silence followed.

Finally, she asked the question he'd been waiting for. "You were at my office, then you followed me to Erin's. Why?"

He hated to bring up such a sensitive issue right now. It didn't seem fair, but what did his father always say? *Where did you get the idea life is supposed to be fair?* He was being paid to do a job. He couldn't guess what Madison Connelly's reaction was going to be, but putting it off wouldn't change things.

"This is about computer security, isn't it? That's what your card said."

"Not exactly. My father owns a company that specializes in corporate security. I'm helping him out while I'm on disability leave. I should be cleared to go back to active duty on Miami PD in the next few weeks." Her expression clouded, and he wondered what she was thinking. For some reason, he touched the wound still healing on his thigh. "I took a couple of slugs in an arrest that didn't go down the way it should have."

Either she didn't care or what he'd told her about himself didn't register. She asked, "Your father wants my business?"

"No. This has nothing to do with your business. This is a personal matter." What in hell was wrong with him? Why couldn't he come to the point? He was progressing with the speed of a glacier. "I need to talk to you about your family."

"Really? I can't imagine why. My father died two years ago of cancer. My mother's remarried." She was regarding him with outright suspicion now, wondering, no doubt, what his angle was. "It's a pretty typical story."

"Would you consider yourself typical?"

She jumped to her feet and went over to the windows. He couldn't help noticing she moved as if she were on a catwalk, not being deliberately provocative but gliding in a smooth, natural way that kicked up his pulse a notch. A second later, she pivoted in place and glared at him. "What do you want from me?" She hurried back to the sofa. "I only own half of Total-Trivia. Aiden Larsen and his wife control the other half. I can't do anything without their approval."

"I'm aware of the situation." He didn't add that he knew her ex had tried his damnedest to take the company away from her during the divorce. But she wasn't just pretty and smart, she was a fighter. "This isn't about your company, it's about you."

"Me?" Her response was a hollow echo in the high-ceilinged room.

"Yes. My father's firm was hired to track you down."

"Me? Why on earth—"

"Someone wants to meet you," Paul replied, easing into what he knew would be a bombshell.

"Who? Why can't they just pick up a phone and contact me? I'm not hard to find." The words came out in a heated rush. She took a deep breath and added, "What's going on? Something's not right."

"There's no easy way to tell you this, so I'm just going to say it straight out. This man might be your biological father. We've been doing the verification for him. That's how we found you."

"What?" She surged to her feet once more. "You can't be serious."

"You're aware of sperm banks." Paul expected a puzzled look, but instead hostility was etched on her face like a death mask.

"Of course," she shot back without taking a breath. "So?"

"That's how you were conceived."

"My parents *never* used a sperm bank. They were totally in love. My mother was devastated when my father died. If they'd used a sperm bank, they would have told me."

Paul knew he wouldn't score any points by reminding Madison that her mother had married less than a year after her father's death. He couldn't see a way to sugarcoat this, and he sensed she was the type of woman who would appreciate directness. "According to my research, your mother was artificially inseminated at the New Horizons Fertility Clinic."

"No way!" she shouted. The retriever shied to one side as if expecting a blow. "My mother would have told me."

You'd be surprised, he wanted to respond. Being a cop had proved to him that unimaginable things could happen. "Are you sure?"

"Positive." She lowered herself to the sofa again and reached down to stroke the head of the frightened dog.

Paul reached inside the jacket of the lightweight sport coat he was wearing and pulled out a folded sheet of paper. He handed it to her. "Is this your mother's signature?"

Brows knit, she scanned the photocopy. "It appears to be her signature. It's hard to say for sure." She thrust the paper back at him. "So? She might have visited a clinic. That doesn't mean—"

"She received sperm donations from donor 8374 on two separate occasions. I can show you documentation to prove it."

Madison stared at him, her intense eyes calling him a liar. "That's ridiculous. I look exactly like my father. Ask anyone. I have his personality, too."

He waited, giving her time to absorb the news. "The insemination dates are just over nine months before you were born."

"I wouldn't know. I haven't seen the so-called documentation."

She had the same stubborn streak the rest of her biological family shared, but he didn't mention it. "I'll have copies of it within the week."

"Why don't you have them now?"

"New Horizons was an unusual facility. They specialized in Mensa donors. Men with high—"

"I know what Mensa is. Eggheads. You have to have a high IQ score."

"You were invited to join, weren't you?"

She tossed her head and flung her hair over one shoulder. "Who would want to hang out with a bunch of nerds?"

He kept his smile to himself. His file on Madison told him a lot about her but there was nothing like an interview to reveal personality. She had attitude in spades, just like the rest of the bunch.

"Don't you want to know more about donor 8374?"

"No. I don't. There's an explanation for this mistake. That donor is *not* my father."

"He was a medical student at Harvard when he sold his sperm. They paid a premium for donors who were extremely intelligent. Know what their next requirement was?" He didn't wait for her to answer. She was gazing heavenward and he was damn sure she wasn't praying. "Other than being Caucasian? Tall. Women seeking sperm donors want tall men. Tall, smart men."

He waited a beat to let that tidbit sink in, then added, "You're a lot taller than either of your parents, aren't you?"

"So?" she shot back, her accusing gaze now directed right at him. "A lot of children are taller than their parents." She studied him a moment as if he were some disgusting bug that had crawled out from under a garbage can. "If this donor lived in Boston, how did his…his sperm get down here? My parents met at Tulane and moved to Miami just after they were married. My father might have gone to Boston on business, but my mother never visited the city until I went to college."

He knew Madison had attended Massachusetts Institute of Technology as a National Science Foundation scholar and had been accepted to a master's program. She'd dropped out and returned to Miami when her father had become ill with terminal pancreatic cancer. That's when she'd met and married Aiden Larsen.

"The clinic in Boston sold some of their inventory to New Horizons."

"Why would they do that?"

"Profit. Do you know how much more valuable sperm is when it comes from Mensa donors with Harvard credentials?"

"Don't forget tall. Women want tall men." She almost cracked a smile, surprising Paul and giving him a captivating glimpse of her disarming sense of humor.

"Right. Tall, smart men with Harvard degrees made New Horizons a bundle. You see, in the Boston area, there are a lot of Ivy League schools, but down here that isn't the case. New Horizons did a ton of advertising. Women flocked to their Miami clinic. There was a long, long waiting list."

"It isn't around anymore?"

"They went out of business in the mid-nineties." He didn't say they'd been sued for false advertising.

"Why? From what I've read, using sperm donors is more

popular than ever. Seems to me, smart, tall men with Ivy League degrees are still in demand."

Some people were book smart, but Madison Connelly was quick on the uptake. He decided now was the time to be honest with her. "The Boston sperm bank stopped using Mensa donors after coming under fire for being too elitist. New Horizons was forced to collect sperm locally. They concocted phony backgrounds to get higher prices for their services. Lawsuits followed and put them out of business."

"I don't know why I asked. This has nothing to do with my parents." She didn't sound as sure of herself as she had a few minutes ago. "What do you want with me?"

"You have a family who would like to meet you. A half brother and a half sister—"

She jumped to her feet again. This time she didn't utter a word as she stalked to the wall of glass where the sun had set in a burst of crimson and gold. "I don't want to meet any of them under false pretenses. I know who my father is. Some photocopy from a clinic that went out of business for illegal practices doesn't prove a thing."

She spun around to face him. "My mother is sailing in the South Pacific right now. It's an extended honeymoon and an adventure she's always wanted. She telephones me whenever she gets to a port." She strode toward the door, covering the distance quickly with her showgirl legs, and flung it open. "I'll call you if she says this is true."

Paul rose slowly. He already knew Madison's mother was sailing around the world with her new husband, a man not much older than her daughter. It could be weeks before she surfaced.

"I regret having to keep being the bearer of bad news. I know now is a terrible moment to tell you all this but I'm afraid we don't have much time. This sperm donor needs a liver transplant or he'll die."

Her flashing eyes telegraphed the anger she was barely

keeping in check. "I knew there was a reason for your visit. That man doesn't want to connect with his supposed long-lost children. He's after an organ donor."

Paul couldn't deny it. "True, but does the name Wyatt Holbrook mean anything to you?"

He could see that it did. Wyatt was well-known in the Miami area for his philanthropic endeavors and his pharmaceutical company. Madison was too smart and too well-read not to recognize the name.

"I've heard of him." The hostility in her voice had dropped a notch. "He's done a lot to help people in Miami."

"Yes. He funded the cancer wing at Miami General and he's given generously to AIDS research projects locally and nationally."

"Fine. So he's a generous man who's helped people." Hostility was still evident in her voice.

"He's the sperm donor I mentioned." He refrained from referring to the man as her father. He could see how sensitive she was about the subject. "He has two children by his late wife but they can't donate."

"Wait a second! Did you say *liver* transplant?" When Paul nodded, she rushed to add, "I was thinking kidney. I've read a little about liver transplants from live donors—"

"It's a relatively new procedure. A donor gives a lobe of the organ and over time it regenerates to almost full size again. The most successful transplants are between blood relatives."

"Isn't it a risky procedure for the donor?"

"There is some risk," he hedged. "It's major abdominal surgery, but there have been very few documented problems."

"It's a lot to ask of anyone, much less a child he dug up just so he could find a suitable organ."

Paul stared at her hard, trying to determine which card to play. "If this were your father, wouldn't you do anything you could to save him?"

She shrugged, but he could see his words hit the mark. He pulled out all the stops. "This man isn't just any ordinary human being who needs help. Wyatt Holbrook is in the process of setting up one of the largest research foundations in the country. The money he contributes will finance countless medical and scientific advances."

He watched these facts register on her pretty face and her composure cracked just a little. "I guess."

Paul pressed his advantage. "Isn't he a man worth saving?"

The words hung in the air, the echo of the truth suspended between them.

She stared at him for a moment, then spoke in a low-pitched voice. "Any human being is worth saving. That isn't the point. I would have given all I have or ever hope to have to prevent Erin's death. I would help this man…if I could. From what I've read, the liver will be rejected unless the two immune systems are compatible. I'm not related to Wyatt Holbrook. The chances of my immune system being a close enough match are astronomical."

"I know you've been through a lot today. I hate to add to your burden. I'm just asking you to think about trying to help a man who has devoted his life to giving to others." He handed her a business card. "Think about it. I'll be in touch."

CHAPTER FOUR

What attracts malaria mosquitoes the fastest?

"WHERE IS EVERYONE?" Madison asked Rob Matthews, Erin's former boyfriend. "There were dozens of people at the funeral home."

It had been three days since she'd discovered Erin's body. The police wouldn't release the body until the coroner certified the autopsy results. Until then, there was always the possibility additional tests might be needed. During that time, Madison had scrambled to plan the funeral and notify as many of Erin's friends and relatives as possible.

It had proved to be a difficult task. Erin had been an only child of parents with almost no living relatives. The second cousins Madison did manage to locate in Missouri barely knew Erin's name. None of them had met her and they weren't interested in attending her funeral.

Erin's employer was fond of Erin and said he would be at the service. Madison contacted a few friends that she and Erin had known in high school. They hadn't stayed in touch with many of them, but several assured Madison they would come. Considering the few people who planned to attend, Madison was astonished when she turned from her place in the first row where she was sitting beside Rob and saw there was standing room only in the tiny chapel operated by the funeral home.

Who were they? she'd wondered. Apparently, they'd read the

notice in the newspaper. Just seeing all the solemn faces cheered Madison. She'd imagined Erin being buried with almost no one to grieve for her. As soon as the brief service was over, Madison had phoned the caterer to order more food and made sure everyone had maps to the Fisher Island home where she was holding the reception.

"Do you think people were intimidated by Fisher Island?" Madison asked Rob. "Is that why they didn't come?"

"I doubt it. Most people never have the chance to visit a private island like Fisher. They wouldn't miss an opportunity."

Madison looked around. Less than a dozen people were clustered in small groups near the lavish buffet. No one was at the bar, where a waiter stood ready to serve drinks.

"So where are they?" she asked. Most of the guests who were present had eaten and would be leaving soon.

"Well…I suspect some of them might not want anyone to know their names." Rob's dark brown eyes telegraphed concern and anxiety. He was obviously grieving but trying to be stoic. He was tall and a little thinner than when she'd last joined him for dinner. He had a warm smile and a great sense of humor, but he was a little offbeat. She could never tell what he was really thinking. In that way, he was a lot like Erin, she decided.

"What do you mean?" she asked.

"The police had a car with a video camera outside the funeral home."

"They did?" Madison had been so shell-shocked from her best friend's death and lack of sleep that she'd barely managed to keep from sobbing as she'd walked into the chapel. She hadn't noticed much.

"I think it's standard after a homicide," Rob replied. "Some killers get a morbid thrill from attending their victim's funerals."

"I know." She'd seen enough crime shows to realize this.

"But people at the funeral were so normal-looking. A lot of them were women. Some seemed to be grandmother and grandfather types. They didn't look like killers."

"What do killers look like?" he asked, his voice pitched so low he was almost whispering.

"I don't know. I've asked myself over and over who could have killed Erin. She never hurt anyone. Who would want her dead?"

"No one. No one we know, anyway."

"Don't bet on it," she replied. "I know the statistics. Homicides are rarely random acts." She didn't mention the details Paul had given her. From what he'd said, the killer knew a lot about Erin's personal habits. The murderer could have been a stalker who spied on her, or someone she knew.

Rob slipped his arm around her shoulders and gave her a reassuring hug. She leaned just slightly against his tall, spare frame. Here was someone who loved Erin as much as Madison had. The only other person at the funeral who had honestly cared about Erin. Whatever had caused Erin and Rob to break up could easily have been Erin's fault. As close as Erin and Madison had always been, it remained a mystery to her why Erin never quite connected with other people.

A lone wolf. That's what her father had once called Erin. The thought of her father brought her back to Paul Tanner and his horrible accusations. She'd tried not to think about what he'd told her.

Madison wanted to reach her mother, but she was still between ports somewhere in the South Pacific with the young hunk who'd replaced her beloved father. Her mother had been so devastated by the loss of her husband that she'd remarried more quickly than she should have, in Madison's opinion. Madison didn't care for the man, but she had to deal with him if she wanted a relationship with her mother.

Though in her heart, Madison knew Zack Connelly was her

father, she just wanted to hear her mother's explanation for visiting a fertility clinic. She'd thought it over and decided her mother must have received some type of fertility drug. That's why what appeared to be her signature had been on one of the clinic's forms. *Forget it,* she told herself. *Focus on Erin, on the present.*

"Who do you think all those people at the chapel were?" Madison repeated the question she'd just asked as she pulled away from Rob. "Why would they care if the police saw them?"

He ran his slender fingers through his dark brown hair, his gaze troubled. "I'm fairly sure they knew Erin from the Everglades Animal Defense League."

"Oh, really?" She hadn't thought of those folks. Erin had been active with the group since her first year in college. Madison had been at MIT at the time, but Erin had told her about being a founding member of the group when Madison came home at Easter. The organization had campaigned hard to stop cosmetic testing on animals. What had begun with pickets and print advertising had escalated into break-ins and arson.

"That's what caused our split, you know."

Madison shook her head; Erin had never wanted to discuss her problems with Rob. Typical Erin. Her friend talked least about what mattered the most.

Not that Rob had been any more forthcoming. Madison had gone to dinner a few times with him, when he'd been kind enough to call and see how she was dealing with her divorce. He'd never brought up his split with Erin. It was as if a steel curtain came down. No one knew the details except Erin and Rob.

"As a vet, I'm sympathetic to the cause," he told her. "But I couldn't condone criminal activity."

She could see his point, yet she shared Erin's concern with the way many animals were treated in labs. "It's wrong to test cosmetics and hair products on animals."

"Like Aspen."

"Dr. Wallace told you?" After finding Erin's body, Madison had taken the golden retriever to Rob's veterinary clinic, but she'd been late for the appointment and his associate had treated Aspen. When Madison had told the police Aspen had an eye infection, it had just been a guess fueled by her desire to get away from the crime scene. Rob's associate had stunned her when he'd informed her Aspen's runny eyes had probably been deliberately inflicted.

"Wally thinks hair spray or maybe spray deodorant was tested on your dog. Not a surprise. Wally interned in a test lab. He knows the signs." Rob hesitated a moment, moved a little closer, then slid his arm around Madison's shoulders again. "Erin called me about midnight the night she died. I hadn't heard from her in months. She told me she'd *found* a dog that someone had abused. Something had been sprayed in his eyes. I told her to come in at noon because I had to leave for a meeting. But that's not why I wanted her there during lunch."

Something in his expression alarmed Madison. She had a feeling she knew what he was going to say.

"I doubted she'd 'found' a dog in the middle of the night. The EADL had been at it again. They'd broken into a test facility somewhere and stolen the animals used for experiments. I agreed to treat the dog but I didn't want it in my records."

Madison knew Rob could lose his license if the authorities charged him with aiding the illegal activities of the Everglades Animal Defense League. She vaguely remembered something she'd seen on TV the morning she'd found Erin's body. There had been a suspicious fire at a local laboratory that conducted tests for cosmetics companies. It appeared to have been set to conceal the theft of the lab's test animals and documents. At the time, it had crossed her mind Erin might have been involved. So much had happened that she'd forgotten about it.

"The television reports never mentioned dogs," she told him. "They said lab animals had been taken, which made it sound like mice or rats."

"Animal rights are a hot issue. People cut labs slack when testing is for cancer or some other medical purpose, but testing cosmetics on dogs could trigger a lot of negative publicity the company doesn't want."

"I see," Madison replied. "Why did Erin have papers saying she bought Aspen for twenty-five dollars from some woman?"

Rob hesitated a moment, then said, "The way I understand it, when the league 'liberates' animals, they shuttle them as fast as they can and as far from the lab as possible. Erin was probably going to drive north, then hand off the dog to someone else who would in turn drive and meet another person. If questioned about the animal, they would have papers."

"I see. Erin never mentioned anything about doing these things."

"That's because she knew you disapproved."

"True. After the fire at the Attleborough Laboratory back when we were in college, I told her how reckless I thought the group was being. Someone could get killed or injured in a fire. I reminded her a man in Oregon who'd set fire to a lab that tested on animals received a five-year prison term. I told her to stop."

"Erin was too stubborn to stop. She just didn't tell you about it anymore."

Madison nodded, sighed. Erin had never said she would drop out of the group. Every time Madison heard about an incident at a lab, she would wonder if Erin was involved.

Rob gave her a slight hug. She was a little uncomfortable having his arm around her so much. She knew he was only trying to comfort her, but it somehow made her feel disloyal to Erin. Her friend had been devoted to this man and he'd left her. Not that Madison blamed him exactly, but the situation made her feel guilty.

Their split had happened just days after Aiden had left Madison. She'd been in such turmoil that she'd been of little help to Erin. When Madison had finally pulled herself together, Erin seemed to have recovered, as well. She never said exactly why Rob left except they didn't agree on life.

"Madison," called a male voice, and she turned to see Erin's boss walking her way. Beside the heavyset, balding Mr. Pinder were two women in black suits. She assumed they all worked in the Tropical Shades office where Erin had been a sales rep.

"We've got to run," said one of the women. "You know how it is on the 95."

She nodded; indeed she did. Take the wrong off-ramp on the trip north and you could be history. A fact that had put a dent in Miami's tourism when several tourists had been killed after taking the wrong exit and finding themselves in no-man's-land.

"I'm sorry for your loss," Mr. Pinder told Madison. "Erin was a wonderful person."

"A treasure," agreed the other woman with him.

"Thank you for coming," Madison made herself say. She doubted if any of the three had more than a passing acquaintance with Erin. She wasn't one to be close to employees in an office she used as a base and visited only when necessary.

Within the next half hour, the others gradually left. Twilight gathered over Biscayne Bay and no one remained except the catering crew, who was busy loading up, and Rob Matthews.

"I've told them to pack up some of the food for you," she said to Rob as they stood by the artful cheese display on the buffet table. "I'm sure the gang in your office can eat it tomorrow."

One of the cheeses was a little strong; the smell wafted up toward her. Madison suddenly remembered malaria-bearing mosquitoes are drawn the fastest by the scent of strong cheese. Humans exuded sweat—particularly from their feet—that was much like cheese and attracted mosquitoes, especially in the tropics. She never ate cheese with a strong smell.

"Thanks. It's a shame to waste so much," Rob replied. "What about your office?"

"There's plenty for both of us and I'm sure the kids in the cube farm will scarf up every morsel." She didn't add that she dreaded going to work tomorrow. She was so angry she was afraid of what she might say. Aiden had known Erin for years. True, the two hadn't cared for each other, but Aiden should have at least put in an appearance at the funeral.

"Maybe we should walk the dog," suggested Rob.

"Good idea. I'll get Aspen." She rushed off toward the bedroom she was using. She'd put the retriever in the room to keep him from slipping out the front door with one of the guests.

"Here, boy," she called as she entered the bedroom. Aspen jumped to his feet and headed in her direction. She noticed he was moving more quickly than he had when she'd first gotten him. Rob's partner hadn't given her much hope that the quality of Aspen's vision would improve, so she assumed he was becoming accustomed to his surroundings. "How about a walk?"

The dog enthusiastically wagged his tail. He was an intelligent dog. In the short time she'd had him, Aspen had learned what "cookie" and "walk" meant. She grabbed his leash off the dresser, clasped it to his collar and walked him out to the foyer where Rob was waiting.

With a smile, he held the door open for them. Outside, it was still warm and the last remaining light from the setting sun glistened on Biscayne Bay. The beauty of nature was eternal, timeless, she thought, unlike the fleetingness of life, where people could be snatched from you in an instant.

"You know, I'm already attached to this dog," she told Rob. "I think Aspen must have been someone's pet. He's well behaved and knows several commands."

"No telling where he came from. Some labs are very careful while others take any dogs they can get."

They paused and waited while Aspen did his business on the greenbelt. An elderly woman dressed to the nines was walking a small white poodle with a Burberry collar nearby.

"What did you tell the police about Aspen?" Rob asked in a low voice.

"Nothing. I took the bill of sale off the counter and stuffed it in my purse before the police arrived. I planned to explain when I went down to the station for the interview, but when Dr. Wallace told me someone had deliberately sprayed stuff in Aspen's eyes, I didn't mention him." She reached down and patted Aspen's sleek head. "I was afraid they would give him back to those terrible people."

"You're absolutely right. They would have."

"Did you tell them Erin called you about Aspen shortly before she was killed?"

Rob shook his head. "No. I can't imagine the break-in had anything to do with her death. Those people are fanatics about animals. They don't go around killing each other."

"But won't the police find your number in Erin's phone records and know she called you shortly before she was murdered?"

"No. She told me she used a pay phone. Animal rights activists are really careful not to leave a trail to others. They won't find anything on her computer or her phones that will link her to the group."

Madison turned, hearing someone calling her name. A paunchy man with gray hair and eyebrows like steel wool was heading their way. She didn't recognize him, and she was fairly certain he hadn't been at the chapel. She'd given instructions to the guards to admit anyone to the island for the reception.

"Ridley Johnson," he told them in a breathless voice. "I'm Erin Wycoff's attorney. Sorry I couldn't get to the funeral. I had a deposition."

Madison stared at the man, not quite believing what she was hearing. Why would Erin need an attorney? She'd never mentioned one. But then, there had been a lot of things her friend had neglected to tell her.

"I have to fly to New York tomorrow morning." He shrugged. "That's the price of being a one-man operation. You're on the go all the time."

Madison tried for a sympathetic smile, but her mind was still on Erin. What else hadn't Erin told her? Maybe if she'd been more open with her, Madison might be able to help the police find her killer.

The lawyer looked at Rob, but spoke to Madison. "Could we talk in private? It's about Miss Wycoff's estate."

Madison almost laughed at the word *estate*. Other than a few pieces of gold jewelry, Erin didn't have much. "This is my friend Robert Matthews. He was also a close friend of Erin's. You can talk in front of him."

The lawyer arched one eyebrow skeptically, then said, "Miss Wycoff had me draw up a will for her about six months ago. She left you everything."

For a gut-cramping second the world froze. "She did? I'm surprised Erin bothered with a will. She didn't have much."

He gazed at her for a long moment in a way that struck her as odd. "Like I explained to the police, the exact worth of her estate won't be clear until the sale of the property is finalized and some back taxes paid. But it's in the neighborhood of eleven million dollars."

Eleven million? The magnitude of this news poleaxed her brain. She managed to whisper, "Are you sure?"

"What property?" asked Rob.

"It's six acres outside Tallahassee. She inherited it from her parents. It was in the sticks when they bought it. The town's spread out and a new shopping center is going in. She agreed to sell the land to the developer. It's in escrow right now."

"Oh my God," Madison whispered. The police were already suspicious of Madison. Now they would have a motive for murder.

CHAPTER FIVE

What does forensic *mean?*

MADISON BROUGHT Aspen to work with her the morning following the funeral. The dog must have spent most of his life in a cage. She refused to lock him up inside the house all day long. There wasn't any yard where she was staying. When she bought her own place, it would need to have an outdoor area for Aspen.

She wasn't exactly sure when she'd decided to keep the retriever, but it had been in the back of her mind since she'd seen her closest friend's dead body. The dog meant a lot to Erin or she wouldn't have taken him home. There was nothing she could do for Erin now. It was too late for that, but she could help the dog. She was positive that's what Erin would have wanted.

"You, like, got a dog," Jade said the second Madison walked through the door. The receptionist's black hair was now a suspicious shade of red and gelled heavenward. "How cool is that?"

"His name is Aspen." She looked around but didn't see Aiden or Chloe in their cubicles. "He'll be coming to work with me until I find a place with a yard."

"I'm sorry about your friend," Jade said as she gave Aspen a pat. "Like, what a terrible thing to happen."

"The worst, believe me. The worst." She let her eyes roam over the small cube farm for a moment. It had been days since she'd been in the office. "What did I miss?"

Jade didn't have an official title. No one but Aiden and Madison were called anything but associates. This had been the cornerstone of their "anticorporate" philosophy, but as part of the divorce settlement, Aiden and Madison became copresidents. Since Jade's desk was up front, she was the receptionist by default to the few visitors. Her main function was to assist Aiden and Madison. Jade's Goth appearance might be offputting, but she was sharp. Madison knew Jade had been on top of everything while Madison was away.

"Not much happened," Jade replied. "I put all the messages on your desk. Aiden may have, like, checked your e-mail for you."

"Why would he do that?"

Jade shrugged and her expression curdled. "I guess he was trying to help. How cool is that?"

"Help with what?" she asked, trying to conceal her anger but hearing its undertone in her voice anyway. Once, they'd flitted in and out of each other's cubicles, checked each other's e-mails and written responses for each other. Those days were over. They no longer visited each other's cubes unless it was absolutely necessary.

"Aiden must have thought you were, like, so busy with the funeral."

But he couldn't be bothered to come to the funeral. Madison doubted Aiden was trying to help. What had he been up to? She realized this was Jade's way of letting her know without being a snitch. She smiled at Jade while silently applauding her own sixth sense. Something had told her Jade would be an asset to the company despite her questionable fashion sense.

"Where is Aiden?" Madison asked.

"He's at the hospital with Chloe."

From Jade's matter-of-fact tone, Madison could tell Chloe wasn't seriously ill. "What happened?"

Jade rolled eyes lined with a paintbrush. "Chloe got headlights. How cool is that?"

"A car accident?" Madison immediately thought of the Porsche Boxster that Aiden had bought for Chloe right after he walked out on Madison.

"No. Like, you know, *headlights*."

"Oh." The light dawned. Headlights were the rage in SoBe, where the babes paraded around with surgically enlarged breasts showcased by skimpy, tight tops. Erect nipples—a total turn-on for guys—crowned perfect chests. To keep them permanently erect, a surprising number of women had their nipples injected with cosmetic fillers that were also used to erase lines and plump up lips.

The whole thing sounded so painful, so ridiculous, that Madison couldn't imagine suffering through the procedure just to attract men. But Chloe was different. Madison had sensed it when she'd interviewed her for a position at TotalTrivia. There was something about Chloe that she hadn't liked, but Madison had been so impressed by her credentials that she'd ignored her instincts.

As time had gone on and Madison had the opportunity to watch Chloe, she began to understand how insecure the woman was. Chloe had a brilliant mind, but she relied on sex to get her what she wanted. How did Aiden feel about this? she wondered. Did he like having a wife who turned heads? Was that what had been wrong with their marriage? Madison was attractive, but men didn't drool when she walked into a room.

"Chloe was so sick the day after her surgery that Aiden canceled his lunch with Luis Estevez."

Luis Estevez! A frisson of alarm skittered down her spine. They'd discussed adding gambling to TotalTrivia and the possibility of using Allied Miami Bank, but they'd put off a decision. Rumors of mob connections and drug money surrounded the bank president who'd left Cuba as a child and had made a fortune in Little Havana, then moved into Miami's financial district.

Madison and Aiden had agreed to wait and think about gambling. No, she mentally corrected herself, she'd told Aiden that she wanted to look into it more. Evidently, he'd gone ahead.

"I'd say you could call him to check in, but Aiden's cell phone has to be off in the hospital."

Her ex was never out of touch; he lived with his cell phone and BlackBerry. Chloe's condition must be serious after all. "She'll be okay. It's not life-threatening. Is it?"

Jade shook her head. "Aiden called earlier. She has a staph infection but they're getting it under control."

"He'll be in later?"

"He doesn't want to leave Chloe if she needs him. How cool is that?"

Touching. Positively touching. Madison reached down and stroked Aspen's silky head. She couldn't help thinking this might be Chloe's just deserts. The woman had been blessed with a brilliant scientific mind, yet she relied on her body to get what she wanted. Chloe had gone after Aiden with the determination of a shark after a fish.

After Aiden had left her for Chloe, Madison had run into an old friend from MIT. Pamela Nolan had gone on to grad school at Stanford, where she'd known Chloe. Pamela had described her as "pathologically sexual" and told tales of the havoc Chloe had wrought upon the grad program while she'd been at Stanford. Pamela didn't know what had happened, but Chloe had left before receiving her master's degree. No one knew why she'd headed to Miami.

Madison had considered telling Aiden, then thought it would sound like sour grapes. What was the gossip worth, anyway? Not much. People always talked about each other. Nothing she could have said would have changed Aiden's mind. He was head over heels in love with Chloe.

A pang, a yearning as familiar as Madison's own reflection in a mirror, hit her. Was there *nothing* Aiden wouldn't do for

Chloe? He'd never once treated Madison with such adoration. Too often her longing to understand his betrayal had a rough edge that morphed into anger or self-pity. *Don't go there*, she warned herself. *Keep your mind on business.*

"I'll be at my desk." Madison jiggled Aspen's leash. He'd settled himself on the floor while they'd been talking. As he jumped to his feet, she remembered the food. Even though it was barely midmorning, heat had purled up from the asphalt parking lot when she stepped out of her car and with it came a suffocating wave of humidity. It would be an oven in less than half an hour. "There's food in my car from the reception. I want to put it out in the break room for everyone to share. Will you help me—"

"I'll get it." Jade popped out of her chair and Madison handed her the car keys. "You have work to do."

"Okay, boy, here we are," she told Aspen when they reached her office. "Find a spot and make yourself comfortable. We'll be here for a while."

Aspen cocked his head and gazed up at her as if he truly understood. He was an amazing animal. She knew from experience that he would nudge her with his nose when he had to go out. He was so well trained that it amazed her he could have wound up in a testing facility. Had he been stolen from someone who'd lovingly trained him?

Madison sat in her swivel chair, wondering as she had many times about the dog. She was tempted to search for his owners, but she was afraid to call attention to Aspen. Rob had warned this could result in the lab being able to prove it legally owned Aspen. She'd already decided that this dog would never be returned to a lab if she could help it. The retriever settled under her desk at her feet.

She sifted through the pile of messages that Jade had placed in her phone message box. Paul Tanner had called several times; he'd also left messages she'd ignored on her cell phone. Would the man ever give up and go away?

Madison was positive she hadn't been conceived through some anonymous sperm donor. She was her father's daughter. Zach Connelly had shared many secrets with her during the final days before cancer claimed him. He would have told her if she hadn't been his biological daughter.

Not that it made any difference. Titles like father and sister were merely words. Erin's death had sent Madison into an emotional tailspin. It was like losing her sister. She wouldn't have loved a real sister any more than she had Erin. That's why Erin's secrets hurt so much. Why hadn't she mentioned that the property her parents had left her had suddenly become so valuable?

Madison tamped down another emotional response and turned her thoughts back to her father. He'd raised her with so much love that she doubted any father and daughter could have been closer. When she spoke to her mother about Paul Tanner's outrageous claim, they'd share a real hoot.

There were stacks of printouts on her desk. She knew most of them were trivia questions programmers wanted to post on the site but worried that players might have problems with. Trivia players were classic nitpickers. If an answer wasn't exactly correct, the site would be inundated with e-mail complaints.

The first question she scanned asked about the tallest mountain on earth. The obvious answer was Mount Everest, but there was another mountain in Africa that was nearly half a mile taller. This was because the earth wasn't round like a basketball, but elliptical, meaning it was wider at the equator. This width translated to additional height, making some obscure African mountain taller than Everest. This was exactly the type of question TotalTrivia gamers adored, but it would have to be phrased properly to add the key element of the shape of the earth.

Madison was usually good at rewriting confusing questions,

but her mind was still muzzy from lack of sleep. She scooted the stack aside and turned on her computer, wondering why Aiden had been in her office. It certainly wasn't to rework questions. Though Aiden was great with the computer and finances, he was terrible at rewrites. He left those to Madison.

Still suspicious about Aiden's motives, she opened her e-mail folder and found hundreds had come in while she'd been away. She could have checked them from home, but she hadn't bothered. Squinting at the screen, she scrolled through the list to see if any of them were really important.

Madison was still answering e-mails when she heard Jade walk into the cubicle. A quick glance at the time on her computer told Madison that nearly two hours had passed.

"There's, like, someone to see you from the police," Jade informed her. "How cool is that?"

Right behind Jade was one of the homicide detectives who'd questioned her at the station the day Erin's body had been discovered. Suddenly there was a weight in the center of her stomach. She ventured a sideways glance under the desk where Aspen was sleeping. The dog couldn't be seen from the opposite side of her desk where the detective stood watching her.

Madison rose, extended her hand and forced a smile. "Detective…"

"Lincoln Burgess." The stout man with sparse gray hair and a walrus mustache shook her hand. A trace of stale cigarette smoke rose from his lightweight sport coat as he moved. "Mind if I sit?"

"Please." Madison slowly sank into her own chair. She'd mentally prepared herself for this moment but now that it had arrived she couldn't help being edgy.

"I just had a few follow-up questions." His tone was conversational but it did nothing to ease her nerves. "It's about the dog."

Dread rolled over her like a silent, all-encompassing fog. She waited with what she hoped was a neutral expression on her face.

"The dog you had with you at the crime scene. Had it been in the house?"

Madison had prepared herself for this interrogation with Rob's help. No sense in lying more than necessary. Forensic experts would know Aspen had been in the house. *Work around this—don't fight it.*

"Yes. Erin told me she had a golden retriever for me. When I came to pick up my cell phone, he was in the kitchen with his bill of sale and everything."

The detective's pale blue eyes narrowed. "When did she tell you this?"

"On Friday night when we went clubbing. Erin said a woman she'd met had a dog she couldn't keep. Erin knew I was looking for a pet and bought him for me."

Two beats of silence. "You never mentioned the dog in your interview."

She ladled on the charm with a vapid smile. There were some advantages to being blond. Men automatically thought you were stupid. "No one asked about Aspen. Why is he important? Aren't you looking for Erin's killer?"

"Her death could be linked to the dog." Detective Burgess's eyes had no depth or light to them. Madison couldn't tell if he'd bought her naive act.

"Really?"

"Do you have the bill of sale?"

"Yes. It's at home. I mean, it's at the home on Fisher Island where I'm house-sitting. Why?"

"We're going to need to see it."

Madison nodded, noticing he hadn't answered her question. She had the sickening sensation that he was going to take Aspen away from her. She cursed herself for not following up on Rob's suggestion that she try to contact the Everglades Animal

Defense League and arrange to shuttle Aspen out of the state to protect him the way Erin would have had she lived.

Out of the corner of her eye, Madison saw Jade hurrying up the aisle with Paul Tanner at her heels. Great! Just what she needed. How could the guy interrupt an ongoing meeting? But a strange, excited feeling feathered through her chest.

Paul Tanner strode through the cube farm wearing arrogance like a second skin. But Madison couldn't help noticing all the female heads turned in his direction. For an instant she regretted taking so little time to dress. She had on no makeup except for lip gloss. Her willful hair was going in all directions this morning and she'd done little to tame it.

What Paul Tanner thought of her didn't matter. Then it occurred to her that a distraction might be useful. She wasn't much good at picking her way through a minefield of lies.

Jade rushed into the cube, saying, "I told Mr. Tanner you were—"

"I thought I might be able to help." Paul Tanner directed his comment to Detective Burgess, who didn't look too thrilled to see him.

"It's okay, Jade," Madison told the girl and she backed out of the cube.

Paul looked directly at her with a tilt of his lips meant to pass for a smile. The beat of her heart suddenly filled her skull. *Get a grip,* she told herself.

"I thought you were still out on leave," the detective said to Paul.

"I am, but I heard you wanted to ask Madison a few questions about the dog. I thought I might be able to help, since I was on the scene immediately after she discovered the body."

Detective Burgess considered this a little longer than Madison thought necessary, considering Paul's presence on the scene was an established fact. "Miss Connelly claims to have a bill of sale for the dog. Did you see it?"

Paul shifted his gaze to Madison and a nimbus of dread snaked through her. What would the man say?

"The envelope on the kitchen counter next to the pizza box?"

Amazing. Paul had been sprinting through the house in response to her screams, yet he'd had time to notice the box and the envelope beside it. From a distance she heard herself answer, "Yes. The bill of sale was in the envelope."

"She never mentioned it during the interview at the station," the detective informed Paul.

Paul shrugged, glanced her way and said, "She probably didn't think it was important. After all, she'd just found her best friend's body."

"Right," Detective Burgess grudgingly agreed. "But the interview was hours later, after she'd taken the dog to the vet for some eye problem."

"Have you made any progress in finding Erin's killer?" Madison asked. Her father always said the best defense was a good offense.

"Her killer might have been the person who sold your friend the dog. He was probably the last person to see her."

Madison said, "The name on the sales receipt I have at my house is L. Morgan. It must be a woman. Erin said a lady couldn't keep her golden retriever."

"Is there a city listed?" Paul asked.

"Miami." She'd already checked the telephone directory. Hundreds of Morgans were listed in the greater Miami area. If Rob had been correct and this dog had been liberated from the lab, his bill of sale had been forged and deliberately made to be untraceable.

"I'll need the certificate," said the detective, "and the dog."

"The dog?" Paul said, a laugh in his tone. "What for? Gonna question him?"

"Forensics might want to—"

"No way," Paul said flatly. "Too much time has passed."

Her brain immediately switched to trivia central. Forensics meant pertaining to or used in a court of law. Too much time had lapsed and Aspen had been too many places to make testing his fur admissible in court. But to be safe she said, "I washed him, then conditioned his fur." It was the truth. Aspen had a strange smell; something they'd put on him at the lab, she'd decided.

"Where is the dog?" asked the detective.

"I'm taking care of him," she replied, knowing he still couldn't see Aspen from where he was sitting. "He's my dog."

"You know where to find her dog if you need him," Paul said.

"I guess," the other man muttered.

"Do you want me to get the bill of sale and bring it in?" Paul asked.

Detective Burgess looked relieved. "It'll save me a helluva lot of time. We're shorthanded as usual."

"I'll bring it to you," Paul said.

Madison didn't like the idea of being forced to spend more time with Paul, but she didn't want Detective Burgess around any longer than necessary. He might change his mind and take Aspen.

Detective Burgess rose and walked toward the exit from the cube. He turned, asking, "When did you learn Erin's death would make you a multimillionaire?"

His words were as sharp as a new razor, but she was ready for him. From the moment the lawyer had told her about the will, Madison had known she would be under even more suspicion. "I found out yesterday, when her attorney came to see me."

A malignant silence filled the cubicle, then the detective asked, "Your best friend never mentioned owning a piece of property worth a fortune?"

"Yes, we talked about it when her parents were killed. At that point, the property was in the sticks and she thought it was worthless. Erin tried to sell it but couldn't. The taxes were killing her. I understand in the last eighteen months there has been a lot of development in the area and a shopping center is going to be built on her land."

Detective Burgess studied her for a suspended moment and she could feel Paul Tanner's eyes on her, too. A chill coursed through her, but she refused to allow her face to reflect her inner emotions. She knew the dead air was a police trick designed to make her talk more, but she didn't. Let them ask their questions.

"What are you going to do with all the money?" the detective asked.

"It's all going to Save the Chimps. That's a refuge for chimps that have been confined to cages for their entire lives and subjected to scientific experiments. It's located in Fort Pierce. According to her lawyer, that's what Erin was planning to do with the money, but she didn't have the opportunity to follow through. I'll carry out her wishes, of course."

"Of course," responded Detective Burgess as he consulted Paul Tanner with a quick glance. "But as I understand it, the deal for the property is still being worked out. Who's to say you won't change your mind and do anything you like with the money?"

CHAPTER SIX

Which fish swims the slowest?

MADISON WATCHED Detective Lincoln Burgess saunter out of her cubicle. She felt as if she'd averted catastrophe, but she knew it was only momentary relief. She hadn't seen the last of the detective.

"Do they have any clues about Erin's killer or am I the only suspect?" she asked Paul.

Two beats of silence. "I don't know. I'm on leave—"

"You said you were in the office this morning. What did you hear?"

He shrugged his powerful shoulders and for a moment, she thought he wasn't going to answer. "Not much. Your prints are everywhere."

She gestured for him to sit in the seat the detective had vacated. "That's not surprising. I was at Erin's on Friday night."

"What about the bottles in the medicine cabinet?" A sardonic note underscored the question.

"I helped Erin move in. I unpacked half of everything in the house. My fingerprints are going to be everywhere."

His blue eyes seared hers and she shifted in her seat, realizing this man exuded masculinity like musk from every pore. Although he wasn't handsome in a conventional way, Paul Tanner had that elusive *something* that made women respond to him.

What she must look like to him hit her again. Madison had rushed out of the house this morning after taking Aspen for a walk. As usual, she was dressed in well-worn jeans, paired today with a blue T-shirt. Her hair had always been sensitive to Florida's humidity.

Enough temptation must come Paul Tanner's way that he would never look twice at a nerd with frizzy hair. Like Aiden, this man would drool at the sight of Chloe and her low-cut tops and straight, sleek hair that fell over one eye. God! What was she thinking? She was in real trouble here.

"Do I need a lawyer?" she asked, to steer her mind back to the problem at hand.

"Wouldn't hurt."

Suddenly all the air in the room went still. Her brain managed to process the information and come up with the gravity of her situation. When she'd asked the question, she'd expected him to say no. "Earlier I realized I might need an attorney, but I don't know any criminal defense lawyers."

"I could give you a few names. Being in homicide, I've run into my share."

"Thanks," she mumbled, and jotted down the names he rattled off. Madison wondered if she could possibly afford to retain an attorney. She would be forced to use the money she'd been saving for a new house. She'd reinvested the rest of her divorce settlement in expanding TotalTrivia and hiring new programmers to keep up with the competition from other Web sites.

Her anxiety mounted as she considered her options. What would she do? The Russerts would return in a little over two weeks. She would have to find another place to live with Aspen.

Paul's measuring eyes continued to study her in a way that gave her the urge to cover herself. It was ridiculous, of course, but she felt he could see right through her and knew all about Aspen. Her fibs about the dog might make him believe she was being untruthful about everything else.

"Did you want to see me about something?" Madison asked as if she hadn't a clue what had brought him here.

He opened the manila folder he'd brought with him. "I know you needed proof that your mother used the services at New Horizons." He handed a sheaf of papers to her. "This is a transcript of her screening interview. It's all there. Just read it."

She took the papers. "Transcription? You mean the interview was taped."

"Yes. The tapes were destroyed but the files still contain transcripts of the screening sessions."

Her mind reeled. A lawyer. A new place to live. How could she deal with this, too? She felt like the slowest fish in the ocean—the sea horse. Bigger, more powerful fish were creating such turbulence in the water around her that she couldn't get anywhere.

She forced herself to scan the first section, which established her mother, Jessica Connelly, was married and living in the small apartment complex that Madison knew had been their home until she was six months old. She glanced over additional information anyone could have discovered about her parents, then told herself to concentrate and read more slowly.

Nurse Avery: How long have you been trying to conceive?

Jessica Connelly: Nearly three years. We've been to fertility specialists and tried everything. That's why I'm here. I want to be artificially inseminated.

Nurse Avery: I've looked over the doctors' records. It seems your husband has a low sperm count. You may become pregnant but it could take more time than you've given it.

Jessica Connelly: We want a baby now. If I conceive again, we'll have two children. If not, we'll be happy with one.

Madison was convinced this so-called interview was bogus. She was an only child, but her parents had assured her that it was by choice. Still, she couldn't help asking herself why a man like Paul Tanner would go to all the trouble to convince her that she had been the result of a sperm donation by a man needing a new liver unless Paul actually believed it was true.

She concentrated on the document before her while covertly studying him. He had a certain rugged appeal most other men lacked. Most assuredly, he was light-years away from Aiden Larsen. But then, Aiden had been a con artist in his own right. Looking back—as she had countless times since he asked for a divorce—Madison could see Aiden's attraction to her had revolved around her ability to construct an online game. Once that had been accomplished, Aiden had become less interested.

What was Paul Tanner's angle? What did he want? She'd done a search online and discovered what little he'd told her about himself seemed to be true. He was a homicide investigator who'd been shot in the line of duty. A Mike Tanner did have a private security agency. He must be Paul's father, but what was in this for them?

Madison knew enough about the psychology of scam artists to know they hooked their "marks" by presenting some facts that could easily be verified. It still didn't make his outrageous allegations true. She was her father's daughter. It was possible that her mother had been to the fertility clinic but hadn't gone through with the procedure.

She'd searched Google further for New Horizons, then used LexisNexis to take an in-depth look at the now-defunct clinic. They'd falsified data, claiming donors had Mensa credentials, and they'd charged for procedures patients hadn't received. An avalanche of lawsuits had been filed and the clinic's owners had left the country. There was no telling why her mother had a file at the clinic or why it had been altered to show she'd undergone the procedure.

She flipped through the pages, not really reading them. *Zeke*. The name exploded off the page with a boom that echoed in her brain. She backtracked and read the entire response, which had supposedly been transcribed from her mother's exact words.

Jessica Connelly: Zeke really wants a son. He says he doesn't care about the sex but I know how much he wants a boy. Zeke had asthma as a child. His mother refused to allow him to participate in sports and his father went along with her decision. Zeke always felt he missed out on the father-son bond other boys enjoyed. He wants a son to share ball games and fishing. You know, guy stuff.

Madison sucked in a stabilizing breath. Zeke. No one called Zachary Connelly anything but Zach or Zachary except her mother. When they were dating, she nicknamed him Zeke. She didn't do it in public for some reason, but at home, especially when she was joking, Jessica Connelly called him Zeke.

This transcript might possibly be authentic. How else would they have come up with the unique nickname? This reinforced an earlier assumption. Her mother had consulted doctors at the clinic. It still didn't prove Jessica Connelly had been inseminated there.

She glanced up and met Paul's eyes. Her doubts didn't show, did they? Her instincts told her this man would exploit any weakness. "How much did the inseminations cost?"

"They ranged from five to seven thousand dollars per session."

A loud gasp exploded out of her like a grenade. "That's a lot of money today. It was even more back then. My parents never had that kind of money, even when I was in high school and my father was at the top of his career. I couldn't have gone to MIT without a scholarship."

"True, but women were desperate to conceive and wanted those Mensa credentials. Your mother could have gone to the clinic—"

"Wait! You said my mother, not my parents. Why?"

He responded with a smile she couldn't quite decipher. What about this seemed so amusing? "Keep reading."

With a growing sense of unease, Madison directed her attention to the next page. It was the last page of the transcript.

Nurse Avery: Mrs. Connelly, the clinic requires an interview with every applicant's husband.

Jessica Connelly: Why? I'm the one having the baby.

Nurse Avery: True, but New Horizons needs to be certain the baby is wanted, by both parents.

Jessica Connelly: What if I were a single mother?

Nurse Avery: Well, that would be different.

Jessica Connelly: I don't see how.

God! thought Madison. The challenging note so obvious on the page seemed exactly like her mother. Jessica Connelly—now Jessica Whitcomb—always confronted people, demanding they explain themselves. The words on the page hit an invisible target she hadn't known existed, a hollow place in her heart. She forced herself to keep reading.

Nurse Avery: In those cases, it's the mother's decision alone…to have a child using artificial insemination. Since she would be the sole parent, the clinic doesn't require—

Jessica Connelly: I understand what you mean, but my case is different. My husband would rather be childless than use a sperm donor. I don't feel that way.

For a moment, Madison was torn by the urge to close her eyes and imagine her mother. Her parents had been close…yet so different. Her father openly loved Madison in a way most fathers reserved for their sons. Zach Connelly had never mentioned sports but he'd always encouraged Madison to participate. No, more than encouraged, now that she thought about it. He had playfully insisted. At some point in junior high school, Madison had realized this was how many fathers in her class behaved with their sons.

Madison had never cared for dolls or dress-up the way other little girls had. She'd been content to read books and experiment with her science kits. Buddy's Bodies had been a favorite.

It required the assembly of the human body from the internal organs outward. Another kit had been Living Chemistry, which involved many simple experiments.

Her father prodded Madison to get out of the house and "exercise." She'd found that she enjoyed sports but she'd never been a real star. It took time and practice that she would rather devote to her kits. She'd earned a spot on her high school varsity tennis team. She wouldn't have stuck with it except her father had assured her that a sport was a necessary component to be awarded an academic scholarship.

He'd been correct. Colleges these days required students to be "well-rounded" and those who qualified for a scholarship needed over-the-top grades, superior SAT scores and a slew of other commendations that would elevate them above the herd. She could thank her father for channeling her energy so that she set herself apart from other high school students across the nation.

From her earliest years, Madison had shown an aptitude for retaining obscure facts. They began playing the child's edition of Trivial Pursuit when Madison was in the second grade. She still remembered her first correct answer. What animal has a day named for it? She could almost hear herself shouting out the answer as she jumped up and down. "A groundhog, Daddy. Groundhog Day." The memory triggered a raw ache. This wonderful man had been her father, not some jerk who'd sold his sperm for cash.

Her mother hadn't been good at arcane facts but Zach Connelly was a trove of information on far-flung subjects. In order to compete and win his approval, Madison had trained herself to remember facts so unimportant that they never registered with most people.

"Does it sound like your mother?" Paul asked in a low-pitched voice.

"A little," she grudgingly conceded.

"What more proof do you need?" he asked.

"Proof?" Madison huffed her disgust. "This so-called tran-script from a defunct clinic that everyone sued for all kinds of illegal things doesn't *prove* anything."

"No?"

"No!" she shot back in a tight, pinched voice. She'd never been a good liar. Evidently, he'd seen or sensed her reaction to several items in the transcript. The air in the room seemed to be charged the way the atmosphere heralds an approaching storm.

"No," she asserted again in her most authoritative tone. "I don't believe I'm related to that man."

"A simple paternity test would prove it one way or the other."

That stopped her. Madison couldn't deny a test would be definitive. "I want to talk to my mother before I do anything."

"Isn't she in the South Pacific on a sailboat? It might be—" he shrugged "—weeks before she telephones you. Right?"

"She should call any day," Madison said quickly. "I heard from her a few weeks ago. She'll phone as soon as she gets to a port with a telephone she can use or when she meets someone with a yacht that has satellite service."

What she said was true. She did expect to hear from her mother. Jessica had called every few weeks since she'd sailed from Fort Lauderdale with the stud-muffin she'd married. But Madison couldn't honestly remember exactly when she'd last spoken to her mother. It could have been two weeks ago, maybe three. Madison had been so caught up with the business and looking for a new home that she hadn't paid that much attention.

She needed to have a heart-to-heart talk with her mother *now*. It occurred to her that she and her mother had shared only one intimate, soul-baring talk. That had been the night her father had died. They'd discussed what a great man he was and how much he'd meant to both of them.

Her mother had been so agonizingly upset at losing the man she'd met in college and married the day after graduation that it came as a physical blow when she'd brought home a much younger man she'd met at a fund-raiser. It was even more up-setting when Jessica Connelly had married him less than a year after Madison's father had died.

What had she been thinking?

Madison still didn't have a clue. She'd always been closer to her father than her mother. It had begun in early childhood when her father had been more willing to play with her. She'd reveled in the attention and as she grew, Madison took her problems and her triumphs to her father first.

"Why don't you at least meet Wyatt Holbrook?" Paul asked. "That way you'll have more to tell your mother when she calls."

Why don't you go to hell. Although she was tempted to yell this at him, Madison kept her temper in check. "I need to talk to my mother before I do anything," she insisted.

She knew she sounded a bit childish, but she did feel the need to talk to…Erin. That's who she would have called about this as soon as Paul Tanner had spouted his wild tale. Erin's death had closed that door irreversibly. Never, ever again would she be able to discuss anything with her best friend.

But even if Erin were here, this was a question for her mother and she might not check in for days or even weeks. When she did, the connection might be a hiss of static the way it was last time. But Madison wouldn't have any choice. She would have to ask this question over the telephone.

She was meeting Rob at Erin's home tonight to decide what to do with her friend's things. She could talk to Rob. He had a level head and he was accustomed to listening to people with sick and dying pets, giving him a wisdom and empathy few others had.

Once she could have discussed this with Aiden, but those days were gone. Even if she could, she knew Aiden would insist Paul's story was true. She could just hear Aiden saying, *Why would a man like Paul Tanner make up such a thing?*

"I understand how hard this has been for you. These last few days have been tough. Why don't we go get the bill of sale for the dog?" Paul suggested. "It may help us decide what's going on here."

CHAPTER SEVEN

PAUL GAZED at Madison for a moment with what he hoped was an encouraging smile. He knew she wanted to get rid of him, to make the whole business with Wyatt Holbrook disappear. Not on his watch. "I'll drive you out to your place. You can give me the sales receipt. Burgess expects me to bring it to him."

She hesitated, then finally responded. "Can't I do it tomorrow? It takes forever to get to Fisher Island and back. I've been out of the office for days. I'm swamped."

"The sooner Burgess tracks down the person who sold your friend Aspen, the sooner he can pursue a valuable suspect or eliminate that person. Don't you want Erin's killer found?"

"Of course I do. It's just that I doubt someone would sell her a dog, then kill her."

"You never know." Privately he agreed and Burgess must have, as well. Aw, hell. Maybe not. Lincoln Burgess was a piss-poor excuse for a detective—not exactly the best choice for a complicated investigation. Around the department, they referred to Burgess as "the missing link." Over the years, it had been shortened to Link. Dumb schmucks thought it was a nickname for Lincoln.

"Well…I guess I—"

Paul stood. "Come on. You can bring the dog with you. I'm in an SUV today."

"What dog?"

Her wide-eyed, innocent stare didn't fool him. "The golden retriever under your desk."

It was a moment before she replied, "You can't see him from there."

"No, but I see a few gold hairs on the carpet. Considering this is your first day back at the office, the dog has to be here." He gestured around at the small cube. "The only place he could be is under your desk."

She rewarded him with the suggestion of a smile that alluringly tipped the corners of her mouth upward. With her wild mane of hair and no makeup, she could have passed for a woman who'd just gotten out of bed. The thought alone sent a rush of heat through his body.

He cataloged every inch of her face while keeping his expression neutral as if he were thinking about the dog. Yeah, right. Something about this woman made his mind wander to sex every time he was around her.

He resisted the urge to allow his eyes to detour lower to where the V-neck of her T-shirt revealed the shadowy cleft between her breasts. His pulse thrummed just thinking about the way she'd looked when he'd walked into her office and had taken the opportunity to give her the slow once-over. True, he hadn't seen below the waist—she'd been sitting—but he liked what he could see.

"You're right. Aspen is under the desk." She rose from her seat in one fluid motion that he found undeniably provocative even though he knew she didn't intend it to be. "I didn't let on I had him because I didn't want Detective Burgess to take him."

As they walked out to his Jeep with the golden retriever at Madison's side, Paul thought about the dog. When he'd heard her screaming and raced into Erin Wycoff's home, he'd charged through the kitchen, barely noticing the envelope on the counter beside the pizza box. Minutes later the envelope and the dog had been gone.

He'd followed Madison from the office and knew she hadn't had the dog with her, but he hadn't realized it wasn't her dog. The way she'd pitched a fit at the scene about the dog needing eye treatment, he'd assumed the dog was hers.

Never assume. When he'd studied criminology at the University of Florida, his favorite professor, Dr. Wells, often tried to trick them into false assumptions that led to erroneous conclusions in the test cases he taught.

All right, all right. He should have known better, but his mind had been busy processing the horror of the scene and trying to decide what type of killer had been responsible for the brutal attack. Hell, he'd been itching to get back into action. He hated being on leave. That was why he'd gone into the station this morning. He was hoping to find that his leave had been terminated. No such luck.

He held the back door of his car open for Aspen. The dog hesitated.

Madison patted the floor in front of him. "Go on, boy. Hop in." The dog leaped up into the car.

They got in and Paul drove out of the parking lot. This close, he caught a whiff of the same scent he had the other time he'd been this near her. Flowery but fresh, not heavy the way some women wore too much fragrance.

He waited until they were down the road before asking, "What did the vet say about Aspen's eye problem?"

"He needs drops twice a day. He'll be fine."

"How did you know to take him to the vet?"

"His eyes were tearing a lot more than normal. At least that's what I thought. I just threw that show-dog stuff at them because I had to get away. I couldn't stand thinking about my friend with all those people walking around her naked body, taking pictures, measuring things, collecting particles of hair and fiber and…I don't know what."

Paul nodded, letting her think he believed her, but there

was a missed beat in the conversation. Something about the dog. What?

"You got him help pretty fast," he remarked, to see if she would reveal something incriminating.

"I took him to Robert Matthews. He was Erin's boyfriend but they broke up last year. I knew he'd get me in right away and he did. I saw his associate."

"That's good." Something in her explanation still sounded off but he wasn't sure what. Evidently the dog meant a lot to her. He had the feeling it was more than the last link to her murdered friend.

"Did Erin leave her boyfriend or was it the other way around?"

She kept staring straight ahead. He couldn't help noticing she had a turned-up nose that gave her profile a cute upward tilt. "I think it was mutual," she finally said.

"She was your best friend. Right? Don't girls discuss stuff like this?" He knew damn well they did. He was pretty sure now that Madison was hiding something. From the first, he'd been positive she hadn't killed Erin Wycoff, but now he wondered if she knew more about the murder than she was admitting.

He reminded himself that he wasn't working on this case. The department could have requested to have him removed from disability leave now that his doctor had approved his return to the force, but they hadn't. He was working for his father and needed to complete this job.

"Women do talk," she told him in a low voice charged with emotion. "But at the time Erin and Rob called it quits, my husband had just left me. I had all I could deal with."

"Wouldn't that have brought you closer to your friend?"

"It did. Erin listened to me whine big-time, but she didn't talk much about herself. It was several weeks before I came out of my fog of self-pity and noticed Rob wasn't around. Erin didn't want to discuss it."

"I see," he said, although he didn't. He didn't have any sisters, and his mother had left them and moved to California when he was seven. His experience with women amounted to sex and not much more.

"You see, Erin was a secretive person. Always." She'd turned to face him as she explained. "Our mothers met when they were pregnant. I've always…known Erin…forever. We were like sisters, but even as a child she kept things to herself. I didn't find it unusual that Erin didn't want to talk about Rob."

The earnest note in her voice told him this was the truth, as she saw it. One thing he'd learned as a detective was the truth often depended on your perspective. "She never mentioned the property she left you."

"Erin believed her parents left her a worthless chunk of property. She never told me it had become valuable or that anyone was interested in buying it."

"She must have mentioned the chimp place—"

"Save the Chimps in Fort Pierce. No, she didn't, but Erin volunteered at a shelter for homeless animals. She probably found out about it there and discussed it with them."

They pulled into the ferry line for Fisher Island. Aspen had hopped up onto the backseat, and Paul rolled down the rear window so the dog could stick his head out and sniff the breeze while the ferry made the short crossing to the island.

The guard recognized Madison and waved them onto the ferry used exclusively by Fisher Island residents. Personally, Paul thought the whole private-island bit was a pain in the ass. It was a hassle to get on and off the place. While guards helped protect residents' privacy, it wasn't a guarantee they were safe. He'd easily gotten onto the island. He could have had a fake police ID and been admitted.

It was almost noon and there were only a few other cars on the small ferry. Neither of them said anything on the short trip. They drove up to the Italian villa where Madison was staying.

Madison jumped out and opened the door for Aspen. It seemed to take the dog a split second longer than necessary to jump down.

Paul got out of the car, asking, "Did the vet say Aspen has some sort of a vision problem, not just an eye infection?"

Madison's eyes became sharper, more focused. "No, but his infection wasn't treated early enough. He has some vision loss, but he's okay now. Aren't you, boy?"

The dog nuzzled Madison's hand. Again, Paul thought there was more to the connection between them than Madison wanted to reveal.

Inside the house, Madison went right to what he assumed was the bedroom she was using. Waiting in the entry with Aspen, he stroked the dog's smooth head and looked into his eyes. "Trouble seeing, huh?"

The dog poked at his hand with his nose. His eyes appeared a little cloudy, as if he had the beginnings of cataracts. He knew dogs could develop cataracts like humans, but Aspen seemed too young.

"Here it is," said Madison, returning to the entry.

Paul took it from her and pulled the certificate out of the envelope. He scanned the document. It immediately raised a red flag. "Someone sold a purebred dog for twenty-five dollars?"

"I guess. Erin told me a woman couldn't keep her dog. I assumed she just wanted to find it a good home, then I discovered this bill of sale."

"What did Erin say exactly?"

Madison silently regarded him for a moment, seeming to weigh her words. "I'm not sure. We were in a club. The music was really loud. She just mentioned the dog. I didn't ask a lot of questions because of the noise."

"You didn't discuss it later when you came back to her house and had pizza?"

"No. She knew I wanted a dog. I've always wanted one but

Mom was allergic to them, then I married a man who didn't want animals of any kind." She shrugged as if her ex-husband didn't matter, but Paul sensed this was still an open wound. Words were pouring out of her too rapidly, which made him think again that she was concealing something.

"We started to talk about the houses I had seen with the Realtor. I forgot all about the dog until I was on the way home. I figured I'd call Erin about it the next day. My first priority was to find a house where I could keep a pet." She waved a hand at the elegant living room beyond the foyer. "The owners will return soon and I need my own place."

It sounded true, but something about the dog situation continued to bother him. He scanned the certificate again. It looked legit but you never knew these days. A lot could be duplicated using a scanner and a computer. Counterfeiters had been so successful at replicating United States currency that the Treasury Department had created new bills just to make it more difficult.

"This says Aspen was born Rudolph Vontreben of Sunnyvale. I guess Sunnyvale is the breeder." He looked at Madison.

She shrugged. "Maybe. I don't really know."

There it was again, the disturbing note in her voice. What was going on? "Don't you want to find your friend's killer?"

"Of course I do!" she cried, then took a deep breath. "I just don't think the woman—"

"What makes you think it was a woman?" He wanted her to repeat what she'd told him earlier. Something wasn't right here.

"I told you. At the club Erin mentioned a woman who couldn't keep her dog. I assume Aspen was that dog."

"But you don't know for sure."

"Well, no. I...ah—"

"It's possible this—" he glanced at the paper again "—L. Morgan used the dog as a ploy and followed her home."

"It's possible," she conceded in a voice pitched low.

"I'll take this to Burgess and let him run down the dog's

owner." He reminded himself this wasn't his case. His agenda was entirely different.

"What about meeting Wyatt Holbrook?" he asked, and immediately saw the change of subject caught her off guard.

"Not until I talk to my mother," she shot back.

"A life hangs in the balance," he reminded her. He was betting a woman who had a soft heart for a dog was someone who would respond to an emotional plea. "He's a lot like Erin, from what you've told me," Paul said, making this up as he went. "He helps others even when the benefits to him aren't observable. We could go over there tonight. He only lives in Palm Beach. You could see for yourself."

"I'm busy tonight. I have to help Rob Matthews sort through Erin's things."

The faint note of irritation in her voice mushroomed into anger so powerful that it must have been festering since the first time he'd told her about her real father. "This man isn't interested in me. He's just—"

"True, Wyatt Holbrook wants to live, but he's a generous philanthropist. He's given millions to worthy causes."

"You already told me about him."

He could see he wasn't getting anywhere. Then something from her bio hit him. "Wyatt's setting up a special foundation to fund promising advances in science and medicine. There just isn't enough money for scientists and it's not likely to get better. The government has too many other priorities."

Madison silently considered what he said. He knew she'd majored in mathematics and had earned a full scholarship to MIT. She was bound to understand how important such a foundation would become.

"Call me tomorrow. I'll see what I can arrange. I'm not promising anything, but I'll think about it."

"Thanks." As Paul left, he was half-tempted to give her a

hug, but he didn't press his luck. *Okay, pard. Get your mind back where it belongs.* He found Madison disturbingly attractive, but this was business. Nothing more.

CHAPTER EIGHT

How long before maggots appear on a dead body?

"Do you want any of these pictures?" Madison asked Rob.

He crossed the small bedroom where they'd been sorting through Erin's things since late afternoon. Madison had kept a few pieces of her friend's jewelry and was packing the rest of Erin's clothes to drop off at Goodwill. She'd come to the lower drawer where she'd discovered a shoe box of photographs. The ones on the top were of Rob with Erin.

Rob looked across the room and looked over Madison's shoulder. "Yeah, save 'em for me." He almost choked on the words. An emotional second passed before he spoke again. "Those are from our trip to New Orleans. You know, before *Katrina,* when New Orleans was still the old New Orleans."

"I'll put them in your box." Madison looked up from the floor where she was sitting and tried for a smile. They'd both brought boxes to save things to remember Erin. So far, there was nothing in his.

"Great. I'll go get it." He headed to the living room, where he'd left the empty box.

Madison sifted through the photos haphazardly thrown into the shoe box. Again, the scent of something like Lysol, only stronger, made her stomach roil. Rob had arranged for a special service to clean Erin's home. None of the bloodstains remained, but the astringent odor was a constant reminder of Erin's brutal death.

Flies.

The image blipped across her brain. In her mind's eye she could see the flies on Erin's body where they'd lay eggs. Maggots would soon follow. It took twenty-four to forty-eight hours for maggots to appear on a corpse. The autopsy and embalming fluids would delay them. But for how long? For once the answer wasn't in the trove of trivia that occupied her brain. She forced her mind back to the task at hand.

There were several pictures of Erin and Madison taken over the years. Not very many, she mused, considering all they'd done together. There were almost no pictures of Erin's parents.

Madison thought of her family. Her mother had taken hundreds of photographs. She'd lovingly compiled them into artistic scrapbooks long before scrapbooking became a fad. Madison missed her mother now in a way that she hadn't before Erin's death. Madison hadn't been able to accept her mother's relationship with Scott Whitcomb. Not only was the guy too young for her, but she'd begun seeing him within months of Zach Connelly's death. It seemed like a betrayal to Madison.

It wasn't until Aiden had walked out on her and the true meaning of loneliness set in that Madison realized her mother's remarriage must have been an attempt to restore the happy life she'd lost. By then, the damage to Madison's relationship with her mother had been done. Jessica Connelly—now Jessica Whitcomb—had left in Scott's sailboat. Madison had turned, as she always had, to Erin.

Now she was truly alone for the first time in her life. She decided to keep the box of photos and sort through them later. Who else would want them?

"Hey," Rob said from the doorway. "Why don't we take a break and grab a bite to eat?"

"Good idea." She stood up and glanced over to the foot of the bed, where Aspen was stretched out, head on his paws, watching her. "Is there someplace where we could eat outside with Aspen?"

"What about Casa Carreta? That's not far and they have a patio."

"Great. Come on, Aspen."

The dog eagerly leaped to his feet. She waited at the bedroom door for him to lumber after her. She'd discovered he couldn't see too far ahead and was more comfortable if he followed her. For an instant, she thought of Paul Tanner. She was certain he suspected something about Aspen.

"The police took the bill of sale that Erin had for Aspen," Madison told Rob as they walked out to the van he'd brought from his animal clinic so they could load Erin's things. "I hope it doesn't show Dicon Labs owns Aspen. I won't let him be hauled back there to be tortured."

Rob opened the sliding door to the back for Aspen. Madison patted the floor and the dog hopped in.

Rob slipped his arm around her shoulders and gave her a slight squeeze. "Don't worry about it. I'm sure the EADL created a certificate that couldn't be traced if it were challenged. I've paid careful attention to the news. The lab hasn't mentioned any lost dogs. Like I told you, I doubt they want *any* negative publicity."

Rob had a slow, deliberate way of speaking that emphasized important words. Madison found him to be very reassuring, exactly what she needed at this point.

She shifted out from under his arm and opened the passenger door. "I hope you're right. We haven't discovered anything to indicate Erin was still part of the group."

She climbed in and waited for Rob to come to his side. They hadn't found anything, but the police had confiscated Erin's computer and all of the records that she'd kept in the small desk in the corner of the bedroom.

Rob settled himself behind the wheel and started the van.

"Trust me. Erin was too careful to leave any trail. There's a firewall between people to protect their identities. Everyone in the group became hyperconscious of security when the FBI began to crack down on what they called domestic terrorism several years ago. A couple of animal rights activists on the West Coast were jailed."

They parked in the lot outside Casa Carreta. During the years Madison had been growing up, Cubans and their culture had spread beyond Little Havana, the area of Miami where the first immigrants from Cuba had settled. Cuban food and coffee and music could be found throughout southern Florida.

It was nearly nine o'clock—early for the SoBe crowd, but late for dinner in this neighborhood. They had no trouble finding a table on the small patio. She directed Aspen to a spot at her feet, under the table so he wouldn't be in the way. The smell of fried plantains reminded Madison that she hadn't eaten since she'd grabbed a few crackers from the platter of goodies in the lunchroom, where Jade had set out the food from the reception.

"Erin used to have the *palomilla*," Rob told her, but he needn't have bothered. Madison knew her friend always ordered the thinly sliced beef laden with grilled onions and spices. Usually it was served with French fries but Erin always substituted fried yucca.

"That's a bit heavy for tonight," she said, her appetite suddenly gone. How many times had she shared a plate of *palomilla* with Erin? Never again.

"Why don't we share it?" Rob suggested with a smile.

She almost said no but stopped. Why not? She would have if Erin were sitting beside her. Rob ordered *palomilla* and *café cubano* to drink.

"Is something bothering you?" Rob asked after the waiter deposited the coffee in cups hardly bigger than thimbles. "Besides Erin's loss, I mean."

As usual, the *café cubano* was so strong that it hit her stomach like a grenade and sent an explosion of caffeine through her system. She realized she hadn't spoken for several minutes. She hadn't meant to be rude, but her mind had been on Paul Tanner and her promise to consider meeting Wyatt Holbrook.

"Sorry," she said, and gazed into Rob's dark brown eyes. He was such a nice guy and he'd loved Erin so much. He had to be suffering even more than she was. She'd been thinking about discussing her problem with him. Now was the time. Maybe it would distract them both from their grief.

"Something strange happened to me and I don't know how to handle it." She paused, not sure where to begin.

"Run it by me. I'll help if I can." He reached across the table and squeezed her hand.

"Okay. A private investigator came to see me." She pulled her hand from his and took a sip of her coffee. The story tumbled out in as succinct a version as she could manage.

"Wyatt Holbrook is your father?"

Rob was clearly impressed—not that she could blame him. Wyatt Holbrook was a big name in Miami, a city with no lack of stellar personalities. But just hearing Rob say that man could be her father made her feel uncomfortably disloyal to her real father.

"That's what Paul Tanner claims." The words were underscored with a hiss of anger. "Like I told you, the clinic closed in a hail of lawsuits for falsifying records and who knows what else."

Rob let the waiter deliver the *palomilla* and two plates to share the platter. With it came a side order of *pan cubano*. The bread had been flattened on a grill and was oozing butter. When the waiter left, Rob asked, "Okay, so they tried to capitalize on some megasperm, but what reason would this private investigator have for manufacturing records to show you were Wyatt Holbrook's child? I could see this as a scam if you were worth megabucks." He shrugged and picked up his fork. "But you're not. Wyatt Holbrook is the one with the money."

Madison took a bite of the savory beef and chewed thoughtfully. This was what had been bothering her, niggling at the back of her mind since she'd read the transcript. "I don't know. There must be some—"

"Look." He reached across the table again and stroked her hand. "I know you loved your father. This doesn't change anything. He raised you and loved you and made you who you are. Still, he might not be your biological father."

She jerked her hand away from his once more and had to bite the inside of her cheek to keep from screaming it wasn't true. "It's not true," she managed to say in an even tone. "When Dad was dying, we discussed *everything*. He would have told me."

Rob offered her a sympathetic smile. "Not if he thought it would change the way you thought about him."

Madison didn't believe this—not for one second. "My father died of pancreatic cancer. He was in tremendous pain and they put him on large doses of painkillers. I doubt he could have resisted telling me the truth. He knew I'd love him regardless. The last words I whispered to him were *I am who I am because you loved me.*"

Rob took another forkful of food and ate it before saying, "Is there any chance he didn't know?"

She remembered the transcript. Her mother seemed to have gone to the clinic initially without her father's knowledge. From the way the nurse had sounded in the transcript, Madison had assumed her father's consent would have been required. *If*—and it was still a really big *if* in her mind—her mother had gone through with the procedure.

"I think the clinic required both parents to sign the consent form."

"Not true of single mothers, of course."

"Of course," she muttered, and put down her fork. Why was she even considering the possibility? She knew she was her father's daughter.

"A paternity test would prove—"

"I know." She ground out the words. "I know." The stricken look on his face upset her. "Sorry I snapped. This investigator keeps pressing me. I truly believe there's some hidden agenda here."

"It's okay." He reached over and stroked her hand with his fingertips. "There is an agenda. This Holbrook guy is filthy rich. How much do you want to bet that he's paying the investigator a bundle of dough to locate his donor-conceived child? So she can be tested to see if she could save his life."

"I don't know why, but I feel there's another reason."

"Madison, I realize you don't want to accept this, and I'm not saying it's true, but I can't imagine why a man like Wyatt Holbrook would waste his time unless he believed you were his daughter."

She had to admit that she agreed. "You're right. I'm sure that man thinks I'm one of his children."

"One?"

"Doesn't the fact he donated sperm once suggest he did it several times since he needed the money? I've read up on it. A single donation of sperm can be divided and used more than once."

Rob rocked back in his chair and thought about it for a second. "Holbrook may have donated several times. Who knows? When I was in veterinary school, there were guys who donated regularly to make money."

"Didn't they care about what happened to their children?"

"I guess not. I never knew any of them well enough to get into it with them."

Each word cracked like a hatchet blow inside her head. Were men really so cavalier? A memory punched through from the night Aiden left her. "You'll be all right," he'd said over his shoulder. "You always are." His words were proof positive men did have a cavalier attitude.

"What I'm concerned about here isn't motivation," Rob said quietly as the waiter removed the dishes. "I'm worried that you might actually be this man's child—"

"I'm not. I *know* I'm not."

He raised his hand. "Hear me out. I'm worried about what would happen should you prove to be his child and an eligible donor."

Madison fought the urge to protest and kept listening. He was her friend—her only friend now—and he was just trying to help.

"This isn't a simple operation. I know a lot about these things from being in veterinary school. Kidneys are fairly routine transplants. They're having a lot of success even with donors who aren't ideally compatible. But a liver transplant is different."

"We all have two kidneys but just one liver." She could have rattled off the statistics about the percentage of the population born with just one kidney but she didn't.

"Exactly. So a liver transplant involves major surgery where they take a lobe of the donor's liver and transplant it into the recipient. It involves a substantial risk to the donor."

"I understand. I looked it up on the Internet."

"It's possible for anyone to donate but you'd need an almost perfect match. There aren't enough people registered as donors to come up with that kind of a match very often. So the best bet is a blood relative.

"That's why this man is tracking down children conceived from his sperm donations." Once again, Rob reached across the table. He took her hand in both of his. "You could die from this surgery, or at the very least be out of commission for weeks."

"I know," she replied, her voice a shade shy of a whisper. For a suspended moment, like holding her breath underwater, her words hung there. She hadn't allowed her mind to take her down this trail until now. Rob's words forced her to consider the possibility this man could be her father. Then she dismissed the crazy idea.

Still, she couldn't help wondering what Wyatt Holbrook was like.

CHAPTER NINE

PAUL HAD NEVER BEEN comfortable in a monkey suit, even though he'd bought this one when he'd needed a tux for a friend's wedding and discovered he was too big to rent one that fit properly. Being a homicide detective required pressed slacks, a sport coat and his nemesis—polished shoes. When he was off-duty, Paul wore jeans or shorts with one of the numerous T-shirts he'd accumulated over the years.

But taking Madison Connelly to meet Wyatt Holbrook tonight required a tux. Paul thought the guy could have cleared some time in his schedule to meet a woman who could possibly save his life. But no, Holbrook was on a treadmill of work and fund-raising to establish his research foundation and consulting with specialists about his illness. The black-tie dinner tonight at his Palm Beach estate was the first opening in his schedule.

Mike Tanner, Paul's father, had explained that the Palm Beach season was ending. How the hell "Big Mike" Tanner, who'd spent his career on the Miami PD and now ran a private security firm, knew so much about Palm Beach society was a mystery to Paul. But then, many things about his father had always been a mystery.

What wasn't a secret was the success of Tanner Security Solutions. Mike Tanner had made a bundle providing security and running background checks for large corporations in South Florida. He employed two dozen people with sophisticated security skills. Some were ex-cops, while others had experience with state-of-the-art alarm systems or were experts in computer security. His father's company didn't tail men's wives to check for lovers or perform any type of divorce work. They restricted themselves to corporate security, but Mike had made an exception to help save Holbrook's life. After all, his father had explained, Holbrook Pharmaceuticals was one of his biggest clients.

Mike claimed the heavy hitters who could contribute big bucks to Wyatt Holbrook's foundation would soon be heading home. The Holbrooks lived in Palm Beach full-time, but many of the other residents did not. Tonight was the final party the Holbrooks would host before the season ended.

Paul waited beside Madison in some damn receiving line in the foyer of the five-acre estate that had been built for a steel tycoon in the 1930s. Holbrook had acquired the place in the late '80s and restored the badly deteriorated mansion to its former glory. Okay, the guy had taken it beyond its former glory to new heights.

Tonight Corona del Mar—houses in this neck of the woods had names—sparkled like the crown jewel in a royal necklace. That's how Paul thought of the string of mansions lining the island's shore in Palm Beach. A royal necklace of money and power. Now referred to as Millionaire's Row, Palm Beach used to be the haven of old money in the days when being a millionaire meant something. Many of the estates had been built at least fifty years ago, but over time they'd changed hands, and self-made men like Wyatt Holbrook had replaced the old-money crowd who'd made their wealth the old-fashioned way: they'd inherited it.

Some of the original mansions had been knocked down and replaced, but not Corona del Mar. It had been lovingly restored. The place was full of what Paul supposed were beautiful people, although most of them were old, with sunbaked hides. But enough glittering diamonds, emeralds as big as eggs and bloodred rubies could make some folks overlook a few wrinkles.

"Oh, my," Madison said in a low voice. "This place is an outstanding example of Mizner Mediterranean architecture."

"Mizner Mediterranean?" Paul had heard of Mizner, of course. The well-known architect had designed many buildings in the Miami area and his name was plastered everywhere.

"Yes. Mizner introduced the Spanish-Moorish Mediterranean style to the area just after the First World War."

Paul glanced up at the dome ceiling painted with bare-assed angles and meringue-style clouds. Like a conga line, the stream of people was snailing its way through the mammoth foyer into the main house. He didn't know much about architecture, but he'd bet the Porsche his father had lent him for the evening that Holbrook could bankroll the foundation he was so hot to establish just by selling this house.

"Do you know a lot about architecture?" he asked, to encourage her to talk. On the way north from Fisher Island through Miami and Bal Harbor, Madison hadn't said much, answering his comments with a yes or no whenever possible.

"I didn't study it, if that's what you mean," she responded, "but one summer I worked as a docent at the Flagler Museum. I learned a lot about the history of the city."

"I get it," he said, mentally noting there had been nothing about this in the detailed profile his father had given him. He wasn't surprised. Madison had a depth to her that most other women lacked. You couldn't capture her on paper. Or predict what she would do. Sure as hell, he hadn't anticipated her phone call, asking to meet Wyatt Holbrook.

He ventured a sideways peek at Madison. Her jumble of blond curls had been swept up into a cluster at the top of her head. A few wisps of hair had strayed and framed her face to give her a charming appearance—a more sophisticated look than she sported at the office.

The black evening dress she wore appeared demure, with a halter top that suggested but didn't reveal much cleavage. Yet when she turned around at her place to pick up her purse, Paul had barely managed to stifle a gasp. The damn dress had no back at all—meaning she couldn't be wearing a bra. So she was still working with her original equipment, unlike so many women who'd had boob jobs, but Madison was sexy as hell even though she wasn't a centerfold candidate.

He leaned close to whisper in her ear and caught a whiff of the fresh floral fragrance he'd come to associate with Madison. Sexy as hell didn't cover it. Everything about her was erotically charged. He was attracted to her, but the feeling clearly wasn't mutual. Even though he'd shaved twice, slapped on some pricey aftershave an old girlfriend had given him and worn his stupid monkey suit, Madison had barely looked at him.

Get over it, he told himself. Madison's mind was on the Holbrooks. His energy should be focused on convincing her to agree to be tested to see if she could be a donor. That's what he was getting paid to do—not drool over a woman who couldn't be less interested.

"That's Garrison Holbrook," Paul whispered to her. They'd moved forward a little and they could see Wyatt Holbrook's children at the head of the line, greeting guests. "His sister, Savannah, is beside him."

Madison cocked her head to look, then she trained her baby blues on him. "Where's Wyatt Holbrook?"

Paul shrugged. "Inside, probably."

"Maybe he isn't well enough to stand around and greet everyone."

"Holbrook doesn't look that ill. He actually appears deceptively healthy." He seized the opportunity to lean closer and sneak a look at her cleavage. "You see, transplants—especially partial transplants where the patient only receives a lobe of the donor's liver—are most successful when the recipient is as healthy as possible. Wyatt has always been very fit and he works out even harder now to maintain his body for a transplant."

"If he has so much money, why does he need a fund-raiser to help a foundation he hasn't even opened yet?"

"Good question. From what I understand, Holbrook wants to have an immense war chest. What he's talking about doing will take more than one person could possibly have. I'm sure he'll explain it all to you when you meet."

Madison didn't respond. Her gaze was focused on her would-be half siblings, Savannah and Garrison. "I don't look anything like them," she told him in a voice so low that the other guests couldn't hear.

"True. Garrison and Savannah favor their mother, Claire Thorndyke Holbrook. She died a few years ago. She was a red-headed beauty from a society family—"

"I know who the Thorndykes were," she snapped. "I didn't expect to look like them because we're *not* related."

Damn. Madison gave a new dimension to stubborn. He'd assumed that since she'd agreed to come tonight, she'd accepted the fact that she'd been conceived through a sperm donation from Wyatt Holbrook. "If you don't believe you can help the man, then why did you come?"

"Curiosity. I'm sure there's a hidden agenda."

Just what he needed—a sexy nutcase who was in this for kicks. Women—weren't they a trip? But, as the saying went, you couldn't live with them and you couldn't live without them. For damn sure he couldn't. He had avoided marriage but had a string of former girlfriends to his credit. You would have thought by now he might have learned his lesson when it came to relationships. Wrong. Dead wrong.

"I assure you, Madison. There's no hidden agenda. Holbrook needs a transplant. You may be able to help. Why don't you agree to have a compatibility test?"

"Do Garrison and Savannah know about me?" she asked, dodging his question.

"I don't know what their father told them," he said in total honesty. His own father wouldn't have told him a damn thing, but who knew how open Wyatt was with his children. "I'm the one who came across your file. My father brought the others to Wyatt's attention."

Her blue eyes snapped with curiosity and he kicked himself for mentioning the files. "What do you mean?"

He kept his voice low. "Like I told you, New Horizons had been sued. Most of the files were in a warehouse where the attorney who agreed to defend the company stored them when New Horizons went bankrupt."

"The file with my mother's name wasn't there?"

He could tell by her tone that this information simply added more kindling to her belief that something suspicious was going on. "No. A handful had been left in the attorney's office. Sloppy filing."

"How many files were in the warehouse?"

"About five dozen," Paul hedged.

"How many half siblings do you suppose are out there?"

That was anybody's guess. A lot. He kept his thoughts to himself. "Clinics claim they limit the number of inseminations from one donor, but this clinic was shady. A handsome guy with Mensa credentials—"

"Don't forget tall. Short Mensa guys need not donate."

Paul stifled a laugh. Madison wasn't joking. "Miami has always attracted money, but it isn't long on major universities with brilliant students like the Boston area. That's why the clinic here was so profitable and why the Boston clinic sold them their samples."

"Wyatt Holbrook ended up here, too. Don't you find that weird?"

"No. Claire's family was local. She attended Boston University. She met Wyatt at a party in Boston and they fell in love, but she wanted to return home after college. Wyatt came with her."

"Six degrees of separation. Wyatt Holbrook could have bumped into any number of his offspring at the local Starbucks or something and not have realized it. No doubt he thought they all were in the Boston area."

"True. We're still going through the records up there, attempting to locate others whose parents moved elsewhere."

"Have you checked anyone else to see if they can donate?"

"Getting confidential records is trickier than you think, especially with the new health privacy laws. We were lucky, because New Horizon's files were warehoused here. We're just going through those now." They inched forward a little as the line moved. "That's how I found you. My father's operatives did find two children in Boston but one had ODed and the other had been killed in a car crash. We've added manpower to locate the rest."

"Obviously, Garrison and Savannah can't donate."

"Right. They both were tested immediately but they don't qualify."

"Savannah's a knockout," whispered Madison as they drew closer.

So what else was new? Savannah Holbrook was a drop-dead gorgeous woman with a killer body and long hair that he supposed some damn fashion magazine would call russet or chestnut or something. It was her eyes that got him. From the first second Paul had met Savannah, he'd wondered if she was wearing contacts that made her eyes such an intense shade of green.

As stunning as Savannah was, her brother, Garrison, was just as striking in his own way. Like a sleek pair of matched thoroughbreds, both of Wyatt Holbrook's children had hit the genetic lottery. They'd inherited their mother's good looks and their father's brains. They both were successful in their own fields.

"Savannah started Salon S. I checked her out on Google and found I already use her products," confided Madison.

From what Paul had heard, the cosmetics were available only in pricey stores. At first, he'd assumed Savannah's business was local, but his father informed him that it was a nationwide operation. He gave Savannah credit for her accomplishments, but Madison was just as successful without the benefit of a huge trust fund.

"What's Garrison like?" Madison asked in a low voice.

"Garrison favors his father. He has his own research company. Apparently he's on the verge of a top-secret breakthrough discovery."

"Really? The Internet said he attended the California Institute of Technology, then did advanced studies and research in Switzerland."

"That's right. Like his father, Garrison is a scientist." Paul didn't add how similar Madison and Garrison were in many respects.

The line moved closer and Paul saw Nathan Cassidy, the family attorney and Savannah's boyfriend, was introducing the guests. Paul had met Cassidy on an earlier visit to the house. The lawyer was in his midthirties, with a surfer's tan and sun-streaked blond hair. Paul resisted the urge to judge the guy by his looks, but he was tempted.

Cassidy's gaze swept over him and Paul knew the lawyer wasn't expecting to see him. He quickly shifted his eyes to Madison, then whispered something to Garrison. Without really thinking about it, Paul put his arm protectively around Madison's waist.

THE ANGEL OF DEATH.

The killer liked that title. It implied a link to another world, to God. The killer was above mere mortals.

A white skull of a moon sulked overhead and the killer

looked up, feeling more a part of the greater universe than of this lowly world. Some people were like that. They were blessed with extraordinary intelligence and insight into the future. Ordinary people were too self-centered. What had Adam Smith said? Something about all interest stemming from self-interest.

That was the trouble with people. They thought of themselves first. Seeing the bigger picture set you apart. The killer had the bigger picture in mind.

The police didn't. Those worthless toads hadn't connected Erin Wycoff's death to the earlier murders. How stupid could they be?

Now another death was necessary.

Some people *deserved* to die.

It wouldn't take much to conceal the link between the homicides. The police weren't going to solve this crime, either.

CHAPTER TEN

Name the largest predator that ever roamed the Earth and is still around today.

MADISON HARDLY FELT Paul's arm encircle her waist. She determinedly stared at the blond man introducing the guests to Garrison and Savannah Holbrook. The man's assessing gaze should have made her uncomfortable but it didn't. A spike of anger hit her, and she realized it had been simmering just beneath the surface all evening.

She wasn't certain where her hostility was coming from exactly. She could blame it on grief over Erin's death and frustration at the police for failing to find her killer. But she had to admit she'd been irritable and edgy since Paul Tanner first suggested Zach Connelly wasn't her biological father.

The more people tried to convince her that this was a definite possibility, the more stubbornly she resisted the idea. She'd always been pigheaded to a fault. Even when Aiden began flirting outrageously with Chloe in the office, Madison had refused to admit she had a problem.

"Paul, good to see you again," said the blond man as he reached out to shake Paul's hand. He'd told her this man was an attorney who'd been dating Savannah for several years. "This is…?" The lawyer kept his eyes on Madison.

"My date, Madison Connelly." Paul smiled at her but she could see it was forced. "This is Nathan Cassidy." He quickly dropped Nathan's hand and spoke to the Holbrooks. "Madison, this is Garrison and Savannah Holbrook."

"Hello. Glad you could come," Savannah responded in a low voice that Madison knew men must find incredibly sexy. For an instant, she wondered what Paul thought of Savannah, but the thought vanished as Garrison spoke.

"Madison Connelly. Your name sounds really familiar. Have we met?" Garrison asked with a smile that made her like him immediately. "Of course not. I'd remember your face."

"No," she replied with what she hoped was an answering smile.

"Enjoy your evening," Savannah said with a quick glance at her brother.

Madison realized Wyatt Holbrook's children had not been told about her. She murmured something and let Paul sweep her into the next room.

"Let's get a drink." Paul guided her, his arm still around her waist, to the bar set up in a living room the size of an airplane hangar. The heat from his hand on her bare skin caused a shiver.

The room reflected Addison Mizner's fascination with Spanish-Moorish architecture, but with a modern twist. Comfortable yet elegant sofas and chairs in muted shades of beige and moss-green were strategically placed. Several coffee tables provided a center for each grouping. Those tables seemed to feature what must be rare shells or pieces of coral.

One table in particular caught her eye. A blue fan shell the size of a coral reef nearly blocked her view of the couple sitting on the sofa beyond the shell. It was such an unusual shade of deep blue with phosphorus highlights that Madison wondered if some decorator had painted it.

More shells and what must be coral were featured on the walls in clusters of prints or watercolors. Even from a distance she could tell they were extremely detailed and Madison suspected they were original Audubons. Had he done shells and coral? She wasn't sure.

In sharp contrast to the casual furniture, black lacquer cabinets were centered at intervals along the walls. They appeared to be English eighteenth-century antiques and were exploding with collections of blue and white Chinese porcelain. She seemed to remember from her days as a docent that wealthy people who'd patronized Addison Mizner had been avid collectors of Chinese porcelain.

She wondered if these pieces had been in Wyatt Holbrook's wife's family. She'd studied his profile on the Internet and had learned he was a self made man, but his wife had come from a wealthy family who had lived in the area before the First World War, when Mizner had been hired to design the first of the megamansions in South Florida.

"Just sparkling water for me," she told the bartender when they reached the bar. She wanted to have all her wits about her when she met Wyatt Holbrook.

"Scotch rocks," Paul said as the bartender handed Madison her drink.

She wondered why she'd agreed to meet the man who obviously had everything he desired—except a healthy liver. She'd told Paul that it was curiosity, but her inquisitive nature was only part of the reason she was here. Rob's reaction had convinced her to at least meet Wyatt Holbrook.

Still—she knew in her heart of hearts—Zach Connelly was her biological father. Her gut instinct rarely failed her, especially when it was this intense. Something else was going on here besides the search for donor-conceived children.

Once she met Wyatt, she felt certain she would be able to figure out what was happening. It could be as simple as an honest mistake. Her mother could have visited the clinic and somehow the records had been mixed up. It wasn't as if New Horizons was the most ethical clinic in the country. Anything was possible.

"Let's get something to eat," Paul said when he had his Scotch. "I'm starving."

Madison was too keyed up to eat but she allowed him to take her through the open doors leading from the enormous room to the oceanfront terrace. Music drifted over the crowd that seemed to be standing around talking to one another like old friends. She didn't know anyone in Palm Beach, but she'd heard about the exclusive enclave's reputation for snobbery.

She didn't care. Even if she made millions, Madison would never want a home here. There were better, more meaningful things to do with money than spend it on a lavish mansion built early in the last century when rich people had scads of servants to maintain homes the size of hotels.

She thought of how Erin had come into a windfall of money yet didn't plan to use it selfishly. She was supporting a worthy cause in Save the Chimps. Madison had investigated them on the Internet and knew the nonprofit group helped chimpanzees that had been used in scientific experiments. Often they had been alone for years, confined to a cage and subjected to horrors she could only imagine. Save the Chimps brought them to a parklike setting where they could live together and roam the grounds in freedom after years of abuse.

It was a much better use of money, she decided. As soon as Erin's murder was solved and Madison had control of the money, it was going to help the chimps. It was what Erin would have wanted.

"Looks like they're carving roast beef over there," Paul said. "Sound good?"

Paul escorted her through the crowd showing off their diamonds and designer clothes to one of several food stations where handsome young men in chef's hats were serving food.

"I think I would rather have the shrimp," Madison said, although she still didn't feel like eating anything. "Let's get your roast beef first."

She waited at his side while the chef carved Paul a generous portion of rare roast beef. Interesting, she thought, she'd expected him to order a well-done portion. Why, she couldn't say. There was something straight-arrow yet wildly unconventional about Paul Tanner.

When he'd shown up tonight, it was all she could do not to drool. He was a striking man who oozed enough testosterone for a dozen guys—under normal circumstances. But when dressed in a tuxedo, there was something overwhelmingly attractive about him. It was a rough-hewn masculinity that stood out in sharp contrast to the other men present tonight. They all seemed slightly effeminate, as if they couldn't hold their own in a fight.

Not Paul Tanner.

She'd watched out of the corner of her eye as they'd waited in the reception line, then made their way outside. Women tracked Paul as he passed and the men looked up and took notice. She wasn't much at reading lips, but she'd caught several gorgeous women whispering: *Who is he?*

"Let's get you some shrimp and find a table," Paul said after he'd been served.

They moved a few feet over to where an ice sculpture of a humongous clamshell showcased a mound of jumbo shrimp. The chef handed her three huge shrimp artfully arranged in a martini glass filled with cocktail sauce.

"Looks good," Paul commented as they moved away.

It was an interesting way of serving shrimp, but her mind wasn't on food. "When do we see Wyatt Holbrook?"

"Tobias Pennington, his personal assistant, will come for us." Paul found a tall round table at the edge of the crowd and placed his plate and drink on it.

Madison set her two glasses beside his. The table came to just above her waist but it was much lower for Paul. Since the tabletop was so small, she had to stand closer to him than she would have liked. "I hope he doesn't make us wait too long."

"Why not? We could dance."

A three-piece group was playing soft rock and a few people were dancing near the pool on a small dance floor that had been put down for the party. Normally, she liked to dance, but she didn't want to find herself in Paul's arms. Something about him kept her on edge. He was far too hot for his own good and kept looking at her in a way that made her uncomfortable. She needed to meet Wyatt Holbrook and leave. What she'd do then, she wasn't sure.

Instead of answering Paul, she picked up a piece of shrimp and nibbled on it. It was delicious. Many people overcooked shrimp, her father often had told her, making it tough. Not this shrimp. It was tender and had just the right amount of cocktail sauce on it from being placed tail up in the martini glass. Her father would have approved and she reminded herself to try this at home, just as soon as she found a new place to live.

"How's the beef?" she asked because Paul was watching her, his square jaw working as he chewed.

"Great." He glanced over her shoulder. "Here comes Garrison."

"He doesn't know why I'm here, does he?"

"From his reaction at the door, I'd say no."

"Don't tell him. I'd like to get in and out of here with as little fuss as possible."

"You don't know Garrison. He's every bit as smart as his father. Maybe smarter. He'll put two and two together and figure out why you're here."

"Getting enough to eat?" Garrison asked as he came up to them, a crystal highball glass in one hand. It appeared to contain vodka on the rocks with a twist of lime.

"Yes, thanks," Paul replied for them.

Garrison turned to Madison. "I didn't get a chance to ask you if you were considering donating to my father's foundation. It's a very worthy cause, you know."

Madison shook her head. "No, I'm here to interview him for a blog, HighKinkz."

Garrison shot her with the old tried-and-true finger pistol as he chuckled. "One one. Real good." Smiling, he stared at her for a moment, then said, "You must be one of my father's...ah...offspring."

She noticed he hadn't used the term "half sister" and realized this was his way of distancing himself. It hit her that this mansion, and the money involved, must make Wyatt Holbrook's heirs feel protective. A half sibling might threaten them somehow.

"I'm certain I'm not one of—"

"Forgive me. Offspring sounds so... silly. The idea of having brothers and sisters I never knew existed takes some mental adjustment. It's great. I mean it. My father isn't just any man. He's extraordinary. Saving his life is really important."

There was no mistaking the sincerity in Garrison's voice. His vibrant green eyes radiated heartfelt anxiety. Madison didn't blame him. She would have given everything she had or ever hoped to have to save her own father.

"I understand." All the anger she'd been harboring vanished.

"You must be from the Boston area," Garrison told her.

Madison knew he believed this because his father had used clinics there while he'd been in medical school. She wasn't sure how much she should say. For reasons she didn't have time to evaluate, she didn't want these people to know too much about her, but she couldn't lie. "No. I live right here in Florida."

"Really?" Garrison's gaze shifted to Paul.

"I found a few files in another location. They led me to Madison."

Garrison's brow creased, but instead of asking Paul for details, he turned to Madison. "What do you do?"

"I work at an online game," she replied, deliberately under-playing her role in the company.

"Interesting," he replied, but, despite his smile, she doubted he gave one whit about online games.

"What do you do?" she asked.

"I have a laboratory." He pronounced it "la-bore-atory," as if he were British. Her initial impression had been favorable. He seemed like a nice man who was terribly worried about his father's health. Now she wondered if he deserved the snobby reputation that was associated with Palm Beach. "I'm developing biologic drugs."

"Ah," she replied, to show him she wasn't an airhead gamer, "drugs made from living organisms."

"Yes," he said, raising his eyebrows in surprise. "Most people don't know much about it."

"I'm afraid I don't know a lot. But I do know that drugs made from living organisms—the new frontier apparently—aren't subject to patent laws like drugs made in the lab by man. Those patents expire, then they become affordable generic drugs."

"True, but biologics are harder to develop than drugs created in a lab. I specialize in using organisms from the sea. The largest predator that ever lived is still alive—"

"The sperm whale," she interjected before she could stop herself. "It's fifty tons or more and roamed the sea back in the days of dinosaurs."

For an instant his eyes narrowed ever so slightly, then he quirked an eyebrow and winked at her. "Correct. Man came from the sea. The most powerful forces in nature, like tsunamis and volcanoes, are in the sea. Answers to health problems in the new millennium will come from—"

"Garrison, here you are," Savannah said as she swanned up to them in the lime-green sheath that fit her like a tattoo, Nathan Cassidy in tow. "We need—"

"You met Madison Connelly. She's here to see if she can *help* Father."

"Oh?" The beautiful redhead stared at Madison as if she'd spotted a deadly snake coiled to strike. "I—I thought we were having trouble locating—"

"Very few records in Boston led to contacts," Garrison informed his sister.

"I found Madison's records here," Paul said.

"Really?" Nathan Cassidy said. "I'm surprised. I thought the records that were located didn't show—"

"There's some question about their authenticity," Madison felt compelled to say.

"Who told you that?" Garrison asked just as an elderly couple approached the group.

"Let's dance." Paul nudged her toward the dance floor.

"Thanks," whispered Madison after they'd moved away from the group. "I don't want to give Wyatt's children false hope."

Paul didn't respond; he had his own theory about the Holbrook children.

"Savannah seems a little…ah…hostile, I guess. Do you think she sees me as a threat?"

Paul swung her into his arms as the quartet began to play a slow tune from the Big Band era. He didn't know its name, but judging by the herd of moon-eyed octogenarians on the dance floor, it was a sentimental favorite. It was almost impossible to move with so many people around. Well, hell, whatever it took. He just wanted to hold Madison. "What do you mean, a threat?" he said into her ear in a low voice.

She cocked her head to one side and gazed up at him. His heart lurched painfully, skipping a beat before settling into its normal rhythm. Honest to God, the woman hadn't a clue how appealing she was. She flexed her leg slightly between his as she moved to the beat. He put his hand on her soft, bare back and a throbbing current of arousal spiraled through him, pooling in his groin.

"Savannah's a true beauty. I'm know I'm not a threat in that way, but I was wondering if she might think Wyatt might… I don't know exactly."

"He might monetarily reward a newfound—what term did Garrison use?"

"Offspring. Could his children—" she stood up on tiptoe to whisper in his ear "—not want him to live?"

"It's a possibility," he admitted. "What makes you ask?"

It took a minute with them moving to the music for her to respond. "Erin. The police made a point of telling me that money is one of the primary causes of murder. I knew it, of course, but until someone you love is killed, it doesn't hit home."

"I don't know," he told her. "The rich are different. Maybe Garrison and Savannah want more than their trust funds."

"It won't matter in my case," she informed him in a low but authoritative voice. "I'm not going to be able to help their father, but someone else might."

Aw, come off it, he wanted to say, but he resisted the urge. Instead, he drew Madison closer, savoring the softness of her body against his, the way her breasts molded against his torso. Rocking to the beat, he skimmed her bare back with his open palm, then lightly stroked the intriguing groove of her spine with his fingertips. His hand reached her neck where a loose tendril curled against the warm flesh. He flicked it aside and traced the curve of her neck with his thumb.

Paul detected Madison's sharp intake of breath and what could only be a sigh. He looked down at her eyes, which were veiled by a golden fringe of lashes. She was staring at the back of a stoop-shouldered elderly man dancing nearby. Okay, so she wouldn't look him in the eye. At least she hadn't pulled away. Maybe, just maybe, he had a chance with her.

The dance ended and the throng around them clapped. Paul refused to release Madison. She made no move to pull away, either. The strains of another waltz began, forcing them to dance again. They swayed to the lilting notes, unable to do much else with so many people trying to dance at once. He held her close and wished to hell that he could think of something clever to say.

Why ruin it? Obviously, they communicated better without words. He leisurely moved his hand up and down her back. They were barely moving now, only rotating their hips, pretending to dance. Another couple bumped into them and muttered an apology. Madison glanced up at him and her arms unexpectedly circled his neck.

What was she thinking?

All right, so he wasn't an ace at figuring out women, but he had enough experience to realize he'd been wrong. This woman wanted him as much as he wanted her.

"What are we doing?" she asked in a husky voice.

"I'm positive Adam asked the same thing in the Garden of Eden."

"Really?" A smile alluringly curved her mouth. "What did Eve say?"

"It'll be all right." He squeezed her. "*Then* she offered him the apple."

She laughed, the first genuine laugh he'd heard from her. "And Adam was dumb enough to fall for it."

Paul chuckled, taken by surprise, another heated rush of desire coursing through him. She had a great sense of humor to go along with a killer bod and a pretty face. Why did he have to meet her on an assignment?

Hell. You couldn't time these things. Sometimes you just had to go for it. Now was one of those times, he assured himself. Madison was different from most women he knew. She was definitely worth the risk of appearing unprofessional. Definitely.

Ignoring the crowd around them, Paul lowered his lips to Madison's soft mouth. Her thick lashes fluttered closed as he eased his hand down from her back to the curve of her buttocks and pressed her against his erection. His tongue invaded her mouth, symbolic of another possession he had on his mind.

Suddenly, he was aware of someone clutching his shoulder. Pissed as hell, he broke the kiss and turned to face the intruder.

"Mr. Holbrook will see you now," Tobias Pennington informed them.

CHAPTER ELEVEN

What is DNA?

MADISON STEELED HERSELF, not sure what to expect as she walked into the massive library. She was still shaken by what had happened on the dance floor. What had she been thinking? Obviously, Paul suffered from testosterone surges that caused him to grab anything in panties.

Well, forget these panties.

But that wasn't the message she'd sent, was it? She'd wantonly slung her arms around his neck and pressed her body against his like some hot-to-trot teenager. Then when he'd kissed her, Madison hadn't pulled away. No. She'd kissed him back. Right there in the middle of the dance floor.

Why had she acted that way? Maybe some part of her brain had responded to him. God knows, it had been ages since she'd been held, been kissed. Her relationship with Aiden had faltered, then they'd separated. She'd dated a few times but refused to get involved with anyone. She didn't know what had happened tonight, but she vowed not to repeat the mistake.

Madison steadied herself and forced her mind to focus on meeting Wyatt Holbrook in the library of his mansion. She had the vague impression of a vaulted ceiling and wood-paneled walls lined with books that had the mellow glow of antique leather. The jarring thumps of her heart blocked other details.

At the rear of the room stood a walnut desk large enough to be a ping-pong table. In front of the desk stood a tall man with a patrician profile. Laser-blue eyes tracked her approach with the same keen intelligence she'd noted in Garrison's eyes. But instead of having rich mahogany-colored hair, Wyatt had sandy hair that must once have been a glistening blond but was now mostly silver.

Nothing about Wyatt Holbrook struck a familiar chord with Madison. She already knew this man wasn't her father and seeing him confirmed her feelings. But Madison couldn't deny there was something impressive about Wyatt Holbrook. Even without speaking, he radiated authority and power.

She was glad Paul was with her. Not that she needed him for moral support or anything, but he'd brought her and she wanted him ready to whisk her away as soon as she'd spoken with Wyatt Holbrook.

"Madison, so glad you could make it." The older man held out his hand and spoke in a friendly tone meant to put her at ease.

"Hello." She shook his hand and held his incisive gaze, not sure what to say next. Paul was right; Wyatt Holbrook did not appear to be ill. Again, she wondered if there could possibly be a hidden agenda here.

"Have a seat," he said, and turned to Tobias Pennington. "Tobias, we'd like champagne."

Madison started to protest and say she needed to leave soon, but Paul grabbed her arm and pulled her onto the love seat near the desk. Two chairs flanked either side of the sofa that was opposite the huge desk.

"I'll have the Veuve Clicquot brought in," Tobias said as he headed out of the room.

Wyatt Holbrook's personal assistant couldn't be much older than Madison, but his tall, lean frame and gaunt face made him look like a long-distance runner in a seersucker sport jacket. His vampire-pale complexion among so many tanned people made her wonder if he'd been ill recently. He certainly looked worse than Wyatt, as if he were the one who needed a transplant.

"Tell me about yourself." Wyatt Holbrook sat in one of the chairs near the sofa.

Madison had no intention of talking about herself. Besides, she knew Wyatt must have been given the same dossier on her that Paul Tanner had read. He could read everything he needed to know.

"I'd rather talk about you," she told him in a clipped tone. "I've been wondering if you ever gave any thought to the other children you could have. Were they okay? Were they being abused?" She paused to glance around at the library and take in the valuable oil paintings and what must be original Remington bronze sculptures artfully showcased in special niches in the paneled walls. "You have so much, while your other children might be starving."

Tobias had returned and was standing directly behind Wyatt. The assistant glared at her with deep-set brown eyes as if to ask: How dare you?

Wyatt didn't appear to be the least bit disturbed by her questions. "When I donated, I was struggling to make it through medical school. A lot of guys were doing it. I honestly didn't give it much thought."

Madison managed a quick nod. She hadn't expected him to be quite so candid.

"Years later, one of my top researchers came to me and said she needed a pregnancy leave. We were right in the middle of FDA trials and Natalie was a key member of the team. She'd always lived for her job, working harder and accomplishing more than three other scientists could have."

Madison silently blessed her father. He'd warned her over and over not to let work consume her. *There's so much more to life than one thing—no matter how fascinating you find it,* he'd told her. *Explore the world around you. Never forget—people count the most.*

"Natalie told me that her biological clock had become a time bomb. She'd spent her life in the lab, never meeting anyone or getting married. She'd undergone artificial insemination. It had taken several tries, but now she was pregnant and needed a leave."

Madison wasn't sure what this had to do with her question, but she found herself listening intently.

"Of course, I gave Natalie a leave and worked out a schedule so she could take care of her baby and spend time in the lab. Her situation made me think of the sperm I'd donated. Back then, most insemination recipients were couples who couldn't conceive. I envisioned helping childless people who would be loving parents. Natalie made me think about single mothers for the first time."

"You never wondered about the children who might not be lucky enough to have both parents."

"I considered the possibility," he admitted slowly, with what might have been a trace of regret in his voice. "I didn't realize until recently that the clinic split my sperm donations and that I could have—may actually have—many more children than I thought possible. I was shocked. Of course, I wondered—"

"But you never tried to contact—"

"There's no easy way to trace these children," Tobias cut in. "Clinics guard patients' privacy tenaciously. The HIPA law has made it even more difficult to access medical records."

The room was silent for a moment, the only sounds the chatter of voices and music drifting in from the party. Finally, Wyatt spoke.

"I didn't try to find any of my offspring," he conceded, "until my doctor told me I had primary sclerosing cholangitis—PSC—and would soon need a liver transplant. The football star Walter Peyton died of the same disease. There is no known cause or cure. The only thing that works is a transplant.

"I hoped Garrison or Savannah could help but neither can. Then I realized I could try to contact children who might have been conceived from my sperm. I was told the first avenue to explore was Internet Web sites where children were attempting to find their biological fathers. They relinquish the confidentiality status of their records, hoping to find fathers or other siblings. We couldn't locate anyone related to me."

"Mike Tanner was able to find two children about your age," Tobias told her when Wyatt stopped speaking. "They'd grown up in the northeast, which is what you'd expect."

Madison was a little surprised that Wyatt's personal assistant knew so much. It appeared that he was closer to his employer than she would have thought. She wondered how long they'd been together.

"I mentioned those children," Paul told her, speaking for the first time since entering the library. She refused to look directly at him. "One ODed, while the other died in an auto accident."

Madison never took her eyes off Wyatt. If the premature deaths of two of his children concerned him, nothing in his expression revealed it.

"How did you find out about New Horizons?" she asked.

"Paul's father, Mike, has handled all my corporate security and…other problems," Wyatt responded. "He's a sharp investigator. He discovered one of the clinics in Boston resold sperm to a so-called Mensa clinic down here called New Horizons."

A waiter arrived with a tray of flutes filled with the expensive champagne. Madison was offered one first and reluctantly took a glass. For an instant she felt like flinging it against the paneled wall. Instead, not sure what to do next, she studied the amber liquid, the bubbles streaming to the surface in an endless parade. Her impulsive trip here now seemed awkward. She had no idea what to say to get out of here. She glanced at Paul but he was taking a sip of champagne.

"Did you locate any other children from the New Horizons clinic?" she asked.

"Mike Tanner gave all the files to Tobias," Wyatt told her. "They had been torn apart to prepare for litigation that ultimately didn't go to court because the clinic declared bankruptcy. Tobias is still sorting through them."

"In other words, the vultures called attorneys couldn't suck any more money out of anyone so they just shoved everything into cardboard boxes," Tobias said.

From the moment Madison had met Tobias, when he found them on the dance floor, he'd struck her as being an angry, bitter man. She felt he resented her. Why? Didn't he want to help Wyatt?

"We thought we had all the files," Wyatt continued, as if Tobias hadn't spoken. "It wasn't until Paul discovered another box of files and found your mother's name that we realized we didn't."

"What made you think to look elsewhere?" she asked Paul.

"There was a list of numbers that corresponded to donors in the master file. Some of them seemed to be missing. It only stood to reason that all of the files hadn't been found in the warehouse."

"It was good work on Paul's part," Wyatt said. "Like father, like son."

"I was the only one in that second batch of files?" she asked Paul. He'd told her about finding the files but hadn't mentioned any other children. She wondered if he had told her everything.

"We're still going through them," Wyatt responded. The way he kept saying "we" made her believe others were doing the work. "I'm afraid Tobias is right. They're a mess."

Madison nodded, not knowing what else to do. A silence enveloped the group. She wanted to leap out of her seat and bolt for the door, but something kept her in place, not saying a word.

"We can arrange for you to take the donor compatibility test at St. John's Hospital."

Madison realized everyone in the room assumed she believed she was one of Wyatt's children and was willing to donate a lobe of her liver if they were compatible. Apparently, Paul hadn't revealed her reservations.

Wyatt broke the uncomfortable silence. "Of course, if you are compatible, we're willing to pay—"

"I'm not interested in money." Madison slammed her untouched glass of champagne on the table beside the sofa. She jumped up and headed for the door. Wyatt Holbrook was right behind her and it took her a few seconds to realize no one else in the room had moved.

"Let me show you something," he said in a low voice.

"All right," she replied slowly, not knowing why she didn't tell him that she was leaving this minute.

He guided her out the door and down a wide hallway lined with more prints of shells and what she assumed were pieces of coral. They came to a closed door. Judging from where she'd been in the house, Madison decided this room must face an inner garden, not the sea or the rambling vista facing the lake with the swans. Wyatt put his index finger up to a button affixed to the doorjamb. It read his fingerprint, she realized with awe. She hadn't noticed any security devices on other doors—just this room. She might expect such high-tech security in an office building, maybe, but not here in this classic Mizner mansion.

"My office," Wyatt explained as he opened the door and waited for Madison to enter. "It's not much, but I'm gearing up to work here full-time after the surgery."

She knew he meant the liver transplant but she didn't know what to say. She stepped into the room as he flicked on the lights. A small wood desk not much larger than the one she used at her office dominated the room. Books lined the shelves, but unlike the library, these volumes appeared to be medical journals. They all were paperbound and some were thicker than most books. Medical and scientific journals, she realized.

"Do you know what DNA stands for?" he asked, sweeping his hand to indicate the wall near the only window in the room.

"It's an acronym for deoxyribonucleic acid, which encodes essential genetic information in every living organism."

"Right," Wyatt said, and she could tell he was impressed. Why? A college student with a biology major could have told him the answer. Then it hit Madison—Wyatt might *not* have seen her personal profile. They thought...thought what? She was merely a video gamer, not a former MIT student.

Wyatt again waved his hand to indicate the wall. "Here is all the research that led to Crick and Watson's discovery of the DNA code."

"Really?" She'd known that years of research had gone into the project and many others had tried—and failed—to break the DNA code. Seeing all the volumes gave her a new respect for the years in many laboratories that it had taken to crack the code.

"This is what I want to be my legacy," Wyatt said in a low voice that rang with conviction. "New frontiers in medicine and science. We've only just begun to glimpse the discoveries on the horizon." He walked toward the desk piled with papers. "I won't be here to help future scientists. That's why I'm establishing the Holbrook Foundation. It will generate enough money for scientists to explore all sorts of possibilities."

"I see," she replied very slowly, because she didn't know where he was going with this and didn't want to be caught off guard.

"I'm not the Getty," he said, his voice suddenly sounding tired. "J. Paul Getty had nearly a billion dollars to contribute to his foundation. It's been wisely invested and continues to grow so the Getty Museum is the richest museum in the world."

"But they still don't have a major collection of art," she responded.

"True. The art they need is already in museums or in countries that won't allow its export." He walked behind the desk and dropped into a chair that was well-worn and appeared to fit the contours of his body. "My point is, my foundation has a sizable amount of money from the endowment I'm setting up, but it needs more funds. Scientists burn through money in search of discoveries that will benefit mankind. It can't be helped. That's the nature of research."

"You're right," Madison said carefully. She didn't know where this discussion was going, but she felt it was his way of persuading her to undergo the necessary tests.

There was a long, heavy silence in the room before Wyatt asked, "Do you know where the scientists in America's labs are coming from?"

She didn't hesitate. "Asia. Mostly India but also Japan, Taiwan and China."

He regarded her for a moment with what she thought might be respect. "Exactly. America's school system doesn't promote the sciences so we aren't producing them. The ones we do manage to nurture to graduate school are overwhelmed by opportunities in the business field."

"Drug companies hire them." She could have said, *Like Holbrook Pharmaceuticals,* but she refrained from taking an accusatory stance.

"Exactly. What I want to do is keep America's scientists in the lab, keep them researching and helping mankind. That's why I need to raise funds for the Holbrook Foundation. It will take more money than I have. After all, my money comes from Xeria, a drug I discovered, not oil like Getty. My funds are limited. I need more. It will take my time and my personal touch to set up this foundation and make sure it's running properly.

"What most people don't realize is medical discoveries are

coming quickly. Twenty years ago MRIs and CT scans were only used in the most advanced medical centers. Now they're commonplace. Fiber optics has made it possible to develop numerous scopes and probes that have led to less invasive surgeries. Other discoveries are on the horizon. That's why I need a liver transplant. It will buy me the time I need."

"What do the doctors say?" she asked, not knowing how to phrase the question delicately. "I mean, how much time do you have?"

He shrugged. "It's hard to say. A year or so. Longer, of course, if I get that transplant."

As far as Madison could tell, this man was totally sincere. He did want to do something that would benefit millions of people. Of course, these discoveries would be worth millions of dollars and would garner a place in medical history. She assumed Wyatt Holbrook sought that place in history. She honestly doubted she could help him, but how could she say no to being tested?

It certainly would be a quick way to prove she wasn't related to this man. Madison knew exactly who her father was. She didn't need a test to confirm it, but she realized these people wouldn't agree. She had to take the test.

She heard herself say, "I'll take the test. I doubt I can help you, but let's see."

CHAPTER TWELVE

PAUL STUDIED the murder book on Erin Wycoff's death. Essentially, in almost a week, the police had no leads and no motive unless you counted Lincoln Burgess's lame theory that Madison had killed her friend to inherit a piece of land that had recently become valuable. Paul wasn't buying the "missing link's" claim, especially now that he knew Madison.

She'd been silent on the drive home last night, but he figured it was best to back off and give her some space. It had taken a supreme effort not to try to kiss her again, but he'd managed. When questioned about the time she spent alone with Holbrook, Madison said she'd agreed to visit Holbrook's office this afternoon. He assumed Wyatt was trying to persuade Madison to be tested to see if she could donate part of her liver, but then she'd informed him that she'd already agreed to take the test.

So why did Wyatt Holbrook want her to come to his office?

He closed the murder book and gazed across the crowded squad room, thinking about last night. The minute he'd taken Madison into his arms he'd felt…something. Aw, hell, he hadn't been laid in a while and she had sex appeal in spades. When he'd held her, Paul could tell she was attracted to him. He wouldn't have guessed it otherwise, but for those few minutes while they'd been dancing, he knew it.

Burgess breezed in, late as usual, but if you asked him, Link would claim he'd been chasing down a lead.

"What are you doing here, Tanner? Aren't you still out on disability leave?"

"Yeah, but I'm curious about the Wycoff case." He stood up. "It's not every day I walk into a murder scene without someone having called the police."

"You're not supposed to be reading the book." Burgess protectively grabbed the three-ring binder. "You're a witness."

Paul decided Burgess didn't want anyone to know that the statements from the main witnesses, including Madison, hadn't yet been typed up and put into the murder book.

"Any new leads?" he asked. There wasn't anything in the book but there was always the wild-ass possibility Burgess was working on something.

Link glanced down at the book he was cradling in his arms. It took a minute before he reluctantly said, "The dog's a problem."

"Really? Got enough to book him?"

"Hysterical, Tanner. Just hysterical." He dropped the book on his desk. "Guess you don't want to know."

Burgess had no sense of humor. So, what else was new? "Of course I want to know what's going on. That's why I came in. I'll help if I can."

That got him. Link was the laziest SOB on the force. How he'd ever made detective was a mystery that couldn't be solved. He was always trying to get someone to do his work for him. Even though this was a sensitive case, Paul wouldn't be surprised to learn Burgess had handed the tapes of the statements given by witnesses to one of the police volunteers to type up. A major no-no because too many volunteers leaked info to the media.

"Forensics found fur from the retriever in the victim's car and on clothing dropped on the floor of her bedroom."

"Not surprising. Erin Wycoff had bought the dog for the Connelly woman." He deliberately avoided giving Burgess the impression that he'd seen Madison since the discovery of the body. "Of course the dog was in the house. I saw it in the kitchen."

Link shrugged again, an annoying habit. "Wilson's working an arson and burglary at Dicon Labs. They were testing some of their products on rabbits and dogs. The firm didn't list any as missing, but the investigators found nothing but charred empty cages. You'd expect a few bones at least."

"Do you think A—the dog—was a lab animal?" Paul stopped himself from using Aspen's name.

Burgess shrugged. "It's a possibility. A friend claimed Erin Wycoff had been involved with an animal rights group but thought the victim had given it up."

Another item not properly noted in the murder book. "If she was still involved, something should turn up on her computer or phone records."

"Nothing so far, but the geeks downstairs are still checking her computer."

"What time was the fire at the lab reported?" Paul asked.

"The alarm went off just before midnight. They'd had several false alarms, so the fire department was slow to respond. When they arrived, no one was around but the night watchman, who hadn't seen anything until flames appeared."

Paul considered this information for a moment. Having been a lab animal would explain Aspen's eye problem and might account for Madison's protectiveness. She struck him as the kind of woman who wouldn't approve of experimenting on animals.

"Plus—" Burgess flashed a shit-eating grin "—we can't track down the name on the bill of sale for the retriever. The address listed is an office complex."

"Well, there's a hot market for stolen purebreds. Maybe someone just wanted to make a quick buck."

Burgess had been present at the crime scene when Madison

said she had to take Aspen to the vet. Evidently, he didn't connect the "eye infection" with testing in the lab. Paul saw no reason to enlighten Link at this point.

"If Erin had been involved, it might explain why she was in the tub at two in the morning. Fire means smoke and soot. You know what clean freaks women are."

The glazed deer-in-the-headlights look in Link's eyes told Paul that the jerk hadn't considered this possibility. "Right…right."

"Do you want me to recheck with the folks at Dicon Labs to see if they are missing any animals?"

"Well…as long as I don't know about it. You're not supposed to be working—"

"Don't worry. I won't mention a thing. Walking in on a murder makes me curious. That's all."

"Do you think it's possible the victim stole something from the lab and someone killed her for it?"

"It's possible," Paul replied. "What was stolen?"

"From what Wilson told me, nothing was reported missing. It could have been some of those animal rights folks, except as I said, no lab animals were listed as missing or dead, either."

"Did any of the local groups claim responsibility or brag about it on the Internet?" Again, Paul could tell Burgess hadn't considered this angle.

"Dunno. I guess Wilson's checking."

Yeah, right. And pigs fly. Torching buildings was a major business in the Miami area, a way of getting an insurance payoff for a failing enterprise. Wilson and the arson task force were overworked and on a tight budget. Paul didn't see them trolling the Internet over a fire where nothing valuable seemed to be missing and no one had been killed or injured.

"The animal rights groups don't usually steal anything but the animals. That's hardly worth murdering someone over."

Burgess dropped into his chair like a load of cement. "Then my money's on the Connelly woman. She'll inherit millions."

"Did forensics tell you if the attacker was right- or left-handed?" All that was in the murder book so far was a preliminary report. A good detective would have asked this question immediately. Madison was left-handed—as were all the Holbrooks—but Paul doubted she was physically strong enough to commit the crime. Not that he believed she'd killed her best friend.

"Forensics didn't say. I guess the knot on the belt around her neck would tell them, right?"

The belt from the robe that had been used to strangle Erin Wycoff hadn't been knotted. Trust Link not to notice such details. Talk about missing a link.

"I suspect the angle of the torque on her neck will tell forensics the tale."

Burgess picked up the telephone and punched the speed dial for the forensic department. Moments later, he hung up the phone with a smile.

"Left-handed. I'm liking Madison Connelly for this one better and better all the time."

MADISON WALKED into the glass and marble lobby of Holbrook Pharmaceuticals just after two o'clock. She'd spent the morning in her own office. Aiden was still with Chloe. The staph infection she'd gotten when her "headlights" had been installed continued to be a problem. Madison had worked, then left Aspen with Jade while she came here.

She'd told herself a thousand times that this was a mistake. She didn't want to get to know Wyatt Holbrook any better, didn't want to feel sorry for him. He was a talented, remarkable man, but he wasn't her father. It would be like hitting the moon with a BB gun should her test show she could donate part of her liver.

The security guard at the desk checked her ID and issued her a temporary badge. He'd just finished explaining that Wyatt

Holbrook's office was on the top floor when her cell phone rang. She wasn't going to answer it, except the digital display told her the Russerts were calling. They owned the Fisher Island home where she was staying. They were still in Italy and wouldn't call unless it was important.

She answered, and Claudia Russert said, "Just wanted to give you a heads-up. We're bored here. It's hot and Tuscany is crawling—absolutely crawling—with tourists. We're coming home early. I hope you don't mind."

Of course she minded. She didn't have anyplace to stay, especially now that she had a dog. "It's okay. When are you coming back?"

"Day after tomorrow."

Oh God! What was she going to do? "Great. I'll have everything ready." She managed to thank Claudia before she hung up. Instead of getting on the elevator to the penthouse, she decided to call her Realtor. Perhaps Karen knew of a short-term rental Madison could take until she bought a home.

It took a few minutes and a call to Karen's cell to reach the agent, who was out of the office. While she waited, Madison walked over to the plate-glass window overlooking the office complex. Two smoke-gray cylindrical buildings of staggered height shot skyward, the shortest being about eighteen stories tall. She'd had no idea Holbrook Pharmaceuticals was this large, but then what did she know? She'd never visited a pharmaceutical company before now.

"Madison, how are you?" The Realtor's bright, too-cheery voice came into her ear. "I've been meaning to call you."

"Really? You found something?" Yesterday, Madison had left a message, saying she had a dog and needed a place with a yard, but Karen hadn't returned her call.

"Not…exactly."

Something in the Realtor's voice rang a warning bell. What was wrong now?

"I was doing a routine prequalification. You remember signing the form…"

"Of course. Prescreening for a loan. What about it? I have excellent credit." She silently amended it to "we" had excellent credit. Much of her credit history she shared with Aiden.

"The funds in your savings account. You know—"

"The down payment."

"Right." Static spit into Madison's ear, almost obliterating Karen's next words. "It isn't there. There's nothing in that account."

It took a second for the words to register. When they did, the blood left her head so quickly that she lurched sideways. "Impossible!" Madison shouted, then lowered her voice. "I put my entire divorce settlement into my savings account."

"Well, I…ah… You might want to check with your bank."

She snapped the phone shut. Shock seeped through every pore, spreading through her body with mind-numbing speed. Her fingers trembling so violently that she could hardly punch the keys, Madison contacted her bank. What Karen had told her was true. She had nothing in her savings account. According to the vice president, the funds had been wire transferred out of her account the day Erin had died.

"Is it possible you've been the victim of identity theft?" the man asked.

Madison hung up, her knees weak, locked by a type of paralysis. Her body refused to move but her mind churned. There were so many ways identity thieves could have gotten into her account. She was a poster girl for the Internet generation. She bought a lot online. She'd been careful and used secure sites. She'd thought she was safe, but this must have been how they'd accessed her personal information to steal the money from her savings account. She wondered if charges had been run up on her credit cards, as well.

Her body felt drained, as if she'd been ill for weeks, but she was able to function again. She called Jade and explained the problem. The receptionist told her she would be happy to contact the credit card companies to see what was happening. Madison didn't like Jade taking time away from the business to do personal things for her, but this was an emergency. She was already late for her appointment with Wyatt Holbrook.

Still light-headed with shock, Madison managed to ride the elevator to the penthouse. The top floor was more marble and glass. It was so quiet that the click-click of her high heels sounded like a hammer. In the distance she saw Biscayne Bay glistening in the afternoon sunlight like a banner of dazzling blue sequins.

The receptionist whose nameplate read Rose Marie Nesbit took her into Wyatt Holbrook's office immediately. She wasn't surprised to find Tobias Pennington there, but she hadn't expected to see Garrison.

"Glad you could make it," Garrison said as he bounded toward her, his hand extended, a welcoming smile on his face. "Thanks so much for coming. It means a lot to my father—to all of us."

"You're welcome," she replied, feeling a little guilty. This man truly loved his father and thought she could help, when she had no doubt that she couldn't. It reminded her of her own father and his fight to stay alive. She understood Garrison's anxiety and for the first time wished she could help.

They shook and she was again struck by how good-looking Garrison was, yet he didn't seem to know it. For a split second, she wondered if he was married. Her Internet search hadn't come across any mention of a wife.

"Garrison has his test labs in the other tower," Wyatt Holbrook told her. "That way we can share some of the same facilities."

"It's more economic," added Tobias.

"I see. The complex's so big. You're doing a lot more

research than I imagined." She hadn't really known what to expect, but certainly not this large an operation. It must employ hundreds of people.

"Like many corporations, Holbrook is known for one product—Xeria. It's a medication for diabetes. It's much—"

"I know," Madison told him. "America is so overweight hundreds of people come down with the disease every day. Sadly, many of them are obese children. Your medication helps them lead more normal lives."

"Yes, well. We've developed a number of other things and we're working on a lot more." Wyatt gave her an encouraging smile. "I want to make a difference in people's lives to help suffering. Our company has a program to help the poor get Xeria at a reduced cost."

Madison had no idea his company was so generous. From what she knew of drug companies, they tried to maximize profits, not caring that the elderly or the poor couldn't afford lifesaving medications.

"It takes years and megabucks to research and develop a drug," Garrison said, echoing what his father had said last night.

"It's easier to show you," Wyatt said, "than try to explain. Let's give her the tour."

Madison was again tempted to remind them that they didn't have to do all this to convince her to take the test. She wasn't related to them. Being tested would be a waste of time, but she had already agreed to do it. She just needed to finish here and straighten out her own financial problems. She could manage if her credit cards hadn't been compromised. She—and Aspen—could live in a residence motel until the mess at her bank was resolved.

She allowed the men to lead her back to the elevator, where they used a special card key to access the fifth floor.

"This is where most of the current research is in the final stages," Tobias Pennington told her.

Aspen was already on her mind and she asked, "Do you experiment on animals?"

"No," Wyatt assured her. "We use mice and rats in some tests but most of our testing is done in vitro." Madison must have had a puzzled look because he explained, "That's experimenting with test-tube cultures of tissue. We also use computers and simulators."

"Tests on animals aren't that reliable," explained Garrison. "Some drugs have looked promising in primate tests, then hit bottom when humans were tested."

"The best example is AIDS," added Tobias, speaking for the first time. "Chimps are very close to man genetically but the AIDS virus doesn't affect them."

"Really?" The mention of chimps made her think of Erin and her plan to use the money from her inheritance to help Save the Chimps in Fort Pierce. Madison had discovered many of those chimps had suffered horribly in clinical trials for years before coming to the sanctuary. She planned to visit as soon as possible.

"Even a medication we use almost daily, aspirin, has caused birth defects in the five other species it was tested on," Wyatt told her. "It costs a billion dollars or more to bring a drug to market. We don't want any mistakes."

They arrived at the fifth floor and stepped out of the elevator into a small room with an armed guard and a security camera trained on them. For a second, Madison's mind strayed to Paul and she wondered if this was part of the security his father provided to Wyatt Holbrook. Everyone, including the Holbrooks, signed the guard's roster before being shown into an adjacent room.

"There are disposable hazmat suits on the shelves," Wyatt said. "We put them on over our clothes. Other sections of the building require full hazmat gear and we have special changing rooms, but this is enough to tour the fifth floor."

Madison left her shoes on a floor rack beside the others and stepped into a green jumpsuit with built-in booties that Garrison had taken from the shelf, shaken out and handed to her. He signaled for her to first put on latex gloves. She stepped into the suit that could easily have fit over a big man like Paul Tanner. Why did she keep thinking about him? What was wrong with her?

She forced herself to watch what the others were doing and slipped a hospital-style cap with a lightweight plastic face mask attached over her hair. It took a moment to adjust the mask so she could see. She followed the men out of the room through a double-wide stainless-steel door with a red biohazard emblem on it. Like cigars in a box, they stood in the small space beyond the locker room.

"The whooshing sound is the bad air being sucked out before we enter the test zone," Garrison said.

It was more like a wind tunnel sound than a whoosh, she thought. Then the noise stopped and the door directly in front of them automatically opened. They went into a large room with banks of high-tech equipment gleaming on sterile white counters. Winking digital displays indicated the equipment was working on something but it was impossible to tell just what.

"We're running a test on a germ we've heated up," Wyatt said.

Garrison added, "That means we exposed the germ over and over and over to antibiotics, which forced the rapid evolution of a drug-resistant strain of the germ."

Madison knew the overuse of antibiotics had created strains of germs that were resistant to them. Her father had been aware of the problem years ago and had argued with Madison's pediatrician not to prescribe antibiotics for her unless it was absolutely necessary.

"We have a new drug that's showing great promise," Tobias told her. "It seems to work on germs that have built a resistance to other drugs."

"It could be the next step in the continuing evolution of medicine." Even though the plastic face shields made their features slightly distorted, Madison could see Garrison's excited smile. "It was my father's brainchild."

"Since the Second World War, there has been a distinct wave of discovery," Wyatt said, "beginning with antibiotics and followed by tranquilizers and hormones. None of these were in use before the war but within ten years had become common. Prior to that there had been many discoveries, of course, but none that impacted the life of the average—"

"Except for aspirin," Madison interjected without thinking. "Wasn't it invented about the time of the Civil War? It's the original wonder drug, right? It reduces pain, breaks fevers and reduces swelling, yet no one can explain exactly how it works."

"That's right," Wyatt said, his approval evident even though she had interrupted him.

"Also, the smallpox vaccine was discovered by Edward Jenner in the nineteenth century," Madison added.

"Antibiotics have become a victim of their own success. This new drug will change that." Garrison pointed at a machine. "We're running the numbers here. Already the results are impressive."

Madison followed them down the long hall, where they peeked in at several workstations where technicians were performing tests. Madison couldn't help being impressed. She'd mentally dismissed the Holbrooks because they were wealthy beyond comprehension. She'd assumed Wyatt merely wanted a measure of immortality by having a foundation with his name on it.

Now she could see that this was his life's work. He seemed to be trying to help others in a way that she hadn't expected event though she'd known about some of his local philanthropic endeavors. She thought about herself. What good was she doing? How could she be critical of the Holbrooks? At least they were doing something worthwhile.

She'd been headed in a scientific direction, too, when she'd gone to MIT. Her field was mathematics with an emphasis on statistics, which could have led to medical research. But her father's cancer had changed everything.

Up to then computer games and trivia had been a hobby, but as her father's cancer progressed, she used it as an escape. He could rest in bed and talk trivia with her. Or she could play computer games with the sound off while she waited beside his bed for the miracle that never happened.

After her father's death, she could have gone back to school. But along came Aiden Larsen. He saw the financial possibilities in the world of computer gamers. It was growing like wildfire as more and more children matured with computer games as part of their lives.

Now she wondered if she'd made a mistake by not returning to school. She could be doing something for mankind, like the Holbrooks, instead of fooling with trivia on a computer game site. Maybe it wasn't too late. Perhaps Aiden could buy her out and add gambling to the site the way he wanted.

But did she want to sell a company that had been her brainchild, a company she'd fought hard to retain in the divorce settlement? She honestly didn't know and realized she didn't have the time to think about it right now.

Wyatt and Tobias hung back to discuss something with a technician while Garrison guided her forward. "My father and I differ on the future of medical research."

"Really?" Madison was surprised. Since they shared facilities and were related, she'd assumed they were on the same page scientifically.

"I think the future is in the sea, not in the lab. There are a million bacteria in every milliliter of sea water and ten million viruses. Can you imagine the potential cures just waiting to be discovered? I call it Neptune's Medicine Chest."

"What about biopharming?"

That got him. His smile vanished, replaced by a tight frown. She knew very little beyond the fact that genetically altered crops could produce pharmaceuticals. Genetically altered corn was already producing a protein that showed extraordinary promise in treating hepatitis B.

"There are a number of possibilities on the horizon," Garrison said, his voice pinched. "I happen to believe the answer is in the ocean. My father likes the lab but he's willing to fund *any* promising research with the foundation he's establishing."

"That's great," she said, a little taken aback by the sudden chill in his tone. "I guess it's impossible to tell exactly where the next revolutionary discovery will be made."

"My father wanted you to see what we're doing," Garrison said, his tone now conciliatory, but the air was fraught with tension.

"Why? I already agreed to be tested."

"True, but…Father believes you're his daughter. If he's right and you test positive, the doctors will explain how difficult the operation will be. It requires extensive surgery that's not without risk. Recovery takes time."

"I'll help if I can, but I doubt—"

The *bring-bring* of her cell phone interrupted them. She walked away, saying, "I have to take this."

They'd come full circle in the building and she was now just outside the changing room where she'd put on the jumpsuit and headgear. This side also had an air lock room. She waited for the whoosh to cease as she ripped open the Velcro on the suit and dug the cell phone out of her pocket. She shouldered her way into the changing room.

"It's me," Jade said when Madison answered. "There's bad news."

Madison wiggled out of the jumpsuit while Jade explained that cash withdrawals on her credit cards had been maxed. She was on credit watch at all three credit-reporting agencies. She clutched the cell phone, concentrating on drawing each breath as panic mushroomed in her chest, making it difficult to breathe. Not only had someone stolen her savings, they had wrung every cent she could raise out of her credit cards. She was flat broke.

"Oh my God." Shaking, Madison dropped her jumpsuit into the disposal bin, then began to peel off the latex gloves. "What am I going to do?"

"Maybe Aiden can help."

"No, no! Don't mention this to him. I'll handle it." She snapped the cell phone shut without saying goodbye. Tears of anger and frustration welled up in her eyes. She didn't have anyone to turn to, but she certainly wasn't going to Aiden with this.

She tried to zero in on her most immediate problem. She needed somewhere to live. With no money and no credit that was going to be a killer. She didn't know how much time it would take to straighten out the credit mess.

Who could she turn to? The friends she'd made at MIT had continued on with their lives when she'd returned to Miami to be with her father. With Erin gone, she didn't have any friends to count on here. Her mother—if she resurfaced soon—could help, but who knew when she'd call? Rob might help her but it would be embarrassing to impose on Erin's ex-boyfriend.

Wyatt Holbrook walked into the room, pulling off his mask. "Is something wrong?"

Trouble must be written all over her face, she decided. "Nah, it's nothing. Your lab is impressive."

The older man studied her for a moment, his blue eyes narrowing slightly as he shrugged out of the jumpsuit. "I appreciate your taking the time to come see the company I've built."

"It's more…extensive than I expected." She couldn't keep the tremor out of her voice. She was penniless and had no one to help her. She needed to get away and think, plan her next

move. "I've got to run. Mr. Pennington has my number. He's
going to arrange for the testing. He'll call—"

"You're upset. Was it something Garrison said? I know he
can be—"

"No." She put up her hand. "He's a great guy. I've got to take
care of a few things."

"Will it wait an hour or two? We were going to catch an early
dinner—"

"I can't. My dog is back at the office. I need to get him and
find a new place to live. I just found out that the couple who
own the home where I'm staying are coming back early. It's
not easy to find a place when you have a pet."

She hadn't intended to tell him anything about her problems
but this explanation seemed necessary somehow. Wyatt Holbrook was a very compassionate man, and she didn't want him
to worry about her. This was easier than going into her financial troubles.

Wyatt smiled and she glimpsed the man he must have been
when he was young like Garrison. A real charmer. No wonder
a wealthy heiress had fallen for him. "I have the perfect
solution. You stay in the guesthouse at Corona del Mar."

"I couldn't possibly," she cried, astounded that he'd offered.

"Why not? It's well away from the main house and has a side
yard for your dog. I assume it would only be for a short time
while you find a suitable place."

"I couldn't," Madison replied, a flimsy splinter of a protest.
This could be a short-term solution to her problem.

"Why not?" he repeated. "You're doing me a favor by taking
the test. The least I can do is let you stay in my guesthouse for
a few days."

Panic evaporated in a dizzy rush, morphing into a fury
beyond anything she'd previously experienced. When she found
the person who'd done this to her...Madison almost thought
she'd kill him. Then the image of her best friend came to mind.

There were worse problems than identity theft. The thought should have calmed her, but it didn't.

"All right. Just for a few days," she reluctantly conceded. "I'm sure I can find a place to live by then."

CHAPTER THIRTEEN

PAUL PULLED UP to the Fisher Island home where Madison was staying. He'd been here often enough that the guards waved him through. Crappy security, but who was he to question the rich? Make that the ultrarich.

A mosaic of clouds tattered the horizon where the sun had already set, leaving a golden glow in its wake. The humidity had kicked up another notch and with it came the fragrant scent of honeysuckle that he hadn't noticed when he'd been here before. Madison's Beamer was parked squarely in front of the home, where the front door was wide open. Clothes were heaped in the backseat and the trunk lid was up, revealing boxes and loose sandals. Was she moving out?

Aspen greeted him in the foyer. The retriever spun in circles, his tail flapping from side to side. Paul gave the dog a few strokes on the head. "Madison, where are you?"

She appeared from the bedroom area with an armload of clothes. A sexy cascade of untamed curls clustered around her face. The skin along the high curve of her cheekbone was flushed from exertion. Her intriguing blue eyes were wide with surprise. Obviously, she hadn't expected to see him. For an instant—maybe two—the world froze as they gazed at each other. He stepped forward, his eyes still on hers, and told himself to keep his mind on business. That's why he'd come here.

"I'm moving out. The owners of this place are coming back

sooner than expected. I guess I brought more stuff than I realized."

"I've got an SUV. I can help." Kicking himself, he wondered why in hell he'd volunteered. He just wanted answers to a few questions, then he could go.

She rewarded him with a smile. He realized with a jolt of shock that she was glad to see him. There was something about her smile that suggested a special bond between them, a sense of intimacy. Or was it just his imagination?

"Where are you moving?"

She hesitated and he could almost see her stiffen, but she kept walking through the foyer toward her car, Aspen at her heels. "I'm using the Holbrooks' guesthouse for a few days. Wyatt said I could stay there and bring Aspen."

I'll be damned. What was Holbrook thinking? The man must be convinced Madison was his daughter and that she could help him. Given Holbrook's medical condition, that was wishful thinking. Even a close relative might not be a perfect match. Wyatt's immune system wasn't normal. The chances of anyone—even his child—matching him were minuscule.

"Really?"

Madison whirled around and leveled those baby blues on him. "He volunteered. I didn't want to accept his offer, but the Russerts are returning early and I don't have anyplace to go." She flung the clothes onto the pile in the backseat of her Beamer.

Her anger thrummed in the air, making his thoughts whirl in his head. He kept circling back to the same conclusion. His experience on homicide, conducting interviews, told him that more was bothering Madison than the sudden need to move out.

Paul put out his hand and touched her shoulder. He resisted the urge to haul her into his arms and hold her close. "What's wrong? Something's happened."

"I've been the victim of identity theft." Anger punctuated

each word. "I don't have any money except the cash in my wallet. Less than a hundred dollars."

"Son of a bitch! How did that happen?"

"I have no idea." He detected more than a hint of desperation in her voice. "I'm usually very careful but…someone got into my savings and my credit cards' cash lines." She explained the situation.

He slipped his arm around her shoulders. "You're not the first and you won't be the last. This is happening at an alarming rate."

"I need a place to stay short-term." She glanced down at the retriever beside them, and he wondered if the glint in her eyes was from unshed tears. Darkness had fallen, making it impossible to be certain. "I have to keep Aspen with me, too. The guesthouse has a side yard. I'm just staying for a few days, until I can straighten out my finances and find a place that allows dogs."

Now was a good time to ask about Aspen, but he couldn't bring himself to add to Madison's troubles. "Have you reported the theft to the police?"

Madison shook her head, her glossy hair swishing across nearly bare shoulders. She was wearing a skimpy blue tank top and shorts. "No. The last thing I want is to see the police again. They think—"

"It has to be reported if you expect the card companies to drop any charges you didn't make."

"From what I can tell, there were no charges, just cash withdrawals. They withdrew the limit from all three of my credit cards."

"Uh-oh. That's a pisser. I thought you could only get so much from an ATM."

"I can't reach anyone who can help me until tomorrow. I'm not exactly sure how they withdrew so much money from my accounts."

A thought hit him. "I'll bet my father has someone who can work on this." He pulled out his cell phone. "I'll—"

"I don't have any money to hire him. Don't—"

"You can pay him when you have the money."

She started to protest but he quieted her with a one-armed hug. His father picked up his cell on the second ring. Didn't Mike have a life? Paul's cell had been off since he drove onto the ferry to Fisher Island. Paul explained the situation and relayed some vital personal information from Madison so his father could access her records.

In typical fashion, his old man didn't ask any questions about Madison. He knew exactly who she was and how important she was to Wyatt Holbrook. Apparently, that was enough for him. S'okay. Paul didn't want to explain his relationship with Madison to his father. Hell, he couldn't even explain it to himself.

He snapped his cell shut, saying, "You have to file a police report. It's not a crime until you report it. It's possible a gang is getting info off the Internet or through a credit card company. The police will know if there have been similar cases."

She heaved a sigh. "All right. It can wait until tomorrow. My cards are maxed and my savings cleaned out. They're not getting anything more tonight."

"Right. Let's get you settled at the Holbrooks'. After a good night's sleep, you'll feel more like facing the police."

Madison gave him an appraising look to let him know she'd *never* feel like seeing the police. *She's hiding something.* He'd suspected as much from the first morning he'd met her, but now he was fairly certain he knew what it was.

"Let's get the rest of your stuff," he said as he guided her back into the house.

Even though Madison had moved in for just three weeks— which turned out to be two—it took several more trips to lug out all her stuff. When you got right down to it, men would never be able to figure out why women needed so much junk.

"Could you bring Aspen?" she asked when they shoved the last load into his SUV. "There's no room in my car."

"Sure," he replied, although the retriever would have to sit on some of her things. He snapped his fingers in front of Aspen's nose and the dog lumbered up into the passenger seat of his car.

"I'll meet you there. Go through the gate, then veer left and follow the road around to the side of the main house. Wyatt told me there are two parking spaces in back of the guesthouse and a stone path that leads from there to the guesthouse."

Paul nodded and climbed into the SUV. He petted Aspen as he waited for Madison to pull out. The retriever gazed up at him with amber eyes that said Paul must have hung the moon. An aching sadness he'd never experienced before swept over him.

This poor dog must have suffered horribly, and yet he still trusted, still loved. People weren't as forgiving. He'd read Madison's file. He knew she'd loved Aiden and given up her education and pitched in her savings to start their business, only to have her husband leave her for another woman.

It wasn't fair. Suddenly, his father's old saying brought him up short. Who said life would be fair?

THE GUESTHOUSE TURNED out to be a three-bedroom home twice as big as the house Paul's father had purchased several years ago. The lights were on and the ceiling fans were going. Holbrook must have had his staff get the place ready for Madison.

The house was decorated in what Madison called "Tommy Bahama" style, which meant plantation shutters and furniture made out of cane. The walls were a cool green that was almost white and all the fabric had some damn fernlike design. A haven in the tropics. Oddly enough, it seemed to suit Madison perfectly.

They lugged in her stuff and deposited it in what Madison

dubbed the "spare" bedroom so she could sort through it later. Aspen tagged along, after taking a detour to relieve himself in the guesthouse yard's lush banks of ferns adjacent to a small swimming pool with a spa.

"Thirsty?" Madison asked Aspen.

"You bet," Paul replied. "I'm guessing this joint has glasses and stuff. What self-respecting guesthouse wouldn't?"

Madison led Paul, with Aspen at his heels, into a good-size kitchen with gloss-black granite countertops and stainless-steel appliances. Not only did the kitchen have dinnerware and pots and pans, but the refrigerator and pantry were fully stocked.

"Not bad." He took the glass she'd found for him and shoved it under the ice dispenser on the refrigerator door. "It'll be hard to beat this."

Madison filled a ceramic soup bowl with water for Aspen. The dog must have a bowl somewhere, but Paul didn't blame Madison for not hunting for it. Poor kid had been through a lot today.

"Let's take a break for a few minutes," he suggested.

She gave him a weary nod and he followed her into the living room. He opened the French doors to the small terrace overlooking the pool and spa. The heady scent of exotic flowers he couldn't name saturated the humid night air. Artsy-fartsy lighting created interesting patterns of shadow and light through the clusters of ferns around the royal palms lining the yard. Paul figured some damn decorator hadn't been satisfied doing just the interior.

The slow, undulating sound of the surf on the shore reminded Paul that the ocean was just over the wall surrounding Corona del Mar. During the day, the guesthouse probably had a view of the water. He turned and went back inside.

Madison sat on the comfy sofa and Paul plopped down near her—but not too close—and put his feet up on an oversize ottoman with a plush cushion top. Aspen settled on the bamboo floor between them. Except when he'd been driving, it was the first time Paul had sat down all day. His leg ached a bit more than he would have liked. Maybe he'd given up on physical therapy sooner than he should have. But then again, this was the first time he'd been on his feet for so long. Usually his father had him sifting through info to locate Wyatt Holbrook's children.

"I don't like coincidences," he announced.

"Meaning?" Her voice, husky and sensual, sent a ripple of awareness through him. Just being around her interfered with rational thought.

He tamped down any erotic ideas and kept to the subject. "Meaning first your best friend is murdered and you're the prime suspect, then someone loots your accounts."

"I don't see how they could be linked." Her tone, her attitude, was dismissive. "I studied mathematics in college, you know. Most people don't understand numbers. For example, how many people would you need to have in a room to find two with the same birthday?"

He didn't like getting off track, but he humored her. "A lot. Fifty, sixty."

"Would you believe two dozen? Most people tackle the problem by thinking there are three hundred and sixty-five days in a year and twelve months. So it seems like there would be a lot of numbers to take into account. Actually, only a few numbers come into play. There are twelve months in a year and a max of thirty-one days in a month. A birthday like mine is 3/7. There aren't that many numerical combinations to come up with for all the possible birthdays."

"Without the year."

She smiled at him and he hoped she was thinking he wasn't dumber than dirt. He'd gone out with a lot of women but none of them had a mind like this. He liked it. Madison kept him thinking, kept him interested in a way no other woman ever had.

"Correct. That's why coincidences are perfectly understandable. Everyone can list a string of coincidences in their lives."

"I still don't like it."

"I know police don't like coincidences. I've seen enough television cop shows to realize this, but I think I'm just another random victim of ID theft."

"We'll know more when my father looks at things. It bothers me that your accounts were looted when you were distracted with Erin's funeral."

"I can't imagine ID thieves killing someone to divert a victim. It's too easy to accomplish without extreme measures."

"True, but what if someone deliberately took advantage of the situation?"

She conceded slowly, "I've considered the possibility."

"Have you spoken with your ex?"

"No!" she snapped. "Aiden would never—"

"Never say never. I've seen worse, much worse, happen after a divorce."

His statement made her seem to consider the possibility more seriously. She gazed off into the distance while the lulling sound of the waves lapping at the sand filled the room.

She finally said, "I'll talk to Aiden first thing in the morning. I don't want to go to the police or waste your father's time if Aiden is involved. Let me talk to him and get back to you."

"Good idea." He swung his feet to the floor even though he was betting that the ex was involved. Better to let Madison discover this for herself. "I'd better get going."

"Wait. You came out to Fisher Island for a reason, didn't you?"

More like an excuse, he thought. He'd told himself it was business, but on the way here with Aspen, he'd been forced to admit the truth to himself. When you got right down to it, he wanted to see her again.

"Have you found out anything about Erin?"

He seized the opportunity to scoot closer to Madison. "A little. I'm not sure how or where it fits."

"Maybe I can help."

"If you'll tell me the truth."

"About what?" There was an edge in her voice that confirmed his suspicion that she was holding back information.

"About Aspen." He reached down and patted the dog on the floor near them. "I went out to Dicon Labs. There had been a fire there the night Erin was killed. The owners didn't report the loss of any lab animals, but I nosed around." She wasn't a very good actress. He could see she knew about the fire, although she'd never mentioned it. "A woman admitted they'd been testing hair spray on eight dogs that were missing."

"Why didn't they report it?"

"Cosmetics companies hate negative publicity. Dicon has been singled out by animal rights groups in the past." He waited for her to comment, but when she didn't he continued. "One of the missing dogs was a male golden retriever."

"You think it was Aspen."

Paul nodded. "Erin had been involved with animal rights groups in the past."

"I think she still was," Madison responded in a tone that sounded hollow, distant, as if her mind was on something else. "Rob—he's her former boyfriend—told me it's what split them up."

Paul decided to play his trump card. "Don't you want her killer found?"

"Of course I do! How can you ask that?" There was the threat of tears in her voice and he knew all she'd been through today had worn her down. He hated pressing her but he couldn't help unless he had the facts.

"Then tell me the truth about Aspen."

Still she hesitated, seeming to search for words. She reached down and stroked Aspen's silky head. "I don't want them to get their hands on him again."

Paul listened while she explained about finding Aspen and the papers in Erin's kitchen. Her murdered friend had never mentioned the dog, never told Madison that she was getting the retriever.

"Don't you see? I *had* to save Aspen. He's almost blind as it is from having stuff sprayed in his eyes." Her voice was spiked with so much fury that he was positive she would have struck anyone from Dicon Labs had they been in the room. "Those insensitive jerks are guilty of animal cruelty. That's why they won't admit they were testing on dogs."

"Probably, but what if something that happened that night caused Erin's death?"

"If I believed that, I would have told the police all about Aspen." She leaned closer to him, her expression earnest. "Look, I don't know how much you know about animal activists, but last year several were arrested."

"On the West Coast. L.A. and Oregon." He hadn't known this until he'd investigated the fire at the lab. He'd used the Internet to check on the better-known groups.

"Right. Now the groups no longer use last names. They have an agenda, carry it out, then disappear. If one person is caught, they can't implicate the others. They're careful not to leave a trail with phones or computers."

He couldn't help wondering if she had been involved. Erin must have been and, as her best friend, didn't that mean Madison was also a member? Or did it? He didn't want to accuse her of anything until he had proof.

"They must exchange some contact info or they couldn't get together," Madison continued.

"They communicate on the Internet."

"Why am I not surprised? It works for child predators. They link up on the Internet often in chat rooms where they can make connections and still keep their identities secret."

"I'm sure Erin intended to drive Aspen to a designated spot, hand him over to another activist who would take him to yet another place, until he was out of state and in safe hands."

Madison sighed and threw up her hands. "Why didn't she tell me anything?"

"I think you're correct. The killer stopped Erin before she could transfer Aspen to the next person. I'm positive he didn't kill her as a result of the raid at Dicon Labs. There must have been another reason or the murderer would have taken or killed the dog." Paul looked at her pointedly. "It's always helpful for the police to have all the facts."

"I know." She clenched her teeth in what he'd come to recognize as her stubborn expression. "I can't let Aspen go back. They'll torture him until he's blind, then kill him."

Paul couldn't argue. If Dicon Labs had been developing a cure for something or a medicine, he might have debated with her. But he'd been out there. They produced nothing worthwhile unless you counted lipstick and hair spray, which he didn't.

"Then you'd better do something about the chip in Aspen's neck behind his right ear. It'll ID him as a Dicon dog if the missing link thinks to have Aspen checked."

It took her a second to realize he wasn't going to give the police the info on Aspen. She threw her arms around him and rewarded him with a grateful hug. He wasn't letting her quit that quickly. His eyes found her inviting mouth and noticed her lower lip was trembling slightly. He kept her in his arms and lowered his mouth to hers before she could say something to stop him.

For a moment Paul didn't think he was getting anywhere. Her lips were warm and slightly open beneath his, but her arms seemed slack around his shoulders. He refused to give up; she wanted him. The way she'd behaved on the dance floor was proof positive. Gradually, his mouth moving against her lips, his tongue nudging its way inside, her arms began to tighten around him.

His body did a slow burn that worked its way down to his thighs, but he kept the kiss gentle, soft…encouraging. His tongue teased hers and he caught the uptick in the tempo of her breathing. He pulled back and gazed into her eyes. The smoldering glint told him all he needed to know.

Beneath her lightweight tank top, he felt her nipples tighten. He kissed her again, but this time there was nothing gentle about the way he slanted his lips over hers and plunged his tongue forward in an age-old mating ritual. His heart thundered against his rib cage and savage heat pooled in his groin.

What was wrong with him?

A kiss or two *never* aroused him like this.

She kissed him back, flattening her body against his as if she couldn't get enough of him. Her soft fingers caressed the nape of his neck and slid into his thick hair.

Desire, dark and urgent, coursed through him, sweeping away all rational thought. He trailed kisses along the ridge of her cheekbone to her ear. Pausing there just long enough to flick his tongue, he pressed hot, smoldering kisses into the sensitive curve of her neck where he detected a lingering trace of the arousing floral perfume he'd come to associate with Madison. She rewarded his efforts with a shuddering sigh that sent his pulse into overdrive.

Had he ever wanted a woman this badly? Why this woman? Why now, when even a dumb schmuck like himself knew better than to get involved?

All the pent-up desire that he'd kept locked away since he'd met her suddenly released itself in his soul-shattering kiss. He slid his tongue into her mouth and rocked against her slightly. Her arms tightened around him and she kissed him back with an openmouthed, hot kiss, her tongue moving against his.

He eased his hand between them and found the soft rise of her breast. Hot damn! She wasn't wearing a bra, a fact he'd noted earlier, but with all the contraptions women wore these days he hadn't been positive. His thumb found the taut nipple and caressed it.

She shivered and pulled back, breaking the kiss. He looked into her amazing blue eyes, just a scant inch from his. The irises were huge, shadowed by the sweep of her long lashes. He thought she might be about to say something to make him stop. To keep her from talking, he kissed her again, still stroking the nipple. A low moan rumbled in her throat. It sent another rush of heat to his groin. In a heartbeat, a rock-hard erection was pressing against his fly.

Aw, man, oh, man. What she could do to him without half trying.

A sharp sound distracted Paul. What in hell? It took a second to realize Aspen had barked. He'd never heard the dog bark. Madison pulled out of his arms just as he glanced sideways and noticed Aspen was standing, hackles raised, growling at the shadowy area beyond the French doors that opened onto the pool. The retriever barked twice, a menacing sound that Paul wouldn't have believed came from Aspen if he hadn't been looking right at the dog.

A second later Garrison Holbrook emerged from the shadows calling, "Hello! Anybody home?"

Son of a bitch, Paul silently cursed as he jumped to his feet. Talk about bad timing. "It's okay, boy," he told Aspen.

The retriever stopped growling but the top of his coat was still bristled skyward like a hedgehog's. Aspen appeared to be just about as thrilled to see Garrison as Paul was.

Common sense kicked in. Time to get out of Dodge. He stood up, doing his best to conceal his erection. "I was just leaving," he told Garrison. Over his shoulder, he said to Madison, "See you later."

He walked to his SUV, his penis aching. She'd gotten him hard two nights in a row. A tragedy, sure, but he was going to have blue balls for a week. Just his luck.

CHAPTER FOURTEEN

How many men have been to the moon?

MADISON KNEW she didn't blush, but she could feel the heat rising up the back of her neck as Paul left and Garrison Holbrook stood between the French doors, watching her.

"I didn't mean to interrupt. I…ah…saw the lights. Dad said you were staying in the guesthouse. I wanted to talk to you."

"It's all right." She motioned for him to come in and have a seat. He stepped around Aspen and walked inside. "Paul helped me move my things here." She knew this must sound lame. How much had Garrison been able to see before Aspen's warning barks?

Garrison offered her a reassuring smile and quickly glanced around the room. It was an open floor plan with a living area and an alcove for dining. Most of the kitchen could be seen from where she was sitting. Only the bedrooms were down the hall and out of sight. She was glad she'd taken her stuff into a bedroom so her things weren't cluttering up the place.

"If there's anything you need," Garrison told her, "dial five. That line goes to the staff office in the main house. They'll take care of you."

The whole setup reminded her of a luxury resort. Madison supposed she should be grateful but resentment crackled inside her. She didn't want to be indebted to the Holbrooks. Someone, probably a total stranger, was responsible for her predicament. Not being able to focus, to direct her anger, was frustrating.

"Everything's fine," she assured him as she reached down to pet Aspen, who'd settled at her feet. "I really appreciate all your family has done. It's taken a load off me to have a few days more to find a place I can rent with a dog."

Garrison studied her intently for a moment, then said, "I came out to see if you needed help setting up an appointment to be tested."

"I assume I just need to call. Right?"

Garrison handed her a business card. "St. John's Hospital is doing all the workups on the prospective donors. Dr. Miller is in charge of the team."

"Isn't it just a simple blood test?"

He hesitated for a moment. "They'll run several tests. My father's blood contains a rare antibody. You'll need to get past that hurdle, then have a health screen and a complete physical. If the results show you're anywhere near compatible, you'll need a bone marrow test."

"Why?"

"My father has an unusual immune system." He shrugged. "I had the test. Your hip's a little sore afterward, but it's not bad. I thought I would be a natural, but turned out I couldn't help."

Madison's thoughts clouded. She hadn't realized there would be anything more extensive than a blood test required when she agreed to do this. No wonder Wyatt had offered her the guesthouse. He'd wanted to make certain she felt obligated to go through with the testing. She wouldn't have backed out, not after seeing his company and coming to understand his value to society. Maybe it was irrational, but she felt pressured.

"They can probably get you in tomorrow," Garrison said. "I'll arrange for Carlos—he keeps everything running around here—to look after your dog."

"I can't tomorrow." She had no idea what she'd have to do

to straighten out her credit mess. She planned to see Aiden first thing. She doubted he had anything to do with it, but she had to eliminate the possibility before going to the police. She also wanted to check with Mike Tanner. Paul's father might have found out something that would help her.

"Why not?" There was more than just a hint of reproach in his voice.

"There are a few things I *must* do tomorrow. I'm not sure how long they'll take."

"My father stands a much better chance of surviving the sooner he gets the transplant. A complete workup on you will take about seven weeks. I know Dad seems healthy but I can see he's going downhill." His eyes telegraphed heartfelt emotion. "We have people who run errands, do things. Let me get someone—"

"No. I have to take care of this myself." Madison knew she sounded stubborn, but she didn't want to explain her predicament to him. The concerned expression on his face bothered her. She tried to put herself in his place. What if her father had desperately needed a transplant? Being secretive and defensive was an inappropriate reaction.

Just tell him the truth, urged an inner voice. What could it hurt? Identity theft happened every day. He'd understand she would need to straighten it out immediately.

She began by explaining, "My best friend was murdered last week."

"I know. I just read Mike's report."

She was a little surprised. Why hadn't he read the report sooner? Maybe the details of a potential donor's life didn't matter. Perhaps his father had kept it from him. After all, Garrison and Savannah had been surprised when Madison appeared at the party.

Once again, she couldn't help wondering if the Holbrook children would inherit a lot of money when their father died.

Even if they would, she decided Garrison cared too much about his father to want him dead. Savannah might. Madison had only met the woman briefly and had no take on the beauty's relationship with her father.

"I'm sorry about your friend." His voice was so charged with sympathy that she wondered if he'd lost someone. "It must be really rough on you."

If Garrison knew she was a suspect in the crime, he didn't mention it. Once again, she was struck by how likable the man was. "It has been. And while I was taking care of Erin's funeral, someone hacked into my bank account and withdrew the funds."

"Oww! That's terrible!"

"You're telling me. It gets worse. They were able to tap the cash lines on my credit cards. They withdrew the limit on each card."

"Do you have any idea how it happened?"

She shook her head. No sense in mentioning Aiden. She knew he was capable of deceit but he wouldn't steal from her. Why bother? Aiden had gotten the best of her in the divorce. He had plenty of money.

"I'll call Mike Tanner. I'm sure—"

"He's already working on it. Paul's been helping me. I have to report this to the police or it isn't considered a crime. Then I have to talk to the bank and credit card companies and I don't know what else, but I will be tied up most of tomorrow." She stared down at the business card. "I'll call the moment I have a chance."

"Thanks," he replied. "That's all we can ask."

He slowly rose and shook out the fold in one trouser. She realized Garrison took great care with his appearance. His stylishly cut hair was always in place and his expensive clothes were never wrinkled. Funny. It didn't seem to fit with being a scientist.

"How many men have been to the moon?" he asked, the question taking her by surprise.

"A dozen," she responded without having to think about it.

"Correct. Man has put more emphasis on space than they have on exploring the ocean on their own planet. Only two men have been down into the Marianas Trench. It's over five miles deep. We have no idea what secrets it might hold."

"Interesting," she responded because she felt she should say something. His abrupt shift in conversation still had her off balance. "You told me your research is based on microorganisms found in the ocean. Right?"

"Yes. My father doesn't agree that the future of medicine will be found in the ocean. Tonight we were *again* discussing what direction his foundation should take. It's important to set up everything properly."

"I guess there's more to starting a foundation than meets the eye."

"You bet. If you expect the work to continue in the direction you want, the foundation must have special directives and written rules." He threw up his hands. "Lots of legal stuff. Lawyers get rich. So what else is new?"

He handed her another card. "Here's my cell number. I'm going down to my place in the Keys. I have a small lab where I do on-site research. It requires a fair amount of diving."

Madison decided he must be collecting fresh samples or something that would take him away from his father and his own work at the facilities they shared.

"Don't hesitate to call," Garrison continued, "if there's anything I can do or if you have any problems."

He headed for the French doors, stopped and half turned, asking, "Do you need money? I could—"

"No, no. Thanks, but I've got it covered," she assured him even though she wasn't sure what she was going to do for money until this mess was straightened out.

KEITH SMITH LOOKED over his shoulder. He'd been doing that a lot lately, he realized. He had the unsettling feeling someone was stalking him. Watching, waiting. It creeped him out. But whenever he turned around, expecting to catch someone—he couldn't. Sometimes there were people nearby but they seemed to be going about their own business. At other times, no one was there at all.

An eidolon, he decided, pleased with his choice of words. Edgar Allan Poe and others of his generation had used *eidolon* instead of *ghost*. The word had gone out of use with the changing times.

Keith prided himself on his vocabulary. He considered himself to be self-educated, having been homeschooled by his mother before entering Brown, where his education was interrupted by his arrest for growing pot in his dorm room. His father had hired an attorney and Keith had been spared anything more serious than a terrifying night in jail, but his father had forced him to return to Florida.

Another semester and he'd had a degree in English lit from Citrus College—not that it did him much good. Being a high school English teacher paid squat, a fact his father used as a verbal bludgeon, reminding Keith every time he came home for dinner.

Keith looked over his shoulder again at the shadowy doorways on the side street not far from Calle Ocho, the heart of Miami's Little Havana. Calle Ocho was a string of small shops like a strand of cheap, unmatched beads, but…aah…the smells. The aroma of sweet Cuban coffee and *coquito,* coconut candy sold from pushcarts, mingled with the heady scent of cigars smoked by the old men playing dominos in sidewalk cafés while reminiscing about Cuba.

Here, blocks away from the main drag, his nostrils were assailed by the overpowering odor of rotting garbage that spewed from Dumpsters in nearby alleys and urine from druggies who lived behind the rusty trash bins. Rats scrabbled between cans, their red eyes catching the ambient light. The stagnant air brought out flies in full force, and they buzzed alongside thousands of no-see-ums that blanketed Miami.

Little Havana was a world unto itself, Keith thought, a world apart from the Miami once ruled by WASPS like his father. *I inhabit a parallel universe, too,* he decided, with a surge of pride. His mother had always told him the determining element in his life was his superior intelligence. His net worth proved her right. He'd like to tell his father—throw it in his face—that he was earning a bundle. But it was best not to rattle his father and disappoint the mother he loved. Neither would approve of the way he really made his money.

Gambling was his first love and always had been. As a kid, he'd bet on marbles, on the number of chips in a bag, on the number of milk cartons a friend could stack before they toppled. He'd won then, and he won now.

He was a winner because he was lucky and he was good at math. He was a whiz at cards because he knew the odds, and he was smart enough to count cards, not just rely on his luck. He played cards whenever he could; it was his bread and butter. It paid for the coke. He gambled on the ships that were nothing more than floating casinos and he played online.

But lately, he'd been going in for live action. Horses and dogs were okay, but cockfights were where the real excitement was. It was a blood sport, with cocks battling to the death with feral savagery.

It probably wasn't like that in the barnyard. Cockfights there—the real deal—were for supremacy and the sole right to the brood of hens. Here cocks were fitted with silver talon extensions that were razor sharp. One cock was certain to die. It usually collapsed in death throes, to the delight of the mob of cheering spectators.

The winner wasn't as lucky. It was removed from the ring,

usually fatally injured. But no veterinarian was waiting nearby.
The cock slowly bled out in a silent, painful death. If it survived,
the cock was bred and its male offspring trained to kill.

Cockfights were illegal, of course, but that added to the excitement. He ventured another look over his shoulder at the
elusive shadows. He saw a couple of men, jabbering in Spanish,
coming his way. Not eidolons. Flesh-and-blood men who were
probably headed to the same backstreet warehouse he was.

Keith slowed down and let them pass. They sauntered by,
dressed to the nines, the way many Cuban men did. Neither
bothered to look at Keith. Men never paid much attention to
Keith, but women did.

Thick sandy-blond hair, big blue eyes and a bod that sported
pecs and abs worthy of a fitness commercial drew women
wherever he went. He knew he had a great personality to go along
with his looks. He was famous for his jokes. He didn't have to rely
on potty gags, either. His humor was always witty, sophisticated.

His father never laughed at Keith's stories, but then his father
didn't have a sense of humor. His mother had been the one to
encourage him as far back as he could remember. His father was
straighter than Cochise's arrow. It didn't matter. The way things
were going, Keith would have the last laugh.

He turned the corner and followed the men to the warehouse door. A bull of a man who looked like a creep from a
horror flick was leaning against the wall, guarding the single
side door to the building. The bouncer. Keith wasn't concerned;
Eduardo had given him tonight's password. The men entered
and an explosion of noise billowed out, then was cut off when
the door closed behind them.

"Media noches." Keith said the phrase that meant a sandwich of ham and cheese with pickles. It was called a midnight
sandwich because Cubans who loved to party traditionally had
them on their way home, closer to dawn than midnight.

The bouncer pushed the door back just far enough for Keith

to squeeze through. Inside, the warehouse was brightly lit, a sharp contrast to the shadowy street leading to it. He squinted against the blaring light and the blue haze of smoke that came from cigarettes and sweet-smelling Cuban cigars. Makeshift bleachers had been assembled in a circle and several hundred screaming, sweating men were sitting shoulder to shoulder like sardines in a can. Others were standing, shouting and waving their gambling chits.

"Keith, *chuce*," Eduardo hailed him, using the short version of the Spanish word, *pachuco,* meaning "bad boy." Keith knew enough YUCAs—Young Urban Cuban-Americans—to realize this was synonymous with "bro." He'd met Eduardo online, playing blackjack. They'd discovered they lived in the same city and had become friends.

"Hey." Keith slapped Eduardo on the back as he looked into the ring. "Did you hear about the two blondes who were sitting on a park bench in Alabama, staring at the moon?"

Eduardo gave him a good-natured smile and shook his head. He was used to Keith's unending supply of jokes.

"One blonde asked the other, 'Which is farther away, Florida or the moon?'"

"Uh-oh," Eduardo said. "What did the other blonde say?"

"'Well, hel-lo. We can't see Florida from here, can we?'"

Eduardo chuckled but his gaze shifted to the ring. The cement floor glistened with blood from the previous fights. Two cocks were going at it. One of them was a prized auburn and black "Macumba." They'd been bred in Cuba specifically for fighting and were considered the most tenacious fighters.

Macumba meant black magic. The Macumba cocks were believed to have the devil in them. That's why they won so often. Keith suspected it was just a matter of breeding. Tonight, the rather ordinary-looking bantam rooster seemed to have the upper hand over the Macumba.

"Ole!" A cheer went up from the crowd as the bantam poked

out the Macumba's right eye. Keith heard himself cheering. It was over in seconds, blood spurting from the Macumba's neck as the other cock ripped his throat open for the kill.

"Bet on the underdog," whispered Eduardo while the annihilated Macumba and the half-dead victor were hauled away.

"Why?" Keith asked, his eyes on the men clamoring at the payoff table in the corner. From the looks of it, the bantam had been a long shot.

"*Heilo.*" Eduardo breathed the word so only Keith could hear.

"Ice?" he whispered. Ice, or crystal meth, was common enough, although he'd never tried it. He didn't like the way it instantly addicted you, but he knew its high made men believe they had supernatural strength. And produced erections that lasted for hours. "Does it work on chickens?"

Eduardo nodded. Two more cocks were brought into the ring in wire cages. Both of them appeared to be Macumbas. The only way to know the underdog was to watch the betting chart being posted on the concrete wall in blue chalk.

"Jesus Willie Christ!" exclaimed Keith an hour later after his fifth trip to the payoff table.

Eduardo smiled at him. "Let's blow this joint." He lowered his voice and added, "If we win too often…"

Keith nodded; he was thrilled with several thousand dollars he hadn't expected, but his sense of fair play made it seem like dirty money. Never before had he cheated. Not that this was cheating—exactly. People received tips all the time. Still, it didn't seem…right.

Eduardo waved his wad of greenbacks in front of Keith's face. "What do you say? Let's spend some of this at Lola's."

Keith found himself grinning. Lola's was a well-known club half a block off Calle Ocho. A neon sign with a woman doing the cancan flashed over the club's entrance. *Lola's* was written in bold script. Smaller letters proclaimed: What Lola wants—

Lola gets. What it really meant was Lola—a beefy woman in her late fifties—would get her customers *whatever* they wanted. No questions asked.

She had a string of strippers with bods that wouldn't quit and the best pole humpers in Miami. She also had back rooms set aside for lap dancing. What went on in them seemed to have little to do with lap dancing as Keith had understood the term before Eduardo had brought him to the club.

"How about another twofer?"

"That's the bomb, dude," Keith replied, repeating what his students often said although he rarely used the term.

They stepped out into the shadowy darkness of the street. The bouncer had deserted his post. He'd probably gone inside to buy a chit. Keith paused a moment to allow his eyes to adjust to the lack of light.

A twofer. Just the thought sent a hot rush to his groin. Two girls—if you could call the pros at Lola's *girls*—for the price of one. The things they could do with those humongous breasts and baby-soft, waxed pussies. The memory alone made him hard.

"Come on, *chuce*. Let's go."

Keith marched beside his friend, positive he could score a bag of coke at Lola's. That would make the twofer an over-the-top fuckfest. He couldn't remember being this happy—ever.

Something made him look over his shoulder and an inexplicable wave of fear, almost like a fever, swept through him. He felt butterfly-shaped rings of sweat form on his shirt. A shape seemed to shift in one of the shadowy doorways. His imagination, he guessed, but the feeling had been with him earlier. Why would anyone be following him?

It occurred to him that cocaine did that to some people. Paranoia set in and they became suspicious of everyone around them. Even harmless shadows seemed threatening. Next thing he knew, he'd be hearing voices from another part of the cosmos.

Maybe he wouldn't buy coke. Perhaps he should try something else.

He'd always wondered about "chasing the dragon." Injecting heroin was so out, so over. Smart guys chased the dragon; they smoked heroin. That might be just what he needed to take the edge off his nerves. The thought made it possible to breathe a little easier despite the foreboding.

"Something wrong?" Eduardo asked.

"No," he assured his friend. "Do you know the difference between guts and balls?"

Eduardo shook his head. Keith immediately felt better. Telling a joke kept his mind off...off what, exactly?

"What is the difference?" prompted Eduardo.

"Guts is coming home late after a night with the guys and being assaulted by your wife with a broom and asking, 'Are you still cleaning or just flying over to your mother's?'"

Eduardo chuckled. "Okay, *chuce*. What's balls?"

"You come home late, smelling of perfume and beer with lipstick on your collar. You slap your wife on the ass and say, 'You're next, babe.'"

Eduardo hooted, the way he always did when he really liked a joke. For a moment, Keith felt himself again. He ambled along with Eduardo toward the lively Calle Ocho and the club where anything was yours for the asking. His friend chattered, but Keith wasn't listening. He barely caught the throbbing beat of salsa music drifting through air so thick you could surf on it. The dread returned, gnawing on him the way rats in the alleyways chewed on garbage. Fear eddied through his stomach and the alley wavered in and out of focus. He couldn't shake the disturbing feeling someone was stalking him.

"Come on, dude," Eduardo said. "Let's get back to those lap dancers."

Keith wished he could respond to the urge to leave and

head for the safety of home, but he didn't want to be a pussy. Cocaine had tinkered with his brain. He was being paranoid for no good reason.

CHAPTER FIFTEEN

Can you name a truly beautiful cannibal?

MADISON SLAMMED on the brakes, nearly sending Aspen to the floor of her Beamer to avoid hitting the sleek Aston Martin that unexpectedly emerged from around the bend as she was leaving the guesthouse. She wouldn't have known the make of the midnight-blue car except Aiden had always wanted one. Until Chloe. Then the man who'd been head of the me-first parade suddenly couldn't do enough for the new woman in his life. He'd bought Chloe the Corvette she'd always wanted and kept driving his Hummer.

The expensive sports car screeched to a halt, its gleaming fender just inches from the Beamer's. Madison recognized the gorgeous redhead behind the wheel. Savannah Holbrook was driving and Nathan Cassidy, her boyfriend, was with her. Did she still live at home?

Savannah leaped out of the car, her hair streaming behind her like a red banner, and beelined for Madison's door. Her cheeks were flushed and her brilliant green eyes seemed to crackle. What now? Madison lowered her window.

"I'm looking for you." Savannah all but shouted the words.

"You've found me." Madison kept her tone level. Out of the corner of her eye, she saw Nathan emerge from the car.

"It won't work." Savannah's voice was lower now but anger

etched each word. She had seemed so pleasant at the party, but now in private her attitude had changed.

"What won't work?" Madison asked, put off by Savannah's attitude.

Nathan had joined Savannah, and he slipped his arm around her waist. Savannah looked at him through eyelashes so long and lush that they had to be extensions. Her expression seemed to say *Does this bimbo think I'm buying her act?*

"Trying to cozy up to Wyatt won't work," Nathan informed Madison in a very sarcastic, superior tone.

"My father's estate is already set. He's not rewriting his will for some brat that crawled out of the sewer."

Anger rocketed through Madison. She wanted to shout that she didn't give a damn about the Holbrook fortune, but she realized these two would never believe her. With an effort, she swallowed a caustic reply.

"We know that's why you finagled your way into staying in the guesthouse," Nathan said. "You're after Wyatt's money."

"You claim to need somewhere to stay with your—" Savannah glanced at Aspen, who was sitting on the seat beside Madison "—mutt. My assistant will find you a place by this evening. I want you out of here."

There was just enough room on the narrow service road to the guesthouse for Madison to wheel the Beamer to the right and shoot around the Aston Martin without responding to their accusations. As soon as she'd cleared the expensive car, Madison hit the gas.

"That was fun!" she told Aspen. "Savannah thinks the world revolves around her."

The dog turned and thrust his nose out the open window to sniff the breeze. She drove as fast as she dared. Not only did anger propel her, Madison wanted to catch Aiden at home. This was a discussion she didn't want to have in the office, where they could be overheard.

Word traveled around the cube farm at work with astonish-

ing speed. Jade called it "new millennium jungle drums."
Madison wouldn't be surprised to discover the majority of
office gossip was circulated by e-mail. Jade was probably
behind most of it. When Madison had a chance, she was going
to find more for the girl to do. Jade was bored because she was
bright and spending each day as a glorified gofer was a waste
of talent.

Madison was too upset with Savannah and her snotty boyfriend to concentrate on what else Jade might do. They thought
they could order her around, take over her life. *I want you out
of here.* Obviously, Savannah didn't have her father's best interests at heart the way Garrison did.

It occurred to her that Savannah might not know about
Madison's financial problems. If she had, the woman probably
would have mentioned money. They couldn't expect her to pay
for a place when she didn't have more than one hundred dollars
to her name.

Madison suspected neither Garrison nor Wyatt had told
Savannah that she was staying in the guesthouse. If they had,
they must have just mentioned it in passing and not given her
the details. More likely someone on staff at the main house had
told her.

Why was Savannah so jealous? It took just an instant for
Madison to come up with the answer. *Because she's insecure.*
Savannah Holbrook might be rich and beautiful and success-
ful but she wasn't sure of her father's love.

The situation reminded her of colorful butterflies. Gorgeous
beauties like Savannah. Most people wouldn't believe that butterflies were cannibals. Many types ate each other. Savannah
had the world—or so it seemed—yet she was ready to eat alive
anyone who threatened her relationship with her father.

Or maybe greed motivated her. Who knew? At this point,
Madison didn't care. She had her own problems. When she'd
gotten a handle on this identity-theft thing, then she would take

the test to see if she was a suitable donor. She knew she wouldn't be. That would end it.

Her mind drifted to Paul, the way it had all last night, waking her often. What was wrong with her? Why did she keep throwing herself at the man every chance she had? She knew better.

Right now she had enough trouble for six women. She didn't need to become involved with a man who…who what? She didn't know much about him except that he was willing to keep his mouth shut about Aspen.

And that she was undeniably attracted to him.

Maybe that wasn't such a bad thing. What had Erin told her that last night they'd been together, sharing cardboard pizza? *Get over Aiden. The past has you trapped.*

Tanner Security Solutions' offices were in a newly refurbished building in Coconut Grove. When Paul had been a kid, "the grove" had been known for its artists and writers and liberal types. Gentrification had transformed the area. Now clusters of trendy boutiques, nightclubs and the endless supply of Starbucks clones had priced out the artists and writers.

The suite his father leased took up the entire third floor. Not bad for a guy who'd retired from the police force with next to nothing except his pension. In a little less than five years, Mike Tanner was *the* go-to guy for private investigations.

Paul rode the elevator up to his father's suite and mentally gave the old man credit for enlisting retired policemen and off-duty officers. He didn't employ guys with drug or gambling problems. He used the best, paid them top wages and produced results for his clients.

Paul stepped out of the elevator and headed for the double glass doors. It was too early for the receptionist to be at her desk. Mike was a workaholic. Paul would bet his last dime that his father was sitting at the walnut desk in his office, just beyond the inner office pod where the computers, laser printer and several copy machines were set up adjacent to an alcove for the coffee machine.

Paul stopped and grabbed a cup of black coffee. Mike never cut corners in his office. Kona coffee, the pride of Hawaii, was his father's favorite. Paul turned the corner in the hall while blowing on the fragrant liquid to cool it.

Sure enough, there he was. Mike Tanner looked up and his sliding smile appeared, then vanished. His father never smiled for more than a second. He had a way about him that seemed friendly, but Paul doubted anyone really knew the man.

"You're out early."

Paul took a sip of coffee and lowered himself into the chair opposite his father's desk. "Yeah. Thought I'd check in and see if you needed me. Then I'm going over to the station to find out if there's any word on my reinstatement."

Mike studied Paul from beneath dark eyebrows. No DNA check was necessary to confirm who Paul's father had been. The older man still had a full head of dark hair just beginning to silver at the temples and a solid frame that hadn't run to fat despite his age. The old guy worked out religiously—an hour a day, seven days a week.

"What's going on with Madison Connelly?" Mike asked.

That's what Paul had come to find out, but he didn't want to rouse his father's suspicions by appearing too anxious. Mike had been a hell of a detective and could pick up a scent like a bloodhound. He shrugged, saying, "She's going to take the tests to see if she's able to donate."

"You said she didn't believe she is related to Wyatt Holbrook."

"She still doesn't." Paul sipped again; the coffee was almost cool enough to drink. "But you know the Holbrooks. They got her out to their offices and she saw what valuable work Wyatt is doing. Yada, yada, yada. She agreed to be tested."

"That's good." Mike fingered a stack of files on his polished walnut desk, where everything was lined up with military precision. "Then maybe we won't have to track down anyone else."

Paul knew he was referring to the list of children conceived through Wyatt's sperm donations. A few might still be in the Boston area, but thanks to New Horizons, more could be in Florida. Paul took some pride in having unearthed those files himself. Of course, his father had never given him any credit. After all, he'd been paid to do a job. That's the way Mike viewed the world. You did what you were paid to do; praise wasn't necessary.

"Madison needs to straighten out this credit card mess before she can check into the hospital for testing."

"What do you think about her?" Mike Tanner responded. "Could Madison have killed her friend?"

How like his father, Paul thought. The man asked a lot of questions. He rarely volunteered anything, particularly about himself.

"I doubt it." In his mind, he could see how upset she'd been. Hell, he could feel her lips under his, feel the softness of her skin beneath his fingers. Could almost... Paul gulped down the last of his coffee, realizing his father was intently staring at him. "She was too shook up about it to be acting."

Paul knew his father would trust his evaluation. Homicide detectives saw more than their fair share of liars. A good detective could smell a lie, could see it in someone's eyes. Paul's ears actually tingled when he was onto someone, a fact he never mentioned because it sounded so absurd.

Mike rocked back in his chair and studied Paul for a moment. "I ask because I had Kirk Bryant on it all last night."

Paul nodded, pleased to hear this. When his father announced he was setting up a private investigation firm to service businesses, Paul had advised him to hire a computer expert. This would attract corporate accounts who would be concerned about computer security.

Paul had been stunned—nah, he'd been blown away—when the old man took his advice and hired a geek and set up a computer security department. Mike had never given him credit, but Paul suspected the department, which had grown from one guy to several, was responsible for the rapid growth of Tanner Security Solutions.

"What did Kirk find out?" Paul prodded when he realized his father, in his typical fashion, wasn't adding anything more.

"The transactions were seamless. Whoever withdrew the funds had all the relevant information. The bank and credit card companies wouldn't have known a thing if Miss Connelly hadn't contacted them."

"She says she does a lot on the Internet—"

"More than half of identity thefts come from sources other than the Internet. Family, friends, coworkers or your trash. Most reputable Internet sites encrypt private information. It's called TLS. Transparent Layer Security."

"I've read about Internet sites as well as bricks-and-mortar companies whose databases have been compromised."

"True," Mike conceded, "but most are quite safe. I always check the percentages first. She's been divorced. That raises a red flag right there. You wouldn't believe the people who don't change their passwords or bank accounts after a divorce."

Paul knew Madison planned to speak to her ex this morning. From the moment he'd first heard about her problem, Paul had wondered if the ex was to blame. Paul had never met the man but he disliked him. What kind of a guy would cheat on a babe like Madison?

Don't go there, he cautioned himself. His father was the next best thing to a mind reader. He didn't want him to know he was involved with Madison. Screw it! His father had probably guessed by now.

"How long do you think it will take for Madison to straighten this out?"

"A year to eighteen months."

"You're kidding!"

"No. Depending on what happened, she'll need to have the credit reporting agencies freeze her accounts so the thieves can't get credit in her name or order more credit cards and run up charges."

Paul knew about identity theft, but he hadn't had any personal experience with it. He did recall it was the fastest-growing theft category in America. Still, he'd thought it would be relatively simple to fix.

"If a gang targeted Madison, the info already went out of state and they've applied for credit in her name. It'll cost the average person around five thousand dollars to clear up the problem."

"Son of a bitch! Why does it cost a victim so much?"

"Sometimes it's necessary to hire an attorney or a credit counselor, especially if other states are involved. Often it's easier to pay off small charges to restore your credit than to fight the system."

Paul almost said it wasn't fair, but he knew what his father would have told him.

"What about getting back the money that was withdrawn from her bank account and credit cards? Doesn't filing a fraud claim help?"

Mike sat forward and realigned a neat stack of papers directly in front of him. "Kirk tells me that she's beyond the processing period. That means after a number of days, the transaction has been processed. The funds are gone. The bank or credit card companies aren't to blame unless you can take them to court and *prove* they knew this was a fraudulent transaction."

"How long is the processing period? She reported this within days."

Mike steepled his fingers and gazed at Paul with blue-gray

eyes that had always reminded him of a wolf. He realized he sounded way too upset for this to be just another case. "Some banks and credit card companies process within three days."

"Can't the funds be tracked? Find out where they went and you'll…have them." He realized it couldn't be this simple or it wouldn't be a nationwide problem.

"Her savings were withdrawn by a person at another branch of the same bank. There's no way to tell who received the funds since they weren't transferred into an account. Same with the cash withdrawals on the credit cards."

Paul took in a deep breath, sucking air through his teeth. He felt like hitting something. How could he tell Madison he couldn't help her? Maybe he was becoming as tightly wound as his father. Unfuckingbelievable. "What should I tell her to do?"

"Reassure her that she's not alone. One person in four is a victim of identity theft."

"I'm sure that'll be *very* comforting."

Mike Tanner arched one brow. "Tell her to check her family and friends. If she finds the culprit, she may get her money back. Go with the odds."

Paul rose, clutching his empty coffee cup. "Thanks. I'll do that."

He was almost out the door when his father said, "I make it a practice not to get involved with clients. It's a lose-lose situation."

Paul didn't answer and kept walking. He dropped his cup in the wastepaper basket next to the receptionist's desk. He'd never been particularly introspective, but long ago he'd realized his inability to have meaningful relationships stemmed from his own relationship with his father. The matter-of-fact comment about getting involved with clients was as close to a personal discussion as they'd ever gotten.

Paul had been seven when his mother kissed him goodbye

and told him to mind his father. Mike Tanner had later explained she'd left them to join the "crazies" in California. Paul had been too young to have any clue what this meant, but he intuitively realized not to question his father.

Back then, Mike had recently received a promotion to the homicide unit. He was too busy to care for his son and had sent him to Woodridge Military Academy in Georgia, the only military school that would accept such a young student. It had taken Paul years to realize this might have been an ill-advised attempt to lure his mother home.

It hadn't worked. His mother had never bothered to contact them. He'd thought about looking for her when he was in college, but decided that would be disloyal to his father.

The only time he saw his father after his mother left was during the holidays. His summers—only slightly less lonely than the winters—were spent at camp. He came to realize his father was the man who paid the bills. That was the extent of the involvement Mike Tanner wanted with Paul.

He'd accepted the situation long ago and had gotten on with life. So why listen to his father's advice now?

CHAPTER SIXTEEN

What is the bestselling record album of all time?

MADISON SLOWED as she drove through the streets of Coral Gables toward the home she'd once shared with Aiden Larsen.

"You could be living here," she told Aspen.

The dog turned from the open window at the sound of her voice and wagged his tail. His soulful eyes brought a smile despite this mess. He was a wonderful animal and for all that had happened to him, the dog deserved a better life. "Don't worry. I'll find another place with a yard for you."

She gazed out the windows at the many homes built from local limestone called coral rock. Coral Gables had been one of Miami's first planned communities when it was developed in the 1920s. Most of the Mediterranean-style homes had tile roofs, lush landscaping and streets bordered with stately trees.

When they'd been house-hunting, she'd desperately wanted a home here. It was still a lovely area, but now its emotional pull wasn't as strong. She'd changed, she realized. That transformation had come very recently. A little over a week ago, she'd had a Realtor looking for a replica of the home she'd lost.

Where she lived no longer seemed to matter. She merely needed a place she could afford that could accommodate Aspen. Erin's death had rocked her world.

Madison had never imagined feeling so truly…alone. With her father gone, her mother missing in action and Erin murdered, the people she was closest to had unexpectedly vanished. Having her identity stolen was the latest blow. It had unsettled her more than she could have imagined because she had no one to turn to.

She parked in front of the Mediterranean villa that used to be her home. She let Aspen out to sniff around. She knew the dog well enough now to realize he wouldn't run away. If dogs could be said to be insecure, then Aspen was. He didn't allow Madison to get too far away from him. And he liked to be on the leash. Probably because he didn't see very well and relied on her to guide him.

She rang the bell and waited. The shutters were closed and there was no sign anyone was inside the house. The morning paper had been picked up, she noticed, glancing over her shoulder to the lawn where Aspen was ambling around, sniffing. A mockingbird trilled from the banyan tree that she'd treasured and the light breeze brought with it the fragrant scent of the neighbor's rose garden.

She rang the bell again and heard its faint echo down the long hall. Had she missed Aiden? She checked her watch; it was too early for him to be in the office. The distant thump-thump of footfalls came through the plank door. A few seconds later, it swung open.

"Madison? What are you doing here?" Aiden stood in the open doorway, his hair still mussed from sleeping. Wrinkled khaki trousers hung from his slim hips. His bare torso was waxed smooth—evidently another of Chloe's innovations.

"I'm sorry. I didn't mean to wake you, but I need to talk to you."

"It's been rough. I almost lost Chloe, you know."

His words smacked her like a slap across her face. He'd never felt so deeply about her, Madison thought with a stab of envy. A second later she realized that maybe there was some measure of justice in this. Chloe was ill after having a stupid, pointless procedure. Then she reminded herself that this was life-threatening. It was a moment before she could ask, "I heard she had a staph infection. Is she better?"

"Yes. She'll be fine."

Madison stepped inside, calling softly over her shoulder, "Here, Aspen. Here, boy."

The dog stumbled up the steps, wagging his tail. She reached out and snapped the leash in her hand to his collar.

"You got a dog."

"Erin's responsible," she replied without bothering to give him any details. Her life was no longer any of Aiden's business.

"Look, I'm sorry about Erin. We didn't always agree on things, but I know she was a good friend to you."

Madison nodded and stepped inside what had been her home, with Aspen at her heels. She should have listened to Erin. Her friend hadn't liked Aiden from the start, but Madison had been too in love to care.

"I would have come to the funeral, but Chloe was having cosmetic surgery, then she developed the infection. She was just released from the hospital last night. She's too weak to use the stairs so she's staying in the maid's room."

Madison realized he'd been speaking very softly. Sounds tended to carry in these older homes that had decorative tile on the walls and marble floors.

Aiden led her to the library just off the large living room where they'd once entertained key sponsors when they'd launched TotalTrivia. She couldn't help noticing Chloe had re-decorated the entire place. Not one stick of furniture remained from her marriage to Aiden. She had to bite back a scathing remark. He could have given her the furniture, but he hadn't mentioned it.

They entered the library and Aiden closed the door. He punched the radio mounted on the wall and Michael Jackson's *Thriller* music softly filled the room.

"The bestselling album of all time—to date," she said automatically.

"Do you think in trivia or do you just do it to show how much you know?" Aiden asked, flipping the radio off again. Apparently he'd changed his mind about the need for music.

It wasn't the first time he'd posed the question. When they'd been married, he'd often accused her of showing off by spouting trivia.

Aiden flopped down on the sofa. From the looks of the bed pillow and lightweight blanket, she decided he'd slept here rather than upstairs to be closer to Chloe, who was in the maid's room off the kitchen. How sweet.

She sat in the chair next to him and began to tell him why she'd come. "I'm sorry to stop by unexpectedly, but this couldn't wait. I've been the victim of identity theft. They've wiped out my savings account and withdrew the limit in cash on my credit cards."

He ran his hand through his already tousled hair. "Jesus! I'm sorry. What a mess."

"Yeah," she agreed. Even though she'd mentally rehearsed what she was going to say, the words wouldn't come.

"You need...money."

"No, no. It's okay." Of course she needed money, but she'd rather starve than ask him for any. "To access my accounts someone would need to..."

Aiden shot off the sofa. "You think I—" he stared down at her "—took your money? That's outrageous! Why would I? I've got plenty and Chloe has her own trust fund."

"You were in my office, using my computer."

"So? That doesn't mean I would raid your accounts. My computer wasn't working and you were gone."

His indignation seemed genuine and what he said made sense.

"No, I didn't seriously think you'd done it, but I wondered

if there was any way someone at work could have gotten the information."

"You changed your account numbers and credit card passwords after the divorce, didn't you?"

"No," she sheepishly admitted. "I meant to, but I never got around to it. I didn't see any point. I knew you wouldn't…"

Aiden dropped back down into the new, plush sofa. Her revelation had taken the steam out of him. "Someone at work?" He considered a moment. "Our personal information is in the files and on the main computer terminal. We both used the same passwords."

"Yes, we did. I assumed you changed yours after we split."

"No, I knew you'd never—" He started to laugh.

She couldn't help laughing with him. For an instant it seemed like old times. They'd been happy once. Very happy, she'd believed.

The library door swung open. Chloe glided in, wearing big fuzzy slippers. Her white robe and pale skin made her seem more like a wraith than the healthy woman that Madison had last seen.

"What's going on?" she asked in a hoarse voice.

Aiden vaulted off the sofa and sprinted to Chloe's side, saying, "Honey, you shouldn't be out of bed."

Chloe leaned against him as if it hurt to stand. She dramatically whispered, "I heard the doorbell." She glanced at Madison through narrowed eyes. "What's she doing here?"

For a moment all the air seemed to have been sucked out of the room. Madison and Chloe had managed to avoid each other at work since the day Aiden had announced he wanted a divorce. Madison had tenaciously hung on to her stake in the company, but she'd been forced to share its turf with her rival.

Now she was in Chloe's home and Madison could see that even in this weakened state the woman harbored tremendous resentment. Why? Chloe had gotten her way. Did she expect Madison would simply give up and slip into the night?

"Why's that dog here? It'll mess up everything," Chloe bleated, and tears sprang to her eyes.

Madison watched as Aiden kissed the top of her head. "It's okay, honey. Madison just came by to warn us. We could have been victims of identity theft."

Why hadn't Aiden told Chloe the real truth? Madison was the victim. Maybe he was protecting Madison from Chloe's anger. Pent-up rage seethed behind the tears. Her reaction to seeing Madison seemed out of proportion.

"Oh, no." Chloe began to sob. "I can't take anything more."

Madison rose and tugged on Aspen's leash, deciding to back up Aiden. "You might want to check your accounts as well as your credit cards to see if there's been any illegal activity."

"Don't cry, sweetheart. I'll take care of everything," Aiden assured Chloe.

Madison walked toward the front door of the home she'd once loved. Forget Aiden Larsen. No one was going to take care of her but herself.

PAUL SAT in Captain Callahan's office and waited while the captain took a long-distance call. Callahan was in his late fifties with a trim midriff and long legs that would look skinny in shorts. He'd shaved his Friar Tuck fringe of remaining hair so he had a bare head like many junior members of the force. If it was supposed to make him more approachable, it didn't work.

Callahan hung up and frowned at the receiver. "Okay, where were we?"

"I'm feeling great. I want to be reactivated. There's a lot going on. You could use me."

Callahan shifted in his chair. He pumped iron but he still had a thin man's shoulders. "I don't like to go against the board. If anything happens to you, then…well, shit, you know. The lawyers will jump all over us and the city will have to settle for a bundle."

"True." He hadn't expected Callahan to allow him to return. "Then is it okay for me to work on the q.t.?"

The captain quirked eyebrows like centipedes. "You wouldn't be paid."

"I understand. I sorta walked in on a homicide. Link's in charge of the investigation...." He let his words hang there. Even the captain—or maybe especially the captain—knew Link's limitations.

"I guess that's all right," he said. "Do you have any hunches about the crime?"

Paul noticed Callahan didn't ask which crime. The man hadn't risen to his position without having a few brains. He'd read the incident reports and knew Paul had been on the scene of Erin Wycoff's murder.

"Not really. I think a profiler will tell us the killer knew the victim and acted with such violence because of it."

"What about the Connelly woman? She has motive."

"Possibly, but I doubt it." He didn't want the captain to suspect he was involved with Madison. His father was one thing, but it would be the kiss of death for his career if the captain discovered the real reason he wanted to work on the case was to help Madison. "I was with her just after she discovered her friend's body. I don't think she was acting. She was stunned."

"Okay, tell Link I said you're to have access to the murder book and all the reports."

Paul stood, realizing he was being dismissed. He walked out and took the elevator down a floor to the homicide division. A few guys were in the office, clacking out reports on computers, but not Link. Paul greeted the men with a wave and responded to their questions about his leg by saying he was ready to return to work.

Erin Wycoff's murder book was in the main file cabinet. It had been updated since Paul had looked at it and contained interviews with key witnesses and friends. He scanned the reports. Other than the forensics report of dog hair on Erin's clothes and in her car, there was no mention of Aspen. He knew he should include the tip he'd received from the Dicon Labs employee, but the woman had sworn him to secrecy for fear of losing her job.

Even if he could have included the information, Paul wouldn't have. For reasons he didn't want to analyze too closely, he'd decided to help Madison. He couldn't see that involving Aspen and possibly having him returned for experiments was going to solve this case. If it did turn out to be important, he could reveal it later.

He was a little disappointed not to find more. Erin Wycoff had been killed over a week ago. The trail went cold a lot sooner than people would think. This murderer had been clever and unless they discovered the "why" of the crime, it might never be solved.

"Hey, dude, what's the haps?" Trey Williams, one of the newer detectives, slapped him on the back.

"Not much. I'm helping out—unofficially—until the board clears me."

"Why don't you help me? I've got my hands full after last night."

"What happened?"

"A couple of gangs shot it out. You add that to the usual shit and—" He waved his hand at a stack of files.

"Anything interesting, unusual?"

"Not really, unless you count someone putting down a man the way you would a dog or horse."

"What?"

"Someone gave a guy a shot of succinylcholine chloride. At one time, it was used to put down animals and is still found in vets' offices," Trey informed him. "It paralyzes the heart and lungs in half a minute. Sometimes it's used in the emergency room. It breaks down in the body very quickly. That makes it hard to detect. We wouldn't have known what killed the man except a nosy neighbor heard a scuffle in the apartment next door and called 911. The killer heard the sirens and dropped the syringe in the alley behind the building."

"No prints on the syringe?"

"Nah. We couldn't get that lucky."

"Did you check to see if it's the type of syringe vets use or the type doctors use?"

Trey banged his forehead with the palm of his hand. "Great idea! Why don't you look through the files to see if anything else jumps out at you?"

Paul agreed and went over to Trey's desk and flipped through the incident reports that would become murder books as soon as they were written up. He wasn't really interested, but he didn't want to appear overly involved in the Wycoff case.

Keith Brooks Smith. That was the man who'd been put down like an animal. If the neighbor hadn't alerted the police, it might not have been listed as a murder.

Interesting.

Something flitted through his brain like a few bars of a song his mind was struggling to remember. Did he know this man? There wasn't much in the report, but Paul didn't think he'd ever met the dead high school teacher. And Smith was a common name.

He set the report aside and rifled through the other incident reports. A gang shoot-out. What else was new? The name kept playing through his mind.

Keith Brooks Smith, Keith Brooks Smith, Keith Brooks Smith.

Why was this man's name so familiar? It was, yet Paul couldn't place it. It had to mean something.

CHAPTER SEVENTEEN

PAUL COULD TELL by the look on his father's face that Mike was more than a little surprised to see him again so soon.

"Did you get reinstated?" he asked.

Paul shook his head. "No. Captain Callaghan gave me permission to help with the Wycoff case, but he can't formally reactivate me until the board gives its okay. Could have legal repercussions."

"Right. Chalk up another one for the lawyers."

"I came by to look at the New Horizons files."

"They're in the security offices at Holbrook Pharmaceuticals. Remember?"

"I assumed you made copies."

"I would have, but Tobias Pennington was hell-bent on getting his staff to sift through the files."

Paul dropped into the chair he'd used earlier that morning. He'd fought the traffic all the way back here for nothing. "Aren't you still working the case? You're paying me to make sure Madison Connelly agrees to be tested."

"Right," his father said in a level voice. "But in case you hadn't noticed, I'm shorthanded. That's why I offered you a job."

Paul hadn't realized this, but he kept his surprise out of his expression. He'd half hoped his father had hired him to help him out while he was on leave. He should have known better.

"Wyatt's security staff is sorting through the records. They'll prepare a list of names—in case the Connelly woman can't donate—and Tobias Pennington will contact other candidates they find. I'm helping only if someone is difficult to locate."

"Makes sense," Paul conceded.

"Why? Has something come up?"

"I'm not sure. I wanted to check on a name in the files. Did you compile a master list of the names at least?"

"Of course." His father sounded offended.

"Could I see it?"

Mike stood up and walked over to the wall of metal file cabinets. He retrieved a manila folder and handed it to Paul.

"What are you looking for?" his father asked.

"A Keith Brooks Smith was killed last night. I thought I recalled that name from the files."

He checked the names on the list in the file folder he'd been given. "Here it is. Mrs. Keith Brooks Smith received Wyatt Holbrook's sperm. She was pregnant on the first try."

"Her husband was killed?"

"No. The murder victim was too young. I'm wondering if it could be their son."

"Smith is a fairly common name. Must be thousands of them in the greater Miami area."

"True, but the exact same name? What are the odds?"

His father shrugged and he could almost hear Madison telling him coincidences were much more common than you'd think. She was damn cute when she took on that soapbox attitude.

"Didn't the jacket on the dead man have his next-of-kin info?"

Paul smiled inwardly. His father had left the force over five years ago, but he still called files *jackets* the way guys on the force did. "No. The dead man was ID'd with his driver's license. Next of kin hadn't been established. The man could have been married. The wife would need to be notified." He handed his father back the file. "I'll check at headquarters later. If it is the same guy, then I'll let you know so he can be removed from the contact list."

"If it's the same guy, I'm not liking this. We've got two dead in the Boston area. If this guy's the third…"

Again Paul kept his smile to himself. Mike had been an ace detective and still reacted like one. "Exactly what I was thinking. But before we worry about it, let me verify it's the same man."

JADE RUSHED into Madison's cube, waving her hands and saying, "You're not going to believe how cool this is. You're, like, going to be blown away."

Madison almost said she couldn't take any more, but then she recalled Chloe whining those same words to Aiden. She braced herself. "Blow me away."

"Guess who's here? So totally cool."

Madison craned her neck to see the front of the office where the reception desk was located. A tall, dark-haired man in a navy blazer and open-neck light blue shirt was waiting near Jade's desk.

"Who is he?" More trouble? she wondered.

"Luis Estevez." Jade whispered the name with something bordering on reverence. Why was she surprised? The man was well-known because he owned a number of nightclubs. Madison suspected Jade spent a fair amount of time at trendy clubs. "Aiden had an appointment with him. He must have forgotten, with Chloe so sick and all."

Great. In addition to the clubs, the Cuban venture capitalist headed Allied Miami Bank. TotalTrivia didn't seem to be a big enough operation for Estevez to be interested. It had to be the gambling angle. What was Aiden thinking?

"Explain to him that Aiden's wife is ill and he'll have to reschedule the appointment." That would buy her time to discuss this with Aiden.

"I did, but he insists on talking to you."

Honest to God. Just when you thought things couldn't get much worse, they did. "All right. Send him down." She swiveled in her chair to pet Aspen at her feet. What was she going to say to the man? *Listen to him, then tell him you'll take it up with Aiden.*

Luis Estevez was a lot younger than she expected, Madison realized when he walked into her office. He'd made money in loans in Little Havana, parlayed that into clubs, then bought Allied Miami Bank. It sounded as if it should have taken years, but Luis Estevez appeared to be just closing in on forty. She didn't know a lot about the man, but rumors had floated around town for years that he was "connected" and laundered money from South American drug dealers. Maybe that was why he was interested in TotalTrivia. It could be a way to launder money.

Luis extended a hand with square buffed nails, clearly from a professional manicure. His grip was firm and his gaze direct as he looked at her with whiskey-brown eyes. "I'm glad you had time to see me."

"Have a seat, Mr. Es—"

"Luis." He sat in the chair opposite her desk.

"I'm not sure I can help you," she told him.

His warm smile seemed to say he thought she could. In a heartbeat she knew it would be foolish to underestimate this man. "I've had preliminary discussions with your husband about adding gambling to your trivia site."

"Ex-husband. Aiden has a new wife."

He nodded, and she was certain he'd known that and deliberately made the mistake to see how she would react. And patsy that she was, she'd snapped at it.

"Right. Ex-husband. He's very receptive to the idea but says you don't want to do it. Why not?"

Madison hadn't quite expected him to be so direct. Aiden would probably kill her for torpedoing his idea, but she decided to say exactly what she believed. "I think too many things in our society revolve around money. We've been doing fine giving gamers a trivia site and earning revenue with ad banners. Why include gambling? We're making money. There's far too much gambling in this country. A lot of people spend more than they can afford on it. I don't want to be a part of that."

She knew she sounded holier-than-thou but it was how she felt. It had been one of her father's pet peeves, too. He claimed gambling came to America like a swift-rising tide and flooded the land. Riverboat gambling, Indian casinos, and practically every state had a lottery.

"Perfectly understandable," he agreed, his tone sincere. "That's why I'm prepared to make you an excellent offer for your half of TotalTrivia."

Madison knew she was staring at him, slack jawed, but she couldn't help it. Why on earth would a man with a huge bank to run and a string of clubs want part of a small online company?

"Look, here's what I'm prepared to do." He went on to explain an all-cash offer that seemed to be more than her share could be worth. He was willing to conclude the deal immediately.

She was tempted to stomp her foot and scream that this was her company. She'd created it and she was proud of her success. But an image of Holbrook Pharmaceuticals intruded. Here was a venture that could help all mankind. Did she want her life's work to be a game?

With this money, she could go back to school and pursue a different career. Considering the way Chloe had acted today, the atmosphere around the office wasn't going to improve. Even though she'd stolen Madison's husband, the woman acted as if she were the injured party. Maybe it was time to leave.

Luis smiled, a captivating grin that said he got his way more often than not. "I take your silence as a 'maybe'?"

It suddenly occurred to Madison that his cash offer would solve her financial problems and buy her time until her identity-theft mess could be straightened out. Just as this thought flashed through her brain, another followed. Could it be coincidence that Luis Estevez was making this offer *just* when she'd become the victim of ID theft and needed the money?

She'd lectured Paul on coincidences. Statistically they were much more common than most people believed. Somehow the urban myth that "there's no such thing as coincidence" had taken root.

Luis Estevez stood and shook out the razor-sharp creases in his beige trousers in much the same way Garrison Holbrook had done. "My offer will be open for a week."

She watched him saunter down the main aisle of the cube farm. Maybe she should be more suspicious of coincidences.

Madison called Jade into her office and asked in a low voice, "Our personnel files are near your desk. Have you seen anyone searching through them?"

"You think someone here obtained your personal information?"

Jade was sharp. She knew exactly what Madison was thinking. "It's a possibility."

Jade drummed shiny black nails on Madison's desk. "I haven't noticed anyone near the files, but I'm at lunch and on breaks. Then there's no one around to see what's happening. But even if one of the guys did get into your file, how would they get your password?"

"Good question." Madison sighed. "Thanks for your help."

"YOU'RE RIGHT," Rob told her as he moved the wand down the back of Aspen's neck just behind the ear. "This dog does have a microchip." He pulled back the wand shaped like a pack of cigarettes and showed her a number on the display screen.

"The owner's name doesn't come up?" she asked.

"No. The way it works is the dog receives an ID number. This is 72340 from Pet Search. That's one of several companies. We'll access the Pet Search Web site and input the number. It should give us owner information."

He led her out of the small examining room toward the main office, where the computers were located. "Now, if a dog is sold, the previous owner should update the info with Pet Search. Unfortunately, too many times an owner moves and fails to update the info or sells the dog and forgets to mention the chip. I can't tell you how many searches are a waste of time."

She touched his arm. "Maybe I don't want to find his owner."

His dark eyes were studying her with a curious intensity. "Let's just see whose number is on the chip. A vet's office or an animal shelter can change the info. Otherwise the original owner *must* be the one to update the chip."

"Wouldn't you get into trouble for doing it when I haven't legally purchased the dog? Erin purchased him—or so the papers say."

"Don't worry about it, babe."

She'd always disliked being called "babe," but coming from Rob, it sounded like a term of endearment. Her mind swung back to this morning and the scene with Aiden and Chloe. No doubt, he called her "babe" all the time.

The office was deserted. Madison had taken the last appointment because her day had been consumed by looking into the identity theft, then going to the office where Luis Estevez had confronted her, but she wanted this chip thing settled before—what had Paul called him? The missing link. Before Lincoln Burgess decided to have Aspen wanded. She didn't want to risk having the retriever returned to Dicon Labs.

Rob clacked away at the computer while Madison stroked the dog's silky coat. Someone had cared enough to chip him, yet something had been sprayed in Aspen's eyes. What was going on here?

"Interesting," Rob said. "Aspen is owned by someone named Bewley Allen. An address on Star Island." He whistled.

They looked at each other in surprise. This was unexpected. Star Island was one of three private islands in Biscayne Bay, where Miami's elite lived.

"Bewley. Do you suppose that's a man or a woman? It certainly isn't the name on the paperwork Erin had."

"Let's look up the name online and find out."

A few clicks later streams of information filled the screen. Madison stared at it in amazement. Bewley Allen was a man— the head of research at Dicon Laboratories.

"Just what I suspected," Rob said, his voice low. He leaned closer to Madison as if to prevent anyone from hearing, even though no one seemed to be around, unless the janitor was disinfecting the back rooms. "Erin and one of the rights groups, probably the EADL, took Aspen and maybe other animals."

"And set fire to the lab." Madison found it hard to believe, at least on one level. Her best friend had kept any sign of illegal activities from her. But when she thought about it, the signs had been there. There were parts of her life Erin hadn't shared. She'd never mentioned the appreciated value of her parents' land or that she intended to sell it and give the profits to Save the Chimps.

Once someone registered disapproval, Erin backed off and shut up. Madison had been quite vocal about the things some animal rights activists were doing. Erin no longer talked about it. Madison thought Erin had stopped. But was that just what Madison assumed? Had Erin ever said this in so many words?

No.

Now, here was proof positive that she'd continued and become more aggressive. Who would set a fire? Someone could have been killed.

"Do you think she was killed because of her animal rights work? Maybe I should tell the police the truth about Aspen."

"No," he responded emphatically. "Why would the activists hurt her? You saw how many people came to her service, but didn't come back to the house. I'll bet most of them were with the animal rights group." He touched her shoulder and looked directly into her eyes. In them she saw the compassion he had for the animals he so gently treated. "The police will give Aspen back to Dicon. Do you want that?"

She glanced down at the retriever. He gazed up at her with eyes that probably couldn't quite distinguish all of her features and swished his tail across the tile floor. He trusted her, and she refused to disappoint him.

CHAPTER EIGHTEEN

PAUL TRIED Madison's cell phone again. He'd called twice before but hadn't left a message. He wanted to talk to her, not to her voice mail. This time she picked up. "It's Paul. Where are you?"

"I'm almost back to the Holbrooks' guesthouse. I took Aspen to the vet. You were right. He did have a chip. Guess who owned him?"

Uh-oh. "Dicon Labs."

"Right. I had his chip updated to show me as the owner."

"Good thinking. Let's not discuss this over the phone. I have several things to tell you. What do you say about pizza?"

"I love it. With anchovies, please."

"Anchovies? You're kidding, right? The world hates anchovies."

Madison laughed. "True. Eighty percent of people ordering pizza cut the anchovies. I'm different. I like 'em."

"I'll have them put on one side only," he said with a laugh. "I'm with the eighty percent."

"Thanks. I appreciate it."

"Okay, I'll pick up a pizza and you open a bottle of wine. I'll meet you at your place—" he checked his Brietling "—in half an hour." He shut his phone, still mulling over everything he'd discussed with his father. This was shaping up to be one hell of a case.

While stopped at a light, Paul dialed Tobias Pennington's

number. Wyatt Holbrook's personal assistant hadn't returned three earlier calls. Now Paul was pissed. And suspicious. Why would the jerk avoid him? He was beginning to wonder if someone in the Holbrook camp didn't want Wyatt to receive a lifesaving transplant.

This time he was put through to Pennington. "Paul Tanner," he said, trying to keep the annoyance out of his voice. Pennington was a prissy little prick who got off vicariously on Wyatt Holbrook's money and power. "I'd like to see the New Horizons files tomorrow morning."

"That won't be possible. My staff is reviewing them."

His arrogant tone made Paul want to slug him. "I'll work alongside them."

"I don't think—"

"I'll be there at nine." Paul snapped the phone shut before Pennington could utter another word.

Something was definitely going on, he decided as he inched along in the slugfest of traffic. Of course, he didn't have any proof, just a tightening in his gut that came with a hunch. Garrison was okay, a bit of a pretty boy, but Savannah and Nathan Cassidy were hard to read.

He wondered about Wyatt Holbrook's will. Actually, people that rich had trusts, not wills. Still, where would Wyatt's money go upon his death? A chunk of it would be used to fund his foundation, but would enough be going to his children to make them anxious to see him die?

What about Pennington? He'd been Holbrook's assistant for years. He might stand to inherit something when Holbrook died.

Paul's cell phone chirped and he flipped it open. It was Trey Williams.

"They've completed the autopsy on that Smith guy."

"So fast?" Usually it took several days. Cases were processed in the order they were received and Miami had plenty of dead people to autopsy.

"Captain put a rush on it. You know, the succinylcholine chloride angle made it unusual."

Paul turned west toward Jo' Mama's Pizza. "What did they find?"

"Blood alcohol twice the legal limit. He'd been snorting coke."

Paul wasn't surprised. Drugs or alcohol figured into half the homicides in the city.

"We know how the killer got to him. There were traces of chloroform in his nostrils, along with the coke, of course."

"A handkerchief saturated with chloroform held over the victim's mouth would have knocked him out. Then he could easily have been injected with the deadly drug."

"Right. The coroner wouldn't have picked up on the chloroform except we asked for a detailed analysis. It's kind of an old-fashioned drug. It isn't used often these days. Couldn't imagine Smith just letting someone give him an injection."

"Any idea where he'd been yesterday?"

"He had a box of matches from Lola's. You know, the pussy bar in Little Havana."

"No shit? Does he have Cuban friends?" Lola's was notorious among cops in Miami. Most of Lola's clients were Cuban. A white teacher like Keith Brooks Smith didn't seem to fit the pattern. But then, who knew?

"I'm still doing background on him," Trey replied. "I had to notify his parents of his death and interview them. Know what? They never told their son that he was a donor-conceived child."

"I'm not surprised," replied Paul.

"Why not? These days we have open adoptions and surrogate mothers up the ying yang—"

"Thirty years ago, things were different," Paul said. That wasn't the real reason he claimed he wasn't surprised. He'd instantly thought of Madison. Her family hadn't told her, either.

"Whatever. The mother bawled when I told her, but you

know, the father didn't seem that shook up. I got the feeling Keith Brooks Smith senior didn't care for the kid. Probably because he wasn't the biological father. I had the feeling he blamed the kid's shortcomings on the donor's genes."

"Could be. Who knows what goes on with families," he said, thinking of his own father. He'd left his parenting responsibilities to a military school. "Did the parents know any of his friends?"

"I got one or two names."

"Take a close look at any women in his life," Paul told Trey. "This kind of crime doesn't take strength."

"There was a struggle, remember? That's why the old lady in the duplex next door called 911."

"I didn't say he didn't resist when he realized what was happening, but there were no signs of forced entry. An average-size woman who works out a little could easily hold him down while she subdued him with chloroform."

"You're right. We're too quick to assume most murderers are men."

"Thanks for updating me," Paul said. He didn't share his suspicions with the detective because that's all they were. Suspicions.

THE BELL OF DESTINY had rung. Keith Brooks Smith had answered the call. Given his life, actually. Not that anyone was going to miss him. A lowlife who used teaching as a cover for his gambling addiction.

The killer sipped a can of Red Bull and thought about the murder. Twice now things had almost spiraled out of control the way the Wycoff killing had taken an unexpected turn. Despite careful planning, Keith Brooks Smith had thrashed about harder than expected, kicking the wall while trying to pry the washcloth soaked with chloroform off his face.

Goddamn nosy neighbors. The old biddy next door had

called the police. Luckily the walls had been thin; her high-pitched voice had come through like an alley cat's screech. There had barely been enough time to give Smith the lethal injection. There had been no time to savor the thrill that was almost sexual in nature. It came with watching life ebb out of another human being.

Intelligent people can overcome the unanticipated, use it to their advantage. That's what set smart people apart from the pack, with their herdlike minds that refused to allow them to think outside the box.

Getting out the back door had been a piece of cake. Watching from across the street, the killer had seen the police arrive within minutes. That meant the body would be examined in an hour or two. A simple blood test would reveal the succinylcholine.

Well, that wasn't the way this murder had been planned. Keith Brooks Smith had been scheduled to die of heart failure. After all, succinylcholine relaxed every muscle in your body until your heart didn't beat and your lungs couldn't move. Upon examination, hours later, the drug would have vanished from his system. The coroner would assume heart failure. True, Smith was a bit young, but it did happen.

Now the police would be suspicious. So what? They couldn't link Keith's death to Erin Wycoff's. They were completely different crimes. That was the beauty of the plan. No one would suspect the same killer was picking off a select number of victims because the murders didn't fit a pattern.

Never underestimate the police. A lot of them, like Paul Tanner, were bright guys. But they were overwhelmed by the sheer number of killings in the Miami area. When they couldn't quickly solve a crime, they were forced to work on those that were easier.

A crack of laughter ricocheted off the walls. Well, it was funny. People got away with crimes all the time because cops were overworked and understaffed. Too bad. That was their problem.

Next up on the list was Madison Connelly. What a piece of work she was! She'd been getting it in spades. No point in killing another person if there was any way around it.

But death might be the only option.

Killing her wouldn't be a cakewalk. She was living in the home of the great Wyatt Holbrook. Her death would cause a ruckus. No doubt the police would be pressured to solve the crime. The whole scheme could unravel.

Could being the operative word. If proper precautions were taken, no one would know. Madison wasn't the type to commit suicide, she didn't have a history of drug use and her death would put Paul Tanner on the case.

An accident might be best for Madison. Happened all the time. People would be sorry, sad, upset, but they would accept it and move on.

What type of accident would generate the fewest questions? There must be a way to throw everyone off track.

"COME IN," Madison called when she heard Paul ring the bell. She'd left the front door open while she changed clothes. The peach-colored shorts and matching tank top were comfortable, she told herself. Truth to tell, she wanted to change clothes and put on a little makeup. She ducked out of the bedroom and into the hall, Aspen at her heels. Ahead she saw Paul standing just inside the door, a large pizza box in his hand. The aroma of pepperoni pizza drifted through the air.

"Let's go into the kitchen," she said.

"Hey, where's the wine?"

She didn't want to admit she'd spent the time primping. "I'll get it." She opened a small wine cooler built into the cabinetry and pulled out a bottle of Pinot Grigio. She handed it to him along with a corkscrew and let him pop the cork while she set the table.

"Aspen's chip claimed he belonged to the head of research for Dicon Labs." She put two glasses on the table.

Paul poured the pale amber wine. "How'd you get the chip changed? I thought only the owner or a vet or animal shelter was allowed to alter ID information."

"Rob did it for me," she told him as she sat down and helped herself to a slice of pizza. Her stomach growled at the aroma of pepperoni, anchovies and cheese. When was the last time she'd eaten? "He thinks she stole the dog along with some others from the lab. He wants to help me keep Aspen."

At the sound of his name, the retriever looked up from where he was sitting beside her and wagged his tail.

"I'm surprised he'd do something illegal," Paul said after he finished a bite of pizza.

"It's no big deal, is it? I wouldn't want to get him in trouble." Sometimes Rob was just a little too friendly, too helpful. For a second Madison wondered if Rob had been coming on to her, then quickly dismissed the thought. He was merely trying to help her while they both were grieving over Erin.

"It's a misdemeanor. I doubt anyone would prosecute unless it was being done on a large scale or if it involved a more serious crime like murder. But still, he told investigators he left Erin because of her activities with the EADL. Sounds like a straight arrow who wouldn't falsify chip info."

Madison put down the rimmed crust of her pizza. She never ate the crusts. Out of the corner of her eye, she saw Aspen. She handed him the crust. He gently took it from her, his tail wagging. "I don't think anyone will find out. Dicon Labs hasn't admitted they were testing cosmetics on dogs. I doubt they'll change their story now."

"You're right." He took a sip of wine and studied her over the rim of the glass.

"Did you ask your ex about using your passwords to access your accounts?" he asked.

Madison nodded. "He didn't do it. I know him well enough to know when he's lying. Actually, he hadn't changed his passwords, either. I could have gotten into his accounts as easily as he could have accessed mine."

Paul shook his head. "I'm not surprised. Happens all the time. Know where most people keep their passwords?"

"No. Where?"

"Taped to the bottom of their keyboards. That's the first place we look when there's a homicide and we want to access a computer."

"What did you want to tell me?" she asked, suddenly recalling what he'd said on the phone.

"Kirk, my father's computer security expert, says there's something called a keystroke logger that could be put on your computer. It records all your keystrokes. That might be the way your password was obtained—and your account numbers, since you do online banking."

"I've never heard of a keystroke logger."

"Apparently, it's a small device that takes just a few minutes to install. You wouldn't be likely to notice it unless you were looking under your keyboard. Tomorrow check your keyboard and let me know. A keystroke logger can enter your computer Trojan-horse-style in an e-mail. Open it, the thing starts recording all your keystrokes and sending them back to a main computer."

"Who would go to all the trouble…" Luis Estevez's face appeared on the screen in her mind. She told Paul about the Cuban's visit and his offer to buy her half of TotalTrivia.

Paul leaned toward her, intensity firing his eyes. He dropped his second slice of pizza back onto the plate. "Jesus H. Christ. That's…weird. Damn weird. I don't know much about Estevez except his reputation. He hasn't been involved in a homicide case that I know about. I could check with the guys in fraud and see what they say."

"I was under the impression his bank financed larger companies. TotalTrivia doesn't seem to be a good fit."

"No, it really doesn't. It seems as if we're missing some pieces of the puzzle."

Madison took a few bites of her second piece of pizza, decided she was no longer hungry and handed it to Aspen. The dog downed it in one bite. She sipped her wine while Paul silently finished another slice. What was he thinking? He was gazing across the room, seemingly lost in thought.

Aspen cocked his head as if to say, *Aw, shucks,* as Paul closed the pizza box and put it in the refrigerator. She silently promised the dog that she would give it to him later. She didn't care for cold pizza.

"Let's go sit in the other room," he said. "I want to talk to you."

She followed him to the sofa facing the swimming pool. Daylight was slowly fading, creating long, dark shadows that melded into each other. The ceiling fan circulated the fragrant aroma of the night-blooming jasmine that grew on the high walls encircling Corona del Mar.

She sat down first and he sat right next to her. *Please,* she thought, *don't let him know how wildly my heart is thumping.*

"I know you're one for facts and statistics," he began, "so what I'm going to say might not seem plausible to you."

Madison nodded and reached down to pet Aspen, who'd settled at her feet. She listened as he explained the strange death of Keith Brooks Smith.

"That's bizarre," she said, "but what does it have to do with me?"

"Maybe nothing, but two of Wyatt's children in the Boston area plus this Smith guy died. Now we have three children who could possibly help Wyatt Holbrook dead."

"How many children do you suppose there are?"

"You're trying to calculate the odds, aren't you?"

"Yes. The other deaths weren't murders. Just this one, right?"

"I wouldn't bet on it. One was a car accident in a relatively new car. Another was a heroin overdose in a young woman who wasn't thought to be a user. Conveniently, drugs and needles were found at the scene."

Suddenly, Madison got the picture. "You think I'm in danger, don't you?"

CHAPTER NINETEEN

What is the largest living organism on Earth?

"IT'S POSSIBLE your life is in danger." Paul took one of her hands in both of his and gazed earnestly at her.

She didn't believe it, but the intensity in Paul's eyes told her that he was dead serious. For an instant her mind snapped back to this morning and the way Aiden had been so protective of Chloe. Madison liked to think she could take care of herself, and she could, but something cracked inside her. Knowing Paul cared appealed to her softer feminine side, the side she liked to deny having.

"I don't think this adds up to my being in any kind of danger," she told him. "The deaths in Boston don't seem to be murder. So what you have is *one* of Wyatt's offspring being killed. That's all."

"It's just a hunch. I admit it, but I can't tell you how strongly I feel I'm right. ID theft, Erin's murder, Luis Estevez's sudden appearance and discovering you're one of Wyatt's—"

"I'm not! I'm just trying to help."

His expression darkened with an unreadable emotion. "So much is going on, a perfect storm of events and you're at the center. We don't have the big picture or we'd know what was happening."

Madison liked to deal in facts. Well, actually, she'd carved out a career from arcane facts. But so much weird stuff was going on around her that she couldn't help wonder. "How can we figure it out?"

"I'll see what the guys in the fraud department have to say about Luis Estevez." He ran his hand through his hair, then added, "I'll also contact an agent I know with the FBI field office here in Miami."

"Good idea." She wouldn't have thought to contact the FBI, but banking crimes did come under federal jurisdiction.

"I'm also going to phone the detectives in the Boston cases and see if there was anything…off about them."

"Off?"

"That just means the lead detective has a hunch something isn't right but can't prove it. They may go with the flow and close the case." He shrugged. "A closed case is a plus for the department. You add it to the 'solved' statistics. Detectives are under a lot of pressure to close cases. It makes it appear as if crime is going down, not up."

"Makes sense," she said.

"I don't want anything to happen to you."

His look was so galvanizing it sent a tremor through her. She believed he was genuinely concerned. Why? He hardly knew her. *Don't kid yourself,* an inner voice cautioned her. This man had already gone out on a limb for her by not revealing Aspen belonged to Dicon Labs. He was interested in her.

And she was interested in him.

It marked the first time since Aiden had walked out that she'd felt anything for another man. She'd tried to date—at Erin's insistence—but her heart hadn't been in it. Paul projected an energy and power that undeniably attracted her. Each time she was with him the pull became stronger.

He scooted closer and slipped his arm around her waist. A delightful shiver of anticipation ran through her. She forced herself to keep her mind on Luis Estevez's offer. "You know, I've been thinking."

He pressed his lips to hers, caressing her mouth more than kissing it. "Can we talk about it later?" he asked with a smile that would test a nun's vows.

"No. Is sex all you think about?"

He considered the question for a moment. "Sometimes I think about food."

She couldn't help laughing…and enjoying being in his arms. He was going to make love to her unless she stopped him, which she knew she didn't have the willpower to do. But she needed to tell him what was on her mind.

"Please help me," she said.

"Name it."

"Really look closely at Luis Estevez. If he wants my half of TotalTrivia for legitimate purposes, I'm inclined to sell it to him." She stared out the French doors at the pool area, a little surprised at herself. She'd been thinking about this, but she hadn't realized she'd actually made up her mind. "Being around the Holbrooks makes me want to do something more with my life than run a trivia game site."

"What have they done other than produce a drug for diabetes?" Paul asked.

"Not a lot," Madison conceded, "but at least they're trying. Wyatt wants to have something that will contribute to society after he's gone. That's commendable. Right?"

"Yes, I guess. I still think they stand to make a fortune."

"While helping people." Madison shook her head. "I'm not helping anyone except to give them a good time. I want to do more."

"You want to make more money."

"It's not about money. When my father was dying, I would have traded anything I had or hoped to have to save him. I'd like to do something to help people. I left MIT before I finished my degree because my father was ill. I'd like to go back— maybe not there—but I would like to complete my degree."

"If that's what you want to do, I think you should."

"There's something else." She didn't know how to explain it exactly. "Chloe took Aiden away from me, and he adores her. I mean *adores* her. Aiden makes no attempt to hide his feelings, yet when I went there to ask about the bank accounts, Chloe went ballistic, like I was a threat or something. Her hatred seemed all out of proportion. It's as if there's a time bomb of jealousy—or something—inside her threatening to explode. It's probably best that I leave the company."

"I never met the woman, but if that's how she behaves and you really want to finish your education, I agree. Sell your half of the business."

"Thanks," she said in a low voice. He had no idea how much she'd needed to talk to him about this. She had no one, no one at all in her life to discuss her hopes, her dreams with. "Check out Luis Estevez. I don't want to sell to a crook."

The concern reflected in his eyes became smoldering desire. She was gathered against a warm, rock-solid body and he covered her mouth with his. He kissed her urgently, hungrily, as if he couldn't get enough of her. She eased her arms around his shoulders and returned the kiss.

Her brain reeled as his tongue slipped into her mouth and mated with hers. In a heartbeat her blood thickened to warm honey. Oh, my, kissing him was even better than she'd imagined.

His hands skimmed the planes of her back and waist. She drew closer to him, using her own hands to test the firm contours of his shoulders. Heavens, his shoulders were wide and powerful. They took their time, kissing, exploring with their hands, but the urgency, the need began to build. She heard herself moaning softly, from deep in her throat, as he adjusted their positions until they were stretched out on the sofa side by side. Instinctively, her body arched into his and he grabbed her bottom with both hands and brought her against his erection.

The turgid proof of his virility pressed against her, his heat searing through her skimpy shorts. His hand glided along her body until it found the swell of her breast and cupped the soft fullness in the palm of his hand. Her fingernails dug into his skin as she fought back a cry of pure pleasure.

His mouth lifted from hers and she opened her eyes, set to protest. The irises of his blue eyes were huge and black and gleaming with desire. His raw masculinity struck a responsive chord in her. "Oh, yes," she whispered.

Yes—what? her brain had the common sense to ask. *Yes, this is the man for me,* came the answer. All the heartache that had gone before had led her here to this man. Now, she was ready to lose herself in him, in this moment, and forget what tomorrow might bring.

She quivered, inhaling sharply as the hand that found her breast eased under the tank top and thumbed the taut nubbin of a nipple through the sheer lace bra. Her body responded instinctively, a shaft of moist heat invading the apex of her thighs.

Passion flared in his heavy-lidded eyes as if he reveled in the reaction he was causing. Then his mouth touched her damp lips again, softly, barely there. She wound her arm around his neck and pulled him as close as possible. The woodsy scent of his aftershave lotion filled her lungs. Madison's sex-starved body kicked into overdrive.

She twined her legs between his, thrusting herself upward, silently offering everything she had to give. It had been so long since she'd had sex, so long since she'd wanted a man that she burned to have Paul make love to her.

His lips left hers to trace a path of moist, lingering kisses down her throat to the sensitive curve where her neck met her shoulder. Somehow he'd unhooked her bra and was now caressing her bare breast while he continued to kiss her. He paused for a moment, breathing like a racehorse.

"Don't stop," she cried.

He rose and swept her wordlessly into his arms. In a few quick strides, they were in her bedroom. The next second they were stretched out on the comforter. He angled himself across her, letting her absorb some of his weight but leaving enough of her exposed for him to touch.

"You know," he said, his voice low and husky, "I had the feeling the first time I set eyes on you that we'd end up in bed."

She grabbed a toss pillow and bopped him with it. "You're conceited."

"Thanks," he said in a tone that would have convinced the toughest jury that he'd just received a supreme compliment.

His mouth captured hers in a fierce, hot kiss and she could feel the rising passion thrumming through his body, flowing like an electric current into hers. The sheer intensity of his kiss took what little breath she had away until she was forced to jerk her head to one side and gasp for air.

"You okay?"

"Never better," she managed to whisper. "Don't stop now."

"Believe me, I had no intention—"

She smothered his words with an openmouthed kiss and arched upward so her bare breasts were thrust against the crisp hair on his chest. What had happened to their clothes? When had he undressed them? Oh, boy. He was just too good at this. A pro really.

Who had he practiced on? asked some distant part of her brain. Did it really matter? came the groggy reply. She tried not to dwell on tomorrow. *Live in the present,* she admonished herself. Still, some little voice in her head reminded her of the heartbreak that could devastate her at a time when she was already oh, so vulnerable.

His slow, erotic kiss robbed her brain of any will to object. Slowly, taking all the time in the world, Paul trailed a series of kisses downward from her lips to her neck to her sensitive breasts. He was tasting her, savoring her as much as kissing her.

All the while, his hand petted and stroked her inner thighs, igniting heat with each caress until she was purring like a kitten and arching upward into the palm of his hand.

Nothing in her life had quite prepared her for this…this pure ecstasy. True, she believed she'd reached the pinnacle of desire on more than one occasion. She'd been wrong. Nothing had felt quite like this.

"You're incredible," he whispered, his voice raspy.

"So…are you," she managed to say.

He angled his body across hers, the weight pressing her down into the soft mattress. The rasp of hair on his chest tickled her breasts and sent yet another bolt of searing heat downward. She wound her arms around his neck and kissed him—everywhere.

His cheeks were stubbled with an emerging beard, but it only added to the erotic sensations coursing through her body. Her tongue explored the patch of soft skin behind his ear. It had the faintest taste of salt. His overheated body exuded a woodsy, musky aroma that spiraled through her in a heartbeat. She moved downward until her lips touched the soft hair on his chest and she felt the thud of his heart against her mouth.

Oh, please, she silently thought. *Let this last for hours and hours. Don't let it end.*

His powerful back was moist beneath her wandering hands, the muscles flexing at her touch. He moved against her, his hard body delightfully heavy as he nudged one leg between hers. His iron-hard erection delved between her legs.

"Oh, my. You're just too good at this."

Instead of responding, his lips nuzzled her nipple, sucking the taut bud deep into his mouth. His tongue played with it while she writhed beneath him. One second she wanted to scream for him to hurry; the next she wanted to demand he slow down, make this last all night.

She felt weak, her body quaking with need. Blood thundered in her temples and it was hard to think coherently. Instead she instinctively reacted and guided his penis into her as she widened her legs to accommodate him.

His mouth claimed hers and he kissed her with a fierce abandon that made her light-headed. He thrust into her in one quick motion that left her gasping for breath. He felt huge and burning hot inside her.

Oh, my. Oh, my.

Nothing registered in her brain for a moment except how thrilling this felt. It was a primal feeling, she dimly realized, a sensation she'd never experienced until this moment. The charged duet of their breathing, their bodies moving in sync seemed so right. So perfect.

"Madison," he moaned in her ear. "You feel…you feel…"

Without completing his sentence, he began driving into her, then pulling out in a series of long, slow strokes. She lifted her hips to deepen the angle of his thrusts. Then, without warning, he picked up the pace, jackhammering into her. She clutched at him, crying his name. "Paul,,,oh, Paul!"

Pleasure rippled through her in shuddering waves and she arched higher, lifting off the bed as she reached the crescendo. Her body contracted in a convulsion of pleasure so mind-blowing that she saw stars. White-hot stars.

Seconds later he drove into her one last time as he found his own release. He collapsed on her, panting, then rolled to one side, their bodies still joined. She felt languid, dazed and utterly incapable of rational thought. They lay silent for a few minutes, cradled in each other's arms, still breathing like marathon runners.

"Well," he said with a typical male smile—a grin really, "am I any good?"

"There's only one way to tell. Let's do it again. This time I'll critique you as we go."

MADISON WALKED through the lobby of St. John's Hospital. The blood tests and physical exam to screen her for organ donation had taken most of the morning. It was almost noon, she noticed, checking her watch. She'd promised Paul that she would examine the underside of her computer to see if a keystroke logger had been attached to the keyboard, then call him. He was probably wondering what had happened to her.

Paul. Lord have mercy. What was she doing? She had no business getting involved with a man right now. Too late! She was involved, if that's what you called making love to a man all night long.

When she woke up alone in bed, she figured it was par for the course. Men were into sex but had no idea what to say to you in the morning. Wrong. Paul had been in the kitchen, scrambling eggs and brewing coffee.

The aroma of the coffee had drawn her like a powerful narcotic, but she made a quick dash into the bathroom to brush her teeth and rake a brush through hair like a tumbleweed blown across Texas. The mirror told her that she could haunt a house and charge by the room, but it didn't keep her out of the kitchen.

Paul had kissed her, then insisted she eat breakfast. He was a little upset to hear she was going to the hospital for testing instead of heading straight to the office to check for the keystroke logger, but she'd promised and didn't feel she could let down Wyatt and Garrison.

"How'd it go?" a male voice asked, breaking into her thoughts.

She looked up, startled to see Garrison walking toward her. What was he doing here? "Fine. It took longer than I expected. I didn't know it would be a complete physical, including a stress test on the treadmill."

"I'm sorry. I hope you didn't miss something at work." His expression was sympathetic and she realized she must have sounded snippy.

"It's okay, really."

"Donating part of your liver involves major surgery. You have to be in excellent physical health."

"I know. Dr. Miller explained the procedure in detail."

"Have you got time to grab a quick lunch?" He gestured toward the cafeteria off the main lobby. "My father's in there, saving a table. He had to have a series of tests this morning, too."

She wanted to say no but couldn't bring herself to do it. True, Garrison and Wyatt had their own agenda, but they'd both treated her with such kindness. The way things were shaping up, she would need to stay at the guesthouse for at least a week. "Thanks. I'll have to make it quick. I need to get back to my office."

Hand on the back of her arm, Garrison guided her into the large cafeteria. It wasn't an ordinary cafeteria, with steam trays filled with dried-out or greasy food. There was a salad bar and turkey being carved by a chef at a make-your-own-sandwich station. Fresh fruit was arranged in bowls on shaved ice.

"They're really into health here," Garrison explained when he noticed her looking around the room. "Nothing fried, no red meat."

In the far corner at a round table for four, Madison saw Wyatt. He waved at her, but she barely managed a smile. At his side was the ever-charming Savannah. If she'd known the woman was going to be here, Madison would have made an excuse, but it was too late now.

Wyatt stood as she approached the table. Savannah smiled, but resentment etched her beautiful face like a death mask. Garrison pulled out a chair for Madison.

"Thanks for beginning the testing process," Wyatt said.

"No problem," Madison replied. He appeared tired even though it wasn't much past noon. She remembered what Garrison said about his father being more ill than he appeared.

"What would you like?" Garrison asked. "A salad or a sandwich?"

"A salad with chicken and iced tea," she said. "Let me help you."

Garrison was already walking away. "I'll get it."

Madison reluctantly lowered herself into the chair. Savannah and Wyatt had partially eaten salads and drinks in front of them. There was a half-eaten sandwich at Garrison's place beside her.

Wyatt nudged his daughter with his elbow. "Savannah has something to say to you."

I'll bet. "Really?"

"I'd like to apologize for the way I behaved yesterday morning," Savannah told her with all the enthusiasm of a woman receiving the last rites. "I was out of line. I know you're just trying to help my father."

Madison couldn't bring herself to say it was all right, because it wasn't. And Savannah wasn't one bit sorry. Somehow her father had found out about the incident and forced her to apologize.

"I was very rude. I don't know what got into me. I guess I'm just overly protective of my father." The gorgeous redhead's tone softened a bit. "I don't want anything to happen to him."

Most people would have assumed Savannah was referring to Wyatt's health, but yesterday morning, Savannah had been upset about her father's money.

"We've been talking about the Holbrook Foundation," Savannah added in a voice that was just a little too perky. *All is forgiven. Get over it,* her tone seemed to imply. She smiled at her father, then asked Madison, "Do you know what the largest living organism on the earth is?"

"Coral reefs," came Madison's automatic reply. Did this woman think a quick "sorry" meant she wanted to have anything to do with her?

For a second Savannah looked stunned. "Oh, I forgot." She rolled her vibrant green eyes. "You're a trivia expert."

"While we were waiting for you, Garrison was trying to explain that coral reefs hold endless possibilities for medical discoveries," Wyatt said.

"Aren't the reefs being killed by global warming and here in Florida from pesticide runoff from golf courses?"

Wyatt smiled at her while Savannah kept talking. "Garrison is nutso over those corn sprouts that have been successfully used to treat hepatitis B."

"That's not from the ocean," Madison replied, not knowing where this confusing conversation was going.

"True, but my son is…well, how can I put it?"

"Bonkers. Simply bonkers," Savannah supplied with an unflinching stare like a vulture. "My brother believes the future of medicine lies not in chemistry but in nature, especially the sea. This hepatitis B discovery only validates his theory. Garrison is determined that Father award the lion's share of the foundation's research money to scientists involved in plant- or sea-based discoveries like the one he's working on."

"It's an ongoing discussion we've been having—"

"Father," Savannah chided. "I wouldn't call it a discussion. It's more like an ongoing fight that my brother won't give up. Garrison thinks he's won this round—"

"Savannah, that's enough." Wyatt smiled at Madison and she had the impression he was embarrassed by his grown children's bickering. "Scientists often disagree on the best method to achieve the same goal."

Madison tried for a smile, but she couldn't help wondering what Savannah's role was. As if reading her mind, Savannah spoke.

"I'm working on skin rejuvenation products from what's left at the bottom of a wine cask. You know, grape skins and seeds. Their antioxidant properties are fifty times more effective than—"

"Vitamin E."

"Exactly," Wyatt said with a warm smile for Madison.

Savannah's eyes narrowed slightly; she didn't even attempt a smile.

Garrison arrived with a large chicken salad and a glass of iced tea. He placed them in front of her. "Thanks. Looks great." She immediately stabbed a chunk of chicken with her fork.

"We've asked the lab to process your blood work as quickly as possible and have Dr. Miller look over the results of your physical. It usually takes three days, but we should know tomorrow. The next day at the latest." Garrison gave her an encouraging smile, then took a bite of his sandwich.

"Did you straighten out the ID theft problem?" Wyatt asked.

"Not yet. Apparently it takes longer and is more complicated than most people imagine."

Garrison touched her shoulder. "Do you need—"

"I'm fine. Just having a place to stay while I straighten out the mess is a huge help." She looked directly at Wyatt. "Thanks."

"You know, every day twenty people die in the United States waiting for a transplant," Savannah said, using her tongue like a whip.

"Savannah!" Garrison scowled at his sister.

She shrugged defiantly and her red hair flowed over her shoulders like molten lava. "It's true. I just—"

"I'm sure Madison understands the gravity of the situation," Wyatt told his daughter in a tone that said Savannah should shut her mouth. "I don't have a lot of time."

"The waiting list for organs is months—even years—long, depending on the type of transplant an individual needs," Garrison added.

Madison thought about this for a moment. She'd meant to go online and learn more, but with everything that had been happening—and Paul—she hadn't had time. "A person can't just jump to the top of the waiting list, can they? What if I match someone who's been waiting longer?" The words tumbled out of her mouth before she had time to think.

Savannah's quick glance at her brother telegraphed…what? Was Madison missing something?

"The person at the top of the list would receive the donation," Wyatt assured her in a level voice. "But if you're related to someone, you can choose to give him the organ instead of the person on the top of the list."

Shock must have registered on her face because Garrison quickly said, "Most living-donor liver transplants are from family members. Few people volunteer to have part of their liver surgically removed for a total stranger."

Thoughts tumbled through her brain like loose change. She recalled Rob telling her that this was a risky surgery and wondered how long the recovery would take. Along with that thought was the realization that this family honestly believed she was related to them. No doubt she would have to sign some sort of document saying she was related in order to bypass the donor recipient list.

Madison would have to admit she was part of this family, and they would have to formally accept her. Legal documents must be involved.

That's what had Savannah in such a snit. She was insecure and didn't trust her father to love her the way he did now if another sibling arrived on the scene with a lifesaving transplant. Or was it more about the money? Madison couldn't be sure. Savannah was hard to read, but Garrison was an open book. He wanted to save the world—the oceans first—and his father. Who knew what Savannah really wanted?

Madison was tempted to assure them of what she knew to be the truth. She was Zach Connelly's daughter. But she could see no amount of arguing was going to persuade this family. Only the facts would.

"They swabbed the inside of my mouth for a DNA test," Madison told them. "How soon will it be run?"

"That takes weeks," Garrison told her. "Best-case scenario. Could take up to two months. By then you'll have gone through the battery of tests necessary before you can donate."

She had the sinking feeling there was much more to this than anyone had told her. Savannah looked away while Garrison took another bite of his sandwich.

Finally, Wyatt said, "I have a very sensitive immune system. I've always been allergic to cats, strawberries, mold of any kind, shellfish…you name it. The doctors will need to see if our immune systems are compatible."

"That means a bone marrow test." The way Savannah said it with such relish told Madison it wasn't going to be pleasant. She'd heard of the test, of course, and Garrison had mentioned it, but she didn't know what was involved.

What had she gotten herself into?

CHAPTER TWENTY

PAUL GAZED across the table at Valerie Branson. The FBI agent was thoughtfully studying the latte on the table in front of her. He'd told Valerie about Luis Estevez's offer to buy Madison's half of TotalTrivia.

"You know I can't comment on any of our investigations," she finally said.

"Of course not. That's why I suggested we meet here to discuss this in general terms, not focusing on a specific case."

They were sitting at a table under a banyan tree at the Daily Grind. Paul had called Valerie while he was driving to Holbrook Pharmaceutical's security offices, where Tobias Pennington and his staff were going over New Horizon's files.

"What I can tell you," Valerie said, "is that Estevez hasn't been indicted…yet, but it's just a matter of time."

Paul nudged aside his mug of *café cubano*. "Can you tell me if Estevez has been acquiring small companies like TotalTrivia?"

She hesitated a moment before saying, "He hasn't, but I'm not surprised. Look at it this way. If you have a lot of money to launder, how are you going to do it without getting caught?"

"Nightclubs and restaurants are good bets. Who's to say how many customers paid in cash? It's difficult to track."

"Nearly impossible," she agreed. "But there's a limit to how much money you can funnel through a club or restaurant on any given night. Anything more than a quarter of a million looks suspicious."

"Whoa! That much?"

Valerie smiled, an easygoing grin that went with her outdoorsy looks—a lanky tomboyish build, brown hair several shades lighter than her dark eyes and a spray of tiny freckles. Paul had met her several years ago at the shooting range when he noticed the woman next to him was a crack shot. They'd started talking and gradually become friends. She'd helped him several times by putting him in contact with agents in the Miami field office to advise him on various cases. This was the first time he'd asked for her direct help.

Valerie leaned across the small café table and spoke in a low voice. "Obviously, you don't do much clubbing. These days, it's not unusual to have what they call private service. You order whole bottles of very expensive premium liquor or wine and have your own waiter who just stands at your table to attend your guests. The tab skyrockets."

"I see what you mean, but at a certain point generating too much money would raise a red flag."

"Right. I'm not aware of Estevez investing in anything but clubs and restaurants, but now that you've brought this to my attention, I wonder if he has decided to expand. It would be a clever move."

"How so? I didn't see any way he could funnel cash through TotalTrivia the way he could a club."

"There's a way. Add gambling to the site. You then have to collect and pay out money. That means a bank—Estevez's own bank, no doubt—will have to handle the finances. Since the game is online, someone could set up a lot of fake accounts who lose money. That way dirty money is funneled into the bank."

Paul sat up straighter, the idea clicking into place and making sense. "Money streams in and it appears legit."

"Exactly. Computer geeks have gotten phenomenally sophisticated. One person on the computer could create lots of fake accounts, using a rerouter that's almost impossible to trace."

"What's a rerouter?"

"It's just one computer sending info to another computer that forwards the same info to yet another computer until it's nearly impossible to find out where the message originated. We'd play hell trying to prove there weren't real people out there losing money."

Paul rocked back in his chair. He didn't know what to think, but he knew he didn't want Madison involved with Estevez. "Drug money. It's killing us, isn't it?"

"Absolutely. We haven't got the manpower to combat it. When there's so much money involved, good people succumb to temptation. From what you've told me, I'd say that Estevez has your friend's ex in his pocket already. That's why he wants to buy her half to close the deal."

"What if she says no? Do you think Estevez would..." He couldn't bring himself to say the words. He could still see Madison the way she'd looked last night, blond hair fanned across the pillow, her body jerking upward as he thrust into her.

"Get rough? It's possible." Valerie stood up. "Gotta go. Tell your friend to be careful."

"I will. Thanks for your help." He sat there and watched Valerie walk away. He wondered if Estevez, who must have a computer whiz or two working for him, had engineered the ID theft. It certainly would put pressure on her to sell. Or was something else going on?

It might be far-fetched, but he believed Madison's problems were somehow linked to Erin's murder. But how? There didn't seem to be any connection, yet his gut instinct told him that he was missing something.

He checked his watch. One o'clock. Why hadn't Madison called? She was supposed to phone as soon as she'd taken the blood test. What was taking so long? Between Estevez and whoever had killed Keith Smith, Madison was in big trouble. Estevez wouldn't bother her...yet, Paul assured himself, because she hadn't turned down his offer. No telling what Smith's killer might do.

His mind replayed them making love last night. All night long. He'd had his share of women, sure, but this woman was different. There was something about her that had gotten to him just after they'd discovered Erin's body and had walked outside.

She was adorable, sexy as hell, but her attraction for him went beyond that. The way she spouted trivia, the way she stood her ground, the way she looked at the world appealed to him. He knew better than to get involved with her but he hadn't been able to resist.

Madison wasn't a woman he was going to be able to casually leave as he had in the past. She represented something much more permanent. Hell, had he ever enjoyed a permanent relationship? No. He didn't go in for psychological bullshit, but even he realized his mother deserting him and being sent to military school had fostered a certain emotional detachment that had undermined his ability to allow himself to be close to a woman. He used his privacy like a shield to maintain his distance from anyone who could hurt him.

He chuckled, recalling how one girlfriend had characterized him. "You're like a dog, Paul. If you can't eat it or hump it, you piss on it and strut away."

She was probably right, he thought. Here he was, almost thirty-six years old, and he walked whenever relationships became too stressful, too involving. Aw hell, whenever a relationship required more than sex, he was outta there.

Not this time, buddy. This time things had changed. Not much for introspection, he still asked himself, How? Why?

Maybe he had changed. Getting shot had been the turning point, he realized. The only permanent thing in his life had been his job. Then one bullet put him out on disability. Hung him out to dry. He was nothing if he wasn't working. Lucky for him, good ol' dad came to the rescue with a job that was a little like what he'd been doing.

How or why he had changed didn't matter, he decided. He wanted Madison Connelly in his life—and not just for one night or a month. He wasn't sure where this was going exactly, but he was determined to give it his best shot.

Paul was on his way to the station when Madison finally called. "I was waylaid by the Holbrooks," she told him. "I had lunch with them."

Paul listened while she explained about Savannah's apology and the family's belief that she was related to them. He didn't give a rat's ass about the Holbrooks. He was too concerned about Madison. She irrationally clung to the belief that she wasn't one of Wyatt's donor-conceived children. What would happen when the DNA came back conclusively proving she was a Holbrook?

"Did you find out anything more by going through the files?"

"Not really. I came across a page of just numbers. Pennington says they went over it, but the list simply assigned numbers to the various women and the children they conceived through New Horizons."

"What about your friend in the field office? What did he say?"

Paul almost corrected Madison and said his friend was a woman but decided against it. What difference did it make? "Estevez hasn't been buying small Internet-related companies, but this could mark a turn in that direction." He went on to explain just how the scam could work.

"Interesting. I guess I'm not selling. I don't want to hand TotalTrivia over to crooks."

"Expect some pressure from Estevez...from your ex."

"Right. I'm pulling into the office parking lot now. I'll check for that keystroke logger and call you if I find it."

"Okay. I'll see you later." He was impressed with the way she was holding up. Most women would be falling apart at this point, but not Madison. "Where would you like to go for dinner?"

"I promised the Holbrooks we would eat with them."

"We? As in you *and* me?"

"That's right. Us. Casual clothes. It's a barbecue."

He disconnected. Us. He liked the sound of it. *Admit it, buddy, you* love *the sound of it.* Most of the time defining moments in life were revealed in hindsight. Not this time. This was a defining moment for him, Paul realized. From now on, he'd be thinking in terms of "us."

MADISON DIDN'T FIND anything attached to the underside of her keyboard. So, that wasn't how her personal information had been obtained. Unless. Unless the device had already been removed. That was possible, she decided. It had been days since someone had accessed her accounts. Once this was accomplished, they wouldn't need to keep the keystroke logger in place. Or it could have been a Trojan horse in an e-mail.

She gazed out across the cube farm, thinking. Jade was bent over a programmer's desk, talking to one of the guys who had recently been hired. Clearly, Jade was flirting with him. The girl did not have enough to do. She was overqualified for a receptionist position. She could earn a lot more elsewhere. Why did she stay?

Madison had seen Jade's résumé but didn't remember much about her background except that she had dropped out of Florida State in her junior year. Being a receptionist didn't require much education so Madison hadn't paid attention to all the details. From what Madison could remember, Jade had worked as a waitress and tended bar. At a club. One of Estevez's clubs? she wondered.

The files were in Aiden's office in the far corner opposite

Madison's office. He was there now; he'd been in his office talking on the phone when she'd arrived fifteen minutes ago. She rose and walked across the cube farm to Aiden's corner. She rapped once on the partition to get his attention.

Aiden looked up, "Hey, Madison. What's up?"

There was a false note of cheer in his voice. "I just want to look at the personnel files for a moment." She walked over to the cabinet where the employee files were kept.

"Look, I'm sorry about the way Chloe acted yesterday. She's been through a lot. She isn't herself. It's not like her to lash out like that for no good reason."

Madison had her back to him and she thumbed the files until she found Jade's. "It was for the best. Her outburst proved I need to sell my half of the business." There! She'd said it. Thinking of selling was one thing, verbalizing it to Aiden made it real.

"Estevez made you an offer."

Madison spun around. "How did you know?"

Aiden shrugged, then said, "Jade told me."

Madison felt a flush creep up the back of her neck. She turned around and pulled Jade's file from the cabinet. Her back to Aiden, she scanned the information. There it was. Just as she suspected. Jade had worked at Barely There—one of Luis Estevez's clubs.

The girl had acted as if she knew Estevez by reputation alone. Obviously, that wasn't the case. Jade could have installed, then removed the keystroke logger. Having Madison in a financial pinch could have been done on purpose to force her to sell.

"You're going to accept his offer." This wasn't a question from Aiden. It was a statement of fact, a foregone conclusion. "It's probably a good idea…considering Chloe and all. I just never thought it would come to this. We were so great together when we started."

Was Aiden being sentimental? It wasn't like him, but then she had to admit he'd changed a lot since he'd married Chloe. They'd never been "good together," but now was not the time to dwell on the past.

"No, I'm not selling to Estevez. He's a crook and you know it. If you're smart, you won't have anything to do with him." She thought back to her conversation with Aiden on the morning she'd found Erin's body. "You said we were going to wait and discuss gambling further, then come to a decision before contacting Estevez."

"Well…things happened fast." Aiden was hedging; there was something he wasn't telling her.

"What things?" she demanded.

"Chloe spoke with Estevez."

Madison shot her ex the coldest look she could muster. She might have known Chloe was responsible. Where it would have taken Madison weeks and a lot of sweet talk, Chloe was able to persuade Aiden with a few words.

"Chloe's more—" he searched for a word and after a moment settled on "—materialistic, ambitious than you are."

Madison believed she was more ambitious than Chloe. Madison had all sorts of plans for expanding the business. But there was no denying Chloe was materialistic. Designer clothes, fancy cars. Yes, it was easy to understand why Chloe would want to wring every last dime out of TotalTrivia. She wasn't really ambitious, just greedy. "Doesn't Chloe know the man's a criminal?"

Aiden snorted a dismissive laugh. "He's never been charged—"

"That doesn't mean he won't be. Get mixed up with him—"

"Who are you planning to sell to?"

"Why don't you buy me out?"

"I—I don't have the same kind of money Estevez does." A

shadow of annoyance darkened his handsome face. "You should accept his offer."

Madison stomped out of Aiden's office. She passed Jade, still chatting up the programmer in the middle of the cube farm. "Jade, I'd like to speak to you."

The girl followed Madison back to her office.

"Jade, why didn't you tell me you knew Luis Estevez?"

Jade fluttered what had to be false eyelashes that fringed her Cleopatra-style eyes. Color seemed to leach from her pale cheeks, which had been powdered several shades lighter than her natural color to enhance the Goth look, "I—I don't know him. I—I mean, I never met him. I did work at one of the clubs he owns."

"You were never introduced?"

"Never. I saw him once…maybe twice. That's all. I swear."

Madison found that hard to believe. "How many employees were at the club?"

Jade thought a moment. "Dozens, I guess. I was one of six bartenders on a shift. Then there were waitresses, busboys, a maître d', three bouncers, parking valets and who knows how many in the kitchen. A lot."

"Has Mr. Estevez ever come here to TotalTrivia before?"

Jade hesitated. "The day your friend was killed, I worked late. When I left, I forgot my cell phone in my desk. I came back and Mr. Estevez was talking with Chloe in Aiden's office."

Chloe again. Why wasn't she surprised?

"Was Aiden around?"

"No. I grabbed my cell and slipped away. They didn't see me."

Madison believed Jade. Not only did her words have the ring of truth, but there was something straightforward in the girl's gaze that said she was being honest. Just because she worked at one of Estevez's clubs didn't necessarily mean she knew the man.

Why was Chloe meeting with Luis Estevez without Aiden? she wondered. Then a faint bell dinged somewhere in the back of her brain. She decided to call Pamela Nolan, the friend from MIT who'd been at Stanford with Chloe. It was time to get the full story on what had caused Chloe to drop out of graduate school.

CHAPTER TWENTY-ONE

PAUL TRIED to concentrate on what Garrison Holbrook was saying, but it was difficult to take his mind off—his eyes off—Madison. She was wearing a pale lavender halter dress. The lilac color made her eyes appear to be a deeper shade of blue than usual. And he couldn't help noticing she wasn't wearing a bra.

Every time his gaze met hers, something inside him seized up. He'd been attracted to other women, but not like this. Madison meant so much to him that he was willing to risk his career by not revealing what he knew about Aspen—for her.

Garrison's voice interrupted his thoughts and Paul tried to appear interested even though he'd rather be in bed with Madison. Garrison kept rattling on about nature's treasure trove of medical cures just waiting to be discovered.

"I say we invest a little money at least," Garrison told his father. "That way we'll have our foot in the door."

"Colombia has long been suspicious of bioprospecting, as we call it." Wyatt directed his comment to Madison, the way he had all evening. "But the U.S. has put enough pressure on them to stop growing opium poppies or coca leaves for cocaine. Allowing farmers to grow crops like medicinal herbs will generate a lot of cash."

They were sitting on the terrace of the main house near the infinity pool, having finished a dinner only someone richer than Midas would call a barbecue. The steaks and grilled vegetables had been barbecued—somewhere—and served by a maid. A chocolate soufflé with espresso gelato the Holbrooks' chef had made had been dessert.

From his chair, it appeared to Paul that the pool was cascading into the ocean nearby. It was just an optical illusion, of course, but in the dim light of early evening, the Holbrook mansion seemed to be surrounded by an endless sweep of water.

"Didn't Merck cut a deal with Costa Rica that gave them the rights to all the naturally occurring substances in that country's plants?" asked Madison.

If the conversation bored her, it didn't show. She kept asking questions and listening attentively. Wyatt hadn't said much, but when he did, most of his remarks were for Madison. Paul had the feeling Garrison harped on his father a lot about investing in nature-based medicines.

"You bet they did," Garrison answered for his father. "Way back in the early nineties. Just cost them a cool million back then. In today's market, the Costa Ricans could get a lot more."

"Why's that?" Paul asked.

"Other countries closed their borders to bioprospectors. Colombia's just opened a crack. It's a real opportunity," Garrison told them.

"Have any discoveries come out of Merck's Costa Rican deal?" asked Madison.

Good question, Paul thought. He was fairly sure she already knew the answer. She had an amazing arsenal of facts in her cute little head—which he imagined on a pillow. No, he didn't think about sex all the time. But when he was around Madison, it was hard to keep his thoughts on anything else. Wasn't it time they got out of here?

"I'm not aware of anything Merck's developed yet," conceded Garrison, "but it takes years of research and testing to bring a new drug to the market. They're probably onto a number of things. Remember, aspirin was originally isolated from the bark of a tree."

"And the Germans were the ones to bring it to the market, right?" Madison asked.

"Right," Wyatt said with a proud smile and Paul had the feeling the older man glimpsed something of himself in Madison. She didn't look much like him but she had his keen intelligence. He reminded himself that like the other Holbrooks, Madison was left-handed and stubborn.

"Why not sell some of the remedies as herbs? Wouldn't that cost a lot less?" Paul asked.

"It would, but it's such an unregulated industry that you'd have knockoffs and phony herbs on the shelf alongside the real deal. People wouldn't trust the herb because sometimes it wouldn't work since they'd taken a counterfeit product. Nope," Garrison concluded with an emphatic shake of his head. "The big money is in prescriptions."

"Some herbs can be really dangerous," Wyatt added, again directing his comment to Madison. "Enebro, a seed from a tree, can be used to successfully treat weight loss, but if you take too much, it causes cardiac arrest."

"Yikes!" exclaimed Madison.

Paul was about to make a sarcastic comment but his cell phone vibrated. He pulled it out and checked caller ID. It was a Boston area code. He rose and walked away so he could talk to the detective who'd worked on the deaths of the two other donor-conceived children.

Detective O'Malley had a thick New England accent. That combined with a three-pack-a-day rasp made him a little difficult to understand at first. Paul walked out onto the footpath along the beach and listened to the man explain how the cases were assigned to him because he had a record for closing files fast and these two seemed simple.

"So you looked into Heidi Thomas's drug-overdose death and Jared Anderson's car accident?" Paul asked.

"Right you are."

"Did either of them seem a little off to you? You know, like perhaps something else was going on?"

Two beats of silence became three. Paul knew cops didn't like being questioned about closed cases. Having a case reopened because you'd screwed up the initial investigation was a humongous black mark.

"Here's what I'm thinking," Paul said. "Both cases in the Boston area were children of the same sperm donor."

"They were? I just pulled the files when I got your message. There's nothing about them being conceived by sperm donation."

"It may not have come up, but check with the parents and you'll see I'm correct."

Paul could hear the other man light a cigarette and suck a puff deep into his lungs. "Now I've got another case down here, which, if we hadn't gotten really lucky, would have appeared to be a death by natural causes." He went on to explain about the succinylcholine murder. Paul figured the more he talked, the better chance he had at putting this detective at ease. Maybe then, he'd speak more freely.

"Well, I dunno. Heidi Thomas's fiancé and roommate swore, and I mean *swore,* she never used drugs. Same thing with her parents. Still, there was no question that she ODed on heroin. There was drug paraphernalia in the room and a stash of heroin hidden in the box springs of her bed."

"Could the stuff have been planted there?"

"It's possible. Hell, anything's possible," the detective admitted. "The parents, the boyfriend were so insistent that I looked into it. But I couldn't find a motive. Heidi was a student with her share of student loans. She had no money and no life insurance policy. There wasn't any reason to kill her."

"What if I told you her biological father is a fantastically wealthy man who is looking for his offspring because he needs an organ donation that must come from a blood relative?"

This time there were three long beats of silence, then, "Aw, shit! How many people knew he was looking? I suppose someone stands to gain—"

"I'm not sure. I'm working on it."

"You think it's someone down there or up here?"

"Good question. I'll get back to you when I know more. What about the auto accident?"

O'Malley sucked in another deep puff and exhaled it into the phone. "A new Lexus. Anderson crashed it. The car was pretty mangled. Nothing obvious had been done to the car that would indicate tampering."

"Did an expert check it?"

"Nah. We didn't spend the money because it didn't seem necessary. The kid had a history of speeding. Tickets up the ying yang. It seemed obvious he was driving too fast in the rain, lost control of the car and rolled it down an embankment."

Great. They didn't want to spend the money. What did he expect? Police budgets everywhere were tight.

O'Malley sighed. "If we'd known about this sperm donation connection, we might have handled these cases differently. Especially since…"

"Since what?" Paul heard something in the man's voice.

"Since they died within days of each other."

Paul lurched forward as if the air had been knocked out of him. Why hadn't he caught that? It must have been in the report his father had given him. He'd read it too fast, too carelessly. He knew better. "Let me do a little checking and I'll call you back. If anything comes up, you have my number."

He snapped his phone shut and stared out at the horizon where two huge cruise ships—floating hotels—were streaming toward the Bahamas. It could be coincidence, he told himself. There was nothing to *prove* any of the deaths were murder, but still… What were the odds of two of Wyatt's children dying in the same week?

Could be that someone in Miami went to Boston—or hired someone to go there—to get rid of children who could possibly save Wyatt. The most obvious suspects would be his children. Possibly Nathan Cassidy. Tobias Pennington was another suspect.

He recalled the conversation after dinner about developing new drugs. Could a rival want him dead for some reason? It seemed unlikely, but stranger things had happened.

He could ask Wyatt, but that would mean getting him alone. It might also upset him and make him suspicious needlessly. This was his father's case, he reminded himself. All he was supposed to do was deliver Madison, which he'd done.

He opened his phone again and punched speed dial to reach his father. As usual, Mike was still in the office. No doubt he'd ordered a pastrami sandwich from the Bayside Bistro and had eaten it at his desk. Paul explained what he'd learned from O'Malley.

"Mmm-hmm," his father grunted. "I'm not liking this. Not one damn bit."

Paul had known he wouldn't. Mike had a cop's view of coincidences. "Do you know who will inherit Wyatt's money?"

"I have no idea," his father replied. "I assume his children, but a chunk of it is going into the foundation Holbrook is setting up. I can tell you one thing. Holbrook has a small firm as far as drug companies go. Most are megacompanies that are publicly held and traded, of course, on the stock exchange. Wyatt's had offers, but he refuses to sell his company."

His father said something else but laughter like a donkey braying came from behind him. He turned and saw Nathan howling at something someone had said. What a fun guy.

"Would you have any objections to me asking Wyatt about his will or trust or whatever?"

"Well, I hate to alarm him needlessly. I mean, we don't really know anything for sure, do we? Why don't you wait and see if you can find out more?"

It wasn't like his father not to immediately jump in, but maybe this account was too important for him to make waves. "I might be able to get him aside and casually ask him. I'm out at his place right now. I was invited for a barbecue."

"Really?" Was it Paul's imagination or did his father sound a little testy?

"Yeah. Madison wanted me to come with her. She's a little nervous around the Holbrooks."

"She's not thinking of backing out, is she?"

"No. She's already taken the preliminary tests."

"Okay. If you think you can ask Wyatt without making the poor guy wonder if his children want him dead, do it. You might also ask about his company or anything they're working on that would make someone want to kill him."

Paul thanked his father and walked back to the terrace where Nathan and Savannah had joined the group. "Sorry, I had to take that call," he told everyone with what he hoped was a sincere smile.

"Official police business?" Nathan asked.

That's a lawyer for you, Paul thought. "I'm still on leave."

"We were just telling everyone how great the new restaurant The Bungalow is," Savannah said, lowering her lashes and leaning toward him slightly so he couldn't miss her impressive cleavage.

Through clenched teeth, Nathan asked him, "Have you tried it?"

Paul shook his head and his gaze strayed to Madison. Savannah in her low-cut black gown and vibrant red hair might be drop-dead gorgeous to most men. But Madison was prettier in her own way and classy. That's what bothered him about Savannah, he decided. Coming from so much money, she should exude class, not flash. There was something in her manner, the way she kept looking at her father and trying to get attention by flirting, that told him the woman was insecure.

He listened to Nathan talk. What the jerk lacked in intelligence he compensated for with enough bullshit to bury Miami. What did Savannah see in him?

The French doors from the house just behind the terrace swung open. Tobias Pennington rushed out. The little weasel was puffing and red in the face. He was fanning himself with a manila file folder.

"I hate to interrupt," Pennington told Wyatt, "but this is important."

"That's all right. We're finished with dinner. I'm a bit tired. I was just about to excuse myself to go to bed," Wyatt said. "I'll talk to you in my study."

"Are you feeling all right?" Garrison asked.

"I'm fine. I was up early. That's all."

"You're sure?" Savannah asked with a concerned expression on her face. She touched her father's arm and he smiled at her.

"Positive. Don't you worry about me."

"We've gotta run, too," Savannah said as she tugged Nathan's arm and turned to leave. "We're meeting friends at a club."

Madison stood. "Thanks for dinner. It was great."

Paul opened his mouth to add his thanks, but Garrison spoke up and said he was leaving, too. Paul shook Wyatt's hand, thanked him and headed toward the guesthouse with Madison.

"Alone at last," he whispered.

"Alone. You want to be alone with me. Why, you naughty man."

Paul laughed and it felt great. Not only was Madison adorable and sexy, she had a quirky sense of humor. He walked her down the path toward the guesthouse. As soon as they rounded a bend and were out of sight, Paul pulled her into his arms. He planted a tantalizing kiss on the hollow of her neck. "I've been dying to do that all night."

"I've been waiting all night for you to kiss me. Don't stop now."

CHAPTER TWENTY-TWO

What part of the country has the most dogs?

PAUL OPENED the door to the guesthouse with Madison's key.
Aspen was waiting right at the door, tail wagging.

"Do you need to go out, boy?" she asked, then turned to Paul.
"I think I should take him for a walk."

"Not alone. I'm coming with you."

Madison couldn't believe how protective Paul was. She'd
thought a lot about what he'd said last night. She really didn't
think she was in any danger, but he had made her promise to
keep her doors locked and carry the can of pepper spray he'd
given her in her purse.

"What part of the country has the most dogs?" Paul asked
as they headed toward the path along the beach.

"What would be your guess?" She unhooked Aspen's leash
and let him wander off the path to do his business. From the
fob attached to his lead, she pulled out a plastic bag to pick up
after the dog.

"I'm thinking the West Coast. Almost everyone in California seems to have a dog or two. It's a big state with a lot of
people."

"Well, you'd be wrong. New England has the most dogs.
Surprisingly, there are a great many in New York City. Many
more than you'd think, considering there are so many high-
rises, which makes having a dog difficult."

The bracing scent of the sea filled the moist warm air, and with it came the heady scent of the gardenias along the path. A full-throated bullfrog that hung out around the koi pond near the main house croaked. Clouds sailed like schooners across the moonlit sky.

"How do you arrive at answers to questions like that? You must do research all day long and have to update, too."

Madison couldn't help smiling at him. Paul seemed genuinely interested in all aspects of her life. Aiden had asked very few questions. He'd mostly talked about himself. It should have been a clue, she thought, but she'd been so upset over the loss of her father that she had rushed into a marriage doomed to failure.

"We consult a lot of databases online. If we need to, we can independently verify the info. In this case, dog licenses tell us the answer."

"But aren't there a lot of dogs without licenses?"

"Not really. Most people take their dogs for a rabies shot. Vets forward the info to the city." Madison noticed Aspen was sniffing the garland of seaweed being pushed ashore by the waves.

"I see," Paul said. "Other facts must be more difficult to compile."

"You bet. If it's even a little iffy, we—"

"Paul, Madison!"

They turned and saw Wyatt striding toward them. "I need to talk to you. Could we go into the guesthouse?"

"Sure." Madison snapped Aspen's leash onto his collar. She would have to walk him again later. "Is something wrong?"

"I'm not certain," he said.

Madison caught Paul's eye and he shrugged as if to say, *Weird.*

They went inside the guesthouse. Paul and Madison sat on the sofa while Wyatt took the chair nearby. Aspen settled at her feet.

"What was the name of your friend who was murdered?" Wyatt asked.

Madison had the instant sensation that something was terribly wrong. "Erin Wycoff. Why?"

"Do you recall her parents' names?"

"Of course—we were best friends since the cradle. Tony and Susie. I mean, Anthony and Susan Wycoff."

Wyatt's eyes were sharp and assessing. "Tobias found their names in the files my security people are going through. The actual file itself is missing. Tobias found part of her record misfiled in another patient's folder, but it appears that she was one of the children conceived through my donation."

Paul's gaze shifted to Madison. She responded with an angry rush of words. "That's impossible! Erin was my best friend. She would have told me."

"What if she didn't know?" Paul asked.

"I don't believe it," Madison replied, but the catch in her voice betrayed her doubts. "Susie was such an open mother. She had us call her by her first name. She'd answer any question we asked. I can't imagine her not telling Erin something this important."

"I don't think it matters," Paul said. "What's—"

"Of course it matters," Madison insisted. "Don't you see?" She paused and turned to Wyatt. "New Horizons was a shady operation. No telling whose sperm they really used on women. I know I wasn't conceived by insemination and I'm positive Erin wasn't, either. You may be wasting your time trying to track children down here. You should concentrate on the Boston area, where the clinics were honest and kept better records."

Wyatt's brows knit together in an incredulous expression, as if he couldn't believe she hadn't accepted that she was one of his offspring.

In the long silence that followed her outburst, the only sound in the room was the lazy swish of the ceiling fan above them.

She reached down to stroke Aspen's silky head. Finally, Paul spoke in a low tone meant to calm Madison.

"All I'm saying is what should concern us is the children being on record as related to Wyatt are dead." He waited a few beats before adding, "Possibly murdered."

Wyatt vaulted to his feet. "What do you mean? Weren't the other deaths accidental?"

Paul motioned for him to sit down and the older man slowly sank into his chair. "I spoke with a detective in Boston. Apparently there is some indication—although nothing has been proved—that those deaths may not have been accidents."

Madison listened intently while Paul explained what he had learned during the telephone conversation after dinner. She assumed he'd meant to discuss it with her but found it strange that he hadn't. Certainly there had been enough time while they were walking Aspen. She decided her fact-based theory on coincidence was so at odds with his cop take on them that he might not have told her until he had more evidence.

"My God," Wyatt responded when Paul concluded. All the color had drained from the older man's face. Madison could see Garrison was right. Wyatt was in poor health and did his best to hide it.

"There's more," Paul said.

His tone of voice sent a tidal wave of apprehension through her. Now what?

"Last night a man, Keith Brooks Smith, was killed with a lethal dose of succinylcholine."

Madison didn't pipe up with her usual trivia response. She was certain Wyatt knew what this drug was typically used for.

"You two probably know the drug disappears rapidly and leaves no trace for a coroner to find."

Madison hadn't known that. She made a mental note to see what TotalTrivia had on the drug.

"If a nosy neighbor hadn't phoned the police, we wouldn't have discovered it was a homicide."

Madison asked, "What does this have to do with—"

Paul directed his answer to Wyatt. "Smith was next on the list to be contacted if Madison can't donate."

Madison gasped. "You're kidding."

"No, I'm not. Now what do you say about the coincidence rate?"

Madison shrugged. This was beginning to spook her. Erin. Identity theft. Luis Estevez. The need to find a new place to live. Her mother. Now that she thought about it, this was the longest stretch she'd had without hearing from her mother. An image of a sailboat foundering on a coral reef filled the screen in her mind. *Please, God. Let her be safe.*

"This is extremely disturbing." Wyatt's voice was like an echo in an empty tomb.

"Is there a way to recheck any of those Boston-area cases?" Madison asked.

Paul shrugged. "It's doubtful. I just don't like the fact that people who could help Wyatt are dead. Two of them died in the same week."

Madison refused to protest again that she wasn't related to Wyatt. The man looked as if he'd stepped off the curb and had narrowly missed being mowed down by a bus. Time would support what she said. DNA tests would reveal the truth.

Paul leaned forward, his elbows on his knees as he asked Wyatt, "Who knew or would have had access to the New Horizons files?"

Wyatt almost flinched as he realized the implications of Paul's question. After a pause that lasted much longer than it should have for him to formulate a response, he said, "Tobias, the staff at Holbrook Pharmaceuticals, my attorney, your father and his staff. You."

"What about the janitorial crew?" Paul asked. "Are the

security offices locked? I know my father has an elaborate alarm system and sophisticated locks. It would have been difficult for anyone to remove the file on Erin Wycoff while those boxes were at my father's office."

Why had someone removed that file? wondered Madison. A sharp splinter of doubt pierced her like the prick of a sharp needle. Was it possible Erin knew and hadn't told her? Her heart said no. But her more rational intellectual side thought, *Maybe*. After all, there had been a lot that she hadn't known about her best friend.

"The executive offices are secure but not state-of-the-art," replied Wyatt. "We don't keep any top-secret information there, like drug formulas or other sensitive material. Your father updated our system. We have all our vital information stored elsewhere."

"How would someone have obtained the names of the people in Boston?" Madison wanted to know.

"That wouldn't have been difficult," Wyatt said. "They were listed at DonorSiblingRegistry.com."

"What about your estate?" There was an edge to Paul's voice.

A smile spread across Wyatt's face for the first time since he'd come to tell them about Erin. "Forget about Garrison and Savannah. They have no reason to want me dead. They won't get a dime from my estate. You see, their mother was immensely wealthy in her own right. Before she died, she set up trusts for both of them. They have plenty of money. Plus, they know I intend to leave what I do have to the foundation I'm setting up."

"What about business competitors?" Paul asked.

"I can understand why you'd ask—being a detective—but let me explain a little about my company." He looked at Madison to make sure she was paying attention. It seemed as if he lost no opportunity, even at a time like this, to tell her about his business. She couldn't help feeling flattered. "I'm a small operation that's family-owned, not a big corporation like most pharmaceutical companies. I have had one big hit and a couple of minor discoveries that are on the market and making money."

Madison couldn't help noticing the trace of pride in his voice. Why not? He'd worked a lifetime and had a lot to show for it.

"The big guys have drugs on the market generating billions of dollars annually. Trouble is many of the patents on so-called 'blockbuster' drugs are expiring and they're going generic."

"Profits will go way down," Paul said.

"Exactly. For example, the world's bestselling drug will go generic in 2010. That's a nanosecond in pharmaceuticals where it takes years and billions to develop a drug. The megacompanies have hit the skids. They've relied on blockbusters for so long that their profits are going to nosedive."

Madison thought there might be a hint of satisfaction in his voice. "Wall Street will have conniptions."

"My very point," Wyatt said with a nod. "When profits go down, the price of your stock goes down. The big guys are scrambling and—"

"They must have some drugs in the pipeline," Madison interrupted. Aspen stirred, then rested his head on her foot.

"You'd be surprised. They've promoted the hell out of their products. How many TV ads have you seen for a drug? They've sacrificed research on the altar of marketing."

"True of many industries," Paul added. "Marketing is the tail that wags the dog."

Wyatt laughed. "I've never heard it put that way but you're right."

Madison realized that though she'd seen Wyatt smile many times, he rarely laughed. His smile was part of his public persona, she decided. He wasn't really that happy. Proud of his accomplishments, but not truly happy.

Why? she wondered. He had two accomplished children who adored him and a successful career. Did he miss his wife? That could be it, she decided. Her own mother had begun acting different after the death of Madison's father.

Maybe he was just afraid he would die before he could get his foundation up and running. It might have nothing to do with his wife or children.

"So, when I die, my company will be gobbled up by one of the giants. The money from the sale is slated to go into my foundation."

"Wouldn't Garrison be interested in running it?" she asked.

"I wish." Wyatt shook his head. "He shares a few facilities with me but his lab is very different. You know how he is about discoveries coming from the sea."

"Passionate," she said.

"Obsessive, according to his sister," Wyatt responded. "The point is both my children have their own money, their own interests. My company will be sold to one of the giants. The conglomerates have time on their side. They've made so much money and are recycling drugs that are altered just enough to be considered new. They can wait me out. These big companies are greedy and the public naive, but I can't see them hiring a hit man to kill me."

Wyatt seemed resigned that his business would be sold to men who cared less about science and helping people than profits. Madison wondered if that was how he really felt. She was having a hard time letting go of TotalTrivia. Selling to a sleaze like Estevez bothered her. Surely Wyatt must be disappointed that neither of his children would take over his business.

"What about employees?" Paul wanted to know. "Would any of them profit from your death?"

Wyatt immediately shook his head. "I pay them well. Everyone from the executives to the cleaning crew gets a bonus at Christmas. I seriously doubt a public company will do the same. They'll probably cut jobs to max profits."

Paul asked, "How many people know you're looking for your donor-conceived children?"

"The whole world could find out. I registered on several Web sites when I found out I would need a relative for a transplant."

"I think we need to take some precautions." Paul's eyes darkened as he held her gaze. "I don't want Madison to be next."

"Mary, mother of God," muttered Wyatt.

"I don't think I'm…" Her voice trailed off. "You're starting to scare me."

A slow smile crept across his handsome face. "Good. It's about time."

CHAPTER TWENTY-THREE

Which is better: a dog's sense of smell or its hearing?

SLIVERS OF MOONLIGHT FOUND their way through the slats of the plantation shutters and cast a pattern across the limestone floor. Madison stared at them, unable to fall asleep. Paul didn't have the same problem. He was stretched out beside her, sound asleep, snuggled close, his comforting arm curled across her lower back. The pressure of his arm was so male, so protective.

Despite the possibility her life was in danger and the fact that her best friend was dead, her finances were a wreck and her mother still hadn't called, Madison felt strangely calm. Wyatt had insisted on paying for a security guard to patrol the grounds around the guesthouse in the evening. He'd even called Paul's father to insist a man be sent out within the hour.

She doubted such extreme and expensive measures were necessary, but Wyatt and Paul had insisted. Paul was still on leave; he would take her to work and pick her up. He was operating on the theory that the killer wouldn't do anything violent. He'd try to stage an accident. Giving the fewest number of people access to her would be her best protection.

If she didn't like Paul so much, she wouldn't put up with all the restrictions because she wasn't convinced she was in danger. But she did like him. *Admit it,* she thought. *You're falling in love with him. Just take it slow. Don't have the same lapse of judgment you had with Aiden.*

After Wyatt had left they'd gone to bed and had taken their time making love. He seemed to know just where to touch her, how to touch her. He asked her what she liked. Aiden had never once said much more than "Are you ready?"

She turned so she could see Paul's dark head against the white pillow. She was conscious of where his warm flesh touched hers. A shiver of excitement rippled through her. How could she have wasted so much time on Aiden? She brushed a gentle kiss against Paul's stubbled cheek, careful not to wake him.

Madison's throat felt as if she'd swallowed sand. She needed a drink of water. Gingerly, an inch at a time, she lifted Paul's arm and slowly slid out from under it. She rose from the bed, taking care not to step on Aspen. Ever alert, the dog awoke, scrambled upright and followed her.

She stopped to grab her robe off the chair where she'd tossed it earlier. Paul liked to sleep in the buff. Another contrast with Aiden, who preferred silk pajama bottoms and insisted she wear Victoria's Secret nightgowns. She wouldn't need them now. But she shouldn't prance around naked with a security guard just outside.

Halfway across the great room, going toward the kitchen, Madison remembered she hadn't checked her cell phone. It had been off all evening because she didn't want to be interrupted at dinner. She found her purse on the table by the sofa. The phone was in the side pocket. She took it out and saw that she had several messages.

What if she'd missed her mother's call? She might sail off, just leaving a message, and Madison wouldn't have the opportunity to ask her why her name was on New Horizons' records. She checked voice mail. Three calls were from Rob; he'd wanted to take her to dinner.

He must be lonely and missing Erin. They'd split some time ago, but evidently, he was grieving. Who could blame him?

Even though Rob and Erin had no longer been together, he had loved her.

"I miss you, Erin," Madison whispered into the darkness. Aspen swished his tail in response. She bent down to his ear. "Good boy," she said softly.

Another message was from Dr. Miller. Evidently her test results were back. She'd call him in the morning. No doubt she would breeze through the preliminary tests. She expected to be eliminated later.

She wasn't sure what to tell Rob. If she had dinner with him, Paul would insist on coming and she hadn't even mentioned him to Rob. It would be awkward, but she didn't want to desert him when he was missing Erin as much as she was.

Erin. What Wyatt had told them came back to her with an unsettling jolt. Could Erin have known she was a donor-conceived child and not told Madison? Did anyone ever really know another person? They'd shared a past full of childhood memories that seemed to bond them, but Erin had always held back a little bit of herself from everyone, even Rob.

He was such a nice man, she thought, putting the cell phone back in her purse. He'd called to ask her to dinner about two weeks after Aiden walked out on her. She told him she wasn't up to going out even with a friend. What a mess she'd been.

Could she have really been that stupid? She'd let the divorce throw her whole life off-kilter. She wandered into the kitchen without turning on the lights. Enough moonlight flowed through the windows to guide her. She took a glass from the cabinet, filled it with water and drank. She set it down on the counter. An odd sensation sent a shiver prickling through her. She tensed and another jolt of uneasiness hit her. Had she heard a low rumble?

"Is that you, boy?" she whispered to Aspen.

There was enough light in the room to see Aspen was growling, a low rasp from deep in his throat and his hackles shot straight up. She stroked his ears. Her pulse skipped a beat, then accelerated. "What is it, boy?"

Dogs had a much better sense of smell than humans and they could detect sounds humans couldn't. "What do you hear, Aspen? What do you smell?"

He growled another warning, louder this time. Nerves fluttered in her chest. Why was she so jumpy? Must be all Paul's talk about the murder—and knowing Erin's murder could also be part of this mess. "Shh! You're freaking me out," she whispered to the dog.

Aspen's nose was pointed toward the French doors that opened from the living room onto the pool area. Maybe the guard was making a pass by the guesthouse and Aspen smelled him. After all, smell was a dog's best sense, hundreds of times better than man's. She tiptoed toward the doors, Aspen at her side, still growling.

Evidently, the lights around the house were on a timer. They were off. The only light came from a full moon overhead. The bushes and the palms created patterns of darkness and light.

One large shadow on the far side of the pool seemed to shift. Was it a person or merely a shadow? A surge of something too intense to be merely nerves shot through her. She was so on edge that she wasn't sure what was real or what she was imagining.

The form shifted again like a ghost and crept closer to the guesthouse. It wasn't her imagination. Someone was out there!

A man emerged from the shadows. He was moving stealthily, obviously trying not to make noise. *Oh my God!* How had he slipped by the security guard? Surely the guard had gotten here by now. Wyatt had made the call several hours ago.

Raw panic slicked her skin like snake oil the instant she realized he had a weapon in his hand. *Paul's here,* her brain reminded Madison. *He has a gun.* She was pivoting when the man tiptoed closer. Garrison Holbrook. The thing in his hand

was an envelope, not a weapon. Sheesh! Talk about being a
nutcase.

She cracked the door and softly called, "Garrison, what are
you doing?"

"I didn't think you'd be up." He waved the envelope at her.
There wasn't the faintest trace of emotion in his voice, yet a
chill tiptoed up her spine. Something *was* wrong. "I was leaving
you a note to call me."

Aspen was still growling. "Hush," she told the dog as she
stepped outside and closed the door behind her so Paul wouldn't
be awakened. "It's okay, boy."

She turned to Garrison; even at this late hour, he looked as
if he'd stepped off a page of *GQ*. She could only imagine what
she looked like after her night with Paul. "What's so important?" she asked.

He hesitated, gazing at her with a level, reflective look. The
air crackled with tension. Or was she imagining it?

"Your blood tests came back," Garrison said in a neutral
voice, but Madison picked up a serious undertone. He paused
for a moment before adding, "I hate to have to tell you this,
but…"

"Tell me what?" She knew by his tone that this couldn't be
good news.

"Madison, I'm afraid it looks like you have a disease called
Chagas."

"An illness caused by a single-cell parasite that feeds on
heart and gastrointestinal tissues. A leading cause of heart
failure in Central and South America." The rote description
came from her mouth as the meaning of his words registered.
"How could I have it? Chagas happens in poor rural areas
where bugs can easily get into homes. The lab must have made
a mistake."

"I wish that were true, but I doubt it. Dr. Miller uses a reputable lab."

Something in his gaze unnerved her. "How could I have caught Chagas?"

"Have you had a blood transfusion?"

"No. Did I catch it from somebody? Miami is loaded with people from—"

"It's a vector-borne illness."

"Transmitted by insects. You can't catch it from an infected person."

"The insect that carries the parasite is moving northward thanks to our friend global warming. All blood banks now test for it. As you might guess, they find quite a few cases in Miami and L.A., but those people contracted it in Central or South America and brought it here. Cases like yours are rare. The doctor said most people who contracted Chagas here were campers or hunters who slept outdoors."

"I went camping in the Everglades twice last year. Maybe I caught it then." She stared up at him, trying to make sense of this. "There must be a drug for this if it's so prevalent south of the border."

Garrison's lips parted in a silent, mirthless laugh. "Drug companies in America expect annual sales of a drug to be over one hundred million or it isn't worth developing. These are poor countries. They can't afford the treatment costs."

"But there is a treatment?" Her voice sounded pathetic even to her own ears.

"What's going on?" Paul was standing at the door, wearing nothing but a towel. If Garrison was surprised to see Paul, his face didn't show it.

"Let's go inside," suggested Madison.

Inside, Madison flicked on the lights, Paul went into the bedroom and put on his pants. They settled on the sofa with Aspen at their feet while Garrison sat in the same chair his father had occupied earlier. It took a few minutes for Garrison to explain to Paul what Chagas was. Madison couldn't recall reading anything about it in the papers or hearing about it on television. It wasn't surprising that Paul had never heard of the fatal disease. Her trivia-filled brain had dredged up the definition, but she'd known little else.

Of all the godforsaken luck, Madison thought. *I have a disease that could kill me.* It made everything else going wrong in her life seem less troubling. Surely there was something she could do. She tried to think where she could go for a consultation. She didn't have health insurance. TotalTrivia had chosen not to offer it. Since it was so expensive and she was young, Madison hadn't thought she needed insurance. It wasn't a smart decision, but it was too late now.

"Wait a minute," Paul said to Garrison. "How did you get Madison's test results? I thought HIPA restricted access to info like this."

A grim smile formed on Garrison's lips. "It does. I went to the hospital after dinner to see if Dr. Miller had your results. I knew he was working late. He was rushing out of his office just as I arrived. His son attends Brown and he was in a serious car crash. Dr. Miller is flying there, not knowing if his son will make it."

"Oh, my. How awful. He's such a nice man." Madison had really liked the doctor. He seemed so much more caring than many of the doctors who'd treated her father. "There was a message from him earlier in the evening asking me to call his office tomorrow."

"He was going to tell you then. When he left me standing near his desk, I confess I couldn't resist the urge to look at your file," Garrison admitted. "He'd told me the results were back. He didn't say anything but there was something in his voice that made me curious."

"I would have looked, too," Madison assured him. There was nothing she wouldn't have done to save her father. How could she expect Garrison to be any different?

"What's the treatment?" Paul asked.

"I used the computer at the nurse's station to access the National Health Service database. People being treated now have had the disease for ten, twenty years. It's a silent killer. The microscopic parasite feeds on heart and intestinal tissues. In your case, I assume it's been discovered early or it would have shown up before now. The only place to go is Olive View–UCLA Medical Center."

"Los Angeles? Nothing here in Miami or the East Coast?" asked Paul.

Garrison shook his head. "Nothing. Olive View–UCLA is the only Chagas treatment center in the country."

"What kind of treatment are you talking about?" Paul asked.

Garrison hesitated. "I don't know what they'll do with Madison. The databases referred to the treatment of patients who've had Chagas for years."

"What aren't you telling me?" she asked.

"Look, I'm not an expert. This isn't my field. From what I understand, there are two drugs known to be effective against the disease. Neither has FDA approval. Many patients can't tolerate powerful drugs with side effects seen most often with chemotherapy."

Stunned, she gaped at him for a second, incapable of speaking. Dread permeated her body, settled into her bones. What was she going to do?

"Aw, hell." Paul put his arm around her and pulled her closer.

Madison's thoughts roiled. Going bald. No money for treatment. Traveling all the way across the country. Funding what must be expensive drugs. Drawing a shuddering breath, she grasped the seriousness of the situation.

"Now, again," Garrison said, responding to what had to be an anguished expression on her face. "This is not my field. I don't know what they do with a case caught in the early stages." He pulled an index card out of his pocket. "Here's the number of the hospital in L.A. Call them tomorrow and make an appointment. They're the experts."

"Thanks." Her voice sounded like a cowering animal's.

Garrison rose and shook each leg for a millisecond to release the crease in his trousers. "I have a trial to run tomorrow. I'd better go."

His father, Madison suddenly thought. What would this do to Wyatt? Tonight she'd seen a side of him that few people saw. He was discouraged and slowly failing. "What about your father? I won't be able to—"

"You won't be able to help him. Not even if you're a perfect match. Chagas, like HIV, automatically eliminates you from consideration." He patted her shoulder. "But having the test was a godsend. Now you know you have an illness and can deal with it."

"I should go to a hotel. I can't—"

"Don't move." He dropped down on his haunches to look directly into her eyes. "You may be his child. Even if we aren't related, my father's not the kind of person to throw someone out who needs help and neither am I." He rose, again twitching to straighten his pants. "You have to call first thing tomorrow and make an appointment. Get the facts, know what your options are. I'll do anything I can to help."

"He's right," Paul said. "We're calling tomorrow at noon. That's nine in L.A. The offices should be open."

Madison heard herself thank Garrison and tell him goodnight, but all she could think about was money. Where would she get the money to fight this? Even if her mother resurfaced, Madison knew she didn't have much money. She'd put what little she had into the blasted sailboat her new husband had wanted.

"I don't have any insurance," she heard a small voice say.

On the floor at her feet, Aspen had his head on his paws, a mournful expression in his eyes. The animal obviously sensed the distress in her voice. She was on emotional overload, she decided. *Stay calm. There's nothing to be gained by panicking.*

Paul put his hand on her shoulder with a gentle, almost tentative touch. The heartrending tenderness in his expression surprised her. "I've got money saved. It's yours."

His unexpected offer affected her deeply. Tears brimmed in her eyes and she blinked them back, a treacherous lump in her throat. "I can't let you do that."

"Why not?"

"You don't know me well enough to waste your hard-earned money on me." She took a deep breath to still the quaver in her voice.

"I know you well enough to know you'd do anything to save an abused animal. I know you well enough to not be able to stop thinking about you. I know you well enough to know I love you. I'm not going to let you die."

She walked into his arms, trembling with happiness. It was a highly charged embrace, but it wasn't sexual. It was like a bear hug you shared after escaping a car crash. He pulled back and gazed down at her. He had the best eyes, eyes that saw right through to her soul. But she couldn't quite make herself say she loved him, too.

CHAPTER TWENTY-FOUR

PAUL LOOKED OUT the kitchen window. The misty half-light of early dawn was giving way to sunrise. He hadn't been able to sleep after Garrison had dropped the bombshell about a disease Paul never knew existed.

Somehow he'd managed to get Madison to sleep by holding her in his arms. When he realized she was asleep, Paul slipped out of bed, went out to his car and brought in his laptop. He didn't know what in hell he'd hoped to find. The Internet search verified everything Garrison had told them. Not that Paul thought the guy was lying. Why would he?

Garrison was self-absorbed. It showed in everything from the way he dressed—never standing for a wrinkle in his trousers—to the way he droned on and on about "discoveries in the sea." Boring, if you asked Paul. But Garrison wasn't a bad guy, not really. He'd cared enough to come all the way out here to deliver the news to Madison and have a referral ready for her to use.

It just seemed strange—downright weird—that so much could happen to one woman. All at once.

Something wet touched his hand. Paul jerked it away and stared down at Aspen's nose. The retriever had been sleeping next to Madison's bed. The dog was incredibly loyal, considering Madison hadn't had him very long. Maybe dogs sensed things in people.

"Do you need to go out, boy?" he asked, his voice low. It was barely dawn, and it would be hours before the clinic in L.A.

opened and they could speak with someone. No need to wake Madison and let her worry.

Paul found the leash on a table near the sofa and attached it to Aspen's collar. He tiptoed out of the bungalow. The salty scent of the sea filled the balmy air. With it came a light breeze that rustled the palm trees.

When he arrived at the path where he'd stood last night with Madison before Wyatt found them, Paul let the dog off the leash. Aspen scampered away but didn't go too far before lifting his leg on a bush. Paul watched, prepared to pick up after the dog with one of the blue bags in a small canister attached to the leash, but his mind was on Madison.

Had he actually told her he loved her? He wasn't usually so impulsive. The words were out of his mouth before he could stop them. It wasn't that he didn't mean them…exactly, but the smart move would have been to tell her how much he cared about her without using the "L" word.

Madison sure as hell hadn't told him she loved him. Maybe she was still in love with that jerk-off of an ex-husband. Or maybe the divorce made her gun-shy. It had been his experience that divorced women had baggage. They were often bitter and felt betrayed. This made new relationships difficult. Paul usually avoided divorced women for this reason.

But Madison had gotten to him—big-time.

He noticed Aspen had deposited a turd the size of Texas on the grass. Paul used a bag from the fob attached to the leash to pick it up. He stood, watching the water while Aspen sniffed around. Garlands of seaweed were being pushed onto the white beach by waves that rolled across the sand.

"Paul, what are you doing here?"

He flinched. How had he gotten the drop on him? Paul usually sensed people before he saw them. It was one of the things that made him a good detective. More than just a little surprised, he turned toward the familiar voice.

"Same question, right back at you," he said to his father.

Mike studied him with that intense cold gaze that seemed to bore right through you. "Wyatt insisted on immediate protection for Madison Connelly. I didn't have anyone so I came out myself. If I'd known you were still here, I could have assigned you the shift."

Paul wasn't about to discuss his relationship with Madison with his father. Hell, what relationship? He wasn't sure where he stood with Madison. "Garrison Holbrook got by you in the middle of the night."

"No, he didn't. I gave him permission to put a note on the guesthouse door."

"Did he tell you what was in the note?"

"No. I assumed it was important. Why else would he drive out here so late at night?"

Paul intended to explain the whole situation to his father and get his take on things. "I assume Wyatt told you Erin Wycoff was one of his children."

Mike nodded. "I don't like it. Too many of these donor-offspring are turning up dead." He paused a second as if he expected Paul to say something, then continued. "He said the file was missing from the box, but Pennington's people found part of her records misfiled. That's why her name wasn't on my master list. We just recorded the names on the file tabs. We didn't have a chance to go through—"

"Just a minute," Paul said. "Let me get rid of this." Aspen at his heels, he walked over to the wicker trash can beside the trail and dropped in the dog's poop bag. He returned to his father's side, saying, "Could anyone have gotten into those files while they were in your office?"

"It's possible. Not likely, but possible. I didn't take any special security measures because I never thought anyone would take them."

It was lighter now and Paul could see another high-rise

condo that was being built across the water. For every one of them, two nightclubs and three trailer parks sprang up. "I'm convinced someone does not want Wyatt to have that transplant. I doubt it's either of his kids. I asked last night and he says they don't stand to benefit from his death. They already have hefty trust funds. We ruled out business competitors. Drug companies are conglomerates and aren't likely to hire hit men."

"When you get right down to it, the killer could just murder Wyatt. It would be a lot less trouble than eliminating so many other people."

"You're right. It doesn't make sense. We're missing something."

"Could be a revenge thing," his father said, seeming to ponder the idea for a moment. "You don't make the kind of money the Holbrooks have without pissing off a few people."

"Is Wyatt known as an asshole?"

Mike shook his head. "His employees seem to love him. Many have been with him for years. But there could be one nutcase out there who wants to see Holbrook suffer a slow, painful death."

"That's why he hasn't killed him."

"Sure. It would take a lunatic to kill this many people so elaborately. It would take time and money—"

"And brains."

"True," Mike said, "which would fit with the stats on serial killers. Most are above average in intelligence. Keep working on it. I've got to head to the gate. An agent's coming to relieve me."

"There's one more thing. We spoke with Garrison last night when he came to put the note on the door." Paul went on to explain that Madison had Chagas. His father hadn't heard of the disease, either.

Mike raked his fingers through his hair. "Son of a bitch! How did she get it?"

"It's a single-cell parasite that's transmitted by a winged insect called a conenose, or a kissing bug because it usually feeds at night. That's how the parasite gets into the bloodstream." He gave his father the other information Garrison had told them. Paul had gone online and learned a few more facts.

"This is way too much to happen to one person all at once."

"Exactly what I think. It made me wonder if this isn't computer-linked somehow."

"What do you mean?"

Paul shrugged. "Check with Kirk, your computer guy. The ID theft could have been done with a computer, right? Couldn't her test results have been altered with a computer?"

"I guess so. That would mean someone close to the family did it. How else would they know Madison had the test?"

"I think it was fairly well-known around the company. Pennington knew. Nathan Cassidy, Savannah's boyfriend, must have known. Quite a few people actually."

"Why? What would be the motive?"

Paul shook his head. He'd been up all night asking himself that. "I wonder if it isn't a way to get her out of town and kill her. You see, the only treatment center is in L.A."

"You're kidding."

"Using a computer, any idiot could check on the Internet and find a rare disease and that there's only one place to go for treatment."

"I don't know what to tell you."

"I have an idea," Paul said as he reached down to pet Aspen. "You run a lot of drug tests for companies, don't you?"

"Sure. Just about every business screens its employees for drugs. Why?"

"I'm thinking your lab will do you a favor and conduct another test on Madison. It must be a simple test if the Red Cross runs it on every blood donation they get. We'll have the results before noon and with luck, she won't have to go to L.A."

For a moment his father looked at him as if he couldn't believe Paul had come up with such a good idea. "I'll phone the lab as soon as I get to my office. I'll call you with the information."

"Thanks. I appreciate it."

His father turned to go. He stopped a few steps away, then came back and stood beside Paul. "You're not getting involved with this woman, are you?"

Aw, shit. His father never—absolutely never—asked him personal questions. So why now? He saw no point in lying. It had to be totally obvious. "You could say we're involved."

"Happened fast."

"True." He wasn't about to justify his actions or make excuses. A full minute passed. "That's how it was with your mother."

Paul didn't know what to say. His father never discussed his mother. Paul had learned—just minutes after he discovered his mother had left them—not to mention her name.

"What I'm saying," his father continued after an uncomfortably long pause, "is to take it slowly. Don't commit until you know her much better. Some women emotionally castrate you. Learn from my mistake."

Paul detected the faint echo of loneliness in his father's voice. He didn't know how to respond, but he knew his father was right. He had jumped in too quickly. He'd told Madison he loved her before he'd thought it through. He realized he did love her. It had happened very quickly. Still, he should have kept his mouth shut until he had a better sense of how she felt. Did she care about him at all? Or was he merely convenient?

He couldn't help but wonder if he allowed himself to really love her, would Madison leave him the way his mother had left his father?

MADISON LOOKED across the desk at Paul's father. The man was staring at her with an intensity that made her uncomfortable.

Mike Tanner was an older version of his son. He was still good-looking in that old Hollywood leading man way. Hair burnished with a touch of silver. Paul's father didn't have that middle-aged bulge around his waist that many men had. Inwardly, she smiled. Paul was a hunk now but he would age well.

And he loved her.

She still couldn't grasp why or how it had happened so suddenly. She didn't quite trust it. She hadn't been able to say she loved him because this was a leap she wasn't ready to take.

Honest to God, she did care about him. Every chance she had she made love to him. It was the best, most satisfying sex she'd ever experienced. But her response wasn't just physical. Her reaction went beyond sex into a part of her psyche she had never explored.

Until Paul said he loved her, Madison hadn't quite realized she'd lost herself. Her very being had been unraveling since Erin's murder. Sometimes there was so little left of the old Madison that she seemed to be living with a total stranger. What could she possibly offer Paul until she got her act together?

"I just received the lab report," Mike Tanner told them.

For a moment Madison's mind had drifted to Paul, but she had bigger problems than her love life. So much had hit her—one knockout punch after another—and now this life-threatening disease. She was suddenly glad she was sitting down. A strange weakness had invaded her limbs.

Paul had insisted she take another blood test at the lab his father used. It was eleven o'clock. In another hour she would call the clinic in L.A. and ask for an appointment.

"What does it say?" Paul asked.

"Madison doesn't have Chagas."

"Thank God," she muttered. Unexpectedly the weakness she'd experienced seconds earlier vanished. Anger coursed through her, hot and deep and astonishingly raw. "Who's doing this to me? Why?"

"Could it be Garrison? He brought the news," Paul said. Earlier he'd seemed to have ruled out Garrison, but apparently now he was having second thoughts.

"I don't think so," his father replied. "I had the lab call Dr. Miller's office. The report they had did indicate Chagas."

"Do you think the report Garrison saw was faulty or did someone tamper with it?" Paul asked.

"It's impossible to say. Drug tests are computerized. It eliminates human errors. There is no paper trail the way there once was. No one can say this was a rare mistake. They do happen. It would take a forensic computer expert months to see if and when the results were altered. The good news is Madison doesn't have to fly across the country for treatment."

"I think there's a real maniac out there who wants to get rid of Wyatt's donor-conceived children," said Paul. "There are too many coincidences in this case."

"I agree," Mike responded.

"Let's shake up the pot," Paul said. "Call Wyatt and let him know there was a mistake. Don't say we think the killer was involved. Just say the chances of Madison having Chagas made us retest her. Their lab made a mistake. I'm betting the killer will go ballistic."

"Wait a minute," Mike Tanner said. "What about Madison? Won't that put her in danger?"

Bitterness like nothing she'd ever experienced filled her. "I'll take my chances. I want to find out who's behind this."

"Don't worry," Paul said. "We'll arrange for your protection. Whenever I can't be with you, I'll make sure someone is or that you're somewhere safe, like your office."

Madison waited while Mike called Wyatt. Her mind was on Wyatt. He'd seemed depressed last night. What was this doing to him? For the first time that Madison could remember she wanted her mother. How long had it been since they'd spoken? She honestly didn't remember. But Madison was overdue for a call.

"Any word on the ID theft?" Paul asked his father. "Could that be a mistake?"

Mike's expression was anything but reassuring. "No, it's for real. Kirk's on it. Looks like they sold the ID info to a ring operating out of Atlanta. They've tried to open several credit card accounts in Madison's name, but the major financial reporting bureaus have a freeze on it."

"Should we let the police know about the tampering with my test results?" she asked.

"And tell them what?" Paul's father wanted to know. "That someone may have altered the records or that the lab itself may have made a mistake?"

Paul offered her a soothing smile. "The police have so many violent crimes to deal with that they aren't going to do anything with so little evidence."

Madison had scoffed at Paul's idea that the deaths of the donor-conceived children weren't coincidences. Then Erin's death had been linked. Now she knew with an eerie certainty her life was in danger.

CHAPTER TWENTY-FIVE

IT IS ALMOST IMPOSSIBLE to round up the wild horses that still inhabit the open range in the western states. Some creative— where would the world be without creativity?—person discovered they could be stampeded using helicopters. That isn't the creative part. Helicopters have been used to herd cattle for a long time.

When in a terrified frenzy caused by the hovering helicopter, horses cannot be herded, unlike cattle that can be herded by the aircraft into pens. The creative person decided to employ a Judas horse. This horse has been specifically trained to act like the lead stallion and run into the slaughter pen.

Once the traitorous horse is with the wild horses it directs them into the death corral, where they pile up on each other. Those that aren't crushed in the total, bloody melee are shot. Of course, the Judas horse dies, as well, trapped at the very bottom of the heap of dead and mortally injured horses.

In an operation of any magnitude, there will be collateral damage.

A lesson worth remembering, the killer reflected. Send in the Judas horse to confuse Madison and trick that nosy bastard Paul Tanner.

There would be losses. There would be death. What could be more satisfying?

MADISON INSISTED Paul take her to her office along with Aspen. She promised not to leave the building until Paul came to get them. She sat in her office and tried to deal with the hundreds of e-mail questions programmers had left for her. She was the final judge about which questions could be used.

Right now she was considering: What is the most popular first name for a man in the world? The programmer who researched the question had put Muhammad.

It was a good choice, she decided. The firstborn male in most Muslim families had that name. What was bothering her was the number-two name could be Juan or Jose. Not enough statistical information was available from South America to be sure, but what they knew from Mexico and more technologically-linked nations such as Costa Rica and Panama made her suspect they might get a different answer if they studied South America more closely.

With her background in statistics, Madison knew she didn't have to rely upon a report from every remote village in South America. She could take the information from the major cities and calculate from there. After all, eleven voters could walk out of a voting booth in New Hampshire and the television stations would project the winner based on a few numbers.

"Got a minute?"

Madison looked up from her screen, having decided to send this question back to the programmer and have him do an analysis of South America.

Aiden so rarely came into her office that she was surprised to see him. And annoyed. After all the time she'd missed between taking care of Erin's funeral and dealing with the identity theft, she was too busy to be interrupted.

"What's on your mind?" she asked.

"Have you given any more thought to Luis's offer?"

"No. I already told you. I don't like his reputation." She wondered about the chummy first-name basis her ex was on with the Cuban.

"He told us that he's really interested."

She didn't have to ask who "us" was. He meant Chloe, of course. Madison saw no reason to tell Aiden about Estevez's offer. "I'm concerned about his criminal connections. I—"

"Luis has never been arrested, even for speeding."

Obviously, the man's notorious reputation had come up or Aiden wouldn't know this arcane fact. "Haven't you asked yourself what that man wants with a small company like ours?"

Aiden tried his charming smile but it seemed smarmy to her now. Compared to Paul, this guy was a total jerk. How could she have wasted time on him?

"Look, if we don't do this, some other trivia site will and our business will hit the skids." Aiden tried his smile again, waiting for her response.

"Why don't you buy me out?" she suggested, as she'd done before. She couldn't believe they were having this discussion again.

"I—I don't have that much cash," he reluctantly admitted.

She wondered if Chloe had burned through all his money already. Well, it was his problem. He loved her. "I'd take less from you. We could work out terms. Then it would be your decision whether or not to get mixed up with this man."

Aiden stood up. "I'll talk to Chloe."

"You do that." She tried to go back to work but her mind wasn't on the business. She really did want to do something more meaningful, but what? She loved math and numbers. She always had, but without a degree she didn't have many options.

An idea hit her, seemingly from out of nowhere, but it must have been lurking in the dark recesses of her mind since she'd met Wyatt Holbrook. She went online and started to do some research to clarify her thoughts.

"Hey, there's, like, this total hunk here to see you. How cool is that?"

Madison looked up at Jade, then checked her watch. Nearly an hour had passed while she'd been researching. As usual, Jade had walked back to Madison's office when she could have used the interoffice phone to tell her she had a visitor. "Who is it?"

"Dr. Matthews."

"Rob's here, not working?" She'd forgotten about his messages on her cell phone and hadn't returned his calls. "Send him back."

Today Jade's hair had a bluish tinge. Madison watched her sashay her way through the cube farm toward the reception area. Why would a person change their hair so often? Wear such weird clothes—noticeable even in SoBe, where it was nearly impossible to appear too strange? The girl was smart but still searching for herself, Madison decided.

"There you are," Rob said as he approached.

Madison left her desk to give Rob a quick hug, saying, "I'm sorry I didn't call you back. So much has been going on."

Rob pulled her closer. "I was worried. That's why I canceled out my morning patients to come here."

Feeling guilty, Madison eased out of his embrace and returned to her chair. She motioned for Rob to sit where Aiden had. How could she have forgotten to return his calls?

"I'm sorry to cause you a problem. I had my phone off and when I picked up your messages it was the middle of the night."

"What were you doing up so late?"

When had she last spoken to Rob? So much had happened. He was such a kind person. Except for Paul, no one else would have missed her. Then she remembered—the day he'd discovered Bewley Allen's name and changed the info on Aspen's chip was the last time she'd seen him. She reached down to pet Aspen, whose head had popped up at the sound of voices.

She wasn't sure how much to tell Rob. Why not? What was happening to her? This was a friend. He'd called her just after Aiden walked out. He'd kept calling and bolstering her spirits through the following months. They'd met for dinner a few times, and he'd invited her to several interesting events. She didn't go because she refused to move on. Whiner that she'd been, Madison preferred to spend evenings alone or with Erin. She didn't want to be with a man, even a friend.

Had she been that pathetic? You bet. Well, those days were over.

"I'm living in Wyatt Holbrook's guesthouse. The Russerts came home early and I had to find a place to stay quickly. I—"

"You should have called me. There's plenty of room at my place." He nodded toward Aspen. "A yard for your dog, too."

He sounded hurt that she hadn't called him. To be honest, the thought had never crossed her mind. "Thanks, that's kind of you—"

"Kind?" Rob leaned forward and gazed at her with an expression filled with hurt. "Madison, I care about you. I'd help you in any way I could."

The way he said this made her a little uncomfortable. "I didn't want to impose, so when Wyatt offered—"

He sat back in the chair and regarded at her with a now unreadable expression. "I guess this means you agreed to be tested."

Rob had advised her against testing, fearing should she be a candidate that the liver operation was dangerous. "I've begun the test process."

"Hopefully you won't qualify."

"I'm sure I won't. Wyatt has some special problems. So he needs a close relative. I know I'm not related to him."

"Did you talk to your mother about that?"

"No. She still hasn't called."

Her telephone buzzed and she picked it up. "Pamela Nolan is returning your call."

Madison had forgotten she'd called her former roommate at MIT about Chloe. She wanted to talk to her, but not now, with Rob in her office. "Tell Pamela I'm in a meeting and I'll call her back."

Rob was looking at her in a way that made her even more uncomfortable.

"Did Erin ever mention being a donor-conceived child?"

Rob nodded. "She did. Erin was worried about not having all her genetic information should we have children. Why?"

Something inside Madison sank like a rock thrown into the bottom of a deep well. Her response was barely a whisper. "She never told me."

"When you went off to MIT, I think she felt… I don't know exactly. I guess *deserted* might describe her reaction. You had a new life that left her behind."

"I called her every week. She was taking classes at Miami City College. I thought she was happy."

"Erin was never much of a student. I think she took classes because she thought it was the thing to do. Her heart wasn't in it."

Madison knew Rob was correct. Erin's sole interest had been animals. She'd taken classes to be a vet tech but had dropped out for some reason. "Even if we did grow apart for a while, we were so close growing up. I would have thought—"

"Erin's parents didn't tell her until she was twenty-one."

Madison supposed that explained it. At that point Madison was still away at college. They talked regularly but she did remember feeling they were growing apart. By then, they only spoke when Madison called. Madison had been looking ahead to graduate school. Her life took an unexpected turn when her father was diagnosed with pancreatic cancer.

"Why are you asking about this?"

"Last night I learned Erin was one of Wyatt Holbrook's donor-conceived children."

Near silence followed this announcement, the only sound the muffled clack-clack of the computers out in the cube farm. "Good God! She never knew that. Amazing. That would have made you half sisters."

A surge of annoyance hit Madison. "Assuming I am one of his children. I'm not convinced."

Rob opened his mouth to argue, then seemed to think better of it.

"The police are wondering if Erin's relationship to Wyatt was the reason she was murdered."

"I don't get it."

"Another of his donor-conceived children was killed here the other night. Not long ago, two others died in the Boston area in the same week."

"Get out!" He stared at her for a moment. "You could be in danger. Sounds like there's a serial killer stalking these people."

She shrugged. "Maybe, or it could be a strange coincidence. The deaths in Boston weren't ruled homicides. I'm not concerned. Wyatt's arranged for security."

"You'll be safer if you take off for a while. No telling what that lunatic might do. I have a condo in Naples. You could go there. I'd come over on weekends."

She was more than a little stunned to realize she had two very protective men in her life. "Thanks, but I can't leave my job. Wyatt has a good security company."

"If there's a will, even the best security can be circumvented."

"I appreciate the offer," she said, firmly but with a smile. "I'm staying. I'm actually not convinced I'm in any danger. If I am, I'm sure that when I'm ruled out as a donor, I won't need any protection."

"I don't like it."

"Neither do I, but that's life."

"Have you had lunch? I'm starving," he said, abruptly changing the direction of the conversation.

She was a little hungry, too. It was after two o'clock. She'd planned to eat a power bar at her desk and finish the backlog. She couldn't leave; she'd promised Paul.

"I already ate," she told him. Not exactly a lie. She had eaten breakfast. "Maybe another time."

"How about dinner?" he asked with an encouraging smile.

Now was the time to tell Rob about Paul, but she didn't. It might make him feel cut off at a time when he was dealing with Erin's death. Plus, he seemed a bit lonely, as if he needed a friend. She knew the feeling. It was exactly how she had felt lately—until Paul.

Erin's death had taught her one thing. Don't take friends for granted. Rob Matthews was a nice man. He had been Erin's longest relationship, so her friend must have truly loved Rob. And he'd helped conceal Aspen's true identity. She didn't want to lose contact with him.

"I'm kind of busy for the next week or so with the Holbrooks and the testing. Let's keep in touch."

She stood to walk him to the door. "I'm sorry you worried about me. Thanks."

"Okay, I'll check in to see how you're doing."

"Don't worry if I don't get right back to you. I'm going in for tests and you have to turn off your phone in the hospital."

"I understand." Unexpectedly, he swept her into his arms. She could feel his uneven breathing on her cheek as he held her close. His mouth moved over hers, devouring its softness. A shudder rippled through her and she pulled away.

"Call me," Rob said as he left.

Madison looked to see if their little scene had attracted the programmers' attention. They were all watching their screens, but Chloe was staring at her from the entrance to Aiden's office and Jade was watching from the reception area.

Great! Just great. She could imagine the office gossip. She'd arrived with Paul and would leave with him. Meanwhile she was carrying on with another man. What did it matter? The important thing to be concerned about wasn't other people's thoughts. It was Rob Matthews.

Evidently, she'd missed the obvious. He wanted to be more than friends. She'd made a mistake. She should have told him about Paul when she had the opportunity.

CHAPTER TWENTY-SIX

PAUL WAITED for Captain Callahan to enter the conference room. It was a little past four. Link Burgess and Trey Williams were with him. Paul had called for this meeting because he hadn't revealed what he'd learned about Aspen. If he planned to have a career, he'd better not withhold more information. They'd had to wait for the captain because he'd been making an appearance with the mayor.

Captain Callahan strode into the room, his military background reflected in his brisk stride and erect posture. He sat at the head of the conference table and spoke directly to Paul. "I assume there's a very good reason that you're keeping two overworked detectives from their jobs and taking up my time?"

"Yes, sir." He rarely used the term *sir* except with the captain. The guy got off on respect. "Last night, I received information that Erin Wycoff was a donor-conceived child of Wyatt Holbrook."

Callahan's jaw didn't drop, but it flexed. No doubt he'd met Holbrook. The captain attended as many public functions as he could justify. It was no secret that he was angling to become the next chief of police.

"So what? That's why you hauled us away from real work?" The missing link snorted. The guy should keep his mouth shut until all the facts were on the table.

Trey Williams got it. "Keith Brooks Smith was also one of Holbrook's children."

Callahan leaned forward ever so slightly. Paul had his attention now. The Smith case was the talk of the department because it was so unique. Erin's murder had generated headlines thanks to the media, who never failed to play to the fear factor to sell papers.

"In Boston two of Holbrook's donor-conceived children died in one week," Paul added. "An accident and an overdose."

"So what?" Link repeated.

Paul realized the two detectives didn't know about Holbrook's need for a transplant. The captain might; it wasn't a secret among Holbrook's friends. Callahan was well enough connected to have heard about it.

"Wyatt Holbrook has primary sclerosing cholangitis. He needs a partial liver transplant. He also has a few complications that means he needs to receive a transplant from a close relative."

"Didn't Walter Peyton have PSC?" Trey asked.

"That's right," Paul responded. "No compatible donor could be found."

The captain was nodding slowly, but Paul couldn't be sure what he was thinking.

"The Wycoff case was supposed to look like an accident," Williams said, which showed why Trey was coming up the ladder fast and Link was stuck in neutral.

"You're saying we've got a serial killer?" asked Link.

"I'm not sure what we have," Callahan responded. "What does Boston PD say?"

"Boston didn't know about the birth angle. They'd closed the cases already," Paul told the group. "They're taking another look, but this guy is clever. They may not be able to prove the two were murdered."

"How did you find out about them?" the captain asked.

"I didn't. My father did. He does Holbrook's security."

There was a moment of heavy, awkward silence. Mike

Tanner's abilities were legendary. If he hadn't taken early retirement, he would have been a serious contender for police chief.

"Tell us what else you know," Captain Callahan said.

Paul filled them in on Holbrook's search for his donor-conceived children. He ended by telling them about the bogus Chagas finding and saying he believed the killer seemed to be after Madison Connelly now.

"Okay, it may look like the kids are clean but—" he nodded at Link "—check their charge records. See if either of them went to Boston."

"Women don't commit—"

"Check anyway," Callahan interrupted Link.

"You might want to look at Nathan Cassidy, Savannah's boyfriend," Paul added.

"Do you have a theory?" Callahan asked Paul.

"Revenge for something. It's probably business-related. I'm meeting with Holbrook tonight with my father. I'm going to find out about any enemies."

"Why didn't the killer just take out Holbrook?" Trey asked.

"He wants to watch him suffer," Paul theorized. "He gets off on it."

"See that you get both Burgess and Williams a copy of your report on any enemies Holbrook may have. It's been my experience that guys that rich make enemies—sometimes unintentionally, but it happens.

"I want you three to e-copy each other about any developments in these cases even if they don't look important or related. Anyone got anything else?"

Link opened his mouth, then shut it, then opened it again. "I don't think it's related, but Erin Wycoff's former boyfriend, the vet, lied. He said he broke off with the victim because of her work with covert animal rights groups. His partner, Dr. Wallace, says he left her because Madison

Connelly was getting a divorce and Matthews was interested in her."

Paul's mouth went dry; he tried to keep his face expressionless. Callahan didn't need to know about his involvement with Madison. He'd never met the veterinarian, but Madison had spoken as if he were a friend, not a romantic interest.

"I'd made this for a love triangle gone bad," Link concluded. "The Connelly woman was the killer."

Paul couldn't help jumping to Madison's defense. "Why would she kill Erin if she'd already stolen her boyfriend?"

"That happened months ago," Link whined. "Could be the situation had changed or something. Plus Connelly stood to gain by the will."

"Why would Erin Wycoff leave money to the Connelly woman if they were fighting?" Trey asked.

"Probably hadn't gotten around to changing her will," Link suggested.

"Did you find any evidence that Madison was dating the vet?" Paul demanded.

"We're still checking."

"Wouldn't the friend who worked with him know?" Paul asked.

"Dr. Wallace said Matthews only discussed it the one time when he'd inquired about Erin. She was around a lot, then she wasn't. He was curious but didn't keep asking because he felt Matthews didn't want to talk about it."

Paul wondered why the vet had lied. It was a simple thing, but it was often those little slips that broke open a case.

"IT'S TOO BAD you can't help my father." Savannah swished into the dining room where Madison was sitting with Tobias Pennington. As usual Nathan Cassidy was a half step behind the gorgeous redhead. It didn't sound as if Savannah was all that upset, but maybe Madison was imagining it.

Paul and his father had escorted Madison from work to have dinner with Wyatt. Tobias had been completing a project with Wyatt in his home office and had been asked to join them.

"You didn't hear?" Tobias said before she could speak. "The lab made a mistake. Madison doesn't have Chagas."

"I was wondering why you were still here. That explains it." She bestowed a smile on Madison. "I'm thrilled your tests were okay. Let's hope you can help my father."

"The lab made a mistake?" Nathan asked. "With computers, isn't an error nearly impossible?"

"Nearly but not absolutely," responded Madison. The last thing she wanted was for anyone to raise the question of tampering. They didn't want the killer to realize they were onto him. Or her. Paul truly believed a woman could be behind this.

"Where's my father?" Savannah asked.

"In a meeting," Tobias said, and Madison had the feeling he deliberately kept the answer short to force Savannah to ask for more information. A power play, or maybe he didn't like the glamorous redhead.

"A meeting at this hour?"

Tobias merely nodded with a smug smile.

"Oh, well. We'll just have to go to the bar for another drink." She motioned toward Tobias and Madison. "Come on. Father can join us there." She didn't wait for a response, sauntering out of the room, Nathan once more at her heels.

Tobias arched one fine eyebrow. "We might as well. I'm sure the staff is waiting to clean up this room."

"Right," she said, and pushed her chair away from the table. She had been enjoying an after-dinner cappuccino made with a Cuban flair while Mike Tanner and Paul interviewed Wyatt. Since it was "official police business," they'd asked Tobias and Madison to wait for them. Tobias was a more interesting man than she'd originally thought. He had a degree in business and a master's in economics from Harvard.

Tobias led the way to the pub-style bar that had six huge flat-screen televisions. "Wyatt is a die-hard Dolphins football fan and a Gators booster. He has a skybox but is often too busy to attend games. He had this room converted to a sports bar."

"Interesting," Madison commented. "Is Garrison a fan, too?"

"No. My brother has never been interested in any sport except scuba diving," Samantha answered for Tobias from her perch on a bar stool. "He learned to dive at nine while we were at our place in the Bahamas."

"It's not legal to certify someone so young here, but outside the U.S. " Nathan shrugged "—they look the other way for enough money."

"In other words, my brother nagged my parents to let him take lessons. He'd been snorkeling since he was five but he was determined to go deeper," Savannah told them. "He's always been obsessed by the sea. Always."

It was a long bar with at least a dozen brass and leather bar stools. Madison wasn't sure where to sit, considering the men should be joining them soon. Tobias settled the question by leaving an empty stool and pulling out the next chair down from Savannah.

"How did you get into skin-care products?" Madison felt she should ask something to keep Savannah talking. Madison certainly didn't want to discuss anything personal with these two.

Nathan handed Savannah what appeared to be a green-apple martini. The woman accepted the drink, took a sip, then said, "My mother was a fantastic woman, a real lady. She took great care to preserve her skin, and it was flawless—hardly a line right up until the day she died. Most people thought she had cosmetic surgery but she didn't. The secret was in hideously expensive Swiss skin care products. I was a whiz at science." Savannah paused to give Madison a smirk of a smile. "The apple doesn't fall very far from the tree."

Madison got the message. She wasn't even a twig on this

magnificent tree. Savannah might want someone to save her father's life, but that didn't mean she had to like the person.

"I started analyzing Mother's favorite product. It took some doing and a little help from my father's lab, and it was almost a year before I could duplicate the product, but I finally did. I was a junior in high school."

Pretty impressive, Madison had to admit. She'd excelled in all her classes and had earned the prestigious National Science Foundation Scholarship, but she hadn't attempted anything quite as ambitious.

"What would you like to drink?" Nathan asked them. He seemed so comfortable behind the bar that Madison guessed he often did this.

"Just sparkling water for me," Madison replied.

"Same here," Tobias added. "We had wine with dinner and I have an early meeting tomorrow."

"Soon I was making stuff for all my friends," Savannah continued as if everyone was dying to hear this when both men must know her story by heart. "I went to college, of course. Georgetown. Then an advanced degree in biology at Emory. You see, by then I was interested in nature's remedies."

"She never gave up compounding creams and lotions even when she was in school," Nathan said with an unmistakable note of pride.

"She's into powerful antioxidants derived from grapes processed for wine," Tobias added, although his tone seemed bored.

"When you slice open an apple, brown forms within minutes. That's oxidation," Savannah informed Madison as if she were a child. "Our skin oxidizes, too, but not as quickly. Antioxidants slow down the process, which ages our complexions."

From the looks of Savannah's flawless complexion, she'd been using something for years. Not a wrinkle showed, even around her eyes.

"For years cosmetic makers have been adding antis to their products," Savannah went on even though the men didn't seem to be listening.

"You mean resveratrol," Madison said, not liking being talked down to; Savannah had already told her about the cures in the bottom of a wine press.

Savannah studied Madison for a moment. "Right. Grape-based products."

Savannah made it sound as if she'd cornered the market. But after their first discussion, Madison had gone online. Dior and L'Occitane had grape-based products, as did several other lesser-known firms.

The prices of their products were stratospheric. When Madison got her hands on some money, she planned to invest a little in grapes. Between wine and beauty products, grapes were bound to go up.

"That's my story," Savannah concluded.

"What about your brother?" Madison asked. She would rather learn more about Garrison than hear Savannah brag. "Was he always into science?"

"Not exactly." Savannah wrinkled her nose as if she smelled one of Aspen's deposits. "He got great grades, but all he wanted to do was study things in the sea. He spent three summers at Woods Hole. We all assumed he'd become a marine biologist."

"He's responsible for the collection of invaluable coral prints and the rare blue coral in the living room," Tobias added.

Savannah gave him a look for cutting her off. She seemed to be getting a little tipsy, yet she motioned to Nathan for another martini. "That's right. When my brother was fifteen, he used money he'd saved for years to purchase the prints at Sotheby's auction in New York."

Madison asked, "They let someone so young—"

"My mother went with him." Savannah said this in a tone that implied Madison was down to her last marble.

"Not your father?" Madison wondered out loud.

"Are you kidding? We rarely saw my father. He was as obsessive as Garrison about his work. Mother busied herself with charity work and me."

There was a pause, then Tobias asked the question for Madison. "Did she have a problem with Garrison?"

Savannah took another sip of her drink, then tossed her head in that provocative way of hers so that her abundant red hair swished across her bare shoulders. Tonight she was wearing an emerald-green dress with a thin strap that held up the gown on one shoulder while leaving the other bare. It skimmed her body until it reached the lowest part of her hips, then the dress descended to midcalf in a series of waves of gold and green fabric that swayed with the slightest move. Obviously it was an outrageously expensive designer gown that made the pale pink halter dress Madison was wearing look like a housecoat.

"A problem with Garrison?" Savannah repeated, as if this were a very amusing question. "No, not a problem exactly. He kept to himself. I guess you would say he was a loner."

"Still is," Nathan added while he helped himself to more Glenfiddich.

"All he wanted to do was go to the Bahamas so he could dive. Then when he was old enough to dive here, all he wanted to do was go to John Pennekamp and dive."

Madison knew the state underwater park well. Her father had taken her there to snorkel. It was an amazing place with an abundance of sea life.

"My mother hated the sun. She never wanted to broil on a boat so Garrison could dive. She was a good mother, though. She had the help take him until he got his license and could drive himself."

"He has a place in the Keys," Tobias added. "That's where he is now."

"Bought it himself and had a lab constructed so he can dive and work there." Nathan shrugged as if to say, *Go figure*.

"Claims to be onto a top-secret cure for a type of lung cancer," Savannah said as if she didn't quite believe it.

"That must be exciting for your father."

Savannah threw her head back and laughed louder than necessary. "Garrison's not sharing this one with my father. You see, Garrison went to Cal Tech. That's when he became interested in science. He became especially interested in the bacteria that sticks to river rocks and is ten times more powerful than manmade glue."

"Caulobacter crescentus," Madison automatically said.

"Of course you'd know. Your life is trivia." Savannah turned to Nathan. "Garrison decided it could be developed into a surgical glue that could replace staples. He told my father, and for the first time, Garrison had his attention."

How sad, Madison thought, fondly recalling her own father. She couldn't remember a time when she didn't have his attention. She'd grown up feeling loved, cherished by both parents, but she'd had a stronger bond with her father.

"It was a very promising idea," Tobias added. "Several other scientists were also experimenting with the bacteria."

"My father found a scientist who was further along. He was in trials already. He backed Swen Torkelsen and brought the surgical glue to market. My brother was pissed off big-time." Savannah laughed again, even louder this time.

Tobias said, "Wyatt felt thousands of lives could be saved if the product came to market as quickly as possible."

"I see." Madison imagined how hurt Garrison must have been, but obviously their relationship had been repaired. "If I understand it correctly, it's not unusual to have several scientists working on the same thing."

"Right," Tobias said. "Happens a lot."

"This time Garrison claims to be onto something unique," Savannah said, accepting another martini from Nathan. "From the sea, of course."

"Wyatt and Garrison have worked on many things over the years," Tobias said. "He understands why his father didn't wait the two to three years it would have taken for Garrison to get his version to trials. From there it would be at least two more years."

"Don't forget to mention Holbrook Pharmaceuticals made a bundle off the discovery." Savannah had clearly had too much to drink; she couldn't keep sarcasm out of her voice.

"What kind of law do you practice, Nathan?" Madison asked to change the subject. Despite her own accomplishments, Madison would bet Savannah was jealous of Garrison and Wyatt's relationship.

Voices from the hall caused all of them to turn toward the door. Savannah slipped off her bar stool and swayed a bit as she headed toward the door.

"I'm in corporate law," Nathan said, his voice low enough so Savannah couldn't hear him. "But if you need me, call. For anything."

Madison was more than a little surprised by Nathan's offer. Wasn't he the man who had accused her of being after Wyatt's money? He'd wanted to get rid of her. So why was he being friendly now? Maybe he was deliberately trying to throw her off-track when he was actually sabotaging her. Could he have the computer skills to rig her blood test and subject her to identity theft? It was possible, she decided. If he didn't do it himself, perhaps he had a resource at his firm or somewhere.

"Father," Savannah greeted Wyatt. If she was surprised to see Mike and Paul with Wyatt, she didn't show it. Nathan did, his eyes narrowing when he saw Paul.

"Father, we have the best news." Savannah grabbed her father's arm, pulled him away from the Tanners and guided him toward the bar. "Nathan and I are getting married. We're going to have a baby right away. We know how much you want a grandchild."

"That's wonderful," Wyatt responded, but he didn't sound all that enthusiastic. "But if you're going to have a baby, I suggest you stop drinking."

Madison couldn't help feeling sorry for Savannah. The woman managed a slight nod, but her father had already turned away to talk to Paul.

CHAPTER TWENTY-SEVEN

What is the only United States monument that moves?

"DID YOU FIND anything out?" Madison asked Paul when they were on their way back to the guesthouse. They'd excused themselves immediately after Wyatt had embarrassed Savannah. The woman had looked so stricken—almost as if she'd received a physical blow—that Madison's heart went out to her.

Mike Tanner had left with them but he'd headed off to his car to go home. Tobias had remained behind. Evidently, he'd been with the family for so long that he was accustomed to their bickering.

Paul slipped his arm around Madison's waist and pulled her close. A shiver of desire rushed through her, but she resisted it. She needed to know what he'd found out. Who was behind all this?

"Look, I wish I could tell you about our interview with Wyatt, but it's an official investigation. I can't."

"Your father's no longer with the force. And you're still on leave." She didn't mean to sound petulant, but her life might depend on what she learned.

"True, but he was a lead detective for many years and now provides security for Wyatt. Captain Callahan trusts him." Paul gave her a one-armed hug. "I can tell you this much. Wyatt has made several enemies, including a woman. I'll bet the ranch that one of them is responsible for the killings."

"What kind of enemies?" She believed Wyatt to be a quiet, compassionate man, but tonight she'd seen another side of him.

"Scientists who claim he stole their ideas."

"Really?"

"Well, Holbrook claims they were all working on similar ideas but he got his to market first."

"Interesting. Listen to this." She told him what she'd learned about Garrison's surgical glue.

"We'll take a much closer look. Maybe this is a pattern of behavior that's now gotten Holbrook into real trouble."

"Maybe Wyatt isn't as altruistic as he seems." She realized she didn't want to think of him that way. She wanted him to be a good man who deserved a transplant so he could continue helping others. "So what? Even if he profited by these drugs, he saved lives."

"How would you feel if he'd stolen your idea?"

She thought about it for a moment and remembered how outraged she'd been when Aiden tried to take TotalTrivia away from her during the divorce. "I'd be upset. Fighting mad, but I wouldn't kill anyone, especially innocent people who didn't have a thing to do with it."

"That's what's so different about this case. That's why I'm going to interview the woman myself."

"The odds are it's a man. They're usually killers, not women."

"Right," Paul agreed. "But the cardinal rule of being a detective is never assume. Don't come up with a theory. Then as you investigate you just try to find facts to support your idea. Keep an open mind. Most people would look for a man. I'm open to it being a woman. Nothing I've seen in any of these murders takes brute strength."

"What about Erin?"

"She was very petite and buck-naked. That put her at a huge disadvantage. A strong woman could have done it. I've thought that all along."

"Maybe you're right," Madison admitted. "In recent years, about five percent of serial killings have had women involved. Usually they are 'black widows' who kill their husbands or angels of death in hospital settings who send patients to heaven prematurely, but women seem to be ramping up their skills."

Paul chuckled. "See? All that trivia does come to good use. Know what bothers me? This could be a duo. Most often women are accomplices and don't act alone. Know anything about those stats?"

Madison thought a moment. She hadn't visited the Murder and Mayhem section of TotalTrivia in…who knew how long. "No, I don't have any idea."

"Serial killings with women as accomplices take on average eight years to solve. It's half that time if it's just a man, acting alone."

She groaned. "I don't want this to drag on that long."

"It won't. I'm not sure this fits a serial killer profile. This one's weird, to say the least."

Paul used his key to open the door to the bungalow. Aspen bounded out with his leash in his mouth. He danced in a circle.

"Somebody wants a walk," Paul said, relocking the door.

"Isn't he cute?" Madison snapped the leash on his collar. "Come on, boy."

They went around the small swimming pool and out to the path by the ocean. Aspen bounced along beside her. The retriever was more comfortable with her, Madison decided. He was becoming playful. She imagined life in a cage and having stuff sprayed into his eyes had taken away some of his spirit, but it was coming back now.

"This is a very unusual case," Paul commented, picking up their conversation again as she unsnapped Aspen's leash and the retriever skipped along the trail cobbled with flat paving stones.

"Like the United States monuments. Most of them are the

same in that they are stationary except for one. It's unique and different. Do you know what monument I'm talking about?"

He laughed, a deep sound that seemed to reverberate in her chest. Suddenly she wished they could laugh all the time instead of having to be so serious.

"I'm thinking the U.S. monument that moves must be San Francisco's cable cars."

"Oh my God," she cried, and playfully punched him in the arm. "How did you know that?"

"I remember being told when I visited San Francisco."

He was pretty amazing, she thought, surveying across the sand. The sea was calm, almost flat, but a full moon made it glisten as if some giant had tossed a handful of diamonds into the dark water. Corona del Mar was as close to heaven as you were likely to get while still on earth, she thought. She inhaled deeply, taking in the scent of the sea and the aroma of gardenias floating on the air.

"Let me ask you about Rob Matthews," Paul said quietly, a little too quietly.

Rob had been on her mind since he'd left her office. It wasn't until he'd kissed her that she realized how he felt about her. Looking back, she should have seen the signs, but she'd been so consumed with her own problems that she'd missed the cues.

"What about him?" she asked.

"When the detectives checked up on him, regarding Erin—"

"Why? He didn't kill her!"

"Passion and money are the main reasons for murder. Matthews had been involved with her for a year and a half. We wouldn't be good detectives if we didn't check him out thoroughly."

"Well, now that you mention it…" She looked up at Paul. The moonlight glowed like a nimbus around his head. She tried to assess his unreadable features. "Rob came to see me today.

He'd called several times yesterday and I hadn't called him back. He was worried enough to cancel his patients and come to my office. After we talked, I realized…he might be romantically interested in me."

"What made you think that?"

She shrugged, then noticed Aspen at their side. If he'd left a deposit, she'd have to pick it up in the morning. She couldn't hunt for it in the dark. She hooked the leash on Aspen's collar.

"I think I've been stupid. I should have seen the signs." She started walking back toward the house. "Rob called just after Aiden left me. He asked me to dinner. I thought he was just being friendly. I didn't go that time but he kept calling to see how I was doing. We went out to dinner several times over the next few months. He asked me to go other places, like to a Dolphins game and a play, but I didn't go."

"Why not?"

"I hate to admit it, but I was wallowing in self-pity." She shrugged her shoulders as if to say she couldn't figure it out herself. "Why are you asking me about Rob?"

"We interviewed his partner, Dr. Wallace."

"I know him. He treated Aspen the day I found Erin's body. He seemed very good. Right away, he suspected something had been sprayed into Aspen's eyes and gave him drops that really helped."

"When Erin and Rob broke up, he claimed it was over her involvement with animal rights groups."

"Unfortunately, that's what split them up. She'd always been—"

"According to Wallace, that's not what caused the breakup." Paul unlocked the door to the guesthouse for them. The new security protocol was to never go anywhere—even to the beach—without locking the door. "He left Erin because you were now available."

Madison stared wordlessly at him, her heart pounding. A shocked gasp escaped her. "You're kidding!"

"That's what he told Dr. Wallace. Question is why Matthews would lie to investigators."

"Oh my God. Erin knew the real reason. That's why she didn't want to discuss the breakup. The poor thing must have been miserable but she hid it from me. Her pride kept her from saying anything." She unhooked Aspen's leash and dropped it onto the end table. "She was brokenhearted and all I did was whine and cry on her shoulder. What kind of friend was I?"

Paul slipped his arm around Madison and pulled her close. "Don't be hard on yourself. If she didn't tell you, how could you help?"

"True, but…" She tried to imagine how Erin must have felt. Disturbing thoughts raced through her mind. She vividly recalled how betrayed and hurt she'd felt when Aiden left her for Chloe. Madison had to battle a white-hot fury every time she saw that woman. She longed to scratch out Chloe's eyes. Was that how Erin had reacted to her? In the end, had her friend actually hated her?

"Honey, can you think of any reason Rob wouldn't have told the truth to the police?" Paul asked, breaking into her thoughts.

She considered the question for a minute. "I really don't know the man all that well. Aiden didn't get along with Erin, so we didn't see them as a couple except when we threw a big party. Then I was too busy to spend time with them. Most of what I know about Rob, I heard from Erin."

"Where did Erin meet him?"

"She volunteered at an animal shelter. Rob donated his services to help give animals shots and stuff so they could find forever homes."

"Forever homes?"

"That's what they call a home when a pet gets a second chance." She thought a moment. "You know, Erin looked up to

Rob. She adored him. Truthfully, when I met him, I was a little disappointed."

"Why?"

She thought about her initial reaction to Robert Matthews as she sat on the sofa and Paul sat beside her. "I'm not sure exactly. He's good-looking—"

"Should I be jealous?" he teased.

"Nah, he doesn't kiss worth—"

"Kiss?" He dragged her into his lap. His nose brushing hers, he asked, "You kissed him? What else did you do?"

He was jealous, she realized, and she couldn't help being secretly pleased. "Just once. Today as Rob was leaving my office, he grabbed me, then kissed me. A quick kiss but not the kind a friend would give you. It was out of nowhere. I hadn't expected it. I thought we were just friends, then I thought back—"

"You have no idea, do you? All that trivia in your head crowds out reality. You're beautiful and sexy as hell. No guy wants to be friends with you unless he's gay."

Madison didn't know how to respond. She honestly didn't. Once, she'd thought herself to be attractive. She'd never had trouble finding guys to date, but the divorce had taken something out of her. Away from her. She hadn't been pretty enough, smart enough or sexy enough to keep Aiden.

Until Paul.

Now she did feel pretty, not beautiful or glamorous like Savannah, but pretty and, most of all, desirable. Her heart swelled with a feeling she thought had died forever. She truly cared about this man in a way that she'd never cared about Aiden.

"You're so sexy that I can't possibly write my report tonight. It'll have to wait until morning." He threaded his fingers through the hair on the back of her head and urged her closer. An exchange of breath, soft yet electric. Again, even longer this time. Madison's mouth parted with a gentle sigh, inviting him to kiss her. His lips finally angled across hers.

She surrendered to the kiss, reveling in the way his powerful arms held her tight yet with such tenderness. His tongue nudged and played with hers, stroking it, coaxing it, imitating the act to come. A sweet ache developed between her legs and her breasts felt heavy and unusually full. She continued to kiss him, savoring every second as pulsing desire spiraled through her.

His free hand explored her bare back. Using the tip of one slightly rough finger, he traced the notches of her spine. The sensation made her breath catch for a second.

Her hands inched up his strong arms to his shoulders, then her fingers dug into his hard muscles. *Oh, my.* She detected the faint aroma of the woodsy aftershave he used. The moist heat between her legs intensified, then ratcheted up a notch when she realized the swelling rod under her bottom was his arousal.

Her head spun as her body did a slow burn while the throbbing between her legs intensified. She needed this, needed to be kissed and made love to by a man who seemed crazy about her. As crazy as she was about him.

The hand cradling the back of her head moved lower and found the clasp at the back of her neck that secured the halter top of the dress. With a snap, it released; he edged his hand between them and pulled down the silky fabric, exposing her bare breasts. She hadn't worn a bra because the dress was backless and she wasn't so busty that she needed one.

His hand fondled one warm breast. The nipple tightened and the breast swelled into his warm palm. He ran his thumb over the taut nub. A fresh rush of moist heat pooled between her thighs while an uncontrollable shudder of pleasure racked her body.

Paul broke the kiss, breathing like a racehorse. Desire shimmered in the air around them. Chemistry, lust and something deeper. She could see it in his heavy-lidded eyes, feel it glowing inside herself.

"You're beautiful," he told her in a rasp of a whisper. "Drop-dead gorgeous."

He stood, bringing her with him, and carried her in his strong arms. One shoe at a time hit the tile floor, but she barely noticed. Three steps behind them trailed Aspen. She marveled at the ease with which Paul carried her as she kissed the curve of his neck, a spot she'd already learned was extremely sensitive.

He gently placed her on the bed and pulled the dress, now half-off, down over her hips. All she wore beneath was a lacy black thong. He left it in place and climbed over her, putting one knee on either side of her body.

She reached up and put her arm around his neck, bringing his head down to hers for a kiss. He allowed her to kiss him, but pulled away. He kissed her neck, tasting and sucking a little as he inched downward to the swell of her breasts with soft seeking kisses. He laved each nipple while he caressed the surrounding flesh with his fingers, stroking lightly.

Her hips lifted off the bed, anxious to press against him, but he was kneeling over her and busy with her breasts. His hand glided over her mound, dipped lower. He teased the nubbin with one finger until she was whimpering with pleasure.

"No fair," she managed to whisper. "You're still in your clothes."

"We'll fix that."

He pulled away, stood and quickly shucked his polo shirt and pulled off his pants and briefs at the same time. He hopped on one foot to get rid of first one sock, then the other. Aspen nosed the pile of clothes and Madison couldn't help giggling. A lab dog had probably never seen the likes of what had been going on in this room lately.

She gazed up at Paul. Lordy, he was the epitome of masculinity. Broad shoulders and a whorl of dark chest hair that arrowed downward to a thicket of dark hair. His erect penis jutted toward her. Huge.

His smoldering gaze was as close to a caress as you could get without touching. Her heart beat lawlessly. She wanted him—now.

"Are you going to stand there all night?" she managed to ask in a breathy voice she didn't recognize.

He reached down to his trousers and pulled something from a pocket. "I have condoms."

They'd agreed after the first night, when they'd been too gripped by lust to think about consequences, to use condoms until Madison saw a doctor and went back on the pill. He ripped open the foil wrapper and pulled out the condom. With mounting anticipation, she watched him quickly work it over his erection.

Paul climbed back onto the bed with a hint of mischief in his smile. He started with her breasts again. Kissing. Tasting. Drawing each nipple deep into his mouth, so deep she felt it in her womb. The quivery heat was almost unbearable now.

"Hurry, hurry," she cried.

He didn't pay any attention to her. A half inch at a time, he worked his way downward. The rasp of his emerging beard was erotic against her soft skin, arousing her more than she'd thought possible. By the time he reached her navel, Madison realized she was on the verge of a climax. And he wasn't even inside her yet.

She steeled herself, clutching the bedcovers with both hands. He worked his way lower and lower until he reached her mound. His tongue found the aching nub and stroked it, played with it until something inside Madison cracked. Her orgasm shot through her like a jolt of lightning.

"Yes! Yes!" she screamed.

He hovered over her, a satisfied smile on his face. She reached up for him and he lowered himself into her arms and turned her on her side. She clung to him, experiencing an emotion that was intangible and frighteningly elusive. It was almost like a mystical experience of some kind.

"I think *wow* covers this," he whispered.

How had she gotten so lucky? Madison asked herself. A great lover with a sense of humor. "*Wow* works for me."

CHAPTER TWENTY-EIGHT

PAUL WAITED inside one of the examining rooms for Rob Matthews. He'd flashed his badge and told the receptionist it was "official business." Actually, it was more of a hunch than anything else. He wasn't supposed to be interviewing anyone, but this morning he'd gotten up—two hours after falling asleep just before dawn—and had sent the report on his interview with Wyatt Holbrook to Captain Callahan, Burgess and Williams.

Madison had still been asleep; making love so many times had wiped her out. He'd taken Aspen for a walk and fed him. While he was taking care of the dog, he decided to investigate as much of this case on his own as he could. He didn't trust anyone else to save Madison.

Save her from what? Paul wished he knew. This whole mess was so perplexing. Nothing seemed to fit together in any way he could see. Yet he felt there was a connection. And it involved Wyatt Holbrook and Madison.

"Hello, Mr. Tanner." Robert Matthews strode into the room. He looked for a pet. Evidently, the receptionist hadn't alerted the vet. "Where's your—"

"I'm here about Erin Wycoff." Paul flashed his badge and studied the man. Tall, dark hair and eyes. Women would probably find him attractive, and he couldn't fault the guy for being interested in Madison. She was a keeper; he wasn't letting anything happen to her.

"I've already been interviewed," Rob protested.

"This is follow-up," Paul said. "Explain to me why exactly you broke off your relationship with Erin."

Rob leaned back against the counter where he would have taken out dressings or medications to treat animals. He appeared to be totally relaxed. Too relaxed, Paul decided.

"Erin was involved in projects the Everglades Animal Defense League endorsed. Sometimes it included breaking and entering. I couldn't risk having my license revoked. It would have been the end of my career. I explained this to Erin, but she wouldn't give up the league."

"When did you tell her the relationship was over?"

Rob shrugged. "Last year. Early spring."

"Were there other reasons?"

Rob remained silent for a long moment. "Well, I was more attracted to a friend of Erin's than I was to Erin." He shrugged. "I wasn't in love with her."

"What friend?" Paul persisted.

Again Rob hesitated, then finally said, "Madison Connelly. She was getting a divorce. I thought the timing was right, but I was mistaken. She was still in love with her husband even though he dumped her for another woman."

"Where were you on the night Erin died?" Paul asked. He knew the answer from the murder notebook, but he wanted to hear what Matthews would say.

"I received a call from Erin at my home about one o'clock."

"Wasn't that unusual? So late."

Matthews paused half a beat before answering, "Not really. Erin was a night owl and so am I. I take the late shift at the clinic most of the time."

"What did Erin want?"

"She claimed to have found a dog with eye problems. I told her to bring it in at noon the next day."

"Why?"

"I knew Erin's history. I figured she'd 'liberated' some dog. If I treated it during the lunch break, it wouldn't appear on our books. I could do a good deed but remain in the clear."

Made sense, Paul decided, but something was missing. "Are you sure that's all that happened?"

"What? I didn't kill Erin." Rob walked backward toward the door. "Do I need a lawyer?"

"No." Paul opened the door for him. "Thanks for your help." He didn't need any trouble. Paul shouldn't even be here. If the captain found out, Paul could get busted down to street patrol in Calle Ocho, the worst of assignments.

TWO HOURS LATER Paul was at Trey Williams's side as they walked into the condo Greta Swensen had leased. "Any priors on Swensen?" Paul asked.

"Nothing. She's clean. For the last eleven years Greta has worked at a dental lab, making implants."

It was a long drop down, Paul thought. Greta had once been in the research department at Holbrook Pharmaceuticals. She had been working on a bone implant that might help patients with spine abnormalities. Holbrook had rushed the technology to market and it had been a success.

Trey rang the condo's bell. A few minutes later a woman with dark hair and challenging dark eyes opened the door. "What are you selling?"

Trey showed his badge. "Official business, ma'am."

"About what?" Greta asked. She was younger than Paul expected, probably about forty. She was short, with the trim, athletic build Paul associated with competitive swimmers.

"Wyatt Holbrook," Trey said, and the woman stepped back quickly as if she'd been zapped with a stun gun.

"What about him?" she asked in a low voice.

Trey flipped open a small notebook from his suit pocket. There wasn't anything written on the pages but Greta couldn't see that. "You had a dispute with Holbrook Pharmaceuticals regarding implant material."

"That's right. That bastard stole my idea." Greta motioned for them to come inside her condo. Thank God; it was sweltering outside. "I was just a kid. What did I know about big business? Wyatt took my idea and had it on the market within the year."

"Doesn't sound fair," Paul commented. "Did he credit you or give you money?"

"Are you kidding?" Greta motioned toward a worn beige sofa, meaning they should sit. Paul and Trey dropped to the sagging cushions.

"You didn't get any compensation at all?" Paul asked.

"No. My position was eliminated, but I knew the truth. Wyatt wanted me out of the way." Greta plopped down onto a chair opposite them. "I've never quite recovered."

"Are you still angry with Wyatt Holbrook?" Trey asked.

"Of course, wouldn't you be?"

Half an hour later they were back in Trey's car, driving away from the complex where Greta lived.

"You don't like her for this one," Trey said.

"No. Greta's bitter and she'd cheer if Wyatt keeled over, but I don't sense the depth of anger it would take to kill innocent people." He shrugged. "Maybe I'm wrong. Check Greta's credit card records. See if she was in Boston recently. I could be too close to this one to call it properly."

"You're involved with the Connelly woman," Trey speculated.

"Are you kidding? Involved with a suspect?" He checked his cell phone. It was vibrating. "I've got a return call from someone I know who used to be in the FBI's profiling unit. I faxed her all the pictures I had of Erin Wycoff's murder scene. Let's see if she has anything for us." He punched in his code, then returned the call. He spoke with the field agent for several minutes, then hung up.

"Well, what's the haps?" Trey asked.

"From the crime scene photos they peg this as a level ten. That's on a one-to-twenty-two scale formulated by a forensic psychiatrist at Columbia University. Level ten is an egocentric killer of persons in his way."

"Shit! That's just how you saw this, right?"

"Absolutely. I just don't know who stands to benefit from Wyatt Holbrook's death. Not his children. Then who? We've got to cast a wider net." Paul told Trey about the way Wyatt had run off with his son's idea for surgical glue. "It's a pattern of behavior."

"We need to keep checking other people Holbrook pissed off," Williams said. "It's our best bet."

MADISON ANSWERED the knock on the bungalow's door, Aspen at her side. Before she unlocked the door, she saw that it was Garrison Holbrook. No doubt the security guard had noted his appearance on the property. No one except Madison, Paul and Mike Tanner knew they suspected the killer had targeted Madison.

"Hey," Garrison said with a smile. "I heard you were working at home today."

"Right." She managed a smile. Paul had insisted she remain in the bungalow while he interviewed suspects. She'd agreed because she didn't want to be around Chloe more than necessary.

"Is it okay if I interrupt for a few minutes?"

"Sure." She opened the door wider and Aspen poked his head out. "Come in. Want coffee? I just made a pot."

"Great," Garrison said as he sidestepped the retriever and followed Madison into the small alcove that served as a kitchen.

Madison poured him a mug of coffee, which he took black. She tossed a small dog treat to Aspen, who was standing at attention near her.

"I hear my father got a little out of hand last night," Garrison said after the first sip of coffee.

Madison wasn't sure what to say. "I think Savannah expected more of a celebration. They're getting married. It's an important event."

"True. If my mother were alive, it would be a memorable occasion. The society pages would be full of it. An engagement bash. Showers. Bridal luncheons." Garrison took another sip of coffee, leaned against the counter, then said, "My father is a different person. He's…" Garrison seemed to be at a loss for words.

"Doesn't he want grandchildren? That seemed to be what Savannah was offering."

"I guess." Garrison shrugged. "My sister has spent her whole life trying to please my father. Where has it gotten her? Nowhere."

"How do you feel about your father?" Madison asked. "Didn't he steal your idea for surgical glue?"

"Heard about that, did you? I wasn't upset. My father didn't steal anything from me. The product was already in trial stages with several scientists. Dad took it to market and made a fortune. At least four other scientists would have brought the glue to market before I did. It was an experience. I learned to keep quiet about discoveries."

"Savannah said you were working on a cure for a certain type of lung cancer."

"What a blabbermouth." Garrison poured the remains of his coffee into the sink. "I am working on a project that will take science to a new level. As you can probably guess, it's all about using elements in the ocean to help us."

"Good," she said, because she couldn't think of anything else to say.

"I just wanted to tell you that my father is a great guy. He was upset last night and lost it because Savannah was acting like my mother."

"Meaning what?"

"Mother was an alcoholic. She turned out for every fund-raiser imaginable and society events. But she wasn't too inter-ested in parenting. My childhood was a parade of nannies and a father who worked nonstop. Savannah was my mother's favorite because she was a girl. Beautiful and smart. I was a big zero until I got to college."

Madison remembered her father and mother with a fondness she hadn't recognized until now. They both had loved her in a way that the Holbrooks hadn't loved their own children. It must have been terrible to be on their own during those formative years, she decided. She'd always been loved. Where was her mother now? Why hadn't Madison heard from her?

"What about Savannah?"

"She's smart and forward-thinking. She's exploring new methods for all kinds of skin-care products. She's been very successful." Garrison was silent for a moment. When he spoke again, his voice was filled with concern. "My father let Savannah have it last night because he's worried she'll turn out like Mother. Heredity is a huge factor in alcoholism. He's just trying to protect the baby."

"I see," Madison said, but she didn't. Her father would have taken her aside and discussed the situation in private. He would never have embarrassed her in front of other people.

"You're working from here today?" Garrison asked, looking at her laptop and papers on the kitchen table.

"Yes. I review questions that go up on the Web site. Right now I'm looking at where tipping is an insult."

"Really? Leaving a tip is an insult? Where?"

"Iceland. But I'm wondering if my programmers looked closely at South America and the Pacific islands, including Christmas Island. It might be insulting somewhere else, as well. That's when we get into trouble."

"Interesting," he said, but he didn't sound too enthusiastic.

"I understand your test results were misinterpreted. What made you get another test? I mean, I'm glad you did, but many people wouldn't have bothered."

"It was Paul's idea. Chagas is an unusual disease. Mike Tanner runs drug tests all the time for companies he represents. It was just a matter of a simple retest."

"Then you're ready for the next set of tests. That's great." Garrison gazed across the room, lost in thought for a moment. "I'm praying you can help my father."

Madison didn't want to say anything discouraging when the Holbrooks had been great about helping her. "How is Dr. Miller's son?"

"The kid pulled through. Dr. Miller will be back at the end of the week."

"That's great. He seems like a nice man. It would be terrible to lose your child."

"Right. It'll also be a huge loss if we can't save my father. A huge loss." Garrison ran his fingers though his hair. "He may have been abrupt with Savannah, but he's a great guy. He's helped a lot of people."

"Do you think he has any enemies?"

"Probably. He's made a fortune. He's bound to have stepped on a few people to get where he is."

Madison wanted to ask more, but she didn't want to arouse Garrison's suspicions. *Let Paul handle this,* she told herself.

CHAPTER TWENTY-NINE

Who was the first president to have a running-water bathtub?

MADISON WAS WORKING through a set of trivia questions on America's presidents. Millard Fillmore had the dubious distinction of being in the White House when the first running-water bathtub was installed. Now who would know that? Even she did not have that obscure fact in her brain. Good. She was making a deliberate effort to stop thinking in trivia and spouting it in conversation. Her life was moving to a new level.

Paul was now a factor, but it wasn't just him. She'd changed. Madison wanted...more. Mostly she wanted out, away from TotalTrivia and Aiden and Chloe.

Her cell phone rang, and she glanced at caller ID, hoping it was Paul. Pamela Nolan was calling. *Oh my gosh!* She'd forgotten her friend from MIT. She had called yesterday when Rob had been in her office.

"Pamela, I'm so sorry. A lot has been happening. I forgot to return your call."

"It's okay. Life happens." Pamela's voice had its usual upbeat tone, and Madison could just imagine her talking on the phone and hooking a strand of long, glistening red hair over one ear as she spoke. Pamela looked like a china doll and spoke with a slight Texas accent. Guys often mistook her for a bimbo, but she was one of the smartest people Madison had ever encountered. She'd gotten into grad school everywhere she'd applied and had chosen Stanford.

"You know, Madison, after I received your message asking about Chloe Barnett, I made some inquiries. There are a few things you might need to know."

"Did you find out about her graduate thesis?"

"I did—it was on Internet gambling. It was part of a larger project being done out of the psychology department. Just to keep it simple, there may very well be an addicting element to online gambling. Apparently, people start out doing it for short periods of time, then find themselves ignoring everything else to gamble."

"Winning produces a chemical reaction in your brain," added Madison. "Gambling is a recognized addiction, with a twelve-step program and the rehab that goes along with it."

"True, but Chloe's theory was younger children could become trained as gamblers by adding a gambling element to various online games."

"That's sick," Madison heard herself say. But she wasn't surprised. There had always been something diabolical about Chloe. Hearing this, Madison was positive Chloe had been the one to approach Luis Estevez.

"Want to hear something even sicker?" Pamela asked, then went on without waiting for a reply. "Remember I told you that she was asked to leave Stanford? It was all very hush-hush."

Madison's sixth sense told her she wouldn't like what was coming next. "Were you able to find out what she'd done?"

"Yes. I've been here long enough to have contacts. It was a big cover-up. She was sleeping with a professor. His project involved saving Monterey Bay. Are you familiar with it?"

"Yes. It's a protected marine area off Northern California. The Monterey Bay Aquarium is world-famous."

"Exactly. It's the subject of one of those green earth-conscious movements that started in California. Professor Hinson set up a Web site with underwater cameras and his students posted info on their research. Part of the site took in donations. You could donate money or stuff like towels for birds that got into oil and mackerel for the injured seals."

"There are quite a few sites like that around. Did Stanford sponsor it?"

"Not officially. They knew about it, but it was Professor Hinson's project. A number of wealthy alums donated heavily. The site was up and running for over a year when one of the grad students working on the project thought donations were less than expected."

"Chloe. How did she do it?"

"Actually, it was pretty ingenious. The online contributions were mostly with credit cards. She electronically diverted many transactions to her own account. To do it, she had to have the financial info off the Web site. You know, personal info like passwords and mothers' maiden names. While she was sleeping with good old Hinson, she was tapping into info on his computer. People didn't complain because their statements confirmed that they'd donated. They didn't have any way of knowing the money had been diverted."

Suddenly, Madison realized the truth. Chloe had taken her money. "Pamela, you're not going to believe this." She explained about the identity theft, the loss of her savings and the devastation of her credit status.

"Oh God. I'm glad I called you," Pamela cried. "I'll bet she did it."

"I made it easy for her," Madison confessed. "I hadn't changed my password after the divorce."

"That's a mistake, but most people don't change their passwords and use the same one for everything."

"What I don't understand is how she got away with it. Weren't charges filed?"

Pamela's laugh was brittle. "No. The university didn't want its reputation tarnished. Wealthy alums give staggering amounts of money to the school. Professor Hinson put his life's savings into the fund to make up the loss. Chloe was asked to leave, but that's it."

"That is so unfair. They cut her loose to do it again."

"I'm really sorry," Pamela responded, and Madison could imagine the concerned look on her old friend's face. "What can I do to help? I've got a little money—"

"Thanks. I couldn't take your money. Besides, I'm okay. I'm with a friend. I just want to get Chloe, to prove she did it. Any ideas?"

"Let me just add that Chloe had a gambling problem. There wasn't any money to be recovered from her. That's why Hinson gave up his savings."

"So, my money is long gone."

"I'm afraid so."

"I don't want her to get away with it." Madison thought for a moment. "There must be a paper trail."

"There must be, even if it's electronic. Her bank records, most likely."

Madison slapped the table with the palm of her hand. Aspen jumped up from where he'd been sleeping at her feet. "That's it. I'll get her records and see if the sums match what's missing from my accounts."

"You'll need a court order, I think."

"I might have her password, if what you say is right and people don't often change their passwords. I'm going to log on to her bank account myself."

"You go, girl. If that doesn't work, contact the local FBI office. They have a whole identity-theft unit."

"Pamela, I'm thinking Chloe applied for a job here just so she could move into online gambling. When I interviewed her, I realized she was overqualified for the position, but I hired her anyway. She saw we were an easy target, then Aiden fell for her and she's in the driver's seat now. What a waste. With her

education, looks and trust fund, Chloe could have built something on her own."

"Wait a minute. What trust fund?"

"Her parents are wealthy San Franciscans. Her grandmother
left her a trust fund. Maybe she gambled through it."

"I think she reinvented herself," Pamela said. "According to
the records on file at the university, Chloe Barnett went to
Berkeley on a scholarship, but still needed a student loan. She
had a loan for grad school. Her parents are high school science
teachers in Fresno."

"Really?" The implications of these lies sent a wave of
excitement through Madison. "I'll bet she invented the trust
fund to explain having money from gambling or ID theft."
Madison bet Aiden fell for it. Served him right.

Madison thanked Pamela and promised to let her know what
happened. She almost called Paul with the news but decided first
to see if she could access Chloe's bank account. She remembered the woman banked with Florida National because Chloe
had written a check for a group wedding gift for a programmer.

She went onto the Web site and typed eolhc1chloe. When
Chloe had first begun working for them, Madison had seen her
type in her password. Her name spelled backward, the number
one, her name again. Every programmer had a special password. They weren't too secretive about them because program-
ming trivia didn't require it.

No luck. Florida National didn't recognize the password.

"Come on, Aspen. Let's go for a walk." She snapped the
leash on the retriever and he happily trotted along beside her.
It was bright outside, a clear, sunny day without the usual
shroud of humidity that was typical when summer neared. It
was a day when it felt good to be alive.

She also felt as if some enormous weight had been lifted
from her. Finding out about Chloe was part of it, but realizing
how much she cared about Paul meant more. Her life was

moving in a new direction. A career change was definitely in order.

Aspen relieved himself, lifting one leg on a gardenia bush. She spotted the deposit he'd left last night and retrieved it. The turd made her think of Chloe.

A bell gonged in Madison's head.

"Here, Aspen. Here, boy." She tossed the deposit into the trash, sprinted toward the bungalow, fumbled with the lock and finally opened the door. Aspen was right at her heels.

"Please, God. Let me be right. Turn the tide here. Let me get out from under one thing at least."

She logged on to Luis Estevez's bank's Web site and typed in Chloe's password. She was betting Chloe had opened an account at Allied Miami as a result of her alliance with the smarmy Cuban. Bingo! Numbers and transaction info filled the screen. She fumbled through the papers in her tote for the information sheets on the missing money from her account. The bank had given her the date and time of each transaction. If she could match it to deposits into Chloe's account, she could prove what had happened.

It was astonishingly simple to match up the withdrawals and subsequent deposits. Chloe had zapped the money out of Madison's accounts directly into her own. Even the cash taken from Madison's credit cards appeared on the screen.

"How stupid." If Chloe had been truly clever, she would have routed the money to another account, combined the money, then transferred it into her own account. That would have made identifying the transactions more difficult. Chloe wasn't stupid, Madison realized, just arrogant. She hadn't taken the extra steps because she never believed she would be caught.

Pamela was right about the money going to pay off gambling debts. There was very little in the account now. Electronic payments had been made to several online gambling companies.

"Print out three or four copies. Get one to Paul, another to his father, and put one in a safe place." Madison was so excited that she was talking to the dog. She reached down and stroked his head. "Wait a minute. I don't have a printer."

She had her laptop but not a printer. If she didn't print out the info immediately it might somehow be deleted. There was at least one printer in the main house. She'd seen it in Wyatt's home office, but she doubted the staff would let her in there. It required a laser fingerprint for entry. Surely, someone on the staff had another computer with a printer.

She grabbed her laptop, locked the door and headed for the main house. Walking fast, she hit speed dial for Paul's cell. It kicked over to voice mail. "Call me. I found the ID thief."

She knocked at the back door and Marcella, the chef, answered. There was no printer in the kitchen or elsewhere in the house. Mr. Wyatt was in his office. They should call him on the house system and ask.

Marcella dialed, then handed Madison the telephone. "I'm sorry to bother you. I know you must be busy—"

"No bother," Wyatt assured her.

"I need to print out something. It'll only take me a few minutes."

"Come down to my office. I'm just going over a few test results. You can use the printer without disturbing me."

The house seemed mammoth; it took forever to get to Wyatt's home office. He was standing in the doorway when she arrived. She maintained a friendly smile but her heart was beating in double time.

He showed her to the printer. It took her a minute to plug in her laptop and it seemed like an hour, but finally the printer kicked out four copies of Chloe's statement. She reconsidered, then went back and printed out the last six months' records, all that was still available online.

Her cell phone rang. It was Paul. "You need me?" He sounded harried or as if he had someone with him.

"I have info on the ID theft. I'm going to have Lance drive me into the fraud unit—"

"Don't do that. I'm not far. I'll take you." She noticed he didn't ask any questions. He was a stickler for not discussing important things over a cell phone.

"Okay." She hung up.

Wyatt was studying her intently. "Sounds like you have your problem solved."

She didn't see any reason not to tell him. "Don't say anything to anyone. I don't want this person to get away with it." He nodded solemnly, and she continued. "It's my ex's new wife."

"Why would she do that to you?"

"She has a history of it, and I made it easy by not changing my password after my divorce."

"That's too bad." He shook his head. "Do you think this will straighten it out?"

"I hope so, but it may not be that easy. The least I can do is alert the authorities and hope they can stop her before she does this to someone else."

"Will you be back in time for dinner? I have a proposition for you. I can see now's not the time."

"Maybe," Madison hedged. She'd hoped to have a dinner alone with Paul. She'd spent the last two with Wyatt.

"Let me walk you back to the guesthouse. I'll tell you what I have in mind and you can think about it."

"Great," she said, although she doubted she could concentrate on anything besides nailing Chloe right now.

"You know I'm setting up a foundation to fund promising medical research. There's a lot to be done. One of the most important things will be finding a director." He held open the door to the terrace. It was the fastest way to the guesthouse. She'd gone in the kitchen door because she hadn't expected him to be home.

She tucked the stack of papers under her arm and walked quickly toward the bungalow. "There must be a lot of well-qualified people who would love the job."

"I don't want some professional foundation person who'll view this as just another business opportunity. I think you should come on board right now and train for the position."

She stopped dead in her tracks. "What? You can't mean that."

"Why not? I've studied your record. A mathematics major trained in sequencing research and statistics. You could analyze projects and evaluate them as well as anyone."

Her breath caught in her lungs and for a moment she was speechless. Finally, she managed to say, "I have no credentials. No one would respect my decisions."

"This foundation won't be up and running for another year or so. I hope I live to see it. You could train on the job." He smiled encouragingly. "A foundation is better off with a well-rounded person than someone like Garrison. He'd just back sea-based research."

"You'd turn down your own son?"

"No. We've discussed it. I think I told you before, Garrison isn't interested."

"Surely there is someone at your company."

"Not really. A couple of guys are possibilities, but they're too close to retirement."

They'd reached the guesthouse, and she took out the key. If Wyatt thought it was unusual for her to lock the door just to go to the main house, he didn't mention it.

"You aren't going back to TotalTrivia, are you? Why don't you come see what we do? Then you can decide."

"May I think about this? It's so, so…unexpected. I've got so much on my mind."

"Of course. Just have faith in yourself and consider this an opportunity."

"I will." She walked into the guesthouse. One thing Wyatt said was absolutely true. Once she turned Chloe in, she couldn't go back to work.

CHAPTER THIRTY

PAUL WATCHED Madison as she told Special Agent Wells about what she'd found in Chloe Larsen's bank records. The FBI agent nodded thoughtfully and glanced down at the sheaf of papers Madison had handed him. Now she gave him copies of her own bank records with fraudulent withdrawals highlighted.

"There's not much we can do immediately," Wells told them. "Her records were obtained illegally."

"Can't you find an excuse to do it?" she asked.

Wells shook his head. "We can watch her, and you bet we will. Apparently, she sold your ID information to a known fraud ring. They've tried to open several accounts in your name, but you were smart enough to have the credit agencies freeze your accounts."

"I can't get any credit, either."

Paul heard the frustration and rising anger in her voice. They'd already been to the police department and were told the same thing. From the moment she'd told him what she'd discovered, Paul had warned her that it would be hard to act on illegally obtained information. The police were sympathetic and noted the information, but Paul knew they wouldn't do anything about it. Paul thought they would have a better chance with the FBI. They had a special identity-theft unit. There were aware of Madison's problems because she had reported the theft to them earlier.

"I'm sure she's going to do it again," Paul told them. "It's just a matter of who the next victim will be."

"Have the employees at your company been warned?" Wells asked.

"No. I didn't think it was necessary. The only ones who make much money are my ex-husband and me."

"What about this woman, Chloe?" Wells asked. "Does she have access to the employees' personal information?"

"She could get it."

Paul said, "You'd better warn them. Even if they don't have a lot of money for her to take, she could sell their personal info to the credit card fraud ring. A gambling habit needs to be fed. She might just get desperate enough to do it."

"He's right. Warn them," Wells advised calmly from behind his desk.

"You might want to contact Professor Hinson at Stanford University. I believe he can give you more information about this woman's activities."

Paul was a little surprised to hear Madison say this. They'd talked over the situation and decided not to involve Pamela Nolan because it might jeopardize her position at the university.

"Oh? What do you think he would tell me?" Wells wanted to know.

"I'm not sure exactly but it's my understanding that Chloe Barnett, now Chloe Larsen, was asked to leave the university after a similar scam. He may have details that you could use."

"Okay, I'll contact him. It's still early on the West Coast." Wells stood up and handed his card to Madison, then gave one to Paul. "We're going to get her. I promise. It just may take a little time. Be patient. Call me if you have any other details."

They thanked Special Agent Wells and left. On the way out of the building, Paul told Madison, "Don't be discouraged. I really think the FBI will do something."

Madison didn't respond. He put his arm around her and gave her a hug.

"It's just so frustrating," she finally said. "I wish there was something I could do to catch her."

"I don't think there is. You should warn TotalTrivia's employees. Don't mention her name. She could sue you."

They got into the Porsche Paul's father was letting him use. "I'm going to drop you off at your office. I'll come back in two hours. Don't go outside of the building."

"Wyatt had an interesting proposition for me," she said.

Something in her tone bothered Paul. "What kind of a proposition?"

"He wants me to work at Holbrook Pharmaceuticals. He wants to train me for the job of foundation president or whatever title a foundation head has."

Why? Paul asked himself. Not that Madison wasn't smart, with a great personality, but her field wasn't medicine or science. "Is this his way of making sure you donate?"

"I don't know. I agreed to consider it. What do you think?"

"I want whatever you want. It's really your decision."

She turned away and looked out the window. "He invited me to dinner tonight to discuss it."

"Go," Paul encouraged. "I'm meeting with Trey Williams this evening to interview one of the guys that Wyatt said might have a grudge. I won't be back until nine or so."

"His offer comes at a good time. I need to get out of Total-Trivia. I don't want to be around that horrid woman. I plan to do more with my life than create a game. I certainly don't want to be a part of anything that encourages gambling."

"I don't think that's a half-bad idea. But are you going to sell to Estevez?"

"No. I want Aiden to buy me out." She thought for a moment, then said, "Did you take a look at Nathan Cassidy?"

"Yes. He didn't make any trips to Boston. At least, none showed on his credit cards. Why?"

"I don't know. There's something about him," she replied.

"You know, these are the kind of people who use private planes."

"Give me some credit," he said in a teasing voice. "I thought of that. Nothing showed up when we checked around. Now there are a lot of small airports. We didn't have the manpower to check them all."

They drove the rest of the way to TotalTrivia in silence. Paul was still puzzled about Holbrook's offer. But it might be just the opportunity Madison needed.

THE MINUTE Madison walked into TotalTrivia's reception area, Jade cried, "There you are. Aiden's been trying to reach you for over an hour."

Madison had turned off her cell phone to go into the FBI field office and hadn't remembered to turn it on again, nor had she checked voice mail. "What does he want?"

Jade rolled eyes that today were coated with violet eyeliner. "I don't know, but he went ballistic when he couldn't reach you. I didn't know where you were. He called the Russerts but they told him you moved out. They didn't know where you were."

"I'll be in my office," Madison told her.

"Aren't you going to see Aiden first?"

"Nope." Madison walked away. Let the jerk stew. She had to admit she was curious. Aiden seldom "went ballistic." He was usually as laid-back as a Malibu surfer. The only time she recalled him actually raising his voice was when she refused to sell her half of TotalTrivia during divorce negotiations.

Aiden was behaving oddly. She'd put it down to money troubles—Chloe having spent more than they had—but now she wondered. Could he be the one after her? Aiden certainly had the computer expertise to alter records. She didn't think he knew about her and the Holbrooks but it wouldn't have been difficult for him to find out. He could have a bug in her office or something.

She walked through the cube farm and nodded at several pro-grammers who looked up as she passed. She had to tell them about the identity theft. She went into her office, dropped her purse in a drawer and placed her laptop on her desk, then took it out of its case. Out of the corner of her eye, she saw Aiden sprinting toward her office. Boy-o-boy, something was on his mind.

A second later, he burst into her office, saying, "Where have you been? I've been trying to reach you for over an hour."

"I was with a friend." She opened her laptop and sat in her desk chair.

"We're in trouble." Aiden collapsed into the chair opposite her desk.

Madison sincerely doubted she could be in much more trouble than she already was. She calmly asked, "What's the problem?"

"We're not going to be able to make payroll."

"What?" she shouted. "Why not?"

"Shush." Aiden put his finger in front of his lips. "We don't want the programmers to walk out."

"We have plenty of money." A cold prickling sensation started on her cheeks, then crept down her back. Aiden always handled the finances. She was good at math, better than he was, but their business was relatively simple and he'd insisted on doing it.

"We're missing a quarter of a million dollars."

"Missing?" she repeated as if it were a foreign word. She was suddenly conscious of the anxiety reflected in Aiden's eyes. A pulsing knot formed in her chest. It was one of those things she just knew without being told. Chloe had taken the money.

"I logged on this morning and it was gone."

"Was it there yesterday?" she asked as she logged on to her computer.

"Yes."

She heard the threat of tears in his voice. The only other time she'd known Aiden to cry was when he told her how sorry he was for hurting her, but he loved Chloe. She typed in Chloe's password. "What is the exact amount we're missing?"

"Two hundred and twenty-five thousand dollars." His voice was still shaky.

There it was sitting in Chloe's account. It was right there on the screen. She opened the drawer, took out her purse and found Special Agent Wells's card. She picked up her desk phone and began dialing.

"Who are you calling?" Aiden wanted to know.

"Where's Chloe?" she asked, continuing to punch in the number.

"At the doctor. What does it matter where she is? Who are you calling?"

"The FBI." The phone started to ring.

"That's ridiculous. They can't help us. This isn't a federal case. I think we should go to Luis Estevez for a loan. I want you to come with me."

Special Agent Wells answered on the second ring. "It's Madison Connelly. I want to report a crime in progress. Can you do anything about that?"

"Depends. What's going on?"

"I'm at my company. Two hundred and twenty-five thousand dollars is missing from our business account. I have Chloe Larsen's personal account up on my screen. Our money is sitting in her account. It was deposited there early this morning."

"What?" Aiden vaulted out of his chair and stormed to her side of the desk. "I don't believe this."

"I'll freeze the account," Wells told her. "As part of a federal investigation I can do that. You'll need to get a lawyer and start proceedings."

"Please hurry," she said, aware that Aiden was reading her computer screen over her shoulder. "You saw how fast my money disappeared."

"It'll take less than five minutes."

"That's not our money," Aiden insisted, his face becoming the color of an eggplant. "That's from Chloe's trust fund."

"Chloe doesn't have a trust fund. Her parents aren't wealthy, but you wouldn't know that, would you? You've never met them."

"They died in an auto accident."

"No. They're alive and well. They're high school science teachers in Fresno."

"I don't believe you." There was a kernel of doubt in his voice.

"I could care less what you believe. I have proof that Chloe took my money. I gave it to the FBI this morning. That's why I had Special Agent Wells's card so handy."

"You're just saying this because you hate Chloe for taking me away from you."

"You're right, I hate her, but she did me a favor by getting you out of my life. I hate her for taking my money. I hate her for taking money from a Stanford University special marine project."

"Where are you getting all this?" Aiden's voice was barely a whisper.

"Sit down, Aiden."

Aiden did as he was told. He slumped down into the chair. Disbelief etched the face she'd once found so handsome. He was a weak man. How could she not have seen it?

"Chloe loves me. She wouldn't do this to me."

"Maybe she does love you, but she loves online gambling more." She went into her purse again and found the card Tobias Pennington had given her. She had the feeling Wyatt's assistant would know a lawyer who handled these kinds of cases..

Madison thought of calling Nathan Cassidy, but there was something about the man that caused her not to trust him. Paul might not have found a link between Nathan and trips to Boston during the time the other donor-conceived children were murdered but that didn't mean Nathan wasn't involved. Instead of contacting Nathan, she dialed the number and Tobias answered on the first ring.

"Hello. It's Madison Connelly. Am I getting you at a bad time?"

"Not at all. What can I do for you?"

"I'm at work. I've discovered an employee has taken a con-siderable amount of money. The FBI has frozen her account, but to get it back I have hire a lawyer. Do you know someone who handles cases like this?"

"Yes, but it's going to cost you and it'll take time. You'd be better off to demand the employee return the money."

"No way. I want her stopped."

"You're just as stubborn as the rest of the Holbrooks," Tobias told her with a chuckle.

Madison didn't bother to argue that she wasn't a Holbrook. She merely wrote down the name and phone number. When she looked at Aiden, he was cowering in the chair like a dog waiting to be kicked. It made her think of Aspen back at the guesthouse.

Madison tried to reach Paul but his cell kicked right to voice mail. She told him to call her, then she called the attorney's office and made an appointment for the following morning. She'd had to use Tobias Pennington's name to get seen so quickly.

Aiden had perked up a bit while she'd been on the phone but he still looked like a man about to face a firing squad. "Where are you going to get the money for a lawyer? Why don't I just convince Chloe to give it back?"

"Nope. I'm filing charges."

"Look, I'll pay you back every cent you lost, too," he pleaded. "Chloe loves me enough to get help for this problem."

"It's an addiction and it's not easy to kick."

"I won't be part of any lawsuit. I'll say I gave her the money." His smug grin reminded her of a used-car salesman. "No lawyer will take your case then. You couldn't pay one anyway."

"Aiden, let me make one thing absolutely clear to you. I will file charges. If you lie, you could be charged, as well. I will chase you with lawsuits for years to come and make your life a living hell." Like a time bomb, anger ticked inside her and was reflected in her low but mean voice. "Do you know where I'm living? In Wyatt Holbrook's guesthouse."

She saw Aiden recognized the name. Most people would, but Aiden always knew the players in Miami and longed to be among them.

"It just so happens that I may be his daughter." She didn't believe this herself but it sounded more threatening.

"No way. I knew your father."

"I didn't realize until recently that I was a donor-conceived child. Wyatt donated a lot of sperm while he was in college. I know he'll lend me whatever money I need." Of course, she knew no such thing, but she was determined to make Aiden take her seriously.

"Oh God, what am I going to do?" Aiden was back to whining mode again.

She felt like laughing and saying, *I told you so*. But she was a better person than that. She'd loved this man once. She'd grieved for him for months. She couldn't bring herself to kick him while he was down. Meeting Paul had changed her view on life. She wanted out of this mess as seamlessly as possible.

"Aiden, listen to me," she said in her softest, kindest voice. "Chloe nearly ruined a professor at Stanford. She slept with him and stole donor information from his key project, spent the money on gambling, and someone exposed her. The poor guy used his life savings to pay back the money. The university asked her to leave rather than charge her and receive a lot of negative publicity."

Aiden threw his head back and stared at the ceiling.

Madison gave him a minute to consider what she'd told him. "It's going to take tough love to change Chloe. She might receive a suspended sentence or a short jail term. But if she gets away with it, the way she did at Stanford, she'll keep doing it."

Jade appeared at Madison's desk. "Is there, like, something I can do?"

Madison knew Jade couldn't have heard their conversation. Madison had seen her on the other side of the cube farm, flirting as usual. Aiden was still staring at the ceiling.

"Yes, there is something I need you to do. Go to each programmer. Ask them to check with all three credit reporting agencies to see if any credit cards have been taken out in their name that they didn't authorize. Then—"

"Kyle and Jeff told me yesterday that they were having problems. Cash had been taken out of credit card accounts."

"Oh, shit," groaned Aiden.

"Check with everyone else. Make them stop whatever they are doing and check with the agencies. If their credit is okay, have them freeze their accounts."

"Have we had a breach or something?" Jade asked.

"Yes. Now hurry up and alert the programmers."

"Oh, fuck! I can't believe this is happening." Aiden slowly rose. "What am I going to do?"

"Aiden, when I leave today, I'm not coming back. That doesn't mean I've changed my mind about filing charges."

"What am I going to do without you?" He shoved his hands into his pockets, his shoulders hunched over like an old man.

"Get Jade to do my job. She's perfectly capable."

"No, I mean what am I going to do about this mess with Chloe?"

"You may want to see an attorney yourself." She took a deep breath, then added, "I want you to buy me out. You can make payments over time or something, but I'm through here."

"What are you going to do?"

"I'm not sure, but Wyatt Holbrook has made me an interesting offer."

CHAPTER THIRTY-ONE

How many bones are in the human body?

MADISON WAS SITTING at the table on the terrace across from Wyatt. Savannah was chattering on and on about wedding plans. Occasionally, Nathan offered a suggestion. Wyatt seemed interested and he didn't make a single comment about Savannah's drinking. Savannah was enjoying her second Lady of the Night. Madison had never heard of this particular type of martini, but Savannah informed her that it was "all the rage." The martini had a floater on it, a thin slice of cucumber topped by a dollop of caviar.

"Now those are our plans, if we get married here in Miami," Savannah told her father. "We're also considering a destination wedding."

"Meaning?" Wyatt asked.

"You know, like Molly Burke's wedding in Florence."

"Right. Make all your friends travel halfway around the world." Wyatt didn't sound thrilled with this idea.

Madison tuned them out and she thought about Paul instead. He'd come right over to TotalTrivia as soon as he'd picked up her voice mail. He'd been able to convince Aiden to turn in Chloe. The last she'd seen of Aiden was as he left for the police station to file a complaint. Chloe would have the police and the FBI after her. Paul expected her to be arrested by evening. The woman might even be in jail right now, Madison thought.

She was surprised to find she felt a little guilty. Here she was having a delicious seafood salad and gazing out at the beautiful ocean while Aiden was dealing with the consequences of Chloe's problems. It would be difficult for him and he didn't deserve it. She'd loved him once and felt sorry for him now.

Maybe he'd become stronger, the way she had after the divorce. Sure, she went through emotional hell, but she came out a better person. And she'd found Paul. She'd been waiting her entire life for this man without knowing it.

"Madison," Savannah said. "Earth to Madison."

"Sorry," Madison replied. "My mind wandered."

"I asked about your wedding."

Madison couldn't imagine how she could contribute anything when such a lavish affair was being planned. "A justice of the peace married us."

Savannah scowled as if she'd just been served a plate of fried ants. "Really?"

"I wouldn't lie."

"Hadn't your father recently died?" Wyatt asked.

"Yes. A church wedding without him to walk me down the aisle was out of the question."

"Well, here comes dessert," Nathan said in a none-too-smooth attempt to change the subject. "Homemade gelato with fresh fruit."

They were served the gelato in shell-shaped silver bowls. One of the maids put a dish of whipped cream on the table. No one spoke for a moment. That was unusual, Madison reflected. This was her third dinner with them. It seemed someone was always talking.

"We'd better enjoy this weather," Nathan said. "In another month we won't be able to eat out here."

"I like to have breakfast here in the summer when the weather's too hot to eat outside in the evening," added Wyatt.

Madison had to admit it was lovely right now. The balmy

air wasn't so humid you felt as if you were wading through it every time you moved. The aroma of the gardenias at the perimeter of the property drifted on a cat's paw of a breeze that was too light to ruffle her hair. It would be perfect if Paul were sitting beside her.

"Where's Garrison this evening?" asked Madison.

Wyatt shrugged.

"Who knows?" Savannah said with a shake of her head that made her hair swish across her shoulders. "Probably at his place in the Keys."

Wyatt finished his dessert and glanced at Madison. She'd eaten the fruit but was toying with the gelato. "Are you finished?" he asked.

"Yes. It's delicious, but I'm full."

Wyatt rose, saying, "Excuse us. We're going into my office to discuss some business."

"Have fun," Savannah said a little too cheerily.

Madison walked beside Wyatt and wondered how much of her troubles at the office she should reveal. It wasn't gory enough for television in a city where crime was rampant, but it might be in the morning papers. She should at least mention it.

Wyatt opened the door to his office and stood aside to allow her to enter first. There was a vase of yellow roses on his desk and their heady scent filled the air. A small model skeleton of a human body stood beside the flowers. *There are two hundred and six bones in the human body,* she thought to herself. *Stop it! Let go of the trivia.*

Wyatt sat down, saying, "Have you had a chance to think about my proposition?"

Madison took the chair opposite his desk. "A little. I'm afraid we had a problem at work that consumed my attention. An employee stole a lot of money."

"That's terrible. You have enough problems already." Wyatt paused, then asked, "You keep money around?"

"No. She took it out of our bank account."

Wyatt nodded, but Madison didn't elaborate. "I did come up with a few questions."

"Shoot," Wyatt said with a smile.

"If I'm not one of your donor-conceived children, will it matter?"

"No, not in the least," he assured her in an oddly gentle tone.

"Will it make a difference if I can't donate part of my liver?"

"No, it won't. With my immune system, I'll be lucky to find a match."

She gazed at him, flashing a quick smile of thanks.

Wyatt leaned forward, elbows on the desk. "I thought of you because you're smart and have a background in statistics. Evaluating research requires a good knowledge of how to interpret test results. An analytical mind is important. Plus, I could train you myself in what time I have left."

Her heart went out to him. She remembered how depressed her father had become when the end neared. He had so wanted to be a grandfather. An ache too deep for tears suddenly came over her. She forced her mind back to the present.

"There's another problem," she told him. "I oppose the use of animals in testing."

"I realize that from previous discussions. It doesn't bother me. I don't believe in it, either, except in rare cases. I believe vivisection will become a thing of the past—soon. Over ninety percent of all drugs tested on animals and declared effective fail in human tests."

"Do you think 3-D computer models will replace vivisection?" she asked, recalling what she'd read online.

"Absolutely. That and microdosing, biochips and nanotechnology."

"What if I don't like the work or you think I'm wrong for the position? Can we agree to be honest and say so immediately?"

"Yes. Being honest is important," he agreed. "Any other questions?"

"Not really. I'm sure I will when you start to train me."

"When can you begin?"

"Tomorrow." She remembered her appointment with the attorney. "In the afternoon."

He arched an eyebrow in surprise. "What about your company?"

"I'm selling it to my ex-husband."

MADISON HAD RETURNED from walking Aspen along the beach and heard her cell phone ringing from her purse, which was in the bedroom. She dashed across the living room, down the hall just as the phone stopped ringing. Maybe it was Paul, she thought. It was just eight, but hopefully he'd finished early or perhaps he was calling to tell her about Chloe.

Voice mail showed two messages. The first was from Paul, saying Chloe had been arrested and would be arraigned tomorrow. Aiden would post bail immediately, she thought.

The second message was from her mother. Thank God! Madison had been worried. Jessica Whitcomb sounded fine and left a 305 area code phone number. She must be home. Great, Madison reasoned. She could discuss this donor-conceived question in person.

She punched in the phone number. Her mother answered on the second ring. "Mom. You're home?"

"I'm back, baby doll."

Madison's heart sang; her mother often called her baby doll. Until Erin's death, she hadn't realized how much she missed her mother. "Where are you? When did you get back?"

Two beats of silence. "Mom? Can you hear me?" What a time for a dropped call.

"I hear you. I came home three days ago. I'm staying with Max and Andy."

"Three days? Why didn't you call me? I've been worried. I hadn't heard from you in so long."

"I'm sorry, honey. It's hard to explain." She sighed. "I didn't want to hear you say 'I told you so.' I'm getting a divorce."

Had she been so cruel about the marriage that her mother hadn't called her for three whole days? "Oh, Mom. I'm sorry. I must have been—"

"You were right. Scott wasn't the guy for me. That man was your father."

"Mom, can you drive over here? I want to see you. Hug you." Tears unexpectedly filled Madison's eyes.

"I don't have a car," she replied. "The boys won't be back for hours."

Max and Andy were gay friends of her mother's. She'd known them both since high school. They were accomplished interior designers whose services were always in demand. They'd made a fortune by restoring fabulous old homes in Coral Gables.

"Are Max and Andy still in Coral Gables?" Even though she'd grown up around these wonderful guys, she'd lost track of them when she'd been married to Aiden. He was as homophobic as they came.

"Yes."

Madison took down the address her mother gave her. "I'll be right over. It'll take me a while. I'm in Palm Beach."

"What are you doing there?"

"It's a long story. I'll explain when I see you." Madison snapped her phone shut, tossed it in her purse and scribbled a note to Paul. She knew he'd be furious that she'd left by herself, but she had to see her mother.

Her car was parked behind the bungalow. She hadn't used it lately because Paul insisted on driving her. "Hop in, boy," she told Aspen. Her mother loved dogs. She'd be thrilled to meet the retriever.

It took less time to arrive than she'd anticipated. Traffic was lighter than usual, since it was after the rush hour. She turned onto the gorgeous tree-lined streets she'd once loved so much. Max and Andy didn't live far from where she and Aiden had bought a house.

She drove up the long cobbled driveway that went around to the back of the house and parked off to the side in case the guys returned and wanted to park in their garage while she was visiting with her mother. Jessica Whitcomb must have been listening for a car. She rushed out a side door, her arms open.

Madison was out of the car in a flash. She ran into her mother's arms and bear-hugged her. "Oh, Mom. I'm so glad to see you. I love you. I missed you so much."

"I missed you, too." Her mother pulled back. "It's too dark out here to see what you look like, see if you've changed."

"Mom, I apologize for how mean I was about you remarrying. I'm sorry it didn't work out. I know how you must have felt after Daddy died. Lonely and upset. I wasn't any help."

"It's okay. You *were* right. We weren't a good fit." She slipped her arm around Madison's waist. "Let's go inside and talk. We've got a lot of catching up to do."

The "boys," as her mother usually called Andy and Max, had restored another huge rambling home to its original elegance. It reminded Madison of the nearby Biltmore, which was Spanish in design, with ornate tiles and mahogany furniture boasting plush cushions.

Her mother led her in through the side door not far from where she'd parked her car. "I can stay here in the south wing until I get on my feet again. The boys are true friends."

"Yes, they are." She hugged her mother again and tears began to trickle down Madison's cheeks. "I'm so glad to see you."

"Don't cry, honey. Everything is okay." Jessica ran her hand through short, curly locks. "Changed my hair."

"I like it."

"It was easier on the boat. Plus, it was time for a new look." She gestured toward a love seat.

They were in a study or a small reading room. It was done in relaxing shades of moss-green. The fabric on the furniture had a palm leaf design.

"I'm so terribly sorry about Erin," her mother said. "The boys told me."

"I found her, Mom."

"Oh my Lord!" Her mother's blue eyes were the same ones Madison saw in the mirror every morning, but now they were filled with genuine sorrow. Her mother hugged her and ran her hand across the back of her head, comforting Madison the way she had when Madison had been a child. "The boys didn't realize that." Her mother released her and gazed lovingly into Madison's eyes.

"I know. The media just said a friend found her. That would be me."

"It must have been terrible. I can't imagine…"

"Devastating. Even worse, the police suspected me."

"They did? Why?"

"Apparently, Erin had some valuable property she'd inherited from her parents. She left it to me. I had no idea. She'd never told me. So the police thought I had a motive."

"They know better now, don't they?"

"Yes, I think so." She didn't want to get into all that yet. There was one question on her mind and it had been nagging at her relentlessly. "Mom, when was the last time we talked? I can't remember. So much has been happening."

"It was over a month ago. Even then I was thinking about flying home, but I didn't mention it. I had to wait until we sailed into a port with an airport nearby. Then I just flew here rather than call."

"I'm so glad you're home."

"I get to start over again," her mother said, attempting an upbeat tone. "I have no money and no job. I'm going to hit you up for a loan."

Madison slapped both hands over her eyes and laughed.

"What's so funny?"

"Mom, I don't have a cent. At least you can get credit. Thanks to identity theft, I don't have any money, but don't worry. I'm fixing the mess."

"Oh, baby doll. That's terrible. The boys will let me stay here and lend me money. There are a couple of places I can apply for a job. It'll work out."

Her mother was always like this. Optimistic. It was uplifting just to hear her voice, know she was home. Where she belonged.

"Mom, there's something I need to ask you. And I need you to tell me the truth."

Her mother gazed at her in shocked surprise. "Haven't I always told you the truth?"

"Yes, of course." It was true; her mother rarely dissembled. Only at the end, when her father was near death, had her mother insisted he was going to make it. Maybe it hadn't been a lie, Madison decided. Her mother had honestly believed a miracle would happen. "Is Daddy my biological father?"

No sooner were the words out of her mouth than she heard furious barking. Aspen. In the excitement of seeing her mother, she'd forgotten him. There wasn't even a window down in the car.

"Oh my gosh." She jumped up. "That's my dog. I forgot him in the car."

"Bring him in. The boys won't mind."

Madison went to the side door that led out of the study to the driveway. She squinted at the darkness and stood there a moment to let her eyes adjust. Aspen was still barking. He rarely barked, she realized. Usually, it was at a neighbor's orange cat that had the audacity to come near the guesthouse.

The driveway was lined with mature trees and tall bushes. Shadows overlapped each other, and she thought she saw something move. Probably another cat was retreating into the bushes to get away from Aspen's frantic barking.

Paul's voice warning her to be cautious sounded in her head. No one knew she was here. Unless she'd been followed. No way. She'd looked in her rearview mirror as she left Corona del Mar. No one had been around, not even the guard. He'd probably been patrolling the other side of the property.

A twinge of guilt crept through her. She'd switched off her cell phone. She didn't want to be interrupted while she had this discussion with her mother. Paul would call the minute he saw her note. And he'd be furious.

"Wait a sec," her mother said. "Let me turn on the lights. The cobblestones are uneven. You don't want to fall."

A few seconds later, floodlights illuminated the driveway, which was cobbled with lacy green baby tears growing between the stones. The boys really had a flair. If she ever had enough money, she'd hire them. She walked up to the car and opened the door for Aspen. He bounded out, tail wagging.

"Come on, boy. Meet my mother." She walked back to the side door. "Mom, this is Aspen."

Her mother stroked Aspen's silky blond head. "Oh, you're handsome." She turned to Madison. "Have you had him long? You didn't mention him when we last spoke."

Madison explained about finding him at Erin's home. She also told her that the retriever had been liberated from a cosmetic firm testing products on animals. They sat down again with Aspen settled at her feet.

There was a moment of silence before Madison's mother said, "You were asking about your father."

CHAPTER THIRTY-TWO

Name the only place on earth where alligators and croco-diles live side by side.

MADISON INHALED a deep breath. So much depended on her mother's answer. "Was Daddy my biological father?"

"Yes, he was. Why on earth would you think he wasn't?"

"There were records at a place called New Horizons Clinic. They had your name on them, and there was this interview for screening—"

"How did you know?" her mother asked, obviously stunned that Madison knew any of this.

"The Holbrooks uncovered the records."

"I did go there," her mother admitted in a low voice etched with emotion. "I never told your father about it. We were having trouble getting pregnant. I took every fertility test imaginable."

"Was there a problem?"

"Not with me," her mother said. "It turned out Zeke had a low sperm count. He said it would happen with time. Several years went by and nothing. I thought maybe I should do something."

"Without telling Daddy?"

Her mother looked away and sighed. "Yes. I knew he wouldn't approve. He kept saying we would get pregnant. He was right. We did. You came along. I never followed through with New Horizons."

Another weight lifted. No one would believe her, but she'd always known in her heart of hearts that Zachary Connelly was her father. A warm glow sang in her veins.

It took Madison a few minutes to explain to her mother about Paul finding her and the Holbrooks believing she was related. She explained about Chloe and the ID theft and how she was living in the Holbrooks' guesthouse and now going to work for him.

"My word! This is amazing. Well, I'm afraid Mr. Holbrook will be disappointed. You aren't related to him. Odds are you're not a match."

"I knew. I knew all along. Daddy was truly my father. No one would listen to me because that clinic had your name down as receiving his sperm."

Her mother drew a deep breath. "I'm not surprised my name was down. The clinic was very expensive. I borrowed the deposit from the boys. When I became pregnant, I went to the clinic and asked for my deposit back. They said it was nonrefundable. I was furious. A friend told me there was a waiting list by that point."

"Was the friend Erin's mother?"

"Yes. Susan told me. How did you know?"

"Go on. I'll explain in a minute."

"I sold my name to another woman."

"Wait a minute," Madison said. "Didn't the clinic know exactly who you were?" Her mother was beautiful even now, but when she'd been younger, she'd been a knockout. People didn't forget her.

"They did, but New Horizons had two locations. One was in Miami, while the other was in Boca Raton. I contacted a woman Susan knew and she willingly purchased my spot. I told her to go to the Boca clinic and say she'd moved there and have the records transferred. I read that later they closed the Boca clinic and just operated out of the Miami office."

"Daddy never knew anything about this?"

"No. I didn't tell him. He would have been angry about it. What was the point?" Her mother touched her arm. "Baby doll, there are some things men are better off not knowing."

"Why did Erin's mother wait until Erin was in her twenties to tell her?"

"Erin was always a difficult child. Reclusive. Susan had expected a highly intelligent child because the father was a Mensa member and a Harvard grad, but Erin really didn't care about school. I think her mother worried that she'd rebel even more if she knew was donor-conceived."

"I think it's what got her killed." Madison went on to tell her mother about the murder of Wyatt's offspring in the Boston area and about the death of Keith Brooks Smith. She then explained about the Chagas scare.

Her mother's eyes darkened with emotion. "Your life is in danger, isn't it?"

"It may have been, but when this news gets out, I'm off the hook."

"Oh God," her mother cried. "I never imagined—"

"Who would? This is a bizarre thing. If someone is so desperate to get rid of Wyatt, why not just shoot him?"

Her mother nodded. "This is a very sadistic person. Very."

"A certifiable lunatic." Madison's body tingled with relief. She was exactly who she thought she was.

"How are you getting along without Aiden? Are you dating again?"

"I met someone wonderful. Paul Tanner. He's a homicide detective. He's been watching over me. You know, in case this maniac comes after me."

"Really? That's wonderful. I can't wait to meet him." Her mother hugged her. "Please be careful. I'm worried about you."

"Don't worry, please." She reached for her purse, which was on the floor not far from Aspen. "I'd better call Paul and let him know I'm coming back soon. He'll worry, too." She checked for messages; there weren't any. *Maybe I can get back before Paul does,* she thought. "Let's get together tomorrow. I'll introduce you to Paul. And if you need money—"

"I'll ask the boys to lend me some. They've already offered, but I assumed you…"

"I may be able to help you out soon. We're working on it." She rose. "Walk me out to the car."

Aspen jumped to his feet and followed her to the door. The lights were still on, and they went slowly toward her Beamer. Neither wanted to part. There was so much to say, but Madison didn't want to upset Paul. As her mother had wisely pointed out, there were some things men were better off not knowing. If she could get back before he did, she wasn't mentioning this trip.

Aspen sprinted ahead, barking furiously. The hackles on his back were up; his tail was down low.

"Are there any cats around here?" she asked her mother.

"I guess. The boys don't have any but I'm not sure about the neighbors."

"Aspen rarely barks except at cats." She watched the dog. He had his nose under the car just below the passenger door, barking for all he was worth. "I'll bet there's a cat hiding under the car."

As they came closer, Aspen's head popped up. He looked at them and began growling, low and deep in his chest, the way he had the night Garrison came to put the note on her door. Madison lowered herself to her knees and peaked under the car. Nothing unless the cat was black. Wouldn't its eyes glow in the dark?

"What do you see?" her mother asked as Aspen continued to growl.

"Nothing. Do the boys have a flashlight?"

"Yes, in the pantry. I'll go get it."

Madison went around to the back of the car and tried to look

from that angle. She caught the gleam of the cat's one red eye.
A one-eyed cat in Coral Gables? Anything was possible, she
decided. After all, the Everglades was the only place in the
world where alligators and crocodiles lived together. That was
Florida for you.

Enough with the trivia, already.

The eye blinked. "Shoo! Shoo!" she shouted.

It didn't move. Aspen was beside her now, barking again,
then growling. The eye blinked again. She realized a second had
elapsed. It blinked again. It wasn't a cat. It was an electronic
something.

Madison stood up and backed away from the car. She pulled
her cell phone out from her purse and hit the speed dial for
Paul's number. He answered, "Hey, babe. I'm on the way there
right now. Took longer than we thought."

"Paul, did you put a tracking device under my car?"

"No, why?" She heard the alarm in his voice. "What are you
doing looking under your car? Why is Aspen barking?"

Her mother came up with a flashlight and stood beside her.
"I'm with my mother in Coral Gables. When I came out—"

"What in hell are you doing there? Is the guard with you?"

"No. I came by myself. My mother returned from the South
Pacific. I had to see her."

"Son of a bitch! You never listen." He cursed again, then said,
"I'm not far. Give me the address. I'll come over."

She rattled off the address and told him, "The thing has a
tiny blinking red light on it."

"Shit! Sounds like an explosive device. Now listen to me. Do
not touch the car. For sure, do not put your key in the ignition."

"Okay. I promise."

"I'm not an expert on bombs, but one thing we've learned
from Iraq is that they can be detonated by cell phone. Get as far
away from the vehicle as you can. I'm calling the bomb squad."

"What's happening?" her mother asked.

"Come, Aspen. Let's go to the front of the house." She took her mother's arm and led her away from the Beamer. Aspen followed. "I looked under the car and saw a blinking red light. Paul thinks it might be a bomb."

"Oh my God!"

"I think Aspen was warning me. I'll bet he was in the car when it was put underneath. That's why he was barking."

"Oh, baby doll. What are we going to do?"

Her mother had never been the hysterical type, but Madison detected something akin to panic in her voice. She felt ice creep into every pore.

They stood out front near the street, under the majestic banyan tree that was artfully illuminated by tiny spotlights. When they'd reached the front of the house, Aspen stopped barking.

She was terrified now, almost trembling, but she tried not to show it. Her mother was upset enough without Madison breaking down. Someone wanted her dead. They meant business.

Paul screeched up a few minutes later in his father's Porsche with a portable police flasher attached to the hood. He jumped out. "Are you okay?"

"Yes. Aspen warned me with a lot of barking and growling. He had his nose under the car," she managed to tell him calmly. She turned to her mother. "Mom, this is Paul Tanner. Paul, meet Jessica Whitcomb."

Paul smiled at her mother, then said, "You have a stubborn daughter. I told her she wasn't safe and not to leave the house."

"She never listened to me, either."

"I'm going to go back and check under the car myself," Paul told them.

"Take this." Her mother handed him the flashlight.

"Maybe I made a mistake," Madison said, praying for this to be true. "You may be dragging the bomb squad out here for nothing."

"Let me check. If the team shows up, send them back."

"Please be careful," she told Paul.

"Well," her mother whispered even though Paul was out of earshot, "he certainly is the handsome, take-charge type."

"The opposite of Aiden." She put her arm around her mother. "We both made mistakes."

A police department panel van pulled up to the curb, followed by two police cars. The sliding door on the van opened and out came two men with German shepherds. Aspen wagged his tail but the professional dogs didn't even look his way, although Madison knew they could smell him.

"The car is around back," Madison said, stepping forward. "Detective Tanner is back there."

A pair of officers approached from the first squad car, one asking, "What's a homicide detective doing here? Nobody's dead, right?"

"He's my boyfriend. I called him about the suspicious thing under my car. He thought it sounded like a bomb so he contacted the bomb squad."

"Gotcha."

The men and dogs headed up the driveway while another man and a young woman unloaded metal boxes of equipment, put the things on a cart and followed the others toward the back of the house. Two more officers emerged from the second squad car, said hello to Madison and her mother, then went after the others.

"We might as well go back into the house," Madison said. "This might take a little time."

They went in through the side door again. Madison waved at Paul so he would know where she'd gone. He nodded but kept watching as the team slid a tray of some kind under her car. She and her mother settled on the sofa with Aspen at their feet. Madison began talking again, as fast as she could, telling her mother about meaningless things just to keep their minds off what was happening outside.

Madison took a deep breath and reached down to pet the dog.

She had been a foot away from death. If it hadn't been for this gentle creature's warning, she would be in a thousand pieces.

"Are you serious about this detective?" her mother asked.

"Yes, but I'm going to take it slowly. I don't want to make another mistake." When her mother nodded, Madison asked about life on the sea.

"Claustrophobic. Boring. So much blue water. Endless blue water. Sometimes we sailed for over a week without seeing land." She shrugged. "It was fun when we were in ports. There others shared their tales and gave advice. But the whole thing got to me. Scott got to me. I missed you and Miami. It's hot and humid and crowded, but it's home."

They were still catching up an hour later when Paul came through the door. *Poor baby,* Madison thought. He looked exhausted. He sat in a nearby chair. Aspen rose and sidled over to him. Paul reached down and petted the dog. "Good boy. You saved her."

"It was a bomb." Madison's breath caught in her throat. She hadn't allowed herself to worry much until now. She'd forced her mind to focus on her mother, but now reality couldn't be ignored. Fear and anger knotted inside her. Who was doing this?

"A crude bomb attached with a magnet. Anyone with a few tools and the Internet could have made it. Took no more than five seconds to affix the damn thing."

"Why did it have that little red light?" her mother asked.

"It's an optional feature that allows the device to be triggered by a cell phone, but this one would have blown you sky-high the second you turned the key in the ignition." Paul shook his head. "Did anyone know you were coming here?"

"No, just Mom."

"You spoke with her over a cell or a landline?"

"On my cell." She groaned. "I totally forgot. I could have used the guesthouse phone. Mom gave the exact address over the cell."

"See anyone following you?"

"No, and I looked. I guess about halfway here I stopped watching," she confessed. "I mean, in the dark all the headlights look the same. I didn't see any strange cars." She thought a moment. "When I came up the street no one was behind me. I checked then."

"I'd bet your cell phone call was monitored," Paul said.

"How does that work?" her mother asked.

"You're just sending out radio waves. With the right equipment, it isn't difficult."

"Wouldn't they have to be nearby recording or something?" her mother asked.

"Not really. Technology these days is pretty amazing," Paul replied. "They could amp the signal and pick it up miles away."

"I was here about ten or fifteen minutes when Aspen began to bark," Madison recalled.

"Coral Gables isn't exactly next door to Palm Beach. That would give our guy time to get here. Could have been up the street, parked with his lights off."

"You know, Mom, before you went to turn on the yard lights, I thought I saw something move in the bushes."

Paul jumped to his feet. "I'll have the guys see if there are any shoe prints in the soil." He was out the door a second later.

"I'm terribly worried about you," her mother said in a troubled voice. "I feel so helpless."

She held her mother's hand. "Please don't worry. Just having you home makes a huge difference. I think if we get out the word that I am not Wyatt's donor-conceived child, I'll be safe. That doesn't mean I don't want this maniac caught, but at least I won't be his target."

"What makes you think it's a man? Earlier you said Paul thought it might be a woman. A woman could have done this or any of the other killings."

"Mom, if there's one thing I've learned recently, it's that I'm not sure of anything."

CHAPTER THIRTY-THREE

IT WAS ALMOST FOUR in the morning when Paul drove Madison into the parking area behind the guesthouse. It was a tight fit with Aspen in the small space behind the sports car's front seats. Paul didn't mind. He'd do anything for Aspen. The dog had literally saved Madison's life. Just like the bomb-sniffing German shepherds, the retriever had smelled something, but how he knew it was dangerous remained a mystery.

They'd spent hours at the station. Madison had been interviewed and Captain Callahan had been called in, even though it was late. He had to approve of Paul's plan, which he did. Paul hadn't expected any resistance. The guy was a publicity hound.

"Do you think they'll find any prints on my car?" Madison asked. Her car had been taken to the yard for examination after the explosive device was removed.

He got out of the car and held his seat back so Aspen could jump out. "I doubt it. But the guy's getting careless. Last time a neighbor called the police in time for us to realize Keith Brooks Smith had been murdered. Tonight he was tripped up by the smartest dog in the world."

Madison was out of the car now. "We'd better let Aspen relieve himself. It's been hours." Aspen had stayed with them at the station; there hadn't been time to take him out.

They skirted the guesthouse and walked along the beach trail the way they had on other nights. The sand glistened, the sea sparkled and the scent of gardenias hung in the air just as before, but nothing was the same for Paul. A golf-ball-size lump formed in his throat and chest-swelling emotion welled up inside him. For a second he thought he might cry.

He'd come unbelievably close to losing Madison. Until now, he'd been running on pure adrenaline. Two nights without sleep and the knowledge that the person he loved the most could be taken away from him in a heartbeat shook him.

Madison released Aspen and the dog lumbered off and immediately lifted his leg on a bush. Paul pulled Madison into his arms. He didn't kiss her; this wasn't about sex. It was about love. He had an all-consuming need for her that he couldn't control, let alone understand. It drove him to protect her, keep her safe at any cost.

"You can't possibly know how much you mean to me," he whispered, his lips against the hair covering her ear. "I almost lost you."

Her arms were around him, hugging tight. "I'm sorry. I should have listened to you. Don't be angry with me."

He pulled back so he could see her face. She was always beautiful, but the moonlight gave her a dreamy glow. "I'm not angry. I was scared. Still am. I've got to get this bastard."

"You think it's a man?"

"Damned if I know. A woman could have put that device together."

"What about the people with grudges against Wyatt?"

He shook his head. "The guy Trey and I went to see tonight, he's one pissed-off nut. Claims the Xeria drug that launched Holbrook's company had been his idea."

"Is there any truth to his claim?"

"I don't think so, but that doesn't mean the guy couldn't be delusional and believe it himself. He was just crazy enough for Trey and I to consider taking a closer look. Trouble is we were interviewing him when someone was attaching a bomb to your car."

"Maybe it's a team. A man and a woman." Madison frowned. "Check to see if Savannah and Nathan have alibis. They were here at dinner. Wyatt and I went into the study to talk. I didn't see them when I came out, but they could have still been around."

"Do you suspect them?" He'd never really believed in women's intuition, but he could be wrong.

"Not really, but Savannah doesn't like me, and she's not going to like me working with her father."

"Come on, Aspen," he called to the dog. "We'd better get to bed. We'll need to get up early to speak with Wyatt before the press conference."

His arm around her, they walked back to the house. He kept feeling he was missing something. A clue was eluding him.

SOMETHING AWAKENED Madison at seven. She was still in Paul's arms. He'd been holding her all night. He was breathing lightly. For a moment she lay in the drowsy warmth of her bed and pretended last night had never happened. *Deal with it,* she told herself. She eased out of his grip and peered over the bed. Aspen was sleeping next to it.

Maybe it was just nerves, she thought as she got up and tiptoed into the bathroom. She was still jumpy and shell-shocked from last night. She went to the bathroom, slipped on her robe, then tiptoed down the hall to use the kitchen phone. She wanted to be sure Wyatt didn't leave for the office before they could talk to him. She left the message with Tobias, who always arrived promptly at seven to have breakfast with Wyatt. The chauffeur drove the men to the office.

Aspen was at the French doors, tail wagging, expecting to go out. After last night, she didn't dare go out alone with him. *He's one smart dog,* she told herself. *Let him go on his own.* She opened the door and Aspen ambled out. He waited, expecting her to come with him the way she usually did.

"Don't even *think* about going out there." Paul's voice came from behind her.

She turned, startled to see him. He slept without clothes and even though she'd seen him nude many times, there was something heart-stoppingly masculine about him. Only the red pocked bullet scar on his thigh marred the perfection. Actually, it didn't, she decided. It made him seem more worldly.

His sex hung heavily between those powerful thighs. Her throat constricted as she realized she wanted to make love to him. Now wasn't the time, she told herself.

"I wasn't going out. I think Aspen's smart enough to go on his own and come back. Don't you?"

"You bet."

"Go on," she told Aspen. "I'll pick up after you later."

As if he understood, Aspen trotted away, his tail in the air like a golden plume.

"I called Tobias and told him that we needed to talk to Wyatt. We're supposed to be there at eight."

"We'd better get in the shower. It's after seven."

"Should I leave the door open for Aspen?" she asked.

"No. Lock it. He's a smart boy. He'll be waiting when we get out of the shower."

Paul's cell phone rang and he sprinted into the bedroom to grab it off the nightstand. While he answered, she headed into the bathroom.

"It's my father," he called to her. "I have to call him back from a landline."

"Okay, I'm in the shower." She turned on the water and stepped in.

A few moments later he joined her. "My father located another of Wyatt's donor-conceived children. Right here in Miami."

"How?" She shampooed her hair.

"Off a Web site where donor offspring can search for

siblings. The registry had posted Wyatt's donor number. I should say numbers, since the clinic used more than one. A woman living in Delray Beach logged on last night, asking if she had siblings."

"So she doesn't know about Wyatt?"

"Not yet." Paul was so tall he had to hunch over to get his head wet. "Don't mention this to anyone. My father phoned the police and they contacted the Web site. Her profile has been taken off. An officer is on his way to see her to warn the woman."

"How many other children do you think could be out there?"

He shrugged. "I don't know. It's an unregulated industry. You're not supposed to have more than twelve siblings, but—get this—one man sired sixty-six. It's like the Wild West. No one's watching over these people."

She closed her eyes and rinsed the suds out of her hair. When she opened them, Paul was staring at her. The heartrending tenderness in his gaze surprised her the way it had last night out on the beach. The look did ridiculous things to her pulse.

"You're gorgeous even wet, without clothes or makeup."

"You're just saying that." She pointed at his erection. "I know what you want."

"Hey, I was too tired last night. Let me make it up to you now."

She shuddered as he cradled her face with his hands and sighed as his lips hovered over hers.

MADISON WALKED beside Paul into Wyatt's home office, where Tobias and Wyatt were waiting for them. They sat down and Tobias poured them coffee from the carafe on the sideboard. She hoped the episode in the shower didn't show on her face. Her body was still aching with pleasure, every nerve ending tingling.

"I have some news," Madison said, accepting the cup from Tobias but directing her comments to Wyatt. "I'm sorry to tell you this after all you've done for me. It doesn't seem fair, but…" She didn't know how to tell him. Wyatt had gone out of his way for her and now she couldn't do anything for him.

"What isn't fair?" asked Wyatt, a concerned look on his face.

"I wish I could help you, but I can't. My mother came home last night. I was not donor-conceived. My mother went to the clinic. That's why her name is in the records. But she became pregnant. She sold her place to another woman."

"Oh, no," Tobias said.

"Do you know her name?" Wyatt asked.

"No. My mother might."

"I'll see what I can do to check it out," Paul offered.

"I'm really sorry. I'll still take the tests in case I can donate, but since I'm not a blood relative, it's doubtful," Madison said.

There was regret in Wyatt's half smile. "You know, sometimes we talk ourselves into things. I thought I saw something of myself in you. I really believed you were my child."

"You did?" She was unexpectedly touched. Wyatt didn't seem to be that close to his own daughter, yet something about Madison had struck a chord with him.

"This doesn't have to change our relationship," Wyatt assured her. "Stay in the guesthouse until things are sorted out."

"There's more," Paul said. "Last night someone put an explosive device under Madison's car." He went on to give them the details.

"I'm so sorry," Wyatt said to Madison, a quaver in his voice. "I don't know what to say. I never meant—"

"I know you didn't," Madison assured him.

"This killer is really deranged," Tobias said, "and cowardly. Why kill innocent people?"

"He or she," Paul responded, "gets a sadistic thrill out of watching Wyatt's hopes for a prolonged life literally die."

There was silence in the room for a moment. Somewhere in the distance a telephone rang.

"Here's what was decided at police headquarters last night," Paul told them. Madison already knew what he was going to say. "Captain Callahan is going to give a news conference. Your name hasn't been associated with the deaths of Erin Wycoff and Keith Brooks Smith. Now it will be. He'll also mention the possibility that the deaths in Boston are linked. Expect reporters and media attention."

"I'll call for extra security," Tobias said. "We won't let them in the building."

"My father is already sending eight guys," Paul said. "Just tell them what to do."

"Maybe we should put another man on here," Wyatt said.

"There is an upside to this publicity," Madison said quietly. "Your donor number will be everywhere. You may find a match."

"Or I'll get more innocent people killed," Wyatt said bitterly.

"ARE YOU UPSET?" Mike Tanner asked Madison as they walked out of the lawyer's office toward his black SUV. Paul wasn't trusting anyone but his father to guard Madison until the danger had passed. That should be tomorrow, after the press conference and the media had a chance to get out the story.

"I'm a little surprised but not angry or upset." She looked at Mike and thought how handsome Paul would be when he was older. "I guess they plea-bargain all the time."

When they'd arrived at the lawyer's office, the attorney had told them that Chloe Larsen agreed to a deal. She gave up names of several ID theft rings to which she'd sold personal identification information. She was going to refund the money to Madison and enroll in a gambling addiction program. In return, the district attorney agreed to allow Chloe to plead guilty to a much lesser charge that might result in little or no jail time.

"The D.A. plea-bargains every day. Saves them the cost of a trial, and sometimes it's for the best."

"Why did the FBI sign off on the deal?"

"They're going after the rings Chloe gave up. They'll shut down a dozen or more people. Unfortunately, that's just a drop in the bucket. ID crooks are everywhere." He opened the door of the SUV for her.

Interesting, Madison thought as she climbed in. Mike let Paul drive that racy Porsche when he could have given him the SUV. He must really love his son. With a surge of guilt, she realized she talked constantly about herself. She'd asked Paul very little. He had mentioned, when she'd been discussing her mother, that his mother had left them when he was very young. Tonight she was finding out more.

They drove toward TotalTrivia in silence. That was a difference between Paul and his father. Mike Tanner seemed not to like her. Perhaps she was imagining things, since she'd only met him this morning when he'd shown up after their talk with Wyatt to escort her to the attorney's office.

"May I turn on the radio?" she asked. "It's about time for the press conference. Maybe it'll be on the news station."

"Good idea."

Back at her office, Madison packed her things. A few minutes later, she glanced up to see Chloe and Aiden coming through the reception area. Madison was still furious at Chloe for what she'd done and wondered if getting off so lightly would actually teach her a lesson. Chloe briefly met her eyes before making a beeline for the restroom.

Madison followed her. Chloe was dabbing at her red-rimmed eyes with a wet paper towel.

"I hope you're satisfied." Madison couldn't keep the anger

out of her voice. "It'll take me at least a year to straighten out the credit mess you caused. Don't tell me that you didn't know what you were doing would hurt people, because I'm not buying it."

This time Chloe refused to make eye contact. "It wouldn't have come to this if you'd sold out to Luis Estevez."

Madison couldn't believe Chloe could be so callous. She realized Aiden's troubles with this woman were probably just beginning.

"You got off lucky. Look at this as an opportunity to straighten out your life. Aiden loves you. He'll help in any way he can, but you've got to do your part. You've already ruined one man's career. Don't destroy Aiden."

Madison walked out of the bathroom without waiting for a response. She didn't want to have another thing to do with Chloe. And though her love for Aiden was a thing of the past, she wished him luck—with Chloe in his life, he'd need it.

THE KILLER WATCHED the press conference on a flat-screen television. The wide-angle shot took in a very military-looking Captain Callahan before the camera. His grim expression was a joke. One look at him and anybody with an iota of intelligence would know the man craved the limelight. No doubt he was angling for the mayor's job or something.

"We have a very unusual case on our hands," Callahan began. "We have linked two very different murders in our city to one killer. Erin Wycoff was strangled and Keith Brooks Smith was injected with a lethal substance."

The jerk probably couldn't pronounce *succinylcholine*.

"We believe they were murdered because they were the donor-conceived children of wealthy philanthropist Wyatt Holbrook."

Philanthropist? Okay, so he gave money away. Just to hide the fact he was an out-and-out thief.

The crowd tittered, obviously surprised. The captain waited for them to quiet down before continuing.

"We have reason to believe three other of Wyatt Holbrook's donor-conceived children were murdered in the Boston area."

"Unfuckingbelievable!" the killer muttered. "They figured it out."

Now the crowd was really buzzing. Several reporters were yapping into their cell phones, probably telling their superiors to get news crews out to Palm Beach and over to the office towers.

"We need the public's help on this one. Last night this vicious killer attached an explosive device to the bottom of Madison Connelly's car. It was thought that Miss Connelly was also one of the donor-conceived children, but that is incorrect. She is not one of those children. Her biological father is the late Zachary Connelly of Miami. Anyone who saw anything suspicious on Hibiscus Lane in Coral Gables or—"

The killer shut off the television, seeing this sham for what it was. They wanted everyone to know Madison wasn't related to Wyatt Holbrook. Those fools believed that information would protect her.

What had Shakespeare once said? "The devil hath the power to assume a pleasing shape." Which play was that? It didn't matter. Madison Connelly was pretty and intelligent. Even if she wasn't related to the Holbrooks, she'd captivated the old coot.

Death was the only way to deal with the devil.

CHAPTER THIRTY-FOUR

What is the number-one city for identity theft per capita?

WYATT SHOWED Madison an office next to Tobias Pennington's after Mike Tanner made sure she was safely inside the building. Outside her new office was a large reception area and beyond it, Wyatt's ocean-view office.

"This was Garrison's office, but he'll move over to the other tower, where he uses the labs."

She gazed around and saw a few of Garrison's things but not a lot.

"He won't mind?"

"Of course not." Garrison's voice came from behind her.

Madison whirled around to find him smiling. "I really can't imagine needing such a large office, if I'm just learning the ropes. I don't want to put you to any trouble."

Garrison's friendly expression welcomed her. "After what you've been through just for trying to help my father, I don't mind moving. I'm usually in the lab anyway, not here in the office."

"You saw the press conference?" his father asked.

"They were watching it on a computer in my lab area when I came in. Jesus. What a mess." Garrison shook his head in disgust. "Are you going to issue a statement?"

"I'm going to work with Tobias on it right now."

"Good. Be sure to emphasize all the positive things you've done for this community." Garrison said.

"Mention your donor number," Madison suggested. "You may find a match."

"Are you serious?" Garrison asked. "I hate to say this, but after what happened to the other donors and the bomb under your car, no one in their right mind is going to come forward."

Wyatt didn't respond, and Madison knew he had reservations about getting anyone else killed. Still, the police had given the number. It would be out there. With luck, the killer would be caught and Wyatt would be saved.

"Rose Marie will move the rest of your things for you," Wyatt told his son.

"I'd rather move the contents of my desk myself," Garrison said.

"Okay, I've got to work on that statement with Tobias," Wyatt replied. "Madison, you have the legal documents for the foundation. Go over them. We'll discuss them later."

"I guess there's a lot of legal stuff behind setting up a foundation," Madison said to Garrison as Wyatt left.

"Absolutely. If a foundation isn't set up correctly, it might be restricted later from doing what it was really intended to do." He sat down behind his desk and began taking things out of drawers and putting them on top. "My father wants this foundation to have great latitude. Scientific advances are coming so rapidly and from different places—"

"Like the ocean."

He chuckled and winked at her. "Exactly. Who knows what we'll find in nature's medicine chests in countries like Costa Rica? Or in outer space."

Rose Marie Nesbit, the receptionist, an older woman with dark hair and intelligent brown eyes, came into the room with a stack of packing boxes. Madison liked her and knew she was the one who kept this penthouse suite of executive offices on track.

"Thanks," Garrison said, taking the boxes. He put them on the floor and began to assemble one.

"Will I bother you if I ask you a few questions while you pack?" Madison said.

"No. I can pack and talk at the same time," he said with a smile.

"It's about the scope of the foundation. I haven't read anything yet, but there's an area I'd like to explore." She sat in the chair beside his desk.

"Oh? What's that?"

"The transplant system in this country. I'm talking about the whole organ transplantation of livers, kidneys, hearts, lungs. It's so unfair. Especially with livers."

"That's true." Garrison moved things from the drawers into the box he'd assembled. "Where you live makes all the difference. It's a matter of geography. The United Network for Organ Sharing is a nonprofit group with a government contract. They broke the country into fifty-eight territories."

"That's what I read, but there are only one hundred and twenty liver transplant centers. If you don't live near one, you aren't getting a liver."

"Even if you do live near one, you may not receive a transplant if there are too many people ahead of you on the list," Garrett told her.

"It's run like a medieval fiefdom." She sighed heavily. "I understand that a liver is viable for up to fifteen hours refrigerated and kept in a special solution. That's enough time to fly it across the country to the patient who needs it most, right?"

He looked up from his packing. "Correct. In a perfect world, that's the way it would be done, but that's not how the system works. I'll give you an example. The area around the University of California at Davis has a population of around two million. That's one small pocket surrounded by a huge population in the San Francisco area of over eleven million, give or take a million, which was put in another region. If you're lucky enough to need a liver in the UC Davis area, you'll get it, while you're more likely to die in San Francisco."

"Isn't there a solution? Couldn't the system be fixed? Wouldn't this be a good project for the foundation?"

Garrison secured the lid on the box he'd been filling and put it on the floor. "It would be an uphill battle. A whole liver transplant runs over a quarter of a million dollars. That's big money to hospitals in the transplant business. They have no incentive to change the system."

"I'd still like to look into it," she replied. "Your father is lucky. St. Luke's in Jacksonville is part of the Mayo Clinic system and does fabulous transplants. It also has a short waiting list."

"He's on it, but with his immune system problems, it's more likely that a partial lobe transplant from a living relative will be the solution. Believe me, I've looked into it."

"Have you thought about going overseas?" she asked.

"Are you going to run the China connection by me?"

"What China connection?"

"The best livers are from young, healthy people who die in car crashes or other accidents, right?" She nodded, and he went on. "China executes thousands of prisoners each year with a single bullet to the head. Lots of good organs there."

"Oh my God. I hadn't heard that. I was thinking of India."

"It's illegal there to buy organs, but it's a desperately poor country and it happens a lot. I guess my father would consider it as a last resort. Problem is you need to be within one hour of the transplant center. I can't see my father sitting in India or China, but who knows what we're going to do if we're desperate."

Madison silently watched him pack the next box. She knew from personal experience how difficult it was to see your father slowly die and not be able to help. If only they could catch this killer, then Wyatt might locate another child who would match and be willing to donate a lobe.

"You know, I'm running a special experiment tomorrow," Garrison said. "If you're around, maybe you'd like to watch."

"Sure," she said. "I plan to be here from now on."

"Don't mention it to anyone," he cautioned. "My work's secret even from my father. Just between you and me, I'm working on an enzyme derived from the saliva of a vampire bat. When a bat bites its prey, its incisors leave tiny pinprick marks that normally would begin to heal in less than a minute. But they don't."

"Because the bat is sucking, keeping the punctures open. Right?"

Garrison shook his head. "That's a myth. Different bats found all over the world lap with long tongues. None of them suck. Feeding time is at least half an hour and they remove about a teaspoon of blood—their sole source of nourishment. The lapping allows air to hit the wound. Air combined with the natural coagulating components of blood should lead to bats licking up clots of blood."

"You'd think."

"You'd be wrong. Bat saliva contains an anticoagulation enzyme. It's perfect for stroke victims."

The excitement was reflected in his voice, his eyes. Madison couldn't help but be enthused, too. This was going to be a great job. She'd be on the cutting edge of wondrous discoveries.

"You see, currently stroke victims must get to the hospital and receive treatment within three hours or the damage is usually irreversible. Most patients don't get to the hospital that soon. With the bat enzyme, doctors will have up to nine hours to treat stroke victims."

"Think of the lives that will be saved," she said, truly awed. A thought occurred to her. "Aren't you working on discoveries from the sea?"

"Yes, but I came across this bat while diving in Costa Rica."

She picked up the sheaf of legal papers on the foundation. "I might as well get started on the legal stuff."

"See you tomorrow. Don't mention my bat saliva," he said with a wink.

"MY MOTHER'S COMING OVER and bringing steaks to grill," Madison told Paul when he walked through the door with an armload of his clothes. She noticed he brought more clothes each time he came. Evidently, he swung by his own house every day. Mike Tanner had driven her from the office back to the guesthouse.

Paul pulled her into his arms and kissed her before answering. "Great minds think alike. I asked my father to dinner. I ran into him going in to see Wyatt. We're planning to discuss strategy."

"What strategy?" She leaned down to pet Aspen. He'd been home alone today. The staff had walked him, but she wanted to start taking him to work, if possible.

"How to guard you. To be sure word is out that you cannot help Wyatt."

"Okay. Let me call Mom. She got a cell today, and a car. I'll have her pick up another steak for your father." She went to the telephone in the kitchen and called her mother, catching her still at the supermarket.

"I'm going to clean off the barbecue," Paul told her after he'd emerged from the bedroom in a black T-shirt with bold white lettering that read Menudo: the Breakfast of Champions. His denim cutoffs were one rip away from unraveling.

She followed him outside, where he found a wire brush in the cabinet under the grill. "Paul, do you see your mother often?"

"Nope." He put the brush back. "This grill is clean. You should see mine."

"There's a lot of staff here. The whole place is immaculate."

Paul put his arm around her. "What do you say we open a bottle of wine while we wait? My father should be along any minute."

"Great. I'll get the glasses," she said as they walked inside. She noticed he'd quickly changed the subject from his mother.

Paul opened a Pinot Grigio someone from the staff had put

into the small wine-cooling unit in the kitchen. She'd placed four glasses on the granite counter. "Where is your mother living?"

Paul didn't look at her. "Beats me. I haven't seen her since the day she walked out on us."

"Really?" She took the glass he offered and touched his arm with her other hand. "Why not?"

"Not every mother is like your mother."

There was a bitter edge of cynicism in his voice that she'd never heard before and she had to remind herself that despite great chemistry, she knew very little about this man. That's why she was taking it slow. She refused to tell him she loved him until she was absolutely positive she wasn't making a mistake.

"It's all right if you don't want to talk about it," she told him.

"Come on. Let's sit outside while the weather is still good, and I'll tell you whatever you want to know." She let him guide her out the door, Aspen at their heels.

They sat in deck chairs facing the pool and sipped the wine in silence for a few minutes. She reached down to pet Aspen.

"One morning when I was seven, my mother kissed me goodbye the way she always did when she handed me my lunch box. I came home that night and she was gone. My father tried to break it to me gently, but even as young as I was I could see he was upset. I didn't believe him. I ran to their room and opened her closet. Everything was gone."

He'd said all this in a flat, emotionless tone, like someone reciting a well-memorized story. Madison felt the pain he wasn't expressing. Losing a parent as an adult was traumatic enough. What must it have been like for a young boy?

"Where did she go and why?" Madison couldn't help asking, even though she sensed he didn't want to talk about this.

"She went to California. She always wanted to move there but my father didn't want to leave Florida. He could have

switched to another police department in California, but my
father is stubborn."

Madison sensed there was more to this than a mother
wanting to live in another state. Mothers didn't just walk out
on children. Did they? She recalled Garrison talking about his
parents. His mother hadn't paid any attention to him and neither
had his father until Garrison showed an interest in research.

"So your father raised you all alone."

There was a long silence punctuated by a bird's warbling call
from a nearby palm. "I raised myself. My father sent me off to
military school—"

"At seven?"

"Yes. My father had no idea what to do with me. He was an
only child, and both his parents were dead. He'd been raised
abroad by an air force father after his mother died. My father
had a career with odd, unpredictable hours. He had no choice."

No choice? Madison wanted to retort. *Of course he had a
choice.* Day care. A nanny. Something. What kind of man sent
a little boy off to a military academy? "What about your
mother's parents? Couldn't they have helped?"

Paul shook his head. "They were in California."

"But you saw your father a lot, didn't you?"

He took another swig of wine before he responded, and
Madison sensed he was stalling. "Not really. I was in Georgia.
He was down here. Sometimes I came home on holidays."

"Sometimes?"

"Not always. Detectives trade holidays. If you work Thanks-
giving, you get Christmas off. See what I mean?"

She absolutely did *not* see. All the happy holidays with
both her parents came rushing into her mind like a whirling
dervish of memories. Love and laughter colored each
memory. That's what nurtured a child. How incredibly lucky
she'd been.

"There were always kids who stayed at school during the

holidays. Mostly kids whose parents lived far away or out of the country. Sometimes I went home with friends."

She wanted to put her arms around him and hug the lonely little boy lurking inside him. Despite the matter-of-fact way he'd told her about this, she knew he must have been lonely. His mother had abandoned him, then his father. It was a wonder Paul was as stable as he was. Maybe he wasn't; perhaps she'd jumped in too soon.

"I don't think your father likes me," she said.

"Don't worry about it. We aren't close. I hardly saw him until I went on disability and he needed extra help at his office."

"I am worried about it. I mean, why would he not like me? He just met me."

He said, "Honey, forget it. My father is a loner. He doesn't trust women. After my mother, he never remarried. I doubt that he even dated."

Just then Mike Tanner walked through the side gate from the path along the oceanfront. He was just far enough away that she doubted he'd overheard them. Madison tried for a welcoming smile, which probably looked like a grimace.

"Madison's mother is joining us for dinner. She's bringing steaks."

"Great." His father sat beside Paul. "Steak sounds real good."

"Let me get you a glass of wine," Paul said.

"Got a beer around?"

"Sure, the fridge is full of everything." Paul went into the bungalow.

How sad, Madison thought. *Paul doesn't know his father prefers beer to wine.* Madison could go shopping for her mother and bring back the right brand of everything.

"So this is the dog that saved you."

"Yes," she replied, and leaned down to stroke Aspen's head. "This is Aspen."

Paul came out with a Corona and gave it to his father. A few minutes later, Madison's mother whirled into the pool area, arms full of grocery bags. Paul and his father both jumped up to help her. Madison caught the appraising look in Mike's eyes. Paul didn't know his father at all. He may never have remarried, but he knew a good-looking woman when he saw one.

Paul took the bags from her mother. Madison introduced her to Paul's father while Paul went inside to put the groceries in the kitchen.

"Excuse us," Madison said to father and son when Paul returned. "We're going into the kitchen to whip up a salad and stuff."

"You didn't tell me Paul's father was so handsome," her mother said in a low voice when they reached the kitchen.

"Don't get interested in him. Mike Tanner is a real jerk."

"You're kidding."

"What would you say about a man who sends his seven-year-old son off to military school when his wife leaves them?"

"My word." Astonishment underscored each syllable. "I wasn't interested. I'm not even divorced."

"Mom, why did you buy five filet mignons when there are only four of us?"

"The boys gave me plenty of money. I'm going to work part-time in their shop to help repay them. I also had several promising interviews today. So when I was at the market, I asked myself who deserved a steak the most. Aspen. He saved my baby doll."

Tears welled up in Madison's eyes even though she was laughing. She hugged her mother. How good it felt to have her home. No matter how terrible the situation with the killer became, there was something immeasurably comforting about having her mother with her.

Paul and his father had moved into the living area to watch the television and see how extensively the press conference was covered.

"It sounds like word is getting out," her mother said a few

minutes later. "Your name has been mentioned on every broadcast. You'd have to be on the moon not to get the news."

"We're not trusting one day of television coverage, Jessica."

It was Paul's father speaking. The guys had shut off the television and moved into the kitchen area.

"We've decided to wait a week and see what happens. When I'm not with Madison, she'll be inside the Holbrook offices where we have extra security, or my father will be with her," Paul told them.

"Why don't we have another glass of wine and enjoy the sunset while the potatoes bake?" Madison asked to lighten the mood.

They talked about other things during dinner by the pool. Madison noticed the way Mike kept sneaking glances at her mother. He was definitely interested; no question about it. But would he call her?

Paul's cell phone rang from his pocket. He pulled it out and checked caller ID, then walked inside to the kitchen and used the landline.

"Well, I learned an interesting fact when I was looking into identity theft," Madison told them. "What city has the most identity thefts per capita?"

Mike rocked back in his chair. "Overall must be a big city like L.A. or New York. Per capita, huh? I'm guessing Palm Beach or some other ritzy small town."

"You're on the right track," Madison responded, noticing whatever Paul was being told on the telephone was making him frown. "It's Newport Beach in California. A wealthy town with a lot of crooks after those IDs. The latest twist is to take out credit in the name of a wealthy child."

"What will they think of next?" her mother asked.

Paul walked through the French doors and dropped into his chair. "Remember the woman in Delray Beach who's one of Wyatt's donor-conceived children?"

"I remember." A cold prickling sensation brought goose bumps up on Madison's skin.

"Sandra Morton is dead. Her husband said she received a candygram supposedly from her sister."

"She just posted last night and her profile was removed. An officer went up there to warn her," Mike said.

"She was warned, but she'd posted on a few lesser-known sites earlier in the evening. Said Godiva chocolate was her favorite. A candygram arrived and she ate a few pieces, then keeled over and was dead when paramedics arrived. Looks like a fast-acting poison that paralyzes the lungs and major organs."

Madison was actually trembling now and she could feel her throat closing up. *That bastard,* she thought, *going after innocent people.*

"Succinylcholine, like what killed that Smith guy?" Paul's father asked.

"My first thought. Trey was right on it with a call to our lab. Succinylcholine can't be injected into candy. It's too unstable with sugar or something."

"What are we going to do?" her mother asked.

"As much as I hate to say it, this might be good news. The killer took out a known donor-conceived child. He didn't come after Madison again."

"I hate to look at it as good news," Madison said. "Someone's dead."

"I think we should take one additional precaution," Mike said. "Corona del Mar is behind walls and a security gate with two guards patrolling all night long. Paul is staying with Madison. You've got the dog, who's proved he'll bark at the first suspicious sign. But I think we're vulnerable from the beach. I'm staying here all night and watching the beach myself to see no one comes up from there."

"I'll help you," Madison's mother said. "I can't go home if my baby doll is in danger."

CHAPTER THIRTY-FIVE

THE KILLER GREETED the new day with a smile. Killing Sandra Morton had been ridiculously easy. People posted so much personal information on the Internet. It made killing her a no-brainer. The others had been more fun because those killings had taken planning and a certain amount of finesse. Nevertheless, this murder brought a smile to the killer's face.

Death by chocolate.

Don't you just love it?

Even though the woman had died in the Delray Beach police jurisdiction, the killer had no doubt Paul Tanner would be involved. Like a cat chasing its tail, the world-class prick would find a woman in a bikini bought the candy at the South Beach store. An hour later another bikinied bimbo brought it back, then paid a hundred dollars extra for delivery to Delray Beach. The killer doubted either of the bimbos would learn of the death by chocolate, but even if one of them went to the police, the killer had taken the precaution of a good—make that great—disguise.

The police would play hell trying to find the poison. The killer actually doubted it could be traced, but maybe given enough time someone would figure it out.

Only the strong survive.

Walk without fear through the camp of your enemies. Death comes when you least expect it.

The killer wasn't finished. Oh, no. The fun was just beginning.

MADISON READ through several reports to get up to speed on other scientific foundations. She understood what Wyatt wanted her to know. Several set up years ago were bound by restrictions and couldn't use emerging technology like stem cells and nanotechnology.

She rummaged through the desk that Rose Marie had stocked with various office supplies and found a yellow highlighter. She highlighted the section of the report that interested her. A second later, her mind drifted to the woman who'd eaten the fatal chocolate.

Who would do something like that? She'd hardly been able to sleep, thinking about it. Her mother had spent the night with Mike Tanner, watching the beach—just in case. Paul felt she was safe, insisting the killer wouldn't care if she couldn't help Wyatt. Madison hoped he was right.

The telephone on her desk rang. From the blinking light on the second button, she knew it was a call from outside the building. Maybe it was Paul, she thought. He'd walked her through a gauntlet of media camped out, and into the building.

Paul had gone down to Delray Beach. She knew how badly he wanted to solve this case. She wouldn't feel truly safe until he did, and her mother would worry about her at a time when she should be rebuilding her own life. Jessica Whitcomb deserved better. She'd been a fabulous mother. Madison hadn't realized how much she'd been loved until Paul had talked about his childhood.

"Hello," she said, and cradled the telephone against her shoulder so she could put the report in the bottom drawer of her desk.

"Still up for watching an experiment?" asked Garrison.

"Sure." Actually, she didn't have much to do now that she'd finished with the report. "Do I have to put on a special hazmat suit or something?"

"Nah. Not for this experiment. Just take the service elevator to the garage."

"You're doing an experiment in the garage?"

"Of course not." He chuckled. "I didn't think you wanted to deal with the pack of media hounds outside. I'm in the other tower. You'd have thought we would have designed a skywalk or something between buildings. We didn't. The only way is to go through the basement garage."

"Good idea. I don't want to deal with the media. I have nothing to say. You know another woman died."

"I heard. Damn it." Anger echoed through the telephone line. "At this rate my father will never find a donor."

"Let's hope the police solve this soon."

"I'm praying, believe me. I'm praying." He sighed. "Do you know where the service elevator is?"

"Yes." The office tower's layout wasn't that complicated. "Should I come down right now?"

"Yes. Just don't mention you're watching one of my experiments. It's a first. My father doesn't get to see what I'm doing."

"Why are you letting me watch?"

"Because you're going to be director of the Holbrook Foundation. One day, you may fund a project of mine. Plus I think you need to understand how experiments are conducted."

"You're right. I know a little from my days at MIT but I could learn more. I appreciate your taking the time to show me. I won't mention it to anyone." She looked out at the other offices, which were glass-walled. "No one's around anyway except Rose Marie. How long will this take? I won't tell her where I'm going, but she'll ask when I'll be back."

"It'll take four hours. We start the process and have lunch in the café in this tower, then go back and see the results."

Madison told Rose Marie that she was going to check out a lab and would be back after lunch. The receptionist was busy on the computer and nodded. Madison found the service elevator and went to the garage.

Garrison was waiting for her in a lab coat.

"Who parks down here?" she asked.

"This is where trucks unload supplies and we keep special bins with hazardous material until it's picked up."

She looked around and saw several huge barrels with biohazard emblems on them. "What's that smell? It's kind of sweet."

"Come with me," he replied with his charming smile. "You'll see."

IT WAS ALMOST NOON and Paul was in his father's office. Mike had arrived a few minutes ago. After pulling an all-nighter on the beach with Madison's mother, Paul's father had gone home for some sleep.

"I've got an ex-cop lined up to guard the beach tonight," his father announced.

"Great, but I don't think that'll assure Jessica. I'll bet she sleeps on the sofa or something." Paul was standing at the window in his father's office. A gull was riding an updraft, floating in a clear blue sky.

"You went to Delray?"

"Yeah. For all the good it did." Paul turned to face his father. "The candy was purchased for cash in South Beach by a blonde in a bikini, then returned an hour or so later by a brunette in a bikini who paid extra to have it delivered to Delray Beach."

"Didn't the clerk think that was strange?"

Paul paced the office. "Come on. It's South Beach. Nothing is too weird down there."

"Any leads at all?"

Paul stopped at the far end of the room. "Nope. One of the girls who purchased, then paid for delivery, might come forward. Trey has the SoBe beat cops asking questions. He has Explorer scouts canvassing the beach. With luck, one of the women will be sunbathing today."

"If the killer's been careful, he will have had a good disguise."

"Probably. But we might catch a break."

"What do you think of Trey Williams? Is he a good detective? He wasn't around when I was there."

Paul sat in the chair opposite his father's desk. He wanted to talk to his father, a discussion that was long overdue. Talking to Madison last night and seeing how her mother treated her had made him think. "Trey's the best detective on the force."

"Better than you are?" his father asked with surprise.

"Yes," Paul admitted. "I'm too close to this case. I care too much about Madison. Trey went to Delray last night even though it isn't in our jurisdiction and convinced them to put the poisoned candy on a plane to the FBI lab in Quantico. That thought didn't occur to me when it should have."

"That was a good idea, but knowing what the poison is might not be the key to the case."

"True, but you never know. Sometimes it's the little things that trip up these lunatics. FBI put a priority on it because it's a serial-killing situation. They promised an answer by noon." Paul checked his watch and saw it was ten minutes until twelve.

His father had an odd look on his face. "Let me ask you something. Would you feel strange if I asked out Jessica?"

Paul stared at his father. "No, of course not. She's very attractive."

"And interesting. We talked a lot last night. I think I'd like to take her out. You know, see what's there."

"Go for it." Paul meant it. His father worked too much. The guy didn't have any hobbies. Paul had been in danger of going down the same path. Until Madison. "Now let me ask *you* something." Paul leaned forward in his chair. "What really happened with my mother?"

A tense silence enveloped the room, then his father spoke, his voice low and awkward. "Your mother left me for another woman."

His father's words were like a knockout punch. For a second, Paul couldn't breathe. Of all the things he'd imagined over the years, this wasn't one of them. Somehow by the time he was around fifteen, Paul had decided his mother had run away with another man. Going to California by herself just because she liked California didn't cut it.

"Remember her art teacher, Annette Webster?" his father asked, his expression bleak. "She came to dinner a few times."

"Not really. I remember Mom painting. She had an easel set up in the garage. She let me use her special paints." He was still trying to come to grips with what his father had told him. "She didn't want me?"

His father hesitated, measuring Paul for a moment. "She wanted you—she loved you very much. But Annette wanted to go to Spain for a while, then on to Italy to study the masters. Your mother didn't want to drag you all over Europe. I told her it would be over my dead body. If she left, it had to be a clean break. She agreed it was for the best."

"She never wrote to me or anything?"

"She wrote, she sent postcards. She even called. When I wouldn't let her have contact with you, she finally stopped."

"Why didn't you tell me?" In his opinion, his father had had no right to keep things from him.

"I didn't want you confused. You were young and it would have been hard to explain what a lesbian is."

"You could have told me when I was older." He hated to criticize but his father had been wrong.

"When would have been a good time? I started to say something a dozen times. Then I'd think you were a teenager. It was a confusing enough time for you without my adding to it."

"What about when I came back here and joined the force?"

"I planned to, but you never asked." His voice was filled with anguish, which surprised Paul. His father never showed emotion. "I decided to leave well enough alone, but if you did ask, the way you have today, I would level with you."

Paul fought back a sarcastic comment, asking himself how he would have handled the situation. What if Madison left him for another woman? A flash of betrayal and despair hit him. No wonder his father didn't trust women.

"You didn't have any idea my mother was…attracted to women?"

"No, I didn't, but looking back I should have. When Annette came to dinner the first time, I felt something wasn't right. I just didn't know what. I realized I was a cop without an interest in art. I figured the women had more in common."

"When was the last time you heard from Mother?"

"Years ago, when you were due to graduate from high school, I told her you had top grades and could go anywhere but you were planning to study criminal justice and would probably join the police force."

"What did she say?" Paul tried to imagine his mother's face, but time had blurred the memory.

His father actually smiled. "Like father, like son."

"Do you know where she is?"

"As a matter of fact, I do." His father tapped on his computer keyboard. "I'm not much good with the computer but I did an online search and found her. She has a Web site for her art."

"You're kidding."

"No. Let's pull it up. She's still with Annette and living in Key West, which makes sense. It's an arty community loaded with gays." He turned the monitor toward Paul.

He looked at the picture and saw a middle-aged woman with dark wavy hair smiling out of the screen at him. "I wouldn't have recognized her if she walked by me on the street."

"Maybe she has," his father said. "Key West isn't that far away."

Paul nodded as he read her personal information on the "Get to Know Me" page. A watercolor artist with several credits for winning shows. Her paintings were in a few collections with names Paul didn't recognize. Molly Tanner lived in a coral and white bungalow typical of Key West. There was a picture of a chunky-looking woman with short iron-gray hair. Annette

Webster, the woman who had lured his mother away from her loving family.

Paul was amazed to feel a surge of anger, or maybe it was hate. What right did that woman have to ruin his father's life and leave a small boy motherless? Then he reminded himself that it had been his mother's choice.

"They have a gallery," Paul's father said. "Grand Designs. It's right on Duval Street. Apparently, they show their own work and sell other artists', as well. There's a phone number."

"Mind if I call her?"

"No," his father said in a clipped voice. "I'll leave and give you some privacy."

"Wait," Paul said, standing. "You're my father. I love you." He realized he did love his father but he'd never said those words. Thank you, Madison. "I just need to talk to her."

"I love you, too, son," his father replied in a choked voice. "I should have been a better father. I just didn't know how."

"It's okay." Paul picked up the desk phone and his father walked out of the room. A man answered the gallery's telephone and informed Paul that Molly and Annette had just gone to lunch. "Tell her that her son called." He left his cell number and hung up.

He went to find his father, who was making himself a cup of coffee. "She wasn't in. I left a message." Paul's cell phone rang and he pulled it from the clip on his belt. Caller ID told him it was Trey, not his mother.

"The report came back on the poison," Trey told him. "It's not much help but I knew you would want to know."

"What was in the candy?"

"Got a pen? You might want to write this down."

Paul found a pen on the counter near the coffee machine and fished a piece of paper out of the wastebasket. "Okay."

"It was venom from a rare Australian blue-ringed octopus. It immobilizes every muscle in the body."

Something clicked deep in Paul's brain. His mind replayed Garrison Holbrook blabbing on and on about the secrets of the sea. Paul slammed his fist down on the table and silently cursed himself. How had he not seen what had been right under his nose? Kicking himself mentally, he wondered why he was a detective. He'd certainly flubbed it this time.

"What's the matter?" his father asked when Paul hit the table again.

"It's Garrison Holbrook," Paul told his father and Trey at the same time.

"You sure?" Trey asked.

"You're kidding," his father said.

"Why would Garrison kill all those people?" Paul asked.

"Wait a minute," his father replied. "What makes you think he did?"

Paul shrugged, not knowing how to put his gut reaction into words. "Garrison is an expert on the sea and he would have access to a rare venom like that. The average person wouldn't."

"True," Mike Tanner responded, "but why…"

"I'm not sure about his motive," Paul conceded. "Maybe it had something to do with his father not backing him with his early discovery. Or who knows? This guy is clearly a nutcase."

"He seems so…normal," his father said.

"That's what they said about Ted Bundy. Handsome, charming. What does a serial killer look like?"

"Normal enough that most people don't notice them." His father studied Paul. "You're sure about this?"

"Positive—and Garrison is in the same building with Madison. If he wants, he'll have the chance to kill her." Just putting his thoughts into words sickened Paul in a way that the most gruesome homicide never had. This was Madison, the woman he loved, and she was side by side with a killer because he hadn't been perceptive enough to see what was happening. "We've got to get Madison out of there."

It took Paul less than five minutes to find out Madison had disappeared from her office in Holbrook Pharmaceuticals. No one could locate Garrison, either. A call to CNBF's news crew staking out the front of the office assured Paul that neither Madison nor Garrison had left through the front door. Only one crew had covered the exit from the underground garage. They hadn't taken any film but reported a black SUV with tinted windows had left the building around eleven.

"She's in that SUV, or he's killed her and dumped her body somewhere in the office building." Paul suddenly felt weak and helpless.

His father was talking on his phone, giving directions to his men to search unlikely places. "Holbrook's security people and my guards are going over the building, room by room."

"He took her away in that SUV. Where would he go?" Paul told himself to think—not to let his emotions override his training as a detective. "Not to Corona del Mar. Garrison has a place somewhere in the Keys."

He reached Rose Marie Nesbit because Wyatt and Tobias were at some meeting in Fort Lauderdale with their cell phones off. She gave him the information they needed. "Thanks."

His father put his hand on Paul's shoulder. "We'll find her, son."

"I have an idea," Paul told him. "It's wild, but it just might work."

CHAPTER THIRTY-SIX

What is prosopagnosia?

MADISON OPENED her eyes slowly. The lids seemed unusually heavy, as if they'd been glued shut. Her throat was parched and her tongue was like a wad of cotton. What was wrong?

She slowly became aware she was in a dark room. Then she remembered being in the subterranean garage at Holbrook Pharmaceuticals with Garrison. She'd smelled something funny, slightly sweet. Suddenly a rag covered her face and she'd melted into a soft blackness.

Oh my God! Garrison had done something to her. She realized her ankles and wrists were bound with tape. A wave of panic swept through her and left her trembling. Her heart kicked strong and fast but she was almost breathless.

Where was she? In the building somewhere? Her terrified brain tried to think but it was difficult. No. Garrison must have taken her somewhere. That's why he'd lured her to the garage.

Unless she could pull off a miracle, she was as good as dead. Icy fear gripped her. Paul. Her mother. She loved them so much. She didn't want to die. Tears stung her eyes as terrified images of the ways Erin and the other donor-conceived children had died filled her brain. *Get a grip. Don't you dare cry. It won't help.*

Suddenly, light flooded the room, blinding her. She squinted and through the slits of her eyes saw Garrison coming toward her. The smile that had deceived her so often was plastered across his face, bigger than ever. A Cheshire cat grin. She choked back a frightened cry, refusing to give him the satisfaction of seeing how terrified she was.

"Nice nap?"

"Where am I?"

"My place in the Keys." He stood over Madison, studying her as if she were some rare specimen. "I told you I wanted to show you an experiment. Well, it's here, not in the lab at Holbrook Pharmaceuticals." He took a pocketknife and slit through the duct tape around her ankles, then yanked it off. He snapped the knife shut and returned it to his perfectly creased linen trousers.

The skin on her ankles burned, but that was the least of her problems. "Why? Why?"

"You really want to know?"

"Of course I do." Madison swung her legs to the floor so she could sit up. She hated having him loom over her. She tried to appear calm but a spasmodic trembling in her chest made her feel weak. If she could get him talking, she might think of something or Paul might discover she was missing and start a search. A long shot, she decided. She'd told Rose Marie that she would be gone four hours. A quick glance at her watch told her it was one-thirty. No one would miss her until around three, if then.

She noticed her purse was on the nightstand, but there wasn't anything in it that could save her. She couldn't get to it anyway with bound hands. Her cell phone was off, otherwise it would send a signal and Paul could locate her using those radio waves. Assuming he was looking.

"You want answers? You got it. My father is a piece of shit. He never paid any attention to me or Savannah. Then I discovered the surgical glue. Did he help his only son? Hell, no. He stole my idea and made millions.

"He neglected his family like you wouldn't believe. My mother had her charity work and Savannah but I had no one. No one. It wasn't until my father became an old man that he spent time with us. Well, by then it was too late. Savannah had her own life, her own business, and I had mine."

The bitterness in Garrison's voice surprised her. He'd skillfully concealed his feelings with a caring tone all the other times he'd talked about his father. She'd foolishly believed Garrison loved his father the way she'd loved hers.

"I thought Wyatt backed another scientist who was further along with the surgical glue. It would have taken you years." Why was she discussing this with a lunatic? To buy time; it was the only chance she had.

"If he'd thrown his resources behind me, my glue would have been ready in no time. Trust me, Wyatt Holbrook thinks only of himself." Anger flared in Garrison's eyes. "When my father became ill, I wasn't one bit sorry. And I damn sure wasn't sorry that my liver wasn't compatible with his. What did he do when neither of his children were suitable donors? He went after the donor-conceived children. He never cared one bit about them until they were of use to him."

"I can't help your father. I'm not related. There's no reason for you to do this." She hated the pleading tone in her voice and doubted it would do any good with such an insane man, but her life was at stake.

"True, and that *almost* saved you."

"Almost?"

"You had to wheedle the position at the foundation out of my father, didn't you? You took my office on the executive floor. Did you really think I wanted to be shuffled aside to the lab?"

His sinister laugh caused a knot to instantly form in her chest. How could she have thought Garrison to be a kind man who loved his father? Was she so easily deceived?

"I didn't wheedle anything. It was his idea, not mine."

"If you say so. It doesn't really matter, does it?"

"Did you kill Erin Wycoff?" If she was going to die, she wanted to know the truth about her best friend.

"Bingo." He pointed a finger like a gun at her and fired. "She was a tough one. She put up a fight, but I finished her off. Keith Brooks Smith was another fighter. I hit him with a dose of chloroform the way I did you. He thrashed and kicked the wall. Damn near got me caught, but in the end, I prevailed."

She was going to have to fight, too. That was her only option. Her eyes darted around the room. A guest bedroom, apparently. The mirrored closet doors reflected her image. Her lime-green linen dress appeared to have been wadded up like a ball of paper then smoothed out. It was hopelessly wrinkled. Her hair, always unruly, looked as if she'd been in a wind tunnel. She didn't recognize the face in the mirror. It was almost as if she had prosopagnosia, a rare condition where a person didn't recognize their own reflection. But this wasn't a rare condition; it was fear.

Garrison had said something about showing her an experiment. That must mean he wasn't going to kill her right here. She had some time and needed to think clearly. *Don't allow panic to muddle your brain.*

"Come on." He grabbed her arm. "You don't want to miss my experiment, do you?"

She lashed out to kick him in the groin with both feet. She was unsteady and he was too quick. His hand clamped around her still-sore ankles and he yanked her off the bed. She landed on the wood floor, striking her tailbone. Pain shot up her spine and stars exploded in her head.

"You won't get away with this." Her voice cracked from the pain. "Paul will track you down. I promise."

"He isn't that smart." He roughly hauled her to her feet. "Let's go. The lab is in the garage."

She screamed, screeching at the top of her lungs.

"Shut the fuck up. There's no one to hear. Don't you think I would put tape on your mouth if I had neighbors nearby? How stupid are you?"

Plenty stupid, she thought or she would have caught on to him.

PAUL SAT beside his father in the helicopter they'd rented and prayed his instincts were correct. His father had put together a backpack for each of them with a variety of supplies, while Paul had changed into spare jeans and a T-shirt that his father kept at the office. He'd needed tennis shoes. On the way to the airport, they'd stopped by a store, dashed in and bought shoes in Paul's size without trying them on first.

"That's Big Pine Key ahead," the pilot told them through the headsets.

Almost to Key West, Paul thought, *where my mother lives. Please, God,* he silently prayed, *don't let me find my mother just to lose the woman I love. Don't let me have guessed wrong about this.*

Big Pine Key was one of the larger islands in the chain of small keys that trailed off the tip of the Florida peninsula from Key Largo to Key West. It had a few homes on it but it was mostly a wilderness of scrub pines and gumbo-limbo trees. Thickets of mangroves lined the banks of the island. Crocodiles preyed on the otters and raccoons. Occasionally, they downed a key deer. The miniature deer had become such a tourist attraction that when one appeared along the side of the road, people stopped to take pictures and traffic backed up for miles.

An aerial shot of Big Pine Key on Google Earth had shown them exactly where Garrison's home was located. It was right on the water with a boat dock nearby. It wasn't large. Three bedrooms and an oversize garage connected to the house. Paul's father thought that might be where his laboratory was. If the asswipe even had a lab. Who knew what he really did out here?

His father tapped his shoulder and pointed to the laptop he'd brought with him. Paul couldn't talk to his father over the noise of the engine. His headset only allowed communication with the pilot. The satellite that updated Google Earth had passed over the area again since they'd last looked. Now there was a black SUV parked in front of Garrison's home.

Yes! Paul thought, silently congratulating himself. He'd been right. The maniac had brought her here for some reason that made sense to a deranged mind. But was she still alive?

A wave of apprehension coursed through him. What would he do if Madison was dead? His stomach clenched tight. He'd tear that bastard Garrison Holbrook apart with his bare hands.

They'd instructed the pilot to drop them off some distance from the house and not to fly anywhere near it. They didn't want to alert Garrison. The chopper touched down, spooking a flock of birds that exploded out of the mangroves into the afternoon sky.

They hopped out and waved the pilot away. The chopper rose upward, leaving a swirl of dust in its wake. The put on their backpacks and ran through the thicket toward Garrison's house.

"THIS IS MY LAB," Garrison said, and there was no mistaking the pride in his voice.

The room had been converted from a four-car garage. It appeared to be as up-to-date as Holbrook Pharmaceuticals. Several computers lined the counter. One screen was running, numbers scrolling down with amazing speed. In one corner was a stainless-steel vat the size and shape of a bathtub. A faintly metallic smell hung in the air.

"I'm running a computer trial on a sea fungus I discovered," he told Madison when he saw her looking at the computer. "It's a fungus that could kill cancer in humans."

"What about that bat saliva? Were you making it up?"

He smiled. Why hadn't she detected the evil lurking behind

his smile? "No, but you don't know shit about science. You aren't qualified to head a foundation. The saliva is already in advanced trials in Germany. It should be on the market next year."

"Your father said neither you nor Savannah wanted to run the foundation."

"The bastard never asked me." Pure venom dripped from every word. "He assumed I wanted to continue with my own work. I do, but I intend to head that foundation. The prick wants to hand the foundation over to a half sibling who turns out not even to be related to him?" He shook his fist in her face. "Know how that makes me feel?"

"Why not just kill him? What on earth did you gain by killing innocent people?"

Again the twisted smile. "I like watching dear old Dad die day by day. Hope springs eternal, you know. He hoped you would be able to save him. Know what he told me? The old fart thought he saw himself in you. He was oh, so positive you were his child. I actually thought I had the biggest thrill when you told him that you weren't his child. I believed it was better than killing you. Then you went after the job."

"I swear I didn't." She barely recognized her own desperate voice.

"Doesn't matter. Know what I learned about myself?"

She couldn't imagine, didn't want to know but if she stood a chance of surviving, she had to stall for as long as possible. She had absolute faith that Paul would figure this out and come after her. "What did you learn?"

He touched her chin with his index finger. "I enjoy killing. It's a high that makes sex seem ordinary. Devising different ways of murdering people to elude the police gives me a major charge."

Oh my God! She could only imagine what he had in store for her.

He nudged Madison forward. "Here's what I wanted to show you. A very promising experiment."

She took baby steps but soon she was standing in front of the stainless-steel tub. The metallic smell was wafting up from the red liquid. Beneath the surface was a stainless-steel mesh net. Her skin crawled as she looked at it. There was a piece of something submerged, just visible on the stainless netting.

"This is an enzyme made from the red tide. My discovery. It's one hundred times more powerful than any man-made acid." He pointed to the small black piece on the net. "Yesterday that was a hundred-and-twenty-pound German shepherd. Great dog. Adopted him from the pound."

Her stomach, already churning with anxiety, heaved. She saw a dog like Aspen in the vat of something more powerful than—she wasn't up on acids—lye. Tears stung her eyes until the vat swam through her field of vision.

"In another hour there will be nothing left. Zilch. Zero. Nada. Amazing thing about Neptune's Treasure Chest, it keeps on surprising me. This solution dissolves everything—even teeth. There won't be one trace of you left for your beloved Paul to find."

Madison gagged on her own bile and brought her bound hands up to her face. She couldn't imagine a more horrible death. Drowning in acid, then dissolving. Why hadn't she told Paul she loved him when she had the chance? All the things she should have said streamed through her mind.

"The only things I've discovered that the red tide acid doesn't destroy are stainless steel and Vaseline. Some things take time for it to dissolve, but it loves to eat people. Takes no time at all."

"You don't think I'm just getting in there, do you?"

"Of course not. I'm going to dose you with more chloroform and put you in the vat myself. I put you in the SUV, then hauled you into the house. No problem. But first I have to put on a full hazmat suit in case you splash. One drop of that acid will burn a hole in my clothes, my skin."

Holding raw panic in check, she said, "Could I leave a message on my mother's answering machine? I want to say goodbye and tell her how much I love her."

His cackling laugh split the air. "You really think I'm stupid. You call your mommy from my phone. Later the police can hit star sixty-nine and get back to my phone."

"No, no. I'm not underestimating you one bit. My cell phone is in my purse in the bedroom. I would use it. I would call the guesthouse and leave a message on that machine. She'd get it later." Her voice cracked. "After I'm gone."

He gazed at her with a sardonic expression that sent another chilling wave of panic through her. Madison knew she was minutes from an unbelievably gruesome death.

"Please let me call her," she begged in a pathetic voice. "If you knew you were going to die, isn't there someone you would want to say goodbye to?"

He shrugged. "Not really."

"I love my mother. She suffered through my father's death from cancer. She just came home. I haven't seen—"

"All right! Shut your fucking mouth." He grabbed her arm so hard that she almost cried out, but stopped herself in time. She had to make this one last call.

They trudged down to the bedroom. Garrison found her purse and pulled out the cell phone. He switched it on, saying, "What's the number? I don't know the guesthouse number."

Madison told him the number. She'd been hoping he'd let her dial. She planned to call Paul's cell and pretend she was speaking to her mother. She was going to get in Big Pine Key so he would know where to look. Not that she wouldn't be half-dissolved when he arrived, but she didn't want the bastard to get away with killing her.

Garrison handed Madison the ringing phone. Using both

bound hands, she held it up to her ear. It kicked over to voice mail. "Mom, it's me. I want to tell you—"

Ding-dong! The doorbell rang.

CHAPTER THIRTY-SEVEN

What is a flashbang?

GARRISON STARED at her in astonishment. "Nobody comes here except UPS."

Madison bolted through the small bedroom, tossing the phone to the floor. She streaked down the hall screaming, "Help! Help! Help!"

She heard the thundering footfalls of Garrison's stylish loafers just steps behind her. She kept screeching, praying whoever was at the door would realize something terrible was happening. He grabbed her from behind just as she reached the living room. She felt the sharp blade of the pocket knife at her throat.

"Shut up or I'll kill you this second."

Whump! Whump! Someone was trying to break down a wood door that appeared to be very solid. *Whump!* This time the sturdy door cracked. *Whump!* Another whack and the door split open, showering splinters onto the floor and bringing in bright sunlight.

Paul tumbled into the room, almost fell, but righted himself. His revolver was aimed directly at them. Relief hit Madison physically. Her knees almost buckled and scalding tears filled her eyes. She couldn't imagine how Paul had found her, but bless him, he had.

"You're dead, Holbrook. You sick fuck."

"She dies first unless you put down the gun." Garrison's calm voice revealed no sign of fear.

Despite the knife pricking her jugular, Madison began to speak. "I love you, Paul. Not just for finding me. I should have told you before. If he kills me, I just want you to know—"

"Oh, pul-leeze. Cut the bullshit." Garrison waved the knife. "Put the gun down. You have two sec—"

Instead of following Garrison's order, Paul put his free hand over his eyes. A half second later a boom like a deafening clap of thunder rocked the room. With it a blinding flash of light as bright as the sun exploded through the room. Garrison released her. Madison couldn't see a thing and her ears were ringing, but she charged forward, knowing she had to get away from that lunatic.

She stumbled over the coffee table but Paul caught her in his arms. "It's okay, honey. You'll be able to see in about ten seconds."

"What was that?" She assumed he had the gun trained on Garrison, who must not be able to see, either.

"A flashbang. It's a type of a grenade, but when it explodes, it doesn't release deadly shrapnel. A loud noise and lots of bright light distract and confuse people without hurting them."

She felt him kiss her cheek, then heard him say, "Don't move, you pervert. We've got two guns trained on you."

"We'd love an excuse to kill you."

Madison recognized Mike Tanner's voice. Her vision was clearing a little. It was like looking through gauze, but she could see Garrison at the far end of the room. Mike was standing in the kitchen doorway. He must have come in through the back door and tossed the flashbang into the living room. She'd heard of them, of course, but experiencing one was quite different.

Garrison turned and dashed down the hallway, running in a zigzag pattern. Paul and his father fired simultaneously but missed. Madison knew even the most highly trained sharp shooter only had a fifty-fifty chance of hitting someone when they ran erratically. The men charged after him.

Madison almost slumped into the nearest chair, then realized they were heading for the garage where the corrosive acid was. She sprinted behind them, yelling, "Stop! Stop! Don't get near the vat with the red water in it."

She wasn't sure they realized the danger. They were still chasing Garrison. She charged after them, her vision clearing, shouting at the top of her lungs. "The red stuff is acid. Stop! Paul, stop!"

They halted at the entrance to the lab. She ran up behind them. Garrison paused in front of the tank. "I choose my destiny. I'm not like my father, waiting around to see if someone can save him."

"We'll get you help," Madison cried, although she couldn't imagine what could be done for such a deranged person or why she was trying to rescue someone who'd been determined to kill her.

"Forget it," Garrison said bitterly. "We'll end this my way."

He plunged into the vat of acid. A big splash sent a wave of water over the side and droplets shot into the air. The red liquid landed on the tile floor and instantly began burning into the tile. The plastered walls were already pocked from the droplets. The vat itself appeared to be boiling. Bubbles churned across the surface.

"He's dead." Madison barely heard her own voice over the ringing in her ears. She wanted Garrison dead; he deserved it. But watching another human being die left sourness in the pit of her stomach.

"Holy shit!" Mike said. "What is that stuff?"

"An enzyme Garrison discovered in red tide. Don't get anywhere near it. We'll need a hazmat team. Maybe we should call the FBI or some agency that is really experienced in hazardous materials. From what Garrison told me, the only thing this acid doesn't dissolve completely is stainless steel and Vaseline."

"I would rather have shot him," Paul said, "than have to watch this."

"Garrison brought me all the way out here to dissolve my body and not leave a trace of me."

"Oh, sweetheart." He pulled her into his arms and gazed down at her with tenderness and love in his eyes.

"Why are we standing here?" Madison asked. "Let's go outside."

"Good idea." Paul handed his father the gun he was holding, then put his arm around her and led her down the hall and through the smashed door.

Outside, she held up her hands so he could use his pocket-knife to cut the duct tape around her wrists. "How did you find me?"

"Thanks goes to Trey Williams. He had the smarts to send the poisoned candy to the FBI lab with a priority order. By noon we knew the poison came from a rare blue-ringed octopus. It clicked. Who else but Garrison?"

"Did he say why?" Mike wanted to know.

"He hates—hated—his father. He blamed him for stealing his surgical-glue idea."

"Obviously, he was severely unbalanced," Paul said, then ripped the tape from her wrists. "Sorry, I know it hurts."

"I don't think it's that simple. Children need to feel loved. Wyatt is a good person in many ways but when he was younger, I don't think he was a great father. His work was more impor-tant than his family. Savannah's mother loved her and they related to each other because they were females. I think Garrison was odd man out and it began eating at his psyche years ago, when he was a child."

"I agree. Feeling loved is important, but it's not the only determining factor," Paul said, and Madison knew he was thinking of his own childhood. "I think this guy was more than a little off."

Madison rubbed her raw wrists. "Believe me, I don't think there is a simple explanation. One thing I know for sure. I was really glad to see you. I thought my life was just minutes from being over when the doorbell rang."

"Thank my father. We came in as a team. I knew he was going to toss a flashbang."

"Thank you," she told Paul's father and the older man smiled. "I was happy to help," he responded, "We couldn't wait for the authorities or a search warrant. We had to do this ourselves. We knew time was critical. Hired a helicopter and flew down here as fast as possible."

"Speaking of the authorities, we'd better call Trey. Tell him to alert the FBI to see about their hazmat team," Paul said. "Since Madison was kidnapped, they can be called in. I think we're going to need them."

While Mike used his cell phone to call, Paul and Madison walked over to the shade of a gumbo-limbo tree. She was jittery now; even Paul's strong arm around her didn't help.

"Do you have any water?" she asked. Her throat was parched and her tongue still felt swollen. She hoped the ringing in her ears would soon go away.

"Sure. I dropped my backpack by the front door. Stay here. I'll get it."

He returned with a heavy backpack and pulled out a bottle of water. She took it from him and opened it. The water was warm but she didn't mind. It soothed her throat and tongue, but her nerves still jangled.

"What's in there?" she asked, then finished the bottle.

"Knives, ropes, guns, pepper spray, another flashbang, screwdrivers, pliers, hammer, lock pick. Stuff my father packed. We didn't know what we'd need when we got here."

"You rang the doorbell. That startled him. Garrison was not expecting it. He said that only delivery men came here."

Paul grinned, the smile that she loved so much. "My father's idea. Get Garrison to the front door while Dad used a lock pick on the back door. I heard you screaming and busted down the door as quickly as I could. I thought he was killing you."

"I didn't know who was at the door, but I wanted whoever it was to know I was in trouble."

"You have a real good set of lungs," he said with a smile. "I came running once before. Remember?"

"I do." She recalled how shocked she'd been to find Erin's body. "Garrison admitted he killed Erin."

"I'm sorry, honey. He was the worst killer I've ever encountered. I knew what he was capable of from his other murders. I was out of my mind with fear for you." He rubbed his shoulder. "It's going to be sore. That was one hard door to bust through."

"You managed, and I'm so grateful. He was going to slit my throat any second." She felt better after drinking the water. "I should call my mother."

Paul took his cell off the clip on his belt and gave it to her. She dialed her mother's cell but Jessica didn't answer. Voice mail came on. "Mom, the killer's dead. I'm with Paul. I'll talk to you later. I love you."

"You love me, too." He kissed her mouth, caressing her lips more than anything. It wasn't a sexual kiss. It was meant to reassure her. "I know we haven't known each other very long, but it doesn't matter. We were meant for each other. You're going to have to marry me."

"Why, are you pregnant?"

He threw his head back and laughed. "You know, your sense of humor is one of the things that attracted me to you in the first place."

"I don't know how I can joke at a time like this."

"It's okay," he assured her. "Cops often joke at crime scenes. Relieves the tension, cuts the stress."

A car drove up to the house and a good-looking man not yet thirty jumped out. Paul introduced her to Trey Williams, then said he was going to take him inside.

"You're not going to believe this. It's one for the books."

Paul was right, she decided. This was one for the books. She just hoped it didn't destroy Wyatt Holbrook. She genuinely liked the man. To have your son do something like this would be positively devastating.

Garrison had a brilliant mind but he was delusional. How had that happened? she wondered. Could it have been prevented? Maybe, she silently conceded. A more nurturing childhood might have changed things.

She had to admit Wyatt—for all the good he'd done and intended to do—wasn't always at his best with his children. He was often rude to Savannah when all she seemed to want was to please him. Madison knew she shouldn't be sorry for Garrison, but she couldn't help feeling that a valuable life had been lost. He could have made a major contribution to society instead of taking innocent lives just to pay back an uncaring father.

The whole situation made her think again of her own father. She'd always felt loved and appreciated. She never would have done anything to hurt him. His loss was still devastating.

Her mother was wonderful, too. Madison had to admit that she'd been extremely lucky. When she had children, she intended to be the best parent possible.

Within minutes of Trey's arrival two police helicopters descended on the street in front of the house. Teams of cops leaped out of each helicopter and rushed into the house. It wasn't long before a television news crew in a chopper was hovering overhead. No doubt they'd been monitoring the police radios.

"We'd better brace ourselves," Paul said, his father at his side. "There's going to be a lot of crime scene stuff to do and interviews to give."

"Just make sure no one gets near that red acid," Madison said with a shudder.

IT WAS NEARLY SEVEN before Paul and Madison were allowed to leave the scene. Madison had to give a statement immediately so she wouldn't forget anything. Paul and his father were interviewed, as well.

"We're getting a ride into Key West with the Key West police," Paul told his father when Mike Tanner walked up to him while he was talking with Madison under the tree.

"We are?" Madison asked. "Why?"

"My mother's there. I want you to meet her." He'd picked up her call on voice mail while he'd been waiting around. "Is that okay?" This question was directed to his father.

"Sure. Tell her I said hello." His father turned toward Madison. "I'm going to see if your mother will join me for dinner. I think she needs to hear about this firsthand. Since the police haven't made a statement yet, there's no telling what the media is putting out there."

"Good idea," Madison responded. "Tell her how much I love her. When you guys miraculously showed up, I was making my last call to her just so she would know how much I care."

"Will do." His father walked over to Trey's car to ride back to Miami. He already had his cell out. He was probably calling Jessica.

"I thought you didn't know where your mother was."

Paul explained what he'd learned today. "I want to see her and I want you to meet her."

"I look a fright. This dress, my hair."

"We can stop on Duval Street and buy you a dress before

we go to the gallery, and your hair looks fine now. When I came through the door, you looked like the wild woman of Borneo, but trust me, you'd never looked better. You were alive."

They rode with the Key West cops, who chattered nonstop about the crime. Big Pine Key was in their jurisdiction so they'd come out to the scene. They weren't much help. Key West was a tourist mecca and didn't have many brutal crimes. Mostly burglary and drunk driving arrests.

Madison fell asleep and was out for most of the twenty-minute drive. The cops let them off on Duval Street. They found a shop and bought Madison a sundress with pink and green flowers. Paul purchased a new polo shirt. The one he was wearing positively stank.

It was almost closing time when they walked into Grand Designs. Paul barely noticed the collection of paintings on the walls or the glass pieces on pedestals. His eyes were riveted on the slim woman with the dark wavy hair. The same woman who'd gazed out at him from the picture on her Web site. She rose, a bit unsteadily, and came toward them.

"Hello, Mother." There was an uneven rhythm to his breathing.

"Paul," she whispered. "Oh, Paul. It is you. When I got the message, I called you. Then you didn't—"

"I was really busy. I came as soon as I was free." His arm was around Madison and he looked at her. "This is Madison Connelly. We're getting married. Madison, this is my mother, Molly Tanner."

His mother stepped forward and gave Madison a hug. "You must be a wonderful woman, and very lucky to have my son love you."

She turned to Paul, but he wasn't ready to hug her. His mother must have sensed this. She backed away, then said, "You turned into a fine man. I knew you would. You look just like your father."

"Dad said to tell you hello." Paul realized he never called

his father "Dad," but he felt differently about Mike after the way he'd leaped into action to save Madison.

"Tell him hello for me."

The sound of his mother's voice affected him deeply. It came back to him with memories of storytime and good-night kisses. He couldn't remember her face, but when he listened to her, Paul recalled her voice.

"Annette's home making dinner. I'm sure there's enough for two more." His mother giggled nervously. "She always makes too much."

"Another time, definitely," Paul said. He needed to be alone with Madison. "I just wanted you to know I was around. I'll come back."

"I'm in Miami occasionally," his mother said, and he heard the heartrending hope in her voice.

"Call us," Madison said. "We'd love to see you."

They said goodbye and left. Walking up Duval Street, his arm around Madison, Paul thought about his mother. She seemed happy, a lot happier than his father, and it bothered him more than he'd expected.

"Why did you come here, if you didn't want to spend more time with your mother?"

"This has been a hell of a day. A real emotional roller coaster. I'm not usually emotional, but now I know what heartache really means." He stopped and put his fist against the middle of his sternum. "My heart literally hurt when I realized that monster had kidnapped you.

"I wanted to see Mother, to start the process, but I need to spend tonight alone with you. Since I met you, I've been thinking a lot. My childhood wasn't happy. I don't believe I can be a good father until I resolve a few things, starting with my mother."

"Father? Are you pregnant?" She tried for the same joke she'd used before.

"No." He chuckled. "But I see children in our future. Don't you?"

"Absolutely."

His lips instinctively found hers. They kissed and kept kissing even though people walking along the sidewalk had to dodge them. They finally broke apart.

"Forever," Paul said, and he meant it. He knew he would love this exceptional woman until the day he died.

EPILOGUE

Eleven months later

PAUL WAITED at the altar, looking down the aisle at Madison. She was wearing a pale lavender strapless gown and her hair was swept up in a wispy arrangement of glistening blond curls. She'd never been more beautiful. Okay, the day he busted down Garrison's door she had seemed more beautiful. Because she was alive. Today was different; this was the beginning of their new life together.

Madison was slowly gliding through the living room of Corona del Mar on the carpet of rose petals some florist provided. She was on Wyatt Holbrook's arm with Aspen walking beside her. A garland of red roses hung around the retriever's neck.

In an odd way, Garrison's death had brought Madison and Wyatt closer. He had taken his son's death hard. Madison had tried as gently as she could to explain the things Garrison had told her in those final moments. Wyatt was truly shocked. He'd never realized his obsession with his work had turned his son against him.

Madison had encouraged him to be more supportive of Savannah. Wyatt had taken her advice and the two now seemed much closer. Savannah had chosen a small private wedding at a chapel in the Bahamas. She, too, had taken her brother's betrayal hard and had decided against a large, flashy wedding.

Madison claimed Wyatt was like many men who were on a fast track to career success when their children were young. They didn't make time for them. But as men became older, they had more time and the grandchildren benefited from the extra attention. Paul knew Madison wished her own father could have lived to see the children they'd someday have.

As for Paul, he was glad his father was around. He could see Mike was going to be a wonderful grandfather. Paul still wished his father had talked to him sooner about his mother. Hell, he should have asked for an explanation. But you couldn't change the past; you had to go forward.

There had been a firestorm of publicity and media coverage following Garrison's death and the revelation he was behind several murders, including Erin's. Madison refused all interviews and remained in the guesthouse. Paul had stayed with her. Wyatt had insisted she remain at Holbrook Pharmaceuticals, which was great. Madison absolutely loved the job. Paul figured her presence helped ease the pain Wyatt felt over his son's crimes.

The foundation was up and running now with Madison as director. She was one smart woman, he thought with pride as she came closer. She found a donor for Wyatt by contacting the woman who'd secretly paid for the sperm donation and used Jessica's name. Twins had been conceived, and one of them was a match.

Madison arrived at the altar. Her eyes were shining with emotion as she smiled up at him. The heart that had literally ached when he realized she'd been kidnapped now swelled inside his chest with love.

"Ladies and gentlemen, we are gathered here today…"

MADISON GAZED out at the small gathering of friends and relatives from across the top of her champagne glass. "I'm Mrs. Paul Tanner," she told her new husband. "You know what's so great about it, besides being married to a hunk of a guy?"

"You'll finally be able to get credit."

Madison giggled. "Exactly." It really wasn't funny. Identity theft took longer to fix than she'd ever imagined.

Madison had been right. Chloe hadn't changed her ways. She'd gotten into trouble again—gambling. Aiden had filed for divorce. He still had TotalTrivia but was just hanging on with it. Madison had told him to keep her share until he got the business running more smoothly.

She refused to allow the credit mess to ruin her wedding day. It would be perfect if her father were still alive—and Erin. Madison had done her best to carry out Erin's last wishes. The estate had been settled and the land sold. She'd given the money to Save the Chimps in Fort Pierce, Florida.

Reviewing so many projects for the foundation had given Madison an appreciation for all the misery animals had undergone in the name of medicine. Chimps had suffered the most. Many of them at the large outdoor facility in Fort Pierce had lived most of their lives in cages, but now had a wonderful new home with lots of space outdoors. It was what Erin would have wanted for them.

She reached under the table to pat Aspen's head. He was always with her. Wyatt allowed her to bring him to the office each day. He couldn't go into the lab area, but he hung out in the executive suite, where Rose Marie had a special jar of dog treats for him.

"Do you want to dance, Mrs. Tanner?" Paul asked with a wink.

"Yes, of course." She rose and walked with him to the dance floor.

Paul swung her into his arms for a waltz. He looked so heart-stoppingly handsome in his tuxedo. But Paul wasn't defined by his looks; he had a depth and power to him that other men didn't have. Now she knew what it meant to be truly loved.

"Do you think your mother and Annette are having fun?"

"I hope so. They don't waltz together, but they've been out dancing the rest of the time."

They saw the couple once every few weeks. At first it was a little uncomfortable because Paul seemed awkward, but the more they were with the women, the better things became. Madison liked them, especially Molly.

Madison noticed that Jade was dancing with Rob—and this wasn't their first dance. A strange couple, she thought, but then, you never knew. Jade's hair was now a fried platinum color. She no longer worked at TotalTrivia. Madison had gotten her a job at Holbrook Pharmaceuticals.

At first, Rob had taken the news of Madison's engagement to Paul hard. He kept coming around to see her. Finally she convinced him that she loved Paul. He'd accepted her decision and allowed Jade to invite him to dinner. From there a romance that Madison could never have predicted took off—and was still hot by the looks of things.

"Do you hear wedding bells?" Paul looked at his father, who was dancing with her mother.

"Wouldn't that be something?"

Madison's mother and Paul's father had been an item since the night after Garrison's death. She honestly didn't know if her mother intended to marry again. Her divorce had been finalized a few weeks ago. She didn't live with the boys any longer. She had her own apartment, but Madison noted that it was very close to Mike Tanner's home.

"Mom's really happy. That's all that counts."

"My father finally has a life and he's happy, too." Paul stopped midwaltz and gazed into her eyes. "How soon do you think we can get out of here?"

"Not yet, silly. We haven't cut the cake."

REQUEST YOUR
FREE BOOKS!

2 FREE NOVELS
FROM THE ROMANCE/SUSPENSE
COLLECTION PLUS 2 FREE GIFTS!

YES! Please send me 2 FREE novels from the Romance/Suspense Collection and my 2 FREE gifts (gifts are worth about $10). After receiving them, if I don't wish to receive any more books, I can return the shipping statement marked "cancel." If I don't cancel, I will receive 4 brand-new novels every month and be billed just $5.74 per book in the U.S. or $6.24 per book in Canada. That's a savings of at least 28% off the cover price. It's quite a bargain! Shipping and handling is just 50¢ per book.* I understand that accepting the 2 free books and gifts places me under no obligation to buy anything. I can always return a shipment and cancel at any time. Even if I never buy another book from the Reader Service, the two free books and gifts are mine to keep forever.

185 MDN EYNQ 385 MDN EYN2

Name _____ (PLEASE PRINT) _____

Address _____ Apt. # _____

City _____ State/Prov. _____ Zip/Postal Code _____

Signature (if under 18, a parent or guardian must sign)

Mail to **The Reader Service:**
IN U.S.A.: P.O. Box 1867, Buffalo, NY 14240-1867
IN CANADA: P.O. Box 609, Fort Erie, Ontario L2A 5X3

Not valid to current subscribers of the Romance Collection,
the Suspense Collection or the Romance/Suspense Collection.

Want to try two free books from another line?
Call 1-800-873-8635 or visit www.morefreebooks.com.

* Terms and prices subject to change without notice. Prices do not include applicable taxes. Sales tax applicable in N.Y. Canadian residents will be charged applicable provincial taxes and GST. Offer not valid in Quebec. This offer is limited to one order per household. All orders subject to approval. Credit or debit balances in a customer's account(s) may be offset by any other outstanding balance owed by or to the customer. Please allow 4 to 6 weeks for delivery. Offer available while quantities last.

Your Privacy: Harlequin is committed to protecting your privacy. Our Privacy Policy is available online at www.eHarlequin.com or upon request from the Reader Service. From time to time we make our lists of customers available to reputable third parties who may have a product or service of interest to you. If you would prefer we not share your name and address, please check here. ☐

BOB09

MERYL SAWYER

77175   KISS OF DEATH   ___ $6.99 U.S. ___ $8.50 CAN.
(limited quantities available)

TOTAL AMOUNT $ _____
POSTAGE & HANDLING $ _____
($1.00 FOR 1 BOOK, 50¢ for each additional)
APPLICABLE TAXES* $ _____
TOTAL PAYABLE $ _____

(check or money order—please do not send cash)

To order, complete this form and send it, along with a check or money order for the total above, payable to HQN Books, to: **In the U.S.:** 3010 Walden Avenue, P.O. Box 9077, Buffalo, NY 14269-9077; **In Canada:** P.O. Box 636, Fort Erie, Ontario, L2A 5X3.

Name: _____
Address: _____ City: _____
State/Prov.: _____ Zip/Postal Code: _____
Account Number (if applicable): _____

075 CSAS

*New York residents remit applicable sales taxes.
*Canadian residents remit applicable GST and provincial taxes.

HQN™

We *are* romance™

www.HQNBooks.com